# HEIR OF BROKEN FATE

ISBN: 978-0-6458037-1-6

*To my younger self,*
*There is always hope to be found*

# Chapter One

No matter how strong I get, I always end up here.

Lifeless, helpless, and hopeless.

I feel it physically first, the burn in my cheek as my skin tears open. The protests of my ribs fighting to stay intact. The blast throughout my body as my knees hit the marble floor and the indescribable pain of my lungs screaming for air as it's stolen from me.

My body sees it coming before I do, locking up every muscle until I'm frozen in place, my blood slowing in preparation to pour out of me. No matter how much I scream no sound slips between my lips. Never mind screaming, it will never do any good. I can never move, never fight. Not with him, never with him.

My father is beating me again.

The one who's supposed to protect me, cherish me, and love me is the one who breaks me every day. Chipping tiny pieces away until I'm nothing but a broken shell of what I used to be. I can never do any good, because it is never enough.

"How dare you disrespect me with such filth!" he booms,

the heel of his boot connecting with my stomach.

I don't dare speak, for the fear of his fists never stopping until I'm buried six feet underground.

"You're an embarrassment to this family. You should be ashamed of yourself," he seethes.

Shame? No.

I never feel anything when this happens—not emotionally. Just the brute force of my father's assault on my body. It's as if my heart can't bear to witness, so it checks out until my father is long gone.

I'm not sure what I did to earn this particular beating. Perhaps it was my horrible training lesson this afternoon. My father doesn't view mistakes as a normal human experience; he sees it as an abomination to not be a perfectly unflawed person.

However, I don't see Easton running to tell him about my little mistake today. He hates my father more than I do.

My father retracts, straightening his rumpled tunic as he slowly eases himself into the dining room chair. Gently picking up the silver cutlery beside his plate, he cuts into his roast, as if nothing happened.

He snaps his fingers once, twice. "Take care of it."

*It.* Not daughter.

Servants are next to me in a flash, gentle hands under my arms lifting me to a standing position. I steal a glance toward my mother, who predictably is staring at nothing. She hasn't been mentally present in a long time, let alone ever stopped this. If she didn't wear the same bruises I do, I'd hate her more than him for sitting by silently while her only daughter is beaten to a bloody pulp.

I don't need to look up to know where I'm going. The aftermath of my father's rage has become as predictable as a ritual. The servants help me walk the long corridors to the nurse's quarters where Annie will suck in a deep gasp and rush forward to tend to my wounds, while trying to inconspicuously wipe away the tears that escape.

Annie was hired as the palace's head nurse before I was born. Besides the graceful ageing of her features, not much has changed over the years. Annie's still got her gorgeous bright red curls pulled into a tight bun on her head, held by her signature white bow. Gold-ringed, kind eyes that see too much and plump, heart-shaped lips that smile extra wide when she sees me. Annie was unable to conceive children, she says it allowed her to focus all her motherly instincts on me over the years. If it wasn't for Annie and Easton…I don't know how I would have survived the past twenty-two years.

"Mean old bastard. I'm surprised he still finds the time to do this, considering the number of people he butchers," she spits.

My cheeks burn red.

There's the shame my father wanted to see.

Annie clicks her tongue. "His barbaric actions have nothing to do with you. You can't so much as drop a pea on the floor without getting hit."

"That doesn't change the fact that my father kills innocent people."

That makes Annie pause. "No, it doesn't," she says quietly.

I lower my voice. "Any updates on the people?"

I know I can trust Annie with my life, and hers with mine, but my father has people everywhere in this castle that kiss his ass to gain the slightest lick of attention from him. Not to mention the spies that riddle these halls.

Annie's features visibly shut down, her face going wholly blank, her telltale sign.

"What?" I ask.

Her only response is a muscle ticking in her jaw, the silence in the room suffocating.

"Tell me what happened," I demand.

"I'll tell you in the morning. It won't make a difference whether you know now or later. Right now, you need to rest," she states.

"How bad is it?" I ask, my stomach sinking as I search Annie's eyes.

"Bad." Hopelessness rings out in her voice.

Everyone's losing hope that the world will change. The prayers for peace are few and far between. I can't say I blame them.

I wince as Annie moves in closer, applying a butterfly bandage to my cheek.

Her voice comes out so quietly, her lips barely move. "There are too many guards around this evening."

Before I can respond the chamber doors burst open so hard, they ricochet off the wall, then slam closed from the force. All six foot two of powerful, taut muscles stride across the room. It only takes a second for him to be in front of me, cupping my face gently in his palms. I lift my head, finding green eyes peering down at me.

A sigh releases involuntary, my body relaxing fully.

Easton.

I scan every inch of him, each passing second of his presence easing the ache in my chest. Short shaggy brown hair that used to be blond but with age has taken on a rustic brown shade. Tan honey skin that makes his forest green eyes twinkle. Easton's rigged jaw, clamped teeth, and scowl can't even make him look unattractive. How can anyone look this attractive while they're pissed off?

"I'm going to kill him," he says vehemently.

"No, you won't," I say gently.

We've had this conversation many times before. I used to argue that despite how horrible my father is, no one deserves to be murdered. I stopped arguing that point a long time ago.

Easton pauses, scanning me head to toe before landing his beautiful eyes on my ice blue ones once more. He dips his head, as if coming to an internal decision.

A lopsided grin spreads across his lips. "Yes I will. Annie will help me set the trap."

"In your dreams, pretty boy. I quite like my fingers and toes," Annie teases, swatting his hands off my face to apply healing lotion to my new bruises.

Easton plants a kiss on my forehead, moving aside to take a seat beside me, his eyes never leaving mine.

*Thank you*, I mouth.

Easton is my best friend, my other half. We've been inseparable since the day we met. His father is the chief guard at the palace, and we met in a truly Easton-fashioned way.

He found me crying, hiding in a bush from my guards in the back garden after falling off my horse and skidding my knees raw. He climbed inside the bush, taking a seat beside me, only to pull one of my braids as he made a raspberry sound. "Stop crying so much, you sound like a girl," he had said.

I then enjoyed giving him a thirty-minute tongue lashing, teaching him the proper etiquette on how to care for someone who is crying. Girl or boy, there was no need to be a sexist pig. I had no idea what "sexist" meant at the ripe age of five; I did, however, hear Annie muttering it under her breath the day before when speaking about my father. Looking back on it now, it was most certainly the right word to use. Learning from his lesson, Easton's now a professional at consoling me. He knows what I need before I do.

"All done. No training tomorrow, you've got two bruised

ribs, and a split lip and cheek." Annie stares me down, her eyes as hard as steel. "I mean it, Delilah Covington. No training tomorrow."

I nod, suddenly too tired for words.

Easton's eyes flash with pain for a split second before his happy demeanor returns. Holding out his hand, he offers, "Come on, I'll run you a bath."

I ease to my feet, Annie and Easton both lunging forward to grab my arms.

Planting a quick kiss on Annie's cheek, I murmur, "Thank you."

Her eyes soften. "Don't thank me. Not for this."

I don't know what home feels like, but I'm certain it doesn't feel like this. The palace itself isn't the problem; it's the most beautiful palace I've ever seen—which doesn't surprise me, as my father has to be and have the best. Cream walls line the corridor with columns painted black, while crimson red-carpet runners contrast the white marble floor. Every ten steps showcase a new art piece, each one having an outrageous price tag attached.

There's color everywhere in the palace. Yet no matter how many flowers or colorful art pieces they place around the halls, it never takes away the slithering cold and detached feeling it emanates.

Walking up the grand double staircase, we reach the top floor, rounding the corner to the east wing. I have the entire wing to myself, while my parents have the west. It's an outrageous amount of room, but I don't complain. I can go days without seeing my father.

Easton shares the east wing with me, his room being

across the hall from mine and as big as my own. When he became my personal guard, I insisted that he stay near me. Convincing my father of my idea for once, I sold the pitch with the safety of his precious *belonging* always being guarded and watched.

Considering Easton and I both have troubled homes and families, I thought it would be best if we stuck together.

In my peripheral, I see Easton glancing my way every second step. I know because I'm counting. I give him ten more steps until he spits out whatever's on his mind.

We pass the black glass side table housing red roses—three steps. A painting of a rainbow arching over the Claremont River—six steps. Then finally, my white ensuite door—nine steps.

"I can come in and keep you company, if you want," Easton offers, taking his tenth step.

"East, you know I love you..." I trail off. "But no."

Like I said, it's a routine at this point and unfortunately, I know it won't change anytime soon.

Wrapping my arms around his waist I lay my head on his chest, listening to the beating of his heart.

"Just give me an hour, okay?" I whisper.

"Okay," he mumbles, laying his cheek on the top of my head.

Disentangling myself I turn around, stepping into my room without a backward glance.

Walking through the center of my dressing room, I enter the attached bathing room. To the left sits my vanity sink and to the right a deep clawfoot bathtub, with a floor-to-ceiling window that can only see out, thank the lords for that sliver of privacy. The view overlooks the eastern Claremont River. Sometimes I sit in the tub for hours and stare at it, fantasizing about where it leads to.

Filling the bath with water, I add oils to help with the new bruises and stiff muscles. Peering down at my hands I watch as they tremble, my fingers shaking wildly as I peel off my clothing. Wincing, I maneuver out of the tight corset.

My knees and arms wobble as I lower myself into the scalding water, the bruises marring my creamy skin disappearing under the bubbles. Tears begin streaming down my freckle-covered cheeks, no matter how hard I try to keep them at bay. This part never gets easier. My heart has finally decided to return to me. I never know where it disappears to when my father hurts me, but I'm grateful he doesn't get the satisfaction of seeing me cry.

I thank whatever gods who listen for that.

The floodgates have opened, and I have no choice but to allow myself to feel the burning rage, disgust, and deep unending sadness. I'd like to think I'd be used to it after all these years, yet it never gets any easier. The worst of it all is the emptiness in my heart as I realize that not only does my father hate me, but I am truly stuck with this miserable life, that there will never be any escaping his fists.

He's the only person I can never fight back against, and I hate myself for it.

My body begins to shake with the force of my sobs, becoming more powerful with every breath I take, my ribs screaming in pain as I do.

Each time, I say never again, next time will be different, I refuse to be my father's punching bag again. Yet when the time comes…I shut down.

I might not be able to fight back, but at least I see him for who he truly is.

I'm no longer a little girl, praying and dreaming every night for the next day to be different.

I no longer spend my nights lying awake crying, wondering why my father hates me.

I no longer dream of waking up to a loving father who doesn't grimace at the mere sight of me.

That dream died years ago.

I chuckle quietly to myself an hour later as I exit my bathing chamber to find Easton sitting in the middle of my bed, devouring chocolates. He has the biggest sweet tooth I have ever seen.

He's also never been able to stay away when he knows I'm hurting.

Sighing, I look around my room. This palace might feel like a cold and detached prison, but I made my room feel safe over the years. The servants and decorators furnished it for a princess, going above and beyond to prove that the heir of Aloriah had the best in all the lands.

A four-poster white bed covered in silk sheets dominates the center of the room, its headboard backed into the very far wall. It's covered in so many pillows it feels like a cloud. Floor-to-ceiling bookcases stretch across the right side of the room, filled to the brim and overflowing with every book I've ever collected in my life. Behind me houses my dressing room and bathing suite. Both sides of the closet are filled with frilly dresses, skirts, tops, and of course accessories. According to my dressers a princess can never have too many pieces of clothing. My favorite spot is to the right of the dressing room. Past the center seat cushions, tucked away in a little corner are my fighting leathers and swords.

The only section the servants aren't allowed to touch.

Settling on the bed beside Easton, I watch as he shovels

creamy chocolates into his mouth, smirking at me with it smeared across his lips.

"I've never seen someone love chocolates as much as you."

Speaking around a mouthful, he taunts, "I've never met anyone so enamored with something so simple as a doughnut."

I gasp. "How dare you question the goodness of doughnuts."

"It's fried dough with a hole in it," he quips.

I snatch the box of chocolates out of his lap, holding them behind me. "Take it back or I'll let the cooks know who's being sneaking into the kitchens and stealing their chocolate stash."

He narrows his eyes. "You wouldn't dare."

"Try me." I smirk.

Easton rolls his eyes as he sighs. "You win by default, pulling the princess card with your connections."

"I would never take advantage of my title," I mock pout, placing a hand over my heart.

There's truth behind my words—the only threats I ever make using my title are against Easton and those are always a joke.

His face turns grave. "Any news about the sectors?"

Just like that, any happiness I was feeling dies.

"Yes, but Annie won't tell me until morning," I say, sliding further into my pillows.

His voice lowers. "Not good news then."

"No."

Easton and I fall into silence.

The only time Annie withholds information regarding the people of Aloriah is when it's horrible. She spends the day fretting about how she's going to tell us. Easton being my personal guard has isolated him. The other guards don't trust gossiping to him about the people of Aloriah, knowing how close we are, so our updates come from Annie.

The sectors started rebelling seventeen years ago when my father, the King of Aloriah, added a long list of laws to an already corrupt system. He became the ruling king when his father died, passing the title down in the family. My father has always been a cruel and wicked man, yet as the years pass, the sliver of kindness in his soul deteriorates.

The people of Aloriah broke the day he announced his new rulings. Their patience and prayers for a better world were not heard. Instead, they were mocked. The protests started peacefully, yet my father didn't see it that way. The first execution was set three days after the new rulings. The so-called "rebels" were few and far between after watching their friends and loved ones be whipped and hung at the gallows.

My father was pleased with the fear that spread throughout the sectors, utilizing his people's pain and fear to control them. His armies and council members revel in the changes, knowing they live behind the capital wall, hidden and safe. Profiting off the sectors' misery.

Then ten months ago, my father started changing the laws again.

Curfews are being set earlier each week. Every crime no matter how small—something as simple as being late for mandatory labor—is punishable by death. Executions are set daily at five p.m., mandatory for all to watch. Those who dare speak ill of the king have their tongue cut out before being executed.

Freedom doesn't exist anymore, not for those who can't buy it.

My father doesn't care that families are lining the streets

at night, that children are starving, morgues are overflowing, the hospitals turn away the ill, and orphanages deny children due to being at max capacity. He doesn't notice that children no longer run around playing, no one smiles in the street, and you rarely smell food burning from the chimneys of homes.

We no longer live in a kind world.

Easton's deep voice drags me from my thoughts. "We should leave."

I groan. *Not this again.* "To where?"

This isn't the first time Easton's brought up running away. If he could get away with it, I believe he'd smuggle me out in my sleep.

"Anywhere but here, as far as we can go."

"I think you're forgetting I'm the princess of Aloriah. There's nowhere I could hide…" I trail off on a whisper. "My father would hunt us."

"It's not right. It hasn't been for a long time."

"I couldn't agree more, but I can do more being here." I sit up, turning to face Easton. "Besides, it's wrong to flee, to leave the people of Aloriah to suffer while I run for a better life they will never see."

Easton's jaw clenches, his eyes focusing on the veranda doors, peering at the lake.

"I know I can't do much…but I have to hold onto hope that one day I'll be reigned queen and be able to fix everything he's broken," I whisper.

Easton turns his forest green eyes to me. "You would make a beautiful queen," he murmurs.

"I don't care about the title or being the best queen. I care about people being able to live a life worth living."

"I know." Easton wraps an arm around my shoulder, bringing me down to lay beside him. "That's why you would make a beautiful queen, Delilah. Because you care."

# Chapter Two

I grit my teeth, breathing deeply through the pain wracking my body. Despite my pain tolerance being high after years of abuse from my father, I know this task would have been easier to do without the new injuries, yet I'm running out of time.

I watch as the palace guards posted in the gardens below leave their post for the changing of shifts. The second the five shadowy figures turn the corner, I swing my legs over the windowsill, wincing as my ribs flare in pain. Balancing on the balls of my toes on the window's ledge, I grip the drain-pipe to my right as I gently close the window at my back, leaving a small crack open to get back inside.

Digging my hands into the chalk in my pants pocket, I lather my hands, coating every inch of my skin with the powder before I begin to climb. I've climbed this drainpipe so often over the years I no longer shake at the knees by the sheer drop. I clear four stories before I reach the roof of the palace, my nails digging into the tiles as I heave my body over, rolling onto my stomach.

Righting myself once more, I run, clearing the east wing

roof, making my way to the outer ledge. I pick up the rope wrapped around the chimney I've had concealed here for years. I tie the free end around my stomach, sliding down the curve of the roof that leads to the stables below. I drop and roll onto the stable roof, the impact making my bones sing in pain.

The skylight window shines in front of me. Untying the rope, I lift the heavy glass and peer inside. I can make out Creseda's shape moving to the far wall, as she knows to make room for me to land. A slow smile spreads across my face at the sight. *Clever horse.*

I've had Creseda for the past nine years, my love running as deep for her as it does for Easton, a true companion in this miserable life.

Landing into a pile of hay with a small *oomph*, I stand, taking her in. The most beautiful Friesian black horse in all the country, six feet tall and thirteen hundred pounds of pure beautiful mammal. Slipping my hand into my pocket, I pull out three large carrots, her mouth tickling my palm as she eats.

"Hi, gorgeous," I whisper. "Are you up for another evening stroll?"

A stomp and a snort have my heart melting.

After getting her saddle ready and taking the reins, I ease Creseda out of the stables, the other horses putting up a fuss that they're still locked in. Sticking my head out the barn door, I check left and right. The grounds are clear, the in-training guards late as usual.

The only time I can get away with leaving the grounds are in the middle of the week, an hour past midnight. The only shift the royal guards allow the trainees to work on. They're all cocky, boasting about their new titles. It makes them sloppy…and late.

Although the curfew laws aren't enforced in the capital, I can't risk being seen leaving the palace grounds. Everyone knows Creseda and who she belongs to. They'd spot her a mile away and inform my father about his precious doll's activities.

Keeping to the shadows, I mount Creseda in one fell swoop, digging my heels into her sides. We take off as fast as lightning into the woods beyond. The crisp night air whips across my face. My hood blows off my head with the speed, my black cloak spreading out behind me as we ride south.

My father keeps the sector prisoners sentenced for executions on the capital grounds. The old egotistical fool that he is, thinks no one in the capital would ever dare betray him and his precious laws.

As the trees begin to part, opening to the view beyond, I spot the silver metal boards of the prison roof. Pulling the reins, I ease Creseda to a stop, finding my usual hiding spot— a large oak alcove, the middle of the tree stump curving in on itself, as if someone cut out a door from it. I dismount Creseda and ease her in backward, hiding her large behind and swishing tail within the oak tree. The rest of her glorious black body camouflaged by the darkness of the night sky.

"I'll be back, you know the drill," I say, planting a kiss on her nose before I back away.

Easing between trees, I make my way to the border of the prison compound, a horrible ugly metal building with no windows and only one way in and out. The metal doors are held together by a deadbolt lock and chain.

A deep chuckle fills the air around me. *Guards.* I grit my teeth as I pull back toward the other side of the building. Lathering my hands in chalk I climb once more, treading carefully on the roof as I pray none of the metal below my feet bends or squeaks.

Crouching onto all fours, I peek over the side of the roof. Three guards are stationed in front of the prison doors.

A young dark-haired male crosses his arms as he puffs out his chest. "Did you take your turn with the whore?"

Another guard smirks. "Which one? The blonde or the brunette?"

The dark-haired man takes a bow. "Both."

As each horrid word enters the crisp air, my blood slows, turning to ice.

How dare they violate the very people they're meant to protect and serve.

Stillness overtakes my body. A silent killing calm.

I feel no guilt as I lunge, free falling to the earth before I land on top of the guard in the middle. A blade imbeds in his gut as another flies from my hand. Before the guard in front of me can so much as blink, a knife is lodged in his leg. Whirling, I roll onto the ground, kicking out my legs and knocking the guard behind me onto his ass before he can so much as touch me. I unsheathe the sword from my back in a breath, bringing the hilt of it down onto the guard's head, rendering him unconscious. With the other two injured they can't stop me as I do the same to them.

There's no need to kill them as punishment for their horrid acts. Once my father finds out what I'm about to do tonight on their watch, he'll have the guards sentenced to the dungeons for failing him. Where they'll never escape, let alone see sunlight again. The sheer violence my father inflicts on those who are disloyal to him are things you only hear about in nightmares.

Lifting my sword over my head, I take one step forward as I plunge it down with all my weight and remaining strength, slicing the chain in two.

I drag open the metallic doors, holding back a gag as the

horrid smell of over a hundred people cramped into the small room assaults my nose. Their bodily fluids mingle with the musty smell. My father likes to herd the prisoners like cattle, making them wait days in their own filth before their execution.

Gasps ring out as everyone shuffles backward. People begin to sob and shake as they believe they're about to meet their end.

I take a step forward into the compound, sheathing my sword behind my back. I pull my black hood off my head. "Who knows how to sail a ship?"

Hushed whispers break out, heads turning this way and that with a mixture of confused and shocked expressions.

A hand shoots up at the back of the room. The sea of people part instantly for the courageous person, revealing the volunteer to be an older, gray-haired man. His hand trembles as it slowly lowers. The man starts to take a tentative step forward before thinking better of it and halting. His mouth opens and closes before a cracked, dry voice stutters out.

The guards clearly haven't given them any water since they've been imprisoned.

"I-I was a sailor, Your Hi-highness." The man takes an audible gulp before he continues, despair coating his words. "Before the capital took over the trading duties."

My heart twists, my throat going dry as my eyes burn.

Many people lost their livelihoods the day my father put his own men in control of the trading duties. Hundreds of families became homeless within that very week, soon dying from starvation.

I take a deep breath, swallowing my emotions. They don't need a crying martyr, they need strength right now.

Striding toward the man, people part for me, scattering away faster than before. Stopping before him, I lift my hand, palm up between us. He hesitates for a moment before placing his in mine. I gently squeeze it, looking into his tired, hopeless brown eyes.

A smile tugs at my lips. "Good, because we need someone to sail the getaway ship."

The room fills with gasps and relieved sobs of joy as the people around me realize I am not their executioner, but their salvation. Whispers spread faster than I can hear.

"It's true…"

"The princess is a rebel."

"…She's going to save us."

"The princess is on our side."

"The heir is the Black Hood!"

I turn, everyone falling quiet as they look at me in my fighting leathers, gently holding the man's hand.

They begin to listen.

"Yes, it is true. I can't explain all the details because we don't have much time. Three miles to the east lies a ship full of supplies to last you a month."

More gasps go up around the room and I finally see hope lining the eyes of my people.

"I will show you the way, yet once you are all on safely, I will leave you." Turning to the older gentleman, I say, "This courageous man will sail you to safety, yet he will need your help. So, I hope we have more than one volunteer."

An array of people—young, old, female, and male—step forward, yelling out their offerings of help.

"I can't give you a safe place in Aloriah. My power over these circumstances is limited," I say soberly. "However, there's land east of here. It's a three-week sail with good weather and it's safe. I've received letters proving so from previous ships I've sent. I promise, you will find no harm once you reach its shores."

The infamous rumors are true. Heir to Aloriah, the daughter of the tyrant running this country, is working on the inside to free as many people as she can. Receiving the letters were the most dangerous part. The first ship I ever sent off, only holding three people, made it to shore safely four weeks later. With my instructions, they addressed a letter to Lady Ophelia, knowing that no one in the palace resides under that name. Befriending the young gentlemen in the mailing room to accompany the lonely princess for weekly tea sessions gave me the access I needed to steal the letters.

Receiving that first letter three years ago was one of the few times in my life I have felt useful toward change in these lands. Ever since, I've been sending as many people as I could to those lands, knowing they're all waiting to help those that arrive.

I look around at all the astonished, hopeful expressions, feeling my heart grow.

"A new world," I declare.

# Chapter Three

I tip my head back, letting the sun shine across my face as I inhale the fresh smells around me—moss, grass, lavender, and sea water. I open my eyes to find the most gorgeous field surrounding me. Colors blossom from every which direction, red and pink leaves adorning the tips of trees, beds of flowers scattering the area. Hearing the trickle of water, I turn to my left, spotting a pool of glistening water as it swirls and flows, the colors of the rainbow shining across it where the sun hits it. Rocks adorn each side of the oval-shaped hole.

It's a mermaid pool.

In awe I take a step closer, my bare feet gliding over soft grass. I've never felt grass so soft before; it feels as if I'm walking on a cloud.

Kneeling before the rock pool, I lean over, stretching out my hand an inch above the surface. My fingers submerge in the water, only to come face to face with ice blue eyes camouflaged in the water blinking up at me.

I tilt my head to the side, the face below doing the same.

I stare at my reflection, scanning the freckles smattered

across my cheeks and turned-up button nose. My pink-tinted, pouty lips. My long auburn hair flowing down my shoulders. Long black eyelashes fluttering as I blink. Nothing has changed, yet something is different. I lower my head to the water, tucking my hair behind my ears, only to find that my ears are pointed. My breath leaves me in a whoosh as I lift a shaking hand, feeling the elongated tip.

Fae.

I look like a Fae.

A loud splash has me snapping my head up. Scanning the pool, a smile spreads across my lips as several tails breach the water.

Tails of all size and color.

I lean as far forward as I can, wishing I could get closer as one glides in front of me, its white tail and hair so stark against the natural color of the water I almost miss the body it's attached to.

"Mermaids," I breathe.

The smell of ocean and pinewood surrounds my senses as strong arms wrap around my waist, my back hitting a wall of muscle as soft lips kiss my cheek.

A dark husky voice whispers in my ear, sending tingles racing through my body.

He sighs in relief. "Angel."

I jolt awake in bed panting, my heart sinking in pain as it longs for the overwhelming happiness and love it felt only moments ago.

Ever since I was a little girl, I've dreamt about the Fae and their lands. As I got older, I began dreaming of the same ocean and pinewood smelling man comforting me, filling my heart with love. Then I awake to a world without magic, Fae, mermaids, and happiness.

My bedroom door bangs open, jarring me from my thoughts as I turn to find Annie strolling into my room looking frazzled. I instantly sit up. "What is it? What happened?"

Annie's eyebrows rise, her pointed stare halting my movements entirely.

"I think you already know why your father is running around like a mad man."

I make my expression blank. "I don't know what you're talking about…Why is he mad now?" She's suspected me of freeing prisoners for years but it's too risky to outright ask the question, especially in a palace filled with my father's spies.

She would never tell a soul. No, Annie would demand to help.

I've never told her because I don't want her to get caught in the crossfire. I don't know what I would do if something happened to Annie, and I refuse to be the one to put her in harm's way.

Annie walks through my dressing room to the bathroom, emerging with the first aid kit that she placed under my wash basin. Returning, she takes a seat beside me on the bed as she addresses my wounds from yesterday evening.

"Your father has requested your presence at a mandatory council meeting," she says, applying ointment to my cut cheek and lip. "I ran into Easton on my way in here. I told him I would tell you myself."

"Will this meeting also include the news you're supposed to tell me?"

Annie lifts her eyes, peering at me below her lashes, her lips twisting into a grimace. "Yes."

I groan. Not only is my father in a horrible mood because

he has no one to execute today, but now he's going to make the council's day a living hell as he takes his temper and wrath out on them.

Myself included.

A flash of memory from my dream floats through my mind. Strong arms wrapped around me, keeping me safe and filling me with love and tenderness.

I stopped believing in fairy tales a long time ago. However, my heart and soul seem to not agree with my mind on that matter.

My love for the Fae lands started when my mother used to read me stories about them when I was a small child. They were the happier stories of the Fae lands, how Fae and humans co-existed, respected each other, and protected one another. Until the Fae lands were destroyed one hundred and forty-eight years ago, along with every single ounce of magic, mystical creature, and sadly the Fae race.

Every single faerie and animal gone in an instant. It's such a tragic story how they died. It was because...

My mind stops abruptly, going wholly blank.

"How did the Fae die?" I ask suddenly, making Annie jump at my abrupt words.

Annie opens her mouth to speak, her eyebrows furrowing. "I don't know," she says quizzically.

*Why can't we remember?*

"Perhaps it's in a Fae history book?" I suggest.

"Good luck finding a book about the Fae. You know your father hates anything to do with magic."

I level her with a flat look. "He thinks it's preposterous because he doesn't have any. He must be the best at everything, and the most powerful."

Annie's eyes sadden. "That's very true." She closes the first aid kit. "All done."

Rising from the bed, I thank Annie for the wound care as she leaves.

In my dressing room, I pick out my finest baby blue dress with a white-lined detail on the corset. Council meetings are where my father shows off his pretty doll, his perfect princess and heir. My father has only ever seen me as an object, something he owns. A chess piece to move around on his board in his game of domination. Which means I can't make any mistakes, disrespect, or embarrass him. I must walk, speak, and look my best—unless I want another repeat of last night.

Taking a deep breath, I get ready for another day in hell.

Strolling out of the east wing, Easton and I make our way to the council meeting room on the first floor. Easton is dressed impeccably in his guard's uniform. Not a single thread is out of place and his armor is so clean I can see my own distorted reflection shining back at me.

"I suppose your father's tantrum this morning was your doing," Easton whispers.

I scan the halls for any loitering guards or workers as I mutter under my breath, my lips barely moving an inch, "Not here, East."

Easton nudges me with his elbow. "Just give me a hint."

Looking into his forest green eyes, I let mine reflect the triumph I feel in my heart that they got free last night. Perhaps a little mischief too.

One side of Easton's mouth tugs into a crooked grin. "You have to take me one of these times. You can't have all the fun." He winks.

All the humor fades from my face.

I can never let anything happen to Easton. I can't even

make a suggestion on what to eat for dinner to my father, and I certainly wouldn't be able to stop him from punishing Easton if he stepped out of line...

Easton has to be protected at all costs.

Passing a group of maids and guards off-duty, Easton bows his head in acknowledgment. I smile at the group as they curtsy to me. But I can hear the whispers at my back as we pass them. I know exactly what they're gossiping about; it's the same every time.

Walking outside, we enter the eastern gardens, our beloved way of getting around the enormous palace. It feels like a maze trying to navigate the gardens, yet the fresh air is always preferred over the coldness that emanates from the palace halls. The garden is beautiful, blossoming with life. It's a sight to behold...and it's also where there aren't as many guards posted.

Once we're halfway through the rose bushes, I turn to Easton, a smirk on my lips. "When oh when will you propose to me, my royal guard?" I ask, fluttering my eyelashes.

Easton sighs dramatically as he takes my hand. "My lady, you know I love you. But I can't in good conscience marry you when I'm in love with your sister."

Dropping Easton's hand, I whack his shoulder. "You always ruin it with your fictional characters!" I chuckle.

He raises his hands in surrender. "I learned from the book lover herself that every story needs a good plot twist."

I chuckle at that. Reading became my escape from reality at an early age. I find comfort in living others' lives, even if it's just for a moment. It brings me immense peace...to be anyone but myself.

It's the only time my anxiety doesn't rear its ugly head.

I roll my eyes, conceding. "Very true."

Easton glances behind us where we left the gossiping staff. "You'd think by now they'd get the hint," he mutters.

Everyone believes Easton and I are lovers. Whenever we're together—which I relent is majority of the time—we're constantly met with whispers and gossip about why we're keeping our union a secret. The reasons vary from my father never approving of me dating someone as "low" as a guard, or that we get a kick out of all the rumors.

The last part does hold some truth—we do find enjoyment laughing at the gossip. However, us being lovers couldn't be further from the truth. Don't get me wrong, I truly do love Easton and I know he loves me, but we're platonic soulmates. Easton is my sounding board, the other half of my soul, yet I don't see him as more than a best friend. Even if I did, Easton loves the other side of the coin. Part of why he hates his father is his father's hatred toward people who love the same gender.

"How are things with Cole?" I whisper.

He glances around the garden. "You know how they are."

I take a deep breath, treading carefully. "Have you reconsidered what he asked?"

Scrubbing a hand down his face, Easton heaves a deep sigh. "You know I can't, Delilah. Things are hard enough with my father as they are. I don't need to be making things worse by coming out in a public relationship with a man."

I take a hold of his hand, gently squeezing. "I will always support whatever decision you make," I vow.

Easton's lips flatten into a line, a sad smile tugging on his lips.

My heart sinks. Easton and Cole have secretly been lovers for over a year. They're perfect for each other and Easton loves him deeply. Except Cole doesn't like being a secret, so he gave Easton an ultimatum: either come out publicly—no more sneaking around—or they were done.

Easton's father did a number on him, and I know he feels shameful, which he absolutely should never feel about the person he loves. But his father's words have dug a deep hole in his mind and Easton is too scared to make that kind of leap yet.

Reaching the west wing, Easton and I walk through an archway, resuming our stroll in silence through the palace corridors. As we turn a corner, we're met with ten palace guards posted outside the meeting room.

Steeling my spine, I lift my chin as I approach, Easton taking his spot outside the door in the hallway. Only my father's personal guards can be present at council meetings.

The guard posted in front of the entry doesn't so much as look my way as he opens the black mahogany door.

The oval-shaped room is styled with white marble tiles. Floor-to-ceiling windows at the far side of the room overlook the western forest, a black steel fireplace adorns the left side of the room, and placed in the center is a twenty-seated, oval-shaped table with white cushioned chairs.

My father sits at the head of the table, dressed impeccably in his black and gold royal clothes. I'm surprised he's not wearing a crown considering his ego needs to be stroked every ten seconds.

Scanning the several council members seated around the table, my stomach drops when my eyes land on my father's second. Duke Harrison, who's seated to the right of my father.

Another reason why I hate council meetings—the insipid man I'm to be seated in front of.

"Thank you for finally gracing us with your presence, Delilah," my father drawls sarcastically.

I slide my gaze to the mounted clock on the right side of the room. I'm not late, I'm ten minutes early, yet because I wasn't here twenty minutes earlier kissing his ass like all these other power-hungry monsters, I'm tardy in his mind.

Ignoring his verbal jab, I take my seat to his left, placing my hands in my lap as I straighten my spine. Glancing toward my father, I pray for him to start this gods-awful meeting.

Leaning back in his chair, my father crosses his arms over his chest. "We've been betrayed again," he says, ice coating his words.

The council members glance around the table at each other. Some have already begun sweating.

"One hundred slaves"—*people, just call them people*, I hiss in my mind—"escaped the holding prison last night." His gaze roams the council members. "No one has seen or heard from any of the slaves. They have completely disappeared!" he bellows, no longer holding the leash on his temper.

"I already have my best men on it, Your Highness," Duke Harrison interjects.

My father's face turns red, the veins in his neck protruding. "We have no one to execute today and I want a solution."

"We could change the curfew and not tell certain sectors," Duke Harrison offers.

Bile burns my throat, making my eyes water.

Suggesting to kill innocent people by their own manipulation and games…

I open my mouth to detest such a horrid idea when my father's laugh booms throughout the room. He smiles. "Brilliant!"

My jaw drops open on its own accord. I can't control the disgust that lines my features. If anyone deserves to be executed, it's the men sitting at this table. Not the innocent people of this country who are trying to get through another day alive. I'm surprised he hasn't halted the killings considering if he keeps it up, there won't be anyone to rule over.

The king flicks his hand to his personal messenger. "Edgar, see to it."

Before anyone can so much as blink, Edgar is scuttling out of the room.

"Any updates on sector three?" my father asks.

Phillip, a scraggly middle-aged man with gray peppered hair, clears his throat.

"Your Highness." He bows, audibly swallowing before he speaks again. "The rebel protests haven't stopped. Sector three is no longer the main rebel group, but sectors four, five, and seven are rioting every day. The damages are insurmountable." Philip casts a wary gaze around the table, wiping sweat off his forehead with a handkerchief. "They're also refusing to work. They've banned together, Your Highness."

My father's jaw hardens. The energy in the room turns palpable, the tension a living thing breathing down everyone's necks. All twenty council members tense, their backs straightening as everyone in the room holds their breath.

There's always been small groups of rebellion in the sectors, yet these past ten months have consisted of outright riots. However, this is the first time in history that the sectors have rallied together and refused to work. The fact that four out of seven sectors are rebelling is a dramatic change of events.

This must have been the news Annie was talking about in regards to the people.

I clamp my mouth shut as my lips threaten to pull into a smile. They're fighting back.

"When was this?" my father replies coldly.

Philip clears his throat. "The past week, Your Majesty."

"And no one thought to tell me?" he barks.

"I had the army sent in to destroy the notion that these sectors have the right to go against their king," Duke Harrison cuts in, saving Philip. "Unfortunately, the efforts to stop this ridiculous act of defiance haven't worked."

"I should have been notified the second it started," my father spits. "The executions aren't taming the rebels." The king slides his gaze around the room as he clicks his tongue, his cold beady eyes assessing each council member. "I'll personally see to it that each sector understands the laws of this mighty kingdom and what happens when you disrespect your king."

My stomach sinks.

I fist my hands in my lap to keep the fear inside of me.

My father never goes to the sectors. He sends his cronies to deal with the "filth". I pray to any god that will listen that he doesn't pick people off the street to make a point.

"Duke, you'll accompany me on the journey. Inform the army to dispatch at first light tomorrow." He turns toward the other members. "I trust that you all understand the ramifications of not telling me what's happening in my own country."

"Yes, Your Majesty," rings out in unison.

Taking a steadying breath, I raise my chin as I address my father.

"Perhaps you could go to each sector and ask what the people want." I keep my voice strong, unwavering. "If you offer them changes, the people might go back to work."

Gasps ring out around the room as my father's head whips toward me faster than humanly possible. His very eyes change, the deep brown turning wholly black, soulless, as his face burns crimson red, the veins in his neck protruding.

"Leave us. See to it that my orders are sent out," he barks, dismissing the council.

I close my eyes as my breathing turns into a wheeze.

I know what happens when his eyes change, when the person behind them vanishes and the monster he keeps on a leash inside of him is released.

I mentally kick myself for speaking at all. I'm only allowed to sit there like a pretty little princess doll, to make our kingdom and court look unified—like a happy family, even if it's anything but. I couldn't sit there any longer and listen to my father's outrageous plans for the innocent people of our country.

The council members leave the room like their asses are on fire, until it's empty save for myself and my father. The clang of the dark mahogany doors slamming shut seals my fate.

"How dare you question my orders?" he seethes.

I blink. "I didn't, Father."

Rising out of his chair, he walks toward me—a predator stalking prey. My body tenses, getting ready for what I know is to come.

I lift my head as he towers over me. His body physically shakes with barely contained rage, and his teeth are clenched so tightly I'm surprised they don't snap.

Quick as a snake, the back of my father's hand whips across my cheek, making my head fly to the side, my hair splaying in a tangled mess over my face. Wetness trickles down my cheek as my cut tears open once more.

Sucking in a breath, I feel my heart leave me until there's nothing but the lingering burn of my father's hand imprinted on my skin.

"You do not *dare* question me in my own court!" Spit flies out of his mouth as he screams.

The second strike I see coming. Frozen in my seat, the heel of his boot comes down on my chest, sending me flying back in my chair to the ground. All the air in my lungs evaporates as my head bounces off the tiles, sending black stars shooting into my vision. Warm liquid trickles down my nape.

He kicks my leg, scoffing. "Useless offspring."

The sound of his boots retreating on the tiled floors make tears spring to my eyes as he leaves his only daughter bleeding on the ground.

It's silent for a moment before I hear Easton, his boots squeaking as he rushes into the room. He skids to a stop beside me on his knees. Those gorgeous forest green eyes lined with tears.

Easton's mouth opens and closes, no sound escaping his lips before he gently scoops me into his arms. I lay my head on his chest, listening to the erratic thumping of his heart as he carries me out of the room.

The sound of the mahogany doors banging behind us rings hollow through my ears.

I place my palm over his chest, my voice breaking as I speak. "I'm okay, Easton."

"Don't lie to me. Never to me," he says vehemently.

Easton takes me to Annie, and so the routine begins again.

For another day is just the same as before. It always will be.

# Chapter Four

The following day, after Annie tried to hide her tears from me while Easton hovered over us, I'm lying on Easton's chest in my bed. It's been silent for what feels like hours. The wind flutters in through the open veranda, but not even the soothing smell of the lake and forest beyond has been able to soothe my aching heart.

I twist my head up to Easton's face. His brows have been pulled down all day, as if his face is frozen in a scowl.

Dragging myself from bed, ignoring the dull pounding in my head, I enter my dressing room. Quickly changing into my riding leathers, I grab my day bag, filling it with my diary, fruit, and the current book I'm reading—which reminds me, I need to go in search of Fae history books—but that can wait until tomorrow. I need to clear my mind.

Walking out of the closet, Easton sits up. I quickly cut him off before he can utter a single word. "No. I need to clear my head. I'm just going to the tree, nowhere else. I promise."

"You shouldn't be going anywhere with a head wound. What if you fall off Creseda riding?"

"Annie checked me out. No concussion, just a little head cut," I state, slinging my day bag over my shoulder.

Easton's brows furrow. "It's not just a *little* head cut. You needed two stitches, Delilah."

I can't argue with that, so I climb onto the bed, giving him a big squeeze. "It wouldn't have done a lick of difference if you were in that room, Easton. Even if you did try to stop it, he would have had you killed just for interrupting." I run my fingers through his hair, cupping his face. "You can't stop him," I whisper.

"I know," he murmurs brokenly, silver lining his eyes.

My heart aches at the sound of his broken voice, for this beautiful caring man to be in such a horrible world where I'm the one contributing to his sadness.

I take a deep breath. "Fine but if I tell you to stop singing a horrible song you must concede," I relent.

Easton's entire face brightens as he smiles down at me. "Are you gracing me with the gift of joining you, Princess?" he teases.

Rolling my eyes, I giggle as we make our way to the stables.

I flit my eyes between Easton's horse and Creseda as we ride through the forest. "I think Creseda and Henry are soulmates," I say in awe.

We're twenty minutes away from our destination when I notice Creseda and Henry, Easton's horse, are playing together and, dare I say, flirting. But they're horses, so you never know what's going through their adorable minds.

Easton bursts out laughing. "Where is this coming from?"

"Look, they're flirting," I say, pointing. Their noses brush for a moment before separating.

Easton tilts his head, looking genuinely puzzled. He has the most adorable face when he's confused. His forehead wrinkles as his lips purse together in deep concentration.

"Huh." He pauses. "They never usually do that."

"Maybe Creseda is finally a free lady and Henry is pouncing on the opportunity," I tease, wiggling my eyebrows.

"Why can't Henry be the free man and Creseda's the one taking the shot?" he objects.

I scoff. "Because Creseda is the most beautiful horse there is."

Easton gasps as he leans forward, patting Henry's neck. He pretends to whisper in his ear, "Don't worry buddy, you're the most handsome horse there is. Don't listen to her horseshit."

"You're weird." I chuckle.

"Switch weird with charming and you're right." He winks. "How far out are we?"

"Ten more minutes." I glance at him sideways. "Why? Are you uncomfortable already?" I tease.

He huffs. "Please, I'm a better rider than you are."

Gasping, I turn around so fast I nearly fall off my saddle. "Take that back!"

Easton lets out a low chuckle, his eyes twinkling with mischief. "I'll race you for it."

I scoff, turning back. "I don't need to race you to prove my riding ability."

"If you say so," he sing-songs.

Narrowing my eyes, I slide my gaze to him. "I'm a fabulous rider."

Easton shrugs. "Then you would have no qualms about racing me for it."

"Fine."

Easton's eyes spark with amusement. "Whoever gets to the treehouse first is the best rider."

Shaking my head, I lift my gaze to Easton as I smirk. "You're on!" Squeezing my legs around Creseda, we take off before he can even register my words.

Easton's voice follows me from behind as he shouts, "You play dirty, Princess!"

I giggle the entire ride to the sound of Easton swearing behind me. Henry's hooves beat the grass, trying to catch up to Creseda and me.

The treehouse comes into view. It's a little under an hour ride away from the palace, and because it's still on the capital grounds my father has no reservations of me going here. I found it when I was a little girl and tried to run away. Back then, for a little girl's imagination, it was heaven on earth. Now being twenty-two years old and five-nine it's extremely small; nevertheless, it holds a dear part in my heart. Whenever I need to escape or have a bad day, I come here for solitude. Over the years I've stocked the one-level, wooden treehouse with knickknacks, books, pillows, and quilts for when it gets cold.

The treehouse doesn't have a door; instead, it has an open arch leading into the four-by-four wooden room. Each wall has a window, showing off panoramic views of the forest. The only way up is the rope ladder, which I've had to replace twice from Easton's large frame snapping it in half.

Dismounting Creseda, I lean against her, crossing my arms over my chest, a smug grin lining my face while I watch Easton trot up beside me.

"Who's the best rider?" I sing-song.

"You are, Delilah," he grumbles, dismounting Henry.

Laughing, I push off Creseda. Pulling out carrots from my bag to feed her. "You're as bad of a loser as I am," I mutter.

Rolling his eyes, Easton matches my movements, feeding Henry.

Once he's done, Easton wraps an arm around my shoulder as he veers me toward the treehouse. "Come on, Princess, read me a story."

Easton and I spend the rest of the afternoon lying amongst quilts and pillows, taking turns reading out loud to each other.

# Chapter Five

My arms are open wide as I sprint through the soft grass, running so fast I practically fly through the field. Tilting my head to the sky, the sunshine streams down my face as I smile so wide my cheeks ache as laughter floats from my throat. A deep husky voice rumbles behind me, the laughter sending peace throughout my body as he chases me through the plush, vibrant forest.

I smell ocean and pinewood before sun-kissed arms latch around my waist, hurtling us up into the sky. I squeal with joy as I hold onto the muscular forearms. Taking in the breath-taking serenity before me, the vibrant colors of the field sing to a part of my soul.

My stomach lurches as the male behind me drops to the ground, the wind pulling my hair as it whips across my face. Stopping at the last second, he gently lands, rolling us onto our backs.

Laughing with happiness in my heart, I lay my palms flat on the grass, planning to sink my fingers through the soft, thick strands. Only to halt the second my palm connects with the field's floor.

Instead of grass, I'm met with ash.

Sitting up, I lift my hands in front of me, watching as gray ash flutters from my palm, sprinkling through the gaps between my fingers as it floats to the ground. The sun making it twinkle.

Looking down, I find I'm sitting on cracked black rock. Horror fills my heart as my eyes connect with the once vibrant forest as it burns, blowing away in the wind.

It's dying. Everything is dying.

A scream of loss rips from my throat as I see everything I love disintegrate into nothing.

I'm jarred awake by my body thrashing, my throat raw from screaming in my sleep. I scramble out of bed for water, drinking deeply from my waterskin. Rushing through my dressing suite, I throw on tailored pants and a maroon satin shirt.

I need to find the history books of the Fae.

It's driving me insane dreaming about the Fae every night and not having answers as to why they're no longer here.

Slipping through my suite door, I check that Easton's room is silent and dark. Heaving a sigh of relief that my screaming didn't wake him, I head out of the east wing, descending the stairs into the family vault below the palace.

Everything of importance is stored in the vaults. There's no point checking the library  I know my father would hate to have any type of book speaking about magic or Fae in his palace.

No guards are stationed throughout the palace, only on

the outside and at the borders, searching for the one who freed the rebels. Guards only monitor the halls around my father's quarters in the west wing. I suppose he only cares whether he lives or dies, not his daughter.

I shake my head, trying to erase the thought and the pang in my heart.

I light the gas lamps lining the vault's corridor. Following the line of fires, I walk the long empty hall until I'm standing in front of the entrance. Its circular door takes up the entire wall, a turning mechanism centered in the middle, designed in the shape of a ship's helm.

Taking out my key, I unlock the door and turn the wheel, heaving at the strength needed to move it. The click as it unlocks echoes throughout the empty hall, and I can only pray that someone has oiled the hinges.

A sigh of relief escapes me when the door opens silently. Plucking a candle off the wall, I enter through the arch. You'd think with all the money my father has he would have built a better vault or at least organized its contents.

The circular room is filled with ancient armor strewn about, books scattered over the floor and any available flat surface, and piles of gold coins tower in every direction. Heirlooms overflow from trunks and odd pieces of furniture lay piled throughout the room.

I huff out a breath as I begin to dig through everything, the dust flying throughout the room mingling with my breath. It's only until what feels like hours later, after picking through half the room's contents, do I finally find anything.

Picking up a heavy leather book, I blow the dust off its cover as I trace my fingers over the raised words. It's an ancient book, well before the Fae lands fell. However, it contains writing about the Fae land—elemental magic, courts, spells, and rituals. I flip through the book, pausing as I reach the different types of magic used in the land—candle, elemental, pure, dark, and crystal magic.

Tucking the book into my bag, I start to pack up. I can go over it tonight without the risk of getting caught snooping. Walking out, I lock the vault, blowing out the flames lining the corridor walls as I sneak back upstairs.

Three days of my father being absent, along with his cronies, has left me with the best sense of peace I've felt in a long time. Annie cleared me to go back to training tomorrow morning. I have a sinking feeling that it's going to be brutal on my muscles after not being able to train for almost a week.

Eating a mouthful of chicken, I lift my gaze to my mother sitting across from me. The past two nights, she's stayed in her own quarters, declining the invitation to dine with Easton and I for dinner. I wonder why she decided to join us tonight.

"Gold is the song she sings," she mutters to no one in particular.

Easton sighs beside me. We're both accustomed to my mother's ramblings, yet sometimes the sadness of it all becomes overwhelming. My mother used to be a beautifully intelligent woman according to Annie. One moment she was here and the next she was gone, as if overnight something snapped her mind in half, spinning and weaving nonsense until nothing made sense.

"I know, Mother, the song is lovely," I say, sipping my water.

I never knew what to say to her when I was younger. I was so confused that one moment my mother was lucid and the next she had seemingly disappeared. With none of the doctors being able to give a medical reasoning for her sudden mental decline, it only confused me further. Over the years I've come to accept that my mother is gone, her lucid moments being few and far between. Now I just go along with whatever she says to calm her.

"Peer inside and find the layers of lives," she whispers.

Ignoring my mother, Easton gazes around the room before lowering his head to mine. "Did you hear the whispers in the palace?"

My brows lower. "No, what is it?"

"The king's army has disappeared."

"The ones with scales see all."

Easton and I lift our heads at my mother's outburst, her face devoid of emotions as her unseeing eyes look past our shoulders to nothing in particular. I resume our conversation when she begins to eat again.

"What do you mean they've disappeared? Did something happen to them?" I ask.

A lock of brown hair falls into his face as he shakes his head. "No one knows. Nobody has seen them since they left."

"When is my father planned to arrive in the seventh sector?" I ask warily.

Concern flashes across his green eyes. "Tomorrow."

I lower my fork, pushing the vegetables around the gold-rimmed plate. I whisper, "We need to pray for the people in sector seven."

Easton's voice wavers as he speaks. "What do you think he'll do?"

The sound of the dining room doors opening snaps both our heads up.

A male server walks in, his face grave as he begins clearing the empty dishes on the dining table. I pick up my glass, taking a sip as all conversation in the dining room stops.

Even my mother seems to hold her breath.

I mean no harm to the servers. The majority of them are lovely people who are trying to survive and make a living, yet I know there's multiple spies that work as servers. It isn't wise to speak around them, for fear of my father hearing every word that comes out of my mouth.

Easton's voice floats through the silent room. "Prepared to kick ass in training tomorrow?"

I grimace. "I am, but my muscles aren't."

Easton rolls his eyes. "It won't be that bad."

I deadpan, "When you were out for two days, you vomited after the warmup."

Cutting into his food once more, he scoffs, "That was entirely different. I was hungover."

"Same thing." I shrug.

"Being hungover and out of shape aren't the same things."

My jaw falls open. "I am not unfit!"

"We'll see tomorrow," he sing-songs.

"That's bullshit and you know it. I'm one of the best trained fighters," I state proudly.

"Yep," he chirps. "Just wanted to hear you sound like an egomaniac."

I lower my voice. "I'm hiding the chocolates from you for a week."

Easton's eyes harden. "You wouldn't dare."

"Watch me."

"The gates were opened. They're watching all of us," my mother blurts.

I frown. That's the most coherent sentence I've heard from her in months.

"What gates were opened?" I ask.

"The devil's," she whispers.

I hold in my sigh. My mother was once a very spiritual woman, praying to the moon on the lunar cycles, worshipping the gods and telling me stories about the universe.

Now she rambles about it.

I'm snuggled in bed later that evening, running my fingers up and down the silk sheets when my bedroom door hinges squeak. Jolting into a sitting position, I find my mother standing in the doorway, holding a lantern beside her, her white dressing gown fluttering to the side from the veranda wind.

I heave a sigh, placing my palm over my pounding heart. "Mother, you scared me."

"I don't have much time," she breathes.

I sit up straighter as she rushes over to my side of the bed.

She sets the gas lamp on the nightstand before taking my hand, her soft creamy skin sliding against my palm before squeezing my hand tightly, forcing me to look into her eyes. My spine stiffens as my gaze connects with clear brown eyes. Not the murky dullness that I've grown accustomed to. I haven't seen my mother lucid in over two years.

"Mom?" I croak, tears pooling in my eyes.

"It's getting worse, and I don't have much time," she rushes out. Digging into her nightgown pocket, her hand returns with a silver-chained crystal pendant dangling between her fingers. Before I can study the pendant, she places the silver chain around my neck, the pendant resting on my chest.

"You must never take it off, Delilah. No matter the truth they try to hide, the darkness isn't as strong as the light."

I open my mouth to speak, my head shaking side to side as disbelief courses through me, but my mother cuts me off.

"In the eyes of the blind it sparkles, whereas the one who wears it prevails."

*She's not lucid.*

Disappointment and sadness flood my heart, the weight of it making me slump. I'm prepared to tell her to go back to bed when she squeezes my hand tighter, her eyes widening.

"Delilah, I'm serious. Please wear this at all times. Hide it under your clothes and show absolutely no one that you're wearing it," she pleads.

The conviction in her voice makes me pause. Her clear eyes tell me she's lucid, yet what she's saying isn't.

She must see my hesitancy and confusion.

"I know dear, but in time it will make sense." She plants a soft kiss on my cheek, then whispers strongly, "I love you."

Tears freely roll down my cheeks as she leaves just as fast as she arrived, taking the glass flame with her, her nightgown flowing behind her.

I wipe my tears away, burying myself in the sheets once more. I cling to the pendant as my tears continue falling, even in my sleep.

# Chapter Six

Easton lunges, his left foot pivoting as his right hand strikes with his blade, yet too slow. I turn, spinning to his vulnerable side. My sword swipes his exposed belly, a smirk dances on my lips as Easton rolls his eyes. We view every training session as a competition. We've lost count over the years, yet I'd say my winning tally is higher than Easton's. I threw myself into training at a young age, at first to be strong, to fight back against my father when he hurt me. Over the years that dream faded away after each hit I wasn't able to stop. I kept up the grueling schedule purely because there's nothing else I'm allowed to do around the palace besides train and appear like a doting, loyal daughter.

It's a miracle in itself that my father believes I shouldn't be completely useless.

If I didn't know any better, I'd say he's been manipulating me all these years to create a carbon copy of himself. Yet for him to do that, he'd have to teach me or speak to me.

Yelling and belittling doesn't count as speaking.

"Okay, I concede for the day." Easton mock bows. "The victory is all yours."

I smile triumphantly despite where my thoughts turned. "Now who looks unfit?"

Easton huffs out a laugh. "Oh get over yourself."

I chuckle as I follow him out the door. "Joining me for lunch today?"

Easton dips his head.

We're strolling through the east wing from the training rink when we hit the first floor of the palace and watch as all hell breaks loose. The halls are buzzing, people running around in every which way. Gasps, whispers, and sobs reach my ears as my feet touch the landing.

In a daze Easton and I turn to each other, making eye contact before we take off for the nurse's quarters, heading straight for Annie.

With everyone running around no one pays us any attention, which in itself is worrisome. I push myself faster. Reaching the nurse's quarters, I bash through the doors, only to stop dead in my tracks.

Annie is huddled in her office chair, her head resting on her knees as her body shakes with sobs. At the sound of our entrance Annie looks up. Her eyes are bloodshot and cheeks blotchy as she covers her mouth with her hand, trying to hide the sounds of her sobs.

I kneel beside her. "What is it? What happened?"

Easton's boots squeak as he steps closer, his warmth radiating behind me.

"H-he killed them," Annie stutters.

My heart begins thumping erratically. "Who? Who did he kill?" I ask, waiting for the answer that will shove the dagger in my heart.

"All of them…Everyone in sector seven."

The moment the words leave her mouth, Annie crumbles, her lips quivering as she cries. I stay on the ground utterly frozen.

"All of sector seven? That's eleven thousand people," I breathe.

Annie's voice cracks. "Everyone's dead. He ordered everyone into the town center, saying he was going to give a mandatory speech... Then he b-bombed them."

My heart stops beating as time pauses. My ears ring so loudly I can't hear anything, yet Annie's lips continue moving. Easton walks around me to Annie, his own eyes full of tears as he hugs her.

I don't feel my body as my feet move on their own accord. As if my body isn't my own. The world might as well have just been pulled out from under me. I knew my father was a horrible person—a murderer—yet I never in a million years thought he'd do something like this.

Executing thousands in one go...

I don't understand any of it.

Why do his men follow him blindly? Why does his army accept his preposterous and horrid orders? It's one thing to receive an order, it's another to follow it.

I exit into the hall, my ears buzzing, fingers tingling and chest heaving as it struggles for oxygen. My vision's blurry as I watch the people around me cry, falling to their knees, while others are vomiting. Some are just as lifeless as I am.

And then I'm running. Suddenly I'm standing in front of Creseda and in the next beat I'm sitting on her bare back as we ride as fast as lightning. I'm not steering her, yet she seems to feel my sadness and knows where to go.

We get no further than a few miles before I'm urging her to stop abruptly. Jumping down, I vomit the entirety of my stomachs contents.

I feel it now. I feel it all.

The bile rising in my throat, the wind slashing across my face, my tears as they stream down my cheeks, the sound of Creseda's worried whines and the tip of her snout nudging me in the back.

I feel the heartbreak, I feel the sadness and I feel the guilt as it begins to kill me from the inside. I feel the grief for every single soul that was taken today.

Eleven thousand people are dead. Innocent people were murdered.

They will never see their family, never feel sunshine on their face, never laugh again, never have a birthday, never see their parents, siblings, and children grow older...because they're dead, they are all *dead*.

I scream.

I scream so loud and viciously my voice cracks as my throat burns.

My knees give out and I hit the ground, a sob wracking my body. My heart hurts...It hurts so much.

My entire being is in unending pain, and it is nothing compared to what those innocent people experienced.

Standing once more on shaking legs, I mount Creseda and urge her forward, getting her to take me as far away as she possibly can.

Creseda halts so suddenly I lurch forward, whacking my forehead as I land on her neck with an *oomph*. Creseda squeals, throwing her head up and down.

"Hey, hey," I soothe, running my hand down her neck. The short black hairs tickling my palm as I do. "What's got you—"

Either I fell asleep on top of Creseda and we're no longer on the capital grounds, or I'm truly going insane.

Words fail me as my jaw hangs open. Three compound buildings sit where my treehouse once was. I'd understand someone destroying it, knocking it down even, except multiple compound buildings being built in under a week? Absolutely impossible.

I check my surroundings, looking for the signature marks around the treehouse. The old unused brick well, half-fallen oak tree, and the red hand paint I placed on the boulder when I was eleven.

I spot them all.

Dismounting Creseda, I find some rope near the old well and create a makeshift rein for her. If I'm going near the mystery building, so is she. Yet when I try to pull her, she stays rooted to the ground.

"Come on, don't be chicken," I pant. "It's just a building."

No matter how much I tug, she won't budge.

Huffing, I pull her toward a tree near the well, tying the end of the rope around it to keep her from bolting. Stroking her snout, I whisper, "I'll be right back, I promise."

Giving her a kiss, I walk toward the buildings.

There's one substantial brick building sitting in the middle between two identical brick buildings half the size, a tiny outback shed sits in the far back. Making my way to the large brick building before me twigs snap and leaves crunch behind me, making me freeze. Unsheathing my fighting knives, I search the area.

I've never been more thankful to be wearing my fighting leathers than in this moment.

I plaster my back against the brick building. Inching around the corner, I stop dead in my tracks. My eyes grow

wide as I take in hundreds of people walking around a courtyard, working in unison. Each second I stay here, the more
my heart beats faster.

Half the people are tall and the other half so short I'd
have to kneel for them to be at eye level with me, yet they're
not children. All their faces are in various stages of ageing,
some young and others old, weathered and peppered with
gray hair.

The air leaves my lungs as I look at each of them, my
eyes darting around the lively courtyard, focusing on one
detail they all have in common.

Elongated ears.

*Fae.*

I ease back around the corner, placing my hand over my
chest to stop my heart from exploding, only to be met with a
pulsing warmth and a zip of electricity as it shoots through
my palm. Pulling my hand away, I dig out the crystal pendant
under my shirt, dropping it the moment I lay my eyes on the
iridescent crystal.

What was once a dull white crystal is now glowing,
pulsing with light.

With each burst of light from the pendant comes a short
breath from my lungs. Squeezing my eyes shut, I try to calm
my breathing.

*In and out. In for four, out for—*

A twig snaps beside me. My voice reacts before my mind
can stop the squeal from escaping. I lock eyes on a small
man, no taller than my thighs, carrying wood. My brows
lower as he walks past me, hobbling from side to side as he
carries the stack of chopped wood in his arms.

He doesn't react to my scream; in fact, he doesn't
acknowledge me at all.

I peek my head around the corner to see if the others

heard me, only to find none of them have stopped their work and no one is looking this way.

Can they not hear me?

Taking a tentative step forward, I tighten the hold on my fighting swords as I edge out into the busy courtyard.

"Excuse me?" I call out.

Nothing. No one acknowledges my presence.

"Hello?"

They truly can't hear or see me.

*I must be losing my mind like my mother.*

That thought alone sends ice down my spine.

Sheathing my swords, I gaze around the courtyard, stunned speechless.

They're truly Fae, albeit some are tiny and pudgy, unlike the strong, tall Fae you read about.

Yet they're all Fae.

Rows upon rows of workers mull about the courtyard, plucking herbs from garden beds, carrying wood, planting seeds, and carrying products into the back door of the main building.

Steeling my spine, I head for the back door.

No one pays me a lick of attention when I join the back of their line. They move as if they're a marching army. It takes less than a minute before I'm in the building, stepping out of the line to the right before I halt.

My eyes nearly bulge out of my head as my hands begin to tremble.

It appears to be a lab with endless rows of tables, covered in glass bottles, boiling pots, burners, tubes of liquid, and tiny glass bottles full of a vibrant orange liquid. The room is so large you could fit my east quarters in here—twice. It's an industrial building with tall ceilings and an open floor plan. Windows line the top half of the walls, beams crisscross overhead, and the floor feels as hard as stone.

*I must have truly gone mad.*

Is this how my mother feels every day? Stuck in her own mind wondering if she's gone insane?

The Fae working indoors are taller than the ones in the garden, their facial features human, yet their ears are elongated and pointed.

None of them stop their work as I walk around to get a better look. None of them talk either. The only sounds I can hear are bubbling liquids, glasses clinking and clashing, and the scuttling of footsteps.

Until a door clangs to my left. Following the sound, I see several Fae exit another room. I stroll toward the door they disappeared through, passing by rows of working Fae.

Opening the steel door, I'm met with the sound of buzzing, so much buzzing it feels like a bee is flapping around in my mind. Confusion mars my features as I enter what appears to be a storage closet. Shelves line the room, creating endless rows like a library, except the shelves are full of only one thing—tiny glass bottles no bigger than the size of my hand.

Descending the small flight of stairs into the room, I pause. Multiple glass jars begin lighting up, glowing with a yellow tinge as small sniffling sounds join the buzzing. I step toward the nearest bottle that's glowing, yet the moment I'm close to it the light extinguishes, taking my air with it.

A sob leaves my mouth. My knees buckle, taking me to the floor where I'm met with more glass jars.

They're all faeries.

Every single bottle contains a tiny faerie, all of them crying.

They're small and yet still have to crouch in the glass,

their tiny opalescent wings folded around themselves as they hug their knees to their chest. Their elongated and pointy ears are so small they're barely visible.

My hand shakes as I reach for the faerie closest to me and pick up the glass bottle. Tears roll freely down my face as the faerie begins to scream and sob as I hold the jar. I gently place it back on the shelf, not wanting to cause it any more pain.

"Can you hear me?" I whisper.

I bring my face closer. It's not looking at me.

"I can help you; can you hear me?"

Holding my breath, I wait for any sign that the faerie can hear me, to no avail. It doesn't stop crying and it never looks my way.

*None of them can hear me.*

How do I free them if they can't see the humans in this world? They'd have nowhere to go, and I couldn't even tell them where to go.

It must be a spell.

It's impossible considering there's been no magic for one hundred and forty-eight years, yet the Fae race died then also, and unless I've lost my sanity, these Fae are very much alive. Standing on wobbly legs, I make a vow to the Fae that I will return and help them. I refuse to see any more innocent people held against their will.

I catalogue every detail as I make my way through the compound back to Creseda, anything that might tell me what they're creating, why they can't see me, how they're here, and why I couldn't see them before now.

Creseda is still spooked when I reach her. Stroking her snout, I ease the rope off and mount her, riding back to the palace as fast as we can.

A new sense of urgency in Creseda's gallop.

Standing in the middle of the vault, I rummage through the remaining books I didn't have the chance to go through. I pluck up any books that have the slightest mention of Fae, their lands, or magic. I'm pumped up on adrenaline, moving throughout the room a lot louder than intended, when Easton's deep gravelly voice drawls behind me.

"What are you doing?"

Jumping as I turn to face him, I hiss, "You scared me!"

"I've been looking for you everywhere," he states.

His gaze lowers to the books in my hand. When he lifts his face to mine, concern and confusion swim in his green eyes.

"What are you doing?" he repeats.

"I'm looking for my mother's journal," I lie, hiding the books behind my back.

I'm a terrible person for lying but I think I make up for it with being a horrible liar. I hate lying to him. It makes my stomach queasy and guilt fill my heart, but I can't stand the idea of him thinking I'm losing my mind like my mother. I can handle a lot of things, but Easton looking at me with disbelief? *That* I cannot handle.

I know how it would sound to him. *Easton, I discovered Fae aren't dead! They can't speak, see, or hear me but they're real!* I'll pass.

"Where did you go?" he asks curiously.

I blink. "What?"

His brows lower. "This morning," he states flatly.

"I went to the treehouse, why?"

"Why? Because one moment you're behind me and the next you've disappeared."

My heart sinks at the reminder of what happened to sector seven.

With everything I saw at the treehouse, my mind short-circuited, making me forget what happened and why I went there in the first place.

Shame and guilt coat my tongue. I can't believe I forgot.

"I needed to be alone," I whisper.

Easton rubs the back of his neck. "Do you want to go for a walk and talk?"

"No. I doubt anyone wants to see a royal right now and I can't handle it if they look at me with disgust."

Easton's eyes soften. "You didn't kill those people, Delilah."

"My father did." My words are coated with venom. "It doesn't matter that I didn't give the order. They're still dead at the hands of my own flesh and blood."

Easton's mouth opens to protest, but I cut him off before he can speak. "I love you Easton, but please don't try to make me feel better about this. I don't deserve to feel better, no one does. Everyone who was involved should be ashamed of themselves."

Easton doesn't say anything. Taking his silence as an opportunity, I pick up the remainder of books lying at my feet.

"I want to be alone right now," I say gently.

Standing, I step forward, wrapping an arm around his waist, letting his warmth and sandalwood smell soothe me. "I'll see you at dinner. We can eat in my room," I offer.

Easton's lips touch the top of my head. "Of course, anything you want."

# Chapter Seven

I've combed through eight books, and nothing mentions a spell that conceals Fae, not to the magnitude of the compound. There must have been at least five hundred Fae working, not counting the poor faeries that were trapped in those glass bottles and the other two buildings I didn't search.

I'm opening a new book on crystal magic when I hear Easton's signature knock on my bedroom door.

"Just a moment!" I yell.

Jumping off the bed, I stash all the books in a loose floorboard beside my nightstand. It's not an ideal hiding place but it will have to do for now.

I open my door to find Easton standing before me, a crooked impish smile on his lips and a small figure beside him staring down at her feet. My head rears back in shock. My mother.

Easton strides forward, bending his head beside my ear as he passes me. "I found her wandering the halls."

With my heart in my throat, I open the door further, gently taking her hand. "Mother, are you all right?"

It feels like an eternity before she finally lifts her head, the movement making any hope I felt seconds before dissipate as I stare into her glazed, vacant brown eyes.

"Black as night yet not alive."

She's not lucid.

Looking over my shoulder at Easton, I frown. "Was she speaking like this in the hall?"

Rubbing the back of his neck, Easton nods.

"Okay, come on, let's eat dinner in my dining suite," I say. Wrapping an arm around her, I guide her to the dining room, placing her in a seat beside mine.

The dining suite in my quarters is simple compared to the main one in the palace. White walls, and a black fireplace with a matching black granite sitting table adorns the room. The kitchen staff has brought up enough food to feed an army. The dining table is full of steamed vegetables, roast chicken, lamb, beef, mashed potatoes, gravy, and an assortment of desserts lining a silver tower dessert tray.

"Busy, busy mutts," my mother mumbles over and over.

"Any news about the sectors?" I ask Easton, distracting myself from the pang in my heart at my mother's ramblings. I place a handful of meat and vegetables onto my mother's plate before serving myself.

Easton helps himself, putting twice the amount of food on his own plate. "No news after the attack. No one's seen or heard from your father since, or his army."

Eyebrows furrowing, I set my cutlery down. "Again?"

Easton dips his head, lowering his eyes to his plate as he pushes his food around.

"The plan was for him to visit each sector. Is he going to do another surprise attack? Is that why his army has disappeared again?" I whisper.

"No one knows, Delilah," he says solemnly. "They've cut off communication."

I lean back in my chair. "What do you mean they've cut off communication?"

Easton sighs, his voice barely above a whisper. "They abandoned the messengers. All of them."

My mouth drops open as Easton's lips flatten. "How did he accomplish that?"

"An elaborate ploy, sending the messengers only for them to return to find their camp deserted."

Shaking my head in disbelief, I pour myself and Easton a large glass of wine.

"The truth will be set free," my mother exclaims.

Turning to my mother, I try to see if she has another riddle for me. "What's going to be set free?"

My mother raises her head, her glassy eyes on me for once. "What should have been righted long ago," she whispers.

Warmth pulses at my chest. Setting down my wine glass, I look from my mother to Easton, his eyes downcast as he shovels mashed potatoes in his mouth. Quickly placing my palm over my chest, my eyes widen as it connects with the warm crystal pendant.

My voice trembles as I say, "What's going to be set free, Mother?"

"The world," she rasps.

I lower my hand from my chest as I let out a long sigh. No more riddles. She's gone back to speaking in a rambling language that only she understands

Turning my attention back to Easton, he begins telling me a new training regime he's created for us. My mother sits perfectly still in her seat as she eats. The pendant hiding under my shirt thrums and warms my chest the remainder of dinner.

It's making me anxious. I need to know why it acts the way it does; I've never had a pendant pulse at my touch or produce its own heat.

By the time dinner finishes, anticipation has me bouncing on the balls of my feet as I stand waiting at my bedroom door. Pressing my ear against the wooden frame, I strain to hear servants milling about in the dining room. I might be paranoid, but I don't want the off chance of anyone coming in here to find magic books strewn about.

It isn't until an hour later when the last of the servants leave, their puffs of air blowing out the candles hanging in the silent corridor, do I move to the side of my bed. Lifting the loose floorboard, I pull out the crystal book I started reading earlier tonight before Easton and my mother interrupted me.

Pulling the crystal pendant off my neck, I place it beside the book, turning page after weathered page. The comforting rustle of paper soothing my nerves as I search for anything that looks familiar to the pendant. About three hundred pages later, I stop.

My heart begins beating so fast I can hear the rapid thumping in my ears. My mouth opens in shock as the air in my lungs leaves me in a whoosh. My mother was lucid when she gave me the pendant; she wasn't insane or jabbering on nonsense. I lift the white crystal pendant, placing it on the page beside a doppelgänger drawing of it.

The title reads "Veil of Truths".

It's not just any pendant or crystal. It's a conduit crystal that had a spell cast to it over a thousand years ago. The crystal pendant unveils spells and truths for those who wear it.

With my now trembling hands, I lower the book to the floor, my fingers making the weathered pages shake. I'm not insane or going mad—there truly are Fae trapped in the human lands.

And how did my mother have the pendant in the first place? She hasn't been lucid since that night so I can't ask her.

Not giving it a second thought, I stand, running out of my room into Easton's.

I barge through the door, my heart hammering wildly. The second I jump onto the mattress, Easton jolts awake, his eyes wide and bleary as he sweeps me head to toe before scanning the room beyond into the hall.

"What is it? What's happened?!"

"I can't explain it. I have to show you," I say, grabbing his arm as I drag him out of bed. I march him into his dressing room and pull out his riding clothes, throwing them at him as he stands there, his face a mix of annoyance and bewilderment. When all he does is stare at me, I clap my hands. "Hurry up!"

Snapping him out of his trance, Easton stumbles as he tries to pull on his pants. "Delilah, you're freaking me out. What is it?"

"If you think you're freaked out now…just you wait."

Leaving his room to change myself, I grab the crystal, safely putting it around my neck and under my shirt.

I'm strapping one of my fighting swords to my hip when Easton strolls into my room, his brows shooting into his hairline when he sees me. "I need swords for this excursion?"

I shrug. "You can never be too cautious."

Without another word Easton turns, only to shortly return with various swords strapped across his back, fighting knives dangling from his hips.

Easing open my window, I hand chalk to Easton, directing him as we shimmy up the drainpipe. Taking the rope down the slope of the roof tile, I show him where to land, trying not to chuckle as Easton lands beside me a moment later with a loud grunt.

"So that's how you sneak out," he mumbles. Easton looks between the roof and myself several times before shaking his head. "I always thought you took the servants' stairs."

Giggling, I open Creseda's skylight window. "Where would the fun be in that?" Creseda moves to the side before I jump. Brushing hay off my clothes, Easton lands beside me less gracefully, grunting and groaning as he falls on his side. "You need to start taking dance lessons. For a guard you move around like a stomping giant."

Easton scoffs as he drags himself into a standing position, his voice gruff. "Sorry that people can't gracefully drop from ceilings."

I roll my eyes. "Stop being so dramatic and hurry up," I whisper as I unlatch the stable door, pulling Creseda out of the barn. It isn't until we've safely made it into the thick forest do Easton and I mount our horses, taking off into the darkened night to the treehouse.

Easton and I tie the reins around the oak tree next to the old well. Taking Easton's hand, I walk him in front of the main compound building. I can't see the Fae walking around the courtyard. They probably have a different routine when it's nighttime. Perhaps they sleep in the other buildings. I can, however, still hear the clanks and clacks of some working inside.

Confusion swirls in Easton's eyes. "Ahh, Delilah…it's just the treehouse," he says hesitantly.

"Not for long," I reply. Removing the pendant from my neck I hand it to Easton.

I turn, coming face to face with the treehouse. I wave my hand at it, knowing the compound lies there behind a veiled spell that only those who wear the pendant can see. It truly is jarring. One moment there's three compound buildings and a large courtyard in the middle of the dense forest, and the next, all I see is my rundown treehouse.

Magic is fascinating.

"It's very pretty but not particularly my style." He chuckles.

"Oh shut up and put it on. You'll be speechless in a moment anyways."

Easton hesitates before taking the pendant out of my palm, but the moment the chain goes around his neck, Easton's expression drops entirely. The color drains from his face as he stumbles backward.

"What the fuck is that?" he yells.

Grabbing his hand, I drag him forward. "Go inside and see."

Wild eyes lock on mine. "Over my dead body am I going anywhere near that thing!"

I roll my own eyes. "It's not a thing, it's a building."

Easton sputters expletives as he shakes his head. "Nope. I don't feel like dying today."

"You won't die. Just go in there and have a look around." I take his hand, rubbing my thumb up and down the inside of his palm. "You can't see it without the necklace. You must go in there alone. I'll stay here and wait for you."

His eyes turn round. "You want me to go in there alone—"

"I can't explain anything without you seeing it for your-self," I interrupt.

"You owe me all the chocolate in the palace for this," he grumbles. Shaking his head, he approaches the compound.

From an outsider's perspective, it looks as if Easton is just walking aimlessly around the woods, but I know he's about to step inside the building in just a matter of—

A deep gravelly scream pierces the night sky as Easton trips over his own feet. I watch as he slowly walks around in circles, taking in the worktables inside the building. He's sheathed his fighting swords, his hands dangling aimlessly as horror fills his eyes. I know he's reached the trapped faeries in the glass bottles when he falls to the ground, his shoulders curving inward as a lone tear runs down his cheek.

Moments later, Easton returns as white as a ghost, every now and then shaking his head in shock. He turns to face the compound once more, his voice quivering. "They're still alive."

I take a step forward, standing beside him. "Alive, yet trapped," I say solemnly.

Easton takes the pendant off his neck, then places it around mine. The compound unveils before my eyes once more.

"What is this?" he asks, voice full of awe, as his thumb brushes the glowing pendant.

"My mother came to me in the middle of the night and gave it to me. She said, 'In the eyes of the blind it sparkles, whereas the one who wears it prevails.'"

I pick up the pendant, holding the warm crystal in my palm as it glows, brightening the forest floor beneath my feet. "At first, I thought she was blabbering on in her usual way, so I didn't give it much thought. I came here the day that sector seven was attacked… I forgot I was wearing it. Imagine my surprise when I not only saw the large buildings but Fae walking around in the courtyard." I shake my head as I stare at the sleeping compound. "The pendant was glowing and radiating warmth against my chest."

Easton and I slowly make our way back to Creseda and Henry as I tell him about the Fae magic books I found in the family vault. Along with the crystal magic book explaining the Veil of Truths spell cast onto the necklace over a thousand years ago.

We take a seat in the grass, gazing at the forest, my eyes seeing the quiet compound while Easton's sees the treehouse.

"In all the books I've read, I haven't found a single one that explains how or why the Fae lands died and whenever you try to ask someone about it...no one seems to remember."

"It was a long time ago, Delilah. Perhaps people have forgotten," he says warily.

I shake my head adamantly. "No, it's more than that. All the books stop entirely. The history is incomplete, like the lands vanished overnight." I turn my gaze to his. "At least one person should remember what happened. It's odd that nobody does."

Easton looks at me anxiously. "Perhaps people at the time didn't want to acknowledge it or the ruling king banned those from talking about it."

"If so, they lived in peace together, East. People had loved ones in the Fae lands. It would have been heartbreaking for many. They wouldn't have dismissed what happened, let alone forget." Taking a deep breath, I continue. "Clearly something happened. We were told all Fae were extinct." I fling my arms in front of me toward the compound. "But they're not, and those Fae in the building couldn't have escaped because they're trapped in a spell."

Easton sits up, his brows pulling low. "You think the Fae lands still exist?"

"What if it's hidden just like this compound?" I suggest.

"Why would they conceal themselves?"

I lower my voice. "What if they didn't do it voluntarily?"

Easton blinks. "Fae were the most powerful beings in this world. How could they all have been trapped?"

"I don't know but clearly something went wrong, and it's not a stretch of the imagination to think the Fae lands are hidden." Turning to the compound, I lower my voice. "There has to be more than five hundred Fae here, Easton, and that's not including the hundreds of trapped fairies in the glass bottles." Disgust mars my words.

I don't voice my suspicions about my dreams being connected. I don't know why I dream about the Fae lands, and Easton already looks sick to the stomach at the idea that they're all still alive yet trapped.

Easton's deep voice pulls me from my thoughts. "Should we set them free?"

I shake my head. "We can't help them if they can't hear or see us. Besides, I think the spell is more complicated than just invisibility to hide them."

"What do you mean?" he asks.

"They move like soldiers. I dare say whoever cast the spell is giving them orders that they can't deny, otherwise they would have left a long time ago."

Both of us turn to the forest as it holds more questions than answers.

Awe lines Easton's words as he speaks. "I can't believe the treehouse you have been going to for your whole life has been hiding this all along."

Perhaps that's why I dream of the Fae.

I shrug. "I call it the In-between now."

"Why?" He chuckles.

"Because it's in between both lands, the humans and the Fae."

His lips lift into a grin. "Did you just come up with that?"

"Yes," I say smirking. "And it's catchy so it's sticking."

Easton's chuckle dies off. "I can't believe Fae are still alive."

My heart pinches, my voice lowering. "I can't believe they've been trapped all this time."

"You're not going to stop here, are you?" he says, quirking a brow.

I lift my chin. "We're going to find the Fae lands," I declare.

"I knew it," he mutters to himself before sitting up. "You'd have to leave the palace and we don't know if there even are Fae in the old lands. What if all that's left are the Fae trapped here?"

"I can't keep sitting around, day in and day out, not doing anything."

*I can't do nothing anymore.*

"You've been freeing as many people as you can. That's not nothing, Delilah," he says softly.

"It's not enough. I can't do anything to help my people. I was kidding myself thinking I could try to help them from within. I mean, look at what happened to sector seven. No one can stop him." For the first time in years, hope flutters through my heart. "Perhaps the Fae can," I breathe. My voice grows with enthusiasm. "We co-existed before they disappeared. What if they can help restore our world to what it used to be?"

"What if there isn't any Fae in the lands to help?" Easton's voice grows solemn. "What if they don't want to help?"

"It's the only hope of change we have."

"Are you ready to go against your father?" Easton whispers.

"No, but I will be." My voice lowers. "I have to be."

No one deserves to live like this anymore.

Easton and I spread out on my bedroom floor the following night, books, maps, and pieces of paper strewn about in all directions. "The old Fae lands are about a two day's ride from the south side palace border," Easton mutters.

I study the map before us. "It's a mystery as to why my father never expanded. Half the country has just been left to rot," I say flatly.

Easton and I searched the family vault together, accumulating more books, trinkets, and an old map of the Fae and human lands. The top northern part of Aloriah is the human lands. The southern half belonged to the Fae, divided by five elemental courts—Earth, Air, Water, Fire, and Essence. The elements of the Fae magic. A large tree sits in the middle of the lands, the Mason River snaking through the courts, linking them together. Starting from the Earth court, moving all the way down to the bottom of Aloriah, and ending in the Essence Court.

I point to the river in the human lands. "We could shorten the trip by taking the Claremont River."

Easton waves his hand in the air. "We'd need a boat for that."

I lift my head as I stare at him blankly.

He chuckles. "Oh, right. Secret mission princess and all that."

Ignoring his teasing, I return my gaze to the map. "I can

get us a rowboat. Anything bigger and I think we'd be drawing too much attention."

Especially after my last prison escape.

Easton rubs his hand over his chin. "How much water and food should we bring?"

"I'd say two weeks' worth of supplies. I don't want to be caught unprepared."

"I think the bigger question is, how are we both going there? There's only one necklace," he says, staring at the apex of my chest where the pendant lies hidden.

I tuck my hand beneath my shirt, pulling out the silver chain. "I've added a longer chain so we can both wear it to get in. It'll be uncomfortable but if the Fae truly are there, I'm sure one of them could place a truth spell onto another crystal similar to this one."

"And if they don't?" he adds warily.

I wink. "Then we'll truly be closer than ever before."

Rolling his eyes, Easton ignores my quip. "When should we leave?"

I grimace. "Before my father returns. It'll be too difficult to get all the supplies out of the palace while he and his cronies are here."

He nods. "We should start moving everything tomorrow night. We can stash it all in the In-between. Take two trips so people don't get suspicious."

"Or we could just leave in the middle of the night. We'll disappear either way, can't get more suspicious than that."

We can't lie and say we're leaving for court business; everyone would know it's a façade. My father doesn't let me leave the palace grounds for anything let alone court duties. He's not a stupid man; if he knew Easton and I were going to the treehouse with weeks' worth of supplies, he'd lock me up faster than I could say no.

"Very true." He sighs. "When do you want to leave?"

I nod at the map. "Tomorrow night," I declare.

Settling into silence, Easton maps out the route we're to take to the Claremont River. Drawing a lined path, his adorable face scrunches in concentration.

"What about Creseda?" I ask, chewing my bottom lip.

"I'll take care of Creseda and Henry." Seeing the anxiety written all over my face, Easton leans forward, covering my hand with his. "Do you trust me?"

"Of course," I answer quickly, not needing any time to think.

Easton winks, returning his attention to the map. "Then there's no need to worry."

# Chapter Eight

After knocking, I stroll into the nurse's quarters. Seeing Annie settled behind her desk has the corner of my lips turning up. Her face brightens as she smiles. "Hello gorgeous, how are you feeling today?"

"Feeling much better, thank you. I was actually wondering if you wanted to come for a stroll in the garden with me. Possibly have some lunch by the river?" I ask, lifting the woven basket, containing the pre-packed lunch I asked the kitchen to prepare.

"Of course, I'd love to!" she exclaims, jumping up from her seat. She grabs a black-wooled coat off the rack against the wall, wrapping it around herself. "After you."

We're silent as we leave the nurse's quarters, not daring to speak with the number of eyes and ears in the palace. The only sound that fills the empty corridor is the heels of our shoes as we move along to the northern gardens, a more private area not traveled.

Reaching the far end of the gardens, the palace a small blip behind us, I lay the white-and-black checkered blanket on the grass.

Annie lowers herself to the ground, crossing her legs as she gazes at the vast forest before us. "Easton already said his goodbyes this morning," she says quietly.

My head whips toward her. "You already know?" I breathe.

"The specifics? No. Easton said it was better that way. However, I do know that this surprise lunch isn't happening purely because you enjoy my company," she teases.

I lower my eyes to the food before me. "You know I enjoy your company. Nevertheless, you're right, it is a good-bye." I lift my eyes to hers, rushing on. "A temporary goodbye."

Annie finally slides her gaze to me, the golden rings around her pupils sparkling as they shimmer with silver. "It's about time."

"I'm not leaving permanently," I scoff. "I could never be that selfish."

Annie clicks her tongue. "I would, and you should."

"I can't do that to my people."

Annie places her soft hand on mine. "It's useless while your father reigns. Nobody can stop him; anything short of killing him will fail."

Her words ring true. People have tried to overthrow my father and kill him in the past. Those who attempted have either been found dead, floating in the Claremont River, or vanished mysteriously. People grew too fearful to continue trying—another moment in history where hope was lost.

I know that I can't do much to help, yet hearing Annie voice it out loud, that nothing would ever work against him unless he was buried in the ground, sends a pang to my heart. The people of Aloriah cannot weather these conditions for more than a year, let alone twenty to thirty, when my father will be on his death bed and I'll be reigned queen.

My voice cracks as I speak, "So we do nothing?"

"No. We play our part." She raises her brows. "Every retaliation counts."

I grimace; she most certainly knows whose been responsible for freeing people over the years.

"Will you be safe?" she asks suddenly, her voice wavering.

"As safe as I can be," I vow.

She gazes into my eyes, searching for the answers she seeks. Patting my hand, she draws back, a smile tugging on her lips. "What did you bring me?"

My own smile flourishes at that. "Cupcakes, lemon tarts, chicken sandwiches, and a fruit platter."

Annie leans forward, peering into the basket at the item I hid for myself. My cheeks heat as she quirks a brow.

"Doughnuts," she mutters to herself. "I awakened an addict."

Chuckling, I hand Annie her lunch, the sound of the wind blowing through the forest filling the silence. Taking a bite of my sandwich, my heart squeezes as dread begins to fill my stomach.

"If we're not back in a month." My voice wavers slightly. "I want you to take Creseda and Henry and leave." I slide my gaze to Annie's, letting the conviction in my voice and eyes show. "Never come back. Ever."

"Don't have to ask me twice. The only reason I stuck around was for you two," she chirps.

My jaw falls open. "I thought you loved your job!"

Her eyes soften. "I used to, very much." She leans forward, tucking a strand of my dark brown hair behind my ears, the ends fluttering at my waist. "However, I don't enjoy the reason behind why I have to attend to wounds so often."

I close my eyes as my breathing hitches.

"I've never thanked—"

"Nope, no need for thank-yous." She waves her hand in the air between us. "I know you're grateful… Blah, blah, blah."

I click my tongue. "Can't we have a nice moment?"

"No, if we have too much of a nice moment, I'm afraid I'll never see you again." She grabs my hand and squeezes. "I plan to have many happy moments with you, Delilah."

My throat tightens as my eyes burn. I pick up the basket beside me, shoving it between us. "Doughnut?" I ask on a wobbly smile.

After saying a tearful goodbye to Creseda, vowing that I'll return as soon as I can while soothing her with a dozen carrots, I'm crouched behind the stable doors, Easton behind my back and whispering in my ear.

"In three, two—"

Before Easton can finish, a blast rocks the very ground below my feet, the force behind it knocking me backward into Easton's chest. My ears ring hollow from the sound. Easton grabs my arms, wasting no time as he pulls me up, running to the other side of the stable to the hunting horse and chariot we prepared, filled with everything we stole last night.

"How much gasoline did you use?" I whisper-yell as Easton drags the stable doors open.

Rushing to the other side of the chariot, Easton and I open the doors at the same time, jumping inside. He leans forward to grab the horse's reins.

"You told me to create a distraction big enough to have all the guards attend!"

"I didn't say to nearly burn the damn palace down!" I snap.

The hunting horse takes off before I can continue speaking, galloping so fast I'm tossed backward into the leather seats with a grunt.

I quickly turn, looking through the glass, my eyes connecting with Creseda's as we're taken away. Her knowing eyes never waver from mine, even as the stable grows smaller, turning into a blip in the distance.

*She will be fine*, I chant to myself, over and over like a prayer.

Once all I see is the night's forest surrounding us, I twist in my seat, jumping as the pad of Easton's thumb wipes across my cheek. I'm surprised to find it damp as he pulls it back.

I didn't realize I was crying.

"She'll be all right, I promise you," he whispers.

I swallow the thick lump in my throat as I nod. "I know, I trust you."

Easton grasps my hand. "I have some news."

"What is it?"

"I spoke with Cole earlier this evening. I've decided to choose myself."

My eyes widen on a gasp. "Does that mean…?"

Easton dips his head as he blows out a rush of air. "I'll be telling my father that I'm in a romantic relationship with Cole when I return."

I fling myself at Easton, wrapping my arms around his neck as I clutch him. "I'm so proud of you, East."

"Thank you."

I lean back in the carriage further. "I can't believe we left," I say in astonishment.

"Phase one complete. Now all we have to do is find the Fae lands that have been trapped for one hundred and forty-eight years, beg them to come back, and help take your father down." Sarcasm drips from his words as he shrugs. "Won't be too difficult."

"Oh, shut up and enjoy the moment. You've been begging me to leave for years."

Easton's smile grows so large it takes up half his face. "I'm so happy we're finally leaving."

"It's not forever," I remind him.

"I know, I know. I'm just happy to get you away from the palace, even for a day."

I take his hand in mine. "Thank you. For coming, for always being there for me, thank you. I truly don't thank you enough…for everything you do for me."

"Together forever," he promises, kissing the back of my hand.

"Together forever," I vow.

Turning his body to the side, one knee up on the seat, he faces me. "So do you think dragons are still alive?"

My head falls back on a laugh. "What is with your obsession with dragons!"

"They're dragons!" He beams. "Not only do they fly, but some have powers!"

"I think everything has magic over there, anything with a life force," I say, remembering a passage from one of the Fae books.

His face drains of color. "Even trees?"

Laughter booms out of me. "Are you afraid of trees?" I ask incredulously.

"If they snatch you up while walking, yes!"

"How adorable, my trusty protector, afraid of trees," I say, giggling.

His eyes glint with mischief. "You're laughing now but if a tree snatches you up, I'd bet gold that you'd soil yourself."

I gasp. "That was one time, and I was eight!"

"Age is nothing but a number. You soiled yourself."

I raise my brows in challenge. "Do I need to remind you of the horse manure incident?"

Easton's eyes grow so large I see the whites of his eyes. "No, we're good."

"That's what I thought." I smirk, satisfaction shining in my eyes.

"You're evil." He laughs, planting a kiss on the top of my head.

Chuckling, I lay my head on his shoulder, the adrenaline that was pumping through my body as we left finally dissipating. Easton's warmth comforts me as my eyes grow heavy, and then sleep pulls me under.

"Delilah! DELILAH!"

Jolting at Easton's voice screaming in my ear, I awake to his face in front of mine as white as a ghost, his chest rising and falling rapidly as his hands tremble on my shoulder.

I sit up so fast I knock him backward. "What is it? What's wrong?"

The next words he utters stop my heart completely, my stomach dropping from my body as my blood turns cold.

"Your father's here."

My body begins running on autopilot. I don't consciously tell my feet to move, yet I start descending the carriage stairs. My breath hitches as I find my father standing in front of me. His appearance is more disheveled than usual—his gray hair tussled, black trousers wrinkled, and his tunic's top buttons are undone. I've only ever seen him in his impeccable court clothing. The sight of him looking like an average man jolts me into action.

"Father, what are you doing here?"

"The same could be said for you, Delilah." His voice demands respect and submission. "Ah, Easton. Of course, wherever Delilah is, so are you."

Easton takes a step in front of me, his jaw clenching as he spits his next words. "Your Majesty."

"You have such disdain for someone that gives you everything. Shocking," my father says coldly.

Taking a step toward him to get his focus off Easton, I say, "We decided to take a camping trip along the river. We'll be back at the palace in three to four days."

"Such a pity that you still haven't learned your lesson yet, Delilah," he says as deadly as the blade strapped to his waist.

"What lesson would that be?" I dare ask.

"That you are never to lie to your king."

King. Not father. He never acknowledges that I'm his daughter.

"I'm not lying—"

His face turns red, a vein throbbing in his neck as he screams, "*Do not lie to me!*" He takes two steps forward, looking down his nose as he glares at me. "Do not disrespect me by lying. Where are you going?" He sneers.

He's walked so close that my back hits the carriage door. My throat turns dry as I speak. "Easton and I are taking a camping trip."

"You lying piece of filth!" he barks, striking my face.

My cheek burns as the force of my father's fist sends stars into my vision. Hit after hit comes as quick as lightning before Easton can reach me.

Silence starts to spread within me as I prepare myself for the onslaught of what's to come. My father never stops until I'm on the ground or bleeding.

Before my father's fist falls again, I hear Easton's growl of rage before he lunges for him, my scream of protest falling on deaf ears. Easton uses all his strength to hit the back of my father's head with the hilt of his sword. My eyes grow wide in horror as my father doesn't move an inch.

I've trained with Easton all my life. That hit alone could have killed him, yet my father doesn't so much as flinch.

My father turns, a predator chasing his prey.

Before I can move my father lunges for Easton, repeatedly striking him in the face. The sight sends unbearable pain and hopelessness pounding through my heart. Before he can hit him again, I'm standing in front of Easton, facing my father's cold and detached face.

"Don't you lay one more finger on him," I seethe.

He barks out a laugh. "What did you say?"

I spit at his feet. "I said, *don't lay a finger on him.*"

The humor fades from his face, only to be replaced by a cold, detached mask. The look that enters my father's eyes is what I have nightmares about, the eyes of a monster.

There isn't even a word I can use to describe it.

It's just…a look.

The moment the light within him snaps—the switch controlling his monster as the beast within him is revealed, his true self—it's the moment that part of himself takes over.

Nothing good ever happens when those eyes devoid of life stare at me.

Before anyone can take their next breath, my father's arm snakes behind me, the corner of my eye catching the reflection of the moon's light glinting off silver.

I glance down. His knife sheath is empty.

My heart lurches out of its cage as hot liquid sprays my back. A choked gurgle, and the indescribable sound of a thump hitting the ground comes from behind me.

As I turn, my brain is slower than usual to take in what my eyes are seeing. Easton is crumpled on the ground, his clothes covered in crimson blood, his chest unmoving. His throat slit from ear to ear, unseeing eyes gazing toward the night sky.

Anguish grows inside of me, as pain like nothing I have ever felt before cleaves my heart in two. My soul leaves my body in a guttural scream.

*He's not moving.*

We were so close to leaving. All he ever wanted to do was leave. He begged me to leave every day. All we needed was ten minutes—*ten minutes*, and he would have been free.

*He's not breathing.*

Each thought passing through my mind makes the hole in my heart grow, my soul scream louder, as the rage becomes an uncontrollable boiling thing inside me.

I turn to my father, my hands shaking with barely restrained anger to find him smiling.

The sadistic man is smiling at killing the person I cherish most in this life.

That smile breaks me.

Taking every single ounce of burning hot fury inside of me, I explode.

My father's face falls as my body trembles from the force of the blaring roar that leaves me. My soul and heart's anguished wail blasts from my body as light burns from within me. Wave after wave of unending gold light barrels into my father until it's the only thing I can see. Panic captures my body as my mind runs havoc.

*What just came out of me?*

Utter shock has me stumbling backward, tripping over a boot and making me fall to the ground.

Warm liquid seeps into my clothes. I'm horrified to see I've landed in a puddle of Easton's blood, his lifeless body lying beside me.

A whimper tumbles from my mouth. My eyes burn as I rush over to Easton, running my hands over his face.

"No, no, no, no, no," I weep. "Easton—Easton wake up." Taking his shoulders, I shake him, screaming. "Wake up! Please wake up!"

I can't control the sobs that escape me as he doesn't move.

Taking one last look at those forest green eyes that I've loved since I was a little girl, I kiss him, feeling the warmth slowly leave his body as my lips tremble against his forehead.

"I'm sorry, I'm so sorry." My voice cracks as I whisper, "Together forever."

Rising on wobbly legs, I tumble to the carriage and take as many bags as I can carry.

Not daring to look at Easton one last time in case I shatter, I run as fast as I can to the rowboat, my vision blurring as the unending tears roll down my cheeks. Branches scratch and poke my arms and legs as I sprint through the forest.

A sob leaves my throat as I reach the small white rowboat, bobbing up and down in the water. My hands shake as I dump all the bags inside and untie the rope tethering the boat to the nearest tree.

Weeping as I row, I push myself, not daring to look back. I row until my arms are burning, shaking with exhaustion. I don't stop until I finally see the fork in the stream that leads to the main river. Not caring anymore as to where I end up, to whether I live or die, I dump the oars in the boat, letting the current choose where to take me as I collapse onto my side.

Sobbing between each wheezing breath, I chant over and over, "Together forever."

# Chapter Nine

Gliding through the Mason River, I lead my sisters to the edge of the border.

Surfacing above the water, I turn to them. "This is as far as we go."

Amelia glides to my side, my second on lookout for any unwanted attention. Feeling the change in the water, in unison, my sisters and I turn, waiting.

Moments later, a small white rowboat floats toward us, a spark of light indicating she crossed the invisible threshold. As one, my seven sisters and I dive below the surface, pulling the rowboat along the river and snaking through hidden channels in the mermaid territory. Those without a tail would find themselves lost at the bottom of the ocean if they dared tread these waters.

The current flows in my bones, through my hair and down my tail. The water slips over my scales, and I feel peace. Finally, the time has come, the day my sisters and I have been waiting to take action for.

*We are ready.*

Reaching Delilah's destination, my sisters and I tie the

boat to the small wooden dock on the far-right side of the river. Nodding in appreciation, I prepare to leave when Amelia's voice stops me.

"Should we heal her?" she asks.

Lifting higher out of the water, I peer into the boat, seeing she's indeed been injured.

I send my magic toward her, receiving images in my mind in return.

"No. Our part is done. Now we wait," I order.

Submerging, my sisters and I leave as fast as we arrived, letting the current sing to us as we swim home.

# Chapter Ten

I open my eyes to find a younger version of Annie peering down at me, so close to my face I can feel the warmth of her breath across my cheeks. Her electric copper red hair is cut to her shoulders, parted in the middle, half of it pulled back as the front pieces dangle beside her cheeks. The color makes her blue eyes stand out, the smattering of freckles across her nose adding to her beauty.

"Annie, where's Easton?" I croak.

Younger Annie tilts her head to the side. "Who's Easton?"

The question jars me, sending a flood of memories through my mind, making my heart break all over again.

Jolting up, I realize I'm not speaking to a younger Annie. My thoughts are confirmed as the woman—or should I say Fae—tucks her hair behind her ears, revealing pointed, elongated ears.

Sucking in a breath, I'm shocked I found another Fae. Or perhaps, she found me?

Gazing around the room, I ask, "How did I get here?"

I'm lying on a single cot pushed up against a brick wall. It's a cozy area, with a small fireplace across from two worn couches and a small kitchen across the hall, its counters visible through the open archway.

"I walked out of my cabin this morning to a rowboat tied to my dock. When I peeked inside, you were lying there unconscious." Her features twist, unease simmering in her blue eyes. "You were badly injured, so I used my magic to heal you."

"Healed me?" I squeak. "Oh, right," I say, feeling stupid. I point to her ears. "Pointy ears and all, you have magic."

The Fae chuckles, her cheeks tinting pink. "I don't know why you're so surprised. You have them as well."

"I what?" I yelp.

Without another word, I slide off the cot, rushing around the room in search of a mirror, startling the poor Fae that looks just as frazzled as I am. Finding a bathroom across the other side of the room, I lock myself inside. Slowly turning to the mirror, I study my reflection.

I see no physical changes to my features or body, yet I somehow look different. My creamy skin appears to be glowing. Taking a deep breath I close my eyes, tucking my long dark brown hair behind my ears before my eyelids flutter open. My mouth falls open as I stumble backward into the bathroom door.

I must be hallucinating.

Taking tentative steps closer to the mirror, I gently bring the tip of my fingers to the top of my ears, finding the shape not round, but elongated and pointed.

*How is this possible? Do you change into a Fae when you cross over? No, that's ludicrous. You must be born Fae.*

That single thought ceases every other that was waiting in line to spring into my mind.

*How am I Fae?*

Panic claws its way up my throat as no answers come to mind.

*It's fine,* I tell myself. *Simply a trick of magic.*

I choose to believe the delusional thought, pushing and shoving every confusing question and emotion away.

It's easier to ask questions as a Fae as opposed to a human. Easton and I never considered that perhaps it was the Fae's choice to cut off all ties with the humans. It's better this way, until I find answers that is.

Lifting my head, I peer at myself once more, staring into the depths of my ice blue eyes.

This is the one thing that I must hide. For all I know, they could find out I'm indeed human and be punished for it. Or worse, poked and prodded until they find out why I turned into a Fae.

Taking one last look at my new ears, I straighten my spine before exiting the bathroom, finding the stunned Fae sitting in the living room.

"I'm sorry about earlier. My mind seems to be a bit all over the place," I mutter.

She nods. "You have a concussion."

My eyebrows jump into my hair line. Her magic told her that?

"I have earth magic. My healing powers are stronger and slightly different compared to others," she explains, seemingly reading my mind.

"Well, thank you for taking care of me. I'm Delilah, by the way."

I don't dare tell her my last name. Knowing that the Covington's have ruled Aloriah by that name for centuries. She'd recognize the human name in an instant.

"That's a gorgeous name!" she blurts, turning her head to the side as she studies me. "Definitely suits you."

Smiling, I wait for her to give me her own name. When it doesn't come, I make a rolling motion with my hand.

Her cheeks burn bright crimson. "Oh! Hazel."

I wink. "Stunning name."

Standing, she moves toward the single cot, pointing to my bags. "I brought them in. I didn't want any animals finding them."

"Thank you, that was thoughtful."

My heart stops cold as I spot Easton's bag beside the cot. In my haste last night, I didn't pay attention to which bags I picked up.

"Who's Easton? You were calling out the name in your sleep. Were you two traveling together?" Hazel asks.

Hearing his name out loud makes my stomach sink as bile rises. I will the tears not to come, blinking rapidly to make them disappear. My voice cracks as I try to speak. "I actually don't remember much."

The lie tastes sour on my tongue, yet the thought of saying what happened to Easton… Speaking the words brings ice to my veins.

"Where are we?" I ask, changing the topic.

"Western border of the Earth Court," Hazel chirps. Walking into the kitchen, she returns with two cups of tea, handing one to me.

Taking a sip, my eyes widen as the flavor of chamomile erupts on my tongue. My mouth salivates over the sweet floral taste, bringing my taste buds to life.

I don't remember ever drinking tea this sweet at home. It—

*My senses are enhanced.*

What else has changed and why?

Hazel's feathery sweet voice drags me from my thoughts.

"Do you want to go for a walk outside? See if you remember anything?"

I set the mug down. "I'd love that."

Following Hazel past the living room, we walk through the arched front door. My hand flies to my mouth as a gasp erupts out of me. The Fae lands are still alive.

A cobblestoned pathway snakes from the cabin to a wooden dock. A small bridge arches over the river, with both sides of the riverbed covered in lively flowers of pink, orange, blue, and purple. Two large oak trees curve toward each other in front of the cabin, creating a canopy archway of vibrant green leaves. Stepping onto the grass, my heart soars; it feels exactly like my dreams, soft and cloud-like. Turning back, I find the small, one-level cabin built of rocks, bricks, and straw. Small puffs of smoke float from the chimney.

Every color I see is magnified, the air I breathe clean and pure. I can hear birds singing from miles away, the grass rustling as tiny insects move between the blades.

All my senses are amplified.

Exactly like my dreams.

Coming to sit beside Hazel on the riverbed, I tentatively touch the water, joy erupting throughout my body as the energy of the water sings through my fingers.

"This place is magical," I breathe.

Hazel chuckles. "Literally."

Internally chastising myself, I realize I need to act as a Fae who's lived here her whole life. My awestruck face probably isn't convincing Hazel.

"How long have you lived here?" I ask.

Hazel's face shudders, her shoulders tightening. "Around one hundred and forty years."

I bite my tongue to keep the surprise in. She doesn't look a day over twenty-five.

The Fae truly age differently.

"Do you remember where you live?" Hazel asks, plucking pink flowers from the garden bed.

Shaking my head, I tamp down on the disgust I feel at the thought of calling the palace home. Brows furrowing, Hazel pauses, the flowers in her hand freezing midair. "You can stay here. Until your memory comes back. I can't in good conscience let you leave with a concussion."

I open my mouth to protest when I remember that Easton isn't with me anymore, that I'm alone with nowhere to go, no one to help me.

"I would appreciate that, thank you," I whisper.

Later that evening, after helping Hazel make chicken stew for dinner and having a mouth orgasm over the richness of food, I'm sitting on the single cot unable to look away from Easton's bag at the end of the bed.

Hesitantly reaching for it, I pick it up, settling it down beside me. With my senses heightened, Easton's smell fills the space around me. My eyes begin to water as I unclasp the front latch. My hands tremble as I take a peek inside, pulling out the worn white cotton tunic sitting on top. Without a second thought, I bring it to my chest, hugging the fabric close to me.

I can't stop the onslaught of tears that escape me.

He should be here.

Easton would have loved this place. I can picture the joy on his face when he realized the Fae lands still exist—that we found them.

It still doesn't feel real. I feel like I'm going to wake up at any moment and run into his bedroom to find him reading.

Where I can cuddle him and tell him all about the nightmare of losing him, as he slowly strokes my hair, reassuring me that he will never go anywhere, never leave me.

I lie down, curling deeper into myself, hugging his shirt to my chest as I let myself quietly fall apart.

I won't stop until I find out if the Fae can help. I absolutely refuse to let Easton die for nothing.

For Easton, *everything* for Easton.

Together forever.

# Chapter Eleven

The next morning I'm sitting beside Hazel in the grass, helping her harvest food in the garden. Rows upon rows of wooden crates full of soil, seeds, and food bursting with life line her backyard. The sunshine warms our backs as it rises for a new day.

I awoke this morning feeling groggy from crying most of the night. Hazel took one look at my red-rimmed, puffy eyes and decided to drag me outside, making me work with my hands. Making me physically exhausted to the point my mind can't drag me into the darkness.

We're both pulling the root of a particularly large carrot when we freeze.

Hazel begins to tremble as a large boom echoes through the air. Life seems to stop around us. Animals pause their scattering, water stops flowing, even the wind pauses, making the trees and grass fall deadly silent. I'm about to ask what's happening when Hazels slaps her hand over my mouth, her eyes wide with terror as she shakes her head, blue eyes pleading with me to be silent. Using her free hand, Hazel takes mine in a death grip, her knuckles turning white as the boom repeats again, louder, closer.

It's a synchronous boom.

*Wings.*

My heart lodges in my throat, my pulse beating erratically as trees down the river to my left part with the force of the wind from the wings. Hazel's entire body is shaking. If she's this terrified by the creature that's attached to those wings, I hope I never meet it. Hazel's fear makes me wish I could disappear as the booming looms closer with each passing second. My thoughts spiral as my anxiety sinks its claws into my chest.

*Take me away, take me away, take me away.*

Hazel's eyes widen as my body tingles, a current of energy zipping up and down my arms and legs. As a dark cloud descends around us an ungodly smell, putrid enough to make me gag, follows right after a slithering energy. The very feel of it has my body screaming for me to run. Then a deafening boom hits my ears. The grass flattens around us, our hair blowing in all directions as the force knocks us to the ground. I squeeze my eyes shut as that horrendous energy becomes stronger, thicker, as if its very essence can sink its claws into my soul.

I refuse to look at whatever creature is large enough to topple two grown women over from the sheer force of wind from its wings.

Faster than it appeared, the shadow is gone, sunshine streaming across my face once more. The booming sound grows quieter as it leaves, life resuming around us a moment later.

Hazel yanking me to a standing position has my eyes flying open. I'm stunned speechless as she manages to drag me inside the cabin. She's incredibly strong for someone so little.

Hazel begins to pace, her palm lying on her chest, her voice trembling as she speaks. "They never come to this area of the woods."

"What was that thing?" I rasp.

Hazel's head snaps up. "You've never seen the beasts before?"

Beast? If a Fae calls a creature a beast, I'll take their word for it.

I change the topic. "How did it not see us?"

"You cloaked us." Hazels brow's furrow. "Did you not know you could do that?"

"No," I squeak.

"It was probably your fear. Emotions can drive magic more than power itself," she mutters more to herself. "Why are they here?" Hazel's breathing becomes erratic, her chest falling and rising in short bursts. "They don't come here."

I take a tentative step forward. "Hazel, it's gone now," I assure her to no avail. Her breathing becomes faster. I take her shaking hand, bringing her to sit on the couch, rubbing her back in slow circles. "You're safe now. Take a deep breath."

Hazel's breath stutters as she tries to inhale air, her eyes darting in all directions around the room. I repeat the mantra over and over, rubbing her back until her breathing returns to normal and her hands no longer shake.

She covers her face in her hands. "That's embarrassing. I'm so sorry."

I move her hands off her face, gently squeezing them. "Anxiety is not embarrassing."

I understand the fear that paralyzes your body, making you feel as if you are slowly dying. It's suffocating.

"They never come here, that's why I moved. I've never seen them in this part of the woods before," Hazel explains.

"There's more than one?" I ask.

Hazel's gulp is audible. "They're everywhere," she breathes.

"What can we do to take your mind off it?" I ask gently.

Hazel lowers her eyes, chewing her lip. "Cooking relaxes me."

I stand, taking her with me as I walk to the kitchen. "Then that's what we'll do."

I'm placing tomatoes in a straw woven basket after offering to collect the rest of the vegetables for Hazel, giving her more time to settle down before coming back outside, when I spot small waves rippling in the water. The river is usually calm and silent, yet there's a fading circle, with small bubbles rising to the surface. Nothing else moves as I walk to the river's edge. I'm about to make my way back to the garden when an iridescent white tail arches out of the water before submerging again.

I've seen drawings of tails like that in the Fae books.

*Mermaid.*

In awe, I race over to the bridge. I look in the direction it disappeared, seeing the stunning fluorescent white tail arch again for a moment before descending. A foggy memory surfaces, pulling me back to the night I left.

*I awake to lying on my side, the splinters from the rowboat poking and prodding into my arm. I turn onto my back, the movement making my head pound, ribs burning with each movement as I lift my head.*

*My vision swims, and as the black stars begin to fade, I slowly piece together where I am.*

*Water surrounds me, a vast deep river with flourishing forests adjacent both sides. Trees fly past me in a blur.*

*I furrow my brows. The boat is moving incredibly fast, faster than a normal current.*

*Groaning, I pull myself into a seated position only to see a long shimmering green tail arch above the water. As the tail descends another one closer to me rises, this one a deep cherry red.*

*Mermaids.*

*I collapse onto the floor of the boat, sobbing with relief that I made it.*

*The Fae lands.*

Mermaids helped me that night. I must have forgotten because of the concussion. Why did they help me? How did they know I was coming?

An endless stream of questions float through my mind, each going unanswered.

I need to do more research. The books at the palace barely covered the Fae lands and the creatures that reside here. I need to know what I'm getting myself into and why they helped me at all that night.

Once Hazel has gone to bed, I waste no time in lighting a candle and rummaging through the bookcase in her living room. I know it's a long shot that a small book collection could answer my questions, but I need somewhere to start.

I scan the titles to find her collection holds mostly books on earth-based spells, herbs, plants, and animals. Placing the candle on the ground, I select one of the animal books and begin flicking through it. Multiple sections cover passages on mammals, insects, birds, reptiles, and fish. I'm flipping through the pages to the fish section, praying the mermaids would be categorized as a fish when another light joins me, making me jump. Turning, Hazel's bewildered face meets me in the middle of the room.

"Are you on the run?" she blurts out. Without waiting for an answer, Hazel rushes to my bags, hastily picking up every single one and the strewn contents of clothes on the cot. "I want no trouble. I follow the laws of the queen and live a simple life. I swear to Faes that I bring no trouble." She finishes off the sentence by dumping the bags at my feet.

"On the run?" Wringing my hands, I shake my head profusely. "I'm not, I swear to you."

"You don't know where you live, you come out of nowhere beaten to a bloody pulp, and you're rummaging through my things in the middle of the night." She throws her hands in the air. "Forgive me if I don't believe you!" she yells, hurt flashing in her striking blue eyes.

I open my mouth to speak when an ethereal voice whispers in my ear, *"Tell her."*

I snap my head to the side. Only, there's no one standing beside me or behind me.

What the hell was that…?

Have I finally gone mad?

*"Open your heart and tell her,"* it whispers again.

Tiny gentle hands begin to push me toward Hazel as the feeling of warmth flows over me, surrounding me, filling me, comforting me, urging me to speak.

"Do you hear that?" I whisper, my gaze roaming the living room for any other signs of life.

Hazel throws her arms up in exasperation. "Hear what? You not explaining why you're spying on me?"

*"Open your heart Delilah,"* the ethereal voice says again.

The voice fills my ears, chanting repeatedly, until it's the only thing I can hear, making my anxiety overtake my body. Panic slithers its way up my throat.

It won't stop. The voice won't stop.

Hazel's mouth moves rapidly yet the only sound to fill my ears is the incessant buzzing of the chanting voice.

"I'm not Fae!" I blurt out.

The second the words leave my mouth; the ethereal voice disappears entirely. I snap my head to Hazel in time to see her roll her eyes as she moves to shove me out her door.

I don't blame her; I feel as if I'm going insane. *What was that?*

"I swear I'm not on the run, Hazel. Please just give me a moment to explain," I rush out, unable to hold back the tears that flow down my cheeks.

I have nowhere to go and no one to turn to.

I have no one.

Hazel pauses in front of the door, assessing. "You have five minutes." she concedes.

Walking further into the room only makes Hazel retreat a step away from me. The movement and distrust make my throat tighten to the point I can't swallow.

"I'm not Fae, or at least, I wasn't before I came here." I say, my voice wobbly as I speak.

"You're not helping your case," she snaps.

"I came from the human lands," I whisper.

Hazel's eyes widen, her mouth popping open to form an O shape.

I think she's stopped breathing entirely. "Hazel?"

"That's impossible," she breathes.

I pull out the crystal pendant from beneath my white linen shirt. "My mother gave me this, blabbering on about truth and veils. I thought it was nonsense until I saw for myself what it can do."

Looking into Hazel's eyes, that warmth washes over me again, and the pull in my gut urges me to continue, to trust Hazel. Sighing, I explain everything that happened, leaving no detail out. Everything pours out of me, like a dam was broken inside me, allowing the floodgates to open. I can't help the sobs that escape me as I recall the horrid details of what happened to Easton and what he meant to me, how much I loved him.

Hazel tears up as I explain what my father did.

"I remembered earlier when I saw the mermaid—"

Hazel takes a step forward, her voice rising to a high-pitched squeak. "You saw a mermaid?"

"Yes, why? Are they nearly extinct?" I ask.

"No, they stick to their own territory. They rarely leave it these days."

I look at her incredulously. "There was one in your river."

"What?!" she yelps, running over to her window to peer at the river.

I'd laugh at her outburst if she didn't seem genuinely shocked.

"I saw the white tail and when I went to get a closer look, a memory surfaced from the night I left…they helped me. More than helped, they were the ones who brought me here," I explain.

Hazel's brows rise to her hairline as she shakes her head. "This is astounding."

"Why?" I ask.

Hazel scoffs. "It's absolutely unheard of that they help people. They're very selfish and territorial creatures."

"Why would they help me then?"

Hazel's head snaps up. "They're psychic."

"Like a tarot reader?" I ask.

"No, they're psychic. They're given messages about the future. What if they were told to help you that night?" she mutters, speaking more to herself. "Why would they bring you to me though?"

I shrug. "Maybe you were the easiest avenue."

"No, there's multiple streams they could have taken from the border. They brought you here purposefully…They don't do anything without reason." Sighing, Hazel flops onto the couch. "My head feels like it's going to explode with all this information."

Chuckling, I take a seat beside her. "How do you think mine felt when I awoke with Fae ears and magic?"

"I wouldn't want to be in your mind, that's for sure."

I throw my head back on a laugh, the first real laugh I've had since Easton.

Hazel's cheeks flush pink on a wince. "Sorry, that was insensitive."

"I take no offense."

"I'm sorry I snapped at you," she says softly.

"I would too if I was in your position." I turn my body to face Hazel's, tucking my feet underneath me. "What happened here? Why did you all disappear? And why are there Fae trapped in the human lands?"

Hazel sits up. "Disappear? We didn't disappear; we were trapped." Hazel leans forward. "What do the humans think happened to us?"

My voice lowers to a whisper. "That you're all extinct, magic included."

"That's—I don't know how to feel about that," she stutters. Hazel jerks back. "Wait, did you say there's Fae trapped in the human lands?"

I dip my head. "That's why I decided to come looking, to see if any other Fae were alive."

Hazel shakes her head. "I have no idea why Fae are trapped in your lands...I can't believe the humans think we're extinct."

"What happened then?" I ask.

A faraway look enters Hazel's eyes as they glaze over. "All faeries and beings in the Fae lands are required to attend the Eclipse Ball, to honor our queens and kings. It was a masquerade ball like all others, absolutely fabulous. Nothing seemed amiss...until the next day. Everybody woke up trying to go about their duties to find that we couldn't cross into the human lands or anything beyond the two islands in our marked territory. You can't see anything but physically it feels as if you're hitting a brick wall, like someone placed a dome over our lands. You can't even escape by sea." A tear falls down her cheek before she wipes it away with the sleeve of her shirt. "That very afternoon, beasts were unleashed upon the lands and attacked the cities," she says, her voice cracking at the end.

My heart breaks for Hazel, for everyone in this land. They've been silently trapped in a prison for nearly one hundred and fifty years.

"No one knows how it happened?"

Hazel's lips flatten. "No one knows how or why. The queen has had her personal army and spies investigating since the moment it happened. We're no closer to knowing who did this than we were when it happened all those years ago."

"That's horrible," I whisper.

We both sit silently, retreating into our own minds as Hazel's words linger in the room. Why would somebody do such a thing? I lower my eyes as I realize our call for aid is worthless, not when they need aid as much as us. "Maybe we can help each other," I mutter, breaking the silence.

Hazel snorts. "I don't know how much help I could be and no offense, but I don't see how a used-to-be human could save us. The older generation Faes don't even know how to help. No one has seen anything like this."

I wave my hand, dismissing her worries. "But you can help me. I know barely anything about your lands. I need someone to teach me everything." My brows furrow. "You're right, I don't have much to offer. Perhaps friendship?" I try to sell it with a smile. Before Hazel can get a word out, I'm gasping, jumping off the couch as I spin to face her. "I can teach you how to fight!" Perhaps it will lessen Hazel's anxiety around the beasts.

Hazel narrows her eyes. "You know how to fight?"

"I've trained all my life," I state proudly.

"You curled yourself into a ball when the beast came."

Rolling my eyes, I plop back down onto the couch. "I was unprepared."

Hazel bursts into a fit of laughter.

"I'm serious! If you teach me about the Fae lands and magic, I can be more prepared when gigantic wings fly over my head," I say, flailing my hand around said head.

Hazel's face is dubious before smiling. "Fine, we have a deal."

"Don't sound too excited," I tease.

A playful smirk dances on Hazel's lips. "Things have been boring around here anyways. I suppose a princess training me to fight will suffice."

Hazel explains the Fae courts to me the next afternoon over pumpkin soup. "The Fae lands consist of five elemental courts, each court housing a major city. Earth Court has Eden; Fire, Ornx; Water, Cardania; Air, Entrile; and lastly, Azalea in Essence."

"Essence Fae aren't limited to one elemental power?" I ask.

Hazel nods. "Essence Fae are those that wield more than one elemental power." Hazel taps her mouth with a piece of cloth. "Every Fae has the power to manipulate the element in which their power comes from. Earth controls Mother Nature and animals, air controls electricity, light, and air. Then of course the water benders and fire breathers." Hazel points her spoon at me. "They don't physically breathe fire; it's the nickname they couldn't shake because their tempers are insurmountable."

I wink. "Don't piss off the fire Fae. Noted."

"Elemental control is the basic form of magic every Fae possesses, yet the majority also wield multiple different gifts. Powerful air Fae can read minds, fire breeds the most powerful warriors, water can change their bodily anatomy, making themselves invisible. They also have the most highly sought-after spell cleavers. Earth Fae"—she gestures to herself—"can wield the power to heal and speak to animals. Although every Fae has the healing power, earth Fae have a deeper well, being able to see things and heal the body in ways others can't." She shrugs. "They're the powers I got. I know other Fae can shapeshift into animal forms."

The clank of my spoon hitting the bowl brings Hazel's eyes up to mine. "You're telling me that I could be walking in the woods with not only animals but Fae lurking in the skin of animals?"

I truly need to pay closer attention to my surroundings when I'm outside.

Hazel chuckles. "Yes, although as you can tell by now"—she waves her hand around the room—"not many Fae come here."

I did notice that. I also noticed how lonely one must get being out in the middle of nowhere. Nobody isolates themselves to this extent without a story behind it.

Changing the subject, I ask, "What are the cities like?"

Hazel's shoulders tense as her cheeks flush pink. "I honestly don't know." She clears her throat. "I haven't been into town in a long time."

My heart tugs at the thought of Hazel, this kind and caring person, hurting so much.

"That's okay," I say. "Why don't you tell me what it was like when you used to go?"

Hazel remains quiet for a moment, yet as she starts to speak, her eyes fill with joy. "The cities were beautiful and full of life. The richest smells and sights you could ever experience. Spice vendors, restaurants, anywhere you went the food was amazing." Hazel pauses. "Well, except for the slums, but nobody goes there unless you want to hire an escort or get so drunk you don't remember your own name." She giggles. "The rest of the city is amazing. Shops with handmade clothing, bookstores, art, and theaters line the streets. Then there's buskers on the street who should be in the theaters."

"That sounds beautiful," I say in awe.

Hazel's lips tug into a grin. "It truly was, and each city is designed after their element." Hazel's eyes lower, voice quieting. "The Fae lands used to be a beautiful place to call home."

Hazel's admission reminds me of how I feel the opposite

about my own home, making guilt burn my throat. I left my people with a monster for a king. I have to remind myself that, yes, I left, but I did not abandon them. I'm working toward getting help. Perhaps what I find will save both the human and Fae lands. I must cling to that small slice of hope in my heart, hope that one day the world will be a better place. Otherwise, life begins to feel meaningless.

"What are the kings and queens of the courts like?" I ask nervously.

Hazel's eyes slowly lift to mine, her face contorting as she grimaces. "They were all murdered the night the entrapment spell was cast."

I choke on the soup, coughing and sputtering for air before I finally get oxygen in my lungs. "All of them?" I exclaim.

"All of them except for the Queen of Air and the heirs." Her voice lowers to a whisper. "The Queen of Air arrived home later that evening from the Eclipse Ball to find her husband murdered." She shakes her head in disgust. "The children were the ones to find their parents butchered. A mass execution of all the court's ruling kings and queens."

I sit back in my chair, a shiver going down my spine. "That's... I don't know what to say."

Hazel lowers her spoon. "Not only was the queen mourning the loss of her husband and friends, she also had an entire kingdom that was grieving the loss of their freedom, her people feeling shackled to the lands. She decided to rule over all the courts until the princes and princesses were of age and no longer grieving their own loss." Hazels voice wavers, full of grief. "The world turned to hell one hundred and forty-eight years ago."

As I tuck myself into bed later that evening, I can't turn my mind off. The conversation earlier dragged up all the horrible things that my people have had to deal with in recent years. The fear, starvation, homelessness, loss of freedom, and the innocent lives taken too soon. What was once a joyous country full of love, warmth, and peace is now a prison. The king has taken every bit of happiness and free will from his supposed people and crushed it with their very souls. The only ones that benefit from how the country is ruled today is the king, the rich, and his cronies.

Determination for change fills my heart as I drift to sleep. Memories of Easton float through my mind, his beautiful face and forest green eyes telling me to fight.

I will fight to save my people, even if it's the last thing I do.

# Chapter Twelve

Dread fills my stomach as I walk down the corridor. I know this hall; I know it all too well.

Unfortunately, I was summoned and when you're summoned…you never dare disobey the order of the king.

Walking through the black stainless steel doors, I make eye contact with my father as he sits proudly in his throne atop the dais. The diamond-filled crown resting on his head shines as bright as a star.

I approach the dais with my chin up, spine straight, and eyes locked on the king. I will courage to fill my veins instead of fear.

Reaching his throne, I bow low. "You summoned me, Your Majesty?"

His grating voice makes the hair on my nape stand on end. "I'm afraid there's been a traitor found living in the palace."

My eyes widen.

How did he find out? No one's ever found the people I set free.

"Bring him in," the king barks.

I turn as the doors open behind me, my heart falling as my stomach twists. I stand frozen in place as three of my father's personal guards drag Easton to the foot of the dais.

I shake my head vigorously. "No, this is a mistake. Easton is innocent!" I scream. No one pays attention to me as they continue to drag Easton to his doom. "IT'S ME! I'M THE TRAITOR!" I scream so loud my throat burns.

The three guards flanking Easton kick the back of his knees, making Easton fall to a kneeling position. The sight of him on the ground in front of my father makes my eyes water.

Easton's honey smooth voice fills my ears. "It's okay, Delilah."

I run to him, screaming profanities at my father as guards suddenly tackle me from behind, knocking the air from my lungs. My father steps off the throne, taking the offered sword from the guard beside him.

My father lifts the silver sword above Easton's head.

A guttural scream leaves me, ringing throughout the room so loud my ears buzz.

I try to wiggle free of the four grown men holding me down when Easton starts thrashing. He twists his murderous, rage-filled face toward my father as he screams, "*Don't you dare touch Del—*"

Easton doesn't get to finish his sentence.

His head thumps to the ground, rolling toward me, stopping inches from my face. Crimson blood scatters across the white tiles, covering me and my clothes as his gorgeous forest green eyes, vacant of life, look up at me.

I lift my head to see my father, covered in Easton's blood, smiling down at me.

I explode.

Red hot flames blast throughout the room. The guards

that were holding me down are flung back by the force, flying into the wall, their bodies hitting it so forcefully they crack the very foundation.

I stand, stalking toward my father, satisfaction coursing through my body as his face drains of color.

"Burn in hell," I growl.

Raising my hands, I roar as fire engulfs my father. I pour all of my rage and grief into blasting him with burning hot fire, sending wave after wave crashing into him. An anguished cry tears through me as my heart breaks for the loss of Easton.

I distantly hear my name being called but I only have eyes for the king—the monster that broke me each day, belittled and hurt me until I was nothing.

"DELILAH!"

The flames around me extinguish abruptly until I'm suffocating.

My throat constricts, tightening until I have to claw at my neck, trying to get—

I jolt, gasping for air as ash coats my tongue. My chest heaves as I look up into Hazel's bewildered eyes. "It's official. You have fire magic," she pants.

Tears roll down my cheeks as Easton's lifeless body flashes through my mind.

Taking a shaky breath, I get up in search of water. "What happened?" I rasp.

Hazel trembles as she sits on the cot. "I heard you scream; it was such a terrifying sound I came to check on you and you were…" Hazel's gaze roams the living room. "The entire room was on fire." She pauses, looking at me. "Yourself included. I don't know how you didn't burn anything; you must have subconsciously known it was a dream."

I rub my eyes with the heel of my palms. "I'm sorry," I sob.

Hazel wraps her arms around me, the tip of her head reaching my collarbone as she squishes me in a hug. "I understand, it's okay," she whispers.

We stand there in the middle of the living room, hugging each other until my crying finally subsides. I wipe the tears away with the sleeve of Easton's shirt. I sleep in his clothes every night.

Hazel pulls back, tugging me down to sit beside her on the couch. "Do you want to talk about it?" she asks softly.

"It was Easton." My voice cracks as my lips tremble. "I don't think I can handle talking about him right now."

Leaning back, she sits with me in silence while I scramble to lock away all the sadness of Easton safely into my heart. The grief of losing him is unbearable and so heavy I have no choice but to bury it. If I feel it, I'll break.

Hazel's unsteady voice cuts through the silence. "I had horrible nightmares when my daughter passed."

I snap my head to her.

Hazel's lip quivers. "It happened the day the Fae were trapped. When the beasts from another world descended and attacked." Her voice cracks on the last word. "I was walking with Luna on Bexery Bridge in Eden, the city of the Earth Court. We were going to pick up supplies to make pancakes." She laughs sadly. "Luna was obsessed with pancakes." Hazel's anguished face lifts to mine. "One moment I'm holding her hand, listening to her vibrant laugh and the next she's ripped away from me, airborne. No one knew what creatures they were or where they came from; it happened so fast. I flew after the beast that had her in its talons, and all I could see was the back of it."

Her breathing stutters as she plays with the ends of her cotton shirt. Tears run down her freckle-covered cheeks. "It dropped her so quickly," she whispers. "I flew as fast as I could to catch her... I got to Luna a second before she hit the ground. I was so worried about catching her in time that I didn't look as I held her to my chest." Hazel squeezes her eyes closed. "I felt warmth soak into my chest, so I checked to see if she was all right."

Hazel's next words cleave my heart in two.

"It had t-torn her open." Hazel's body shakes from the force of her sobs. "Luna was dead before it decided to drop her."

I have no words that could comfort Hazel, that could begin to heal the horror of what she experienced. The pain of losing your own child, a part of your soul, in such a horrendous way. I lean forward, wrapping my arms around Hazel, returning the gesture she so kindly gave me. I let Hazel lean against me as she falls apart.

# Chapter Thirteen

"We're going to see a mermaid," Hazel announces as she walks into the room two days later.

I jump off the couch with excitement. "How do we find them?"

She dumps a sack on the ground, its contents rattling and clanking. "We summon them through offerings. We can't enter their territory, that would be a suicide mission. There's a swimming hole that we can visit. You lay respectful offerings on the rocks surrounding the pool of water and wait for a mermaid to appear." Hazel adds, rolling her eyes, "If they feel like it."

I furrow my brows. "Have you done this before?"

Hazel's eyes widen. "God no. Mermaids are horrendous creatures."

I stare blankly at her as confusion mars my face. If they're such horrendous creatures then why did they help me?

"They're manipulative and deceitful; they live for playing games with Fae. They're also terrifying," Hazel explains, moving throughout the room as she finds her boots.

"I thought they looked beautiful," I say.

Hazel sits on the couch as she ties her laces. "Their beauty is part of their manipulation. They're stunning creatures with cold cunning hearts. We have to be vigilant, and you must choose your words carefully. If you don't ask your questions correctly, they'll give you a bogus message."

I frown. "What the hell is the point? How will we know if they're telling the truth?"

Hazel picks up the sack, handing it to me. "They helped you that night. For whatever reason, it worked in their favor. Games are one thing, but actively searching for you to bring you here…They have their own reasoning behind it."

Trepidation lines my stomach, each word coming out of Hazel's mouth makes my anxiety rear its ugly head.

I peer into the sack in my hands. It's filled with oyster shells, pearls, hand mirrors, and funnily enough, hairbrushes. "I can't believe you can summon a mermaid with brushes."

"Stop laughing at them and hurry up," she calls over her shoulder as she exits the cabin.

"I'm sorry, it's just…brushes?" I chuckle.

"Don't be fooled, mermaids aren't just pretty fish. They all have individual power, and we don't want them to use it against us. So play nice."

I trail behind Hazel, walking into her front garden as I try to imagine what type of powers mermaids could possess when her other words ring through my mind.

"You don't think I'm nice?"

Hazel bursts out laughing. "From all of that, that's what you take away?" She shakes her head on a chuckle. "You can be pushy sometimes. Don't push them."

"Some would call me persistent," I tease.

Hazel stares at me flatly. "Are you ready?"

I wave my hand around. "Yes, I was waiting for you to start walk—"

Shimmering red wings blossom from Hazel's back. Stretching to their full wingspan, they glimmer where the sun shines on them.

My mouth drops open as I stumble back, kicking up dirt as I fall on my behind. I sputter, "You—I—Wings, you have wings!" Of course Hazel has wings; she spoke about flying in her story…yet seeing them in front of me is another thing entirely. They're magnificent.

Hazel's boisterous laugh pulls me out of my shock.

"Warn a girl next time!" I shriek.

"It was worth it to see your face!" Kneeling over with laughter, her wings fold around her like a shield.

I stand, moving toward her wings to see what they feel like. My hand's outstretched when Hazel snaps up.

"Don't!" she blares.

I retract my hand quickly. "Sorry! I just wanted to know what they feel like. They look smooth and shiny, yet leathery."

"It's very personal to touch a Fae's wings. Some will bite your head off if you do it without their consent," she explains. "They're made entirely of muscle and bones so they're hard to the touch but soft as silk. It's a very intimate thing…to touch a Fae's wings."

My cheeks heat. "Sorry."

"It's okay, now you know. I should have explained but I couldn't stop laughing." Her eyes shine with humor. "Are you ready now?"

"We're not walking, are we?"

"Not today," she sing-songs.

"If you drop me"—I point my index finger at her—"I will haunt you for eternity, and that's a long time for a Fae."

Hazel rolls her eyes. "Don't be dramatic. I've only fallen once or twice."

Before I can respond I'm in Hazel's arms, airborne. I let out a yelp, closing my eyes tightly as I wrap my arms around Hazel's neck. Her chest shaking on a laugh.

My hair is pulled in every which direction, the crisp cold air seeping through my fighting leathers. The sound of the wind roars in my ears.

The moment I open my eyes, my heart soars.

We're flying so fast I can barely make out the ground below me. The vast expanse of green forest canopy and mountain hills sprawl out before us. Peering down, the ebb and flow of the forest mingles with the blossoming life of flowers. Every now and then I can see an opening in the forest floor, a peek into what's below the treetops.

Suddenly, the river's blue flow appears, gliding through the forest like a snake, veering off into different paths as if it's a maze.

This must be the river channels the mermaids pulled me through.

I tip my head back, a smile playing on my lips as the sun shines on my face. I have never felt freer than I do in this moment. I splay my arms out, the air rushing through my fingertips, as I soak up the feeling of euphoria.

Hazel's voice drags me away. "Hold on!" she exclaims.

I lift my head. An opening appears, showing a trailed path on the forest floor. Hazel banks, dropping into the opening so fast I tighten my arms around her as she swoops low, following the natural curve. We bank and turn, the path cutting in every which direction before Hazel begins to slow down, the trees in front of us parting to a wide field. Grass and flowers bloom around the open circular meadow.

Hazel lands gracefully in the center, setting me down on the ground.

Amazement fills my features as I face Hazel, yelling over the deafening roar of water that surrounds us. "Please tell me all Fae have wings and I can magically pop some out too."

Hazel's head flies back on a laugh, her smile wide and full of life.

"The majority of Fae have wings. I don't know if you will though, considering your…odd circumstances," she says, flailing her hand at my body. "Come on, let's get this over with."

I turn to follow Hazel, completely awestruck as I do.

The meadow leads to a river that winds into a large swimming hole. The deafening roar comes from a gorgeous waterfall, concealing what appears to be a cave pool behind the falls.

"This is the most beautiful sight I've ever seen," I breathe.

Hazel grimaces. "If the tree folk and gremlins didn't live nearby, I'd come all the time."

"I take it those creatures are bad?" I deadpan.

"Oh, we will do a full lesson tonight on which creatures to avoid," she mutters.

Hazel walks in front of me, weeding through the shin-length grass before her entire body freezes midstep. I look up to see what's startled her. A pod of mermaids stares back at us in the swimming hole.

They have beautiful pointy ears, similar to Fae yet made of scales. Long hair flows in an array of different colors, making it appear like a rainbow. They all bear sharp facial features and vibrant colored eyes. There's one mermaid in front of all others. Her white hair is slicked back, a turquoise jewel glowing on her forehead, her red eyes solely on mine. Chills scatter down the length of my body. They're beautiful, yet not a single one of them shows an ounce of emotion.

The pure essence of them is sensually sinful.

The white-haired mermaid's beautiful, husky voice glides to my ears. "Delilah."

They know who I am.

I blink rapidly, trying to contain my shock. Blindsided is an understatement.

"We mean you no harm," Hazel says sternly.

The white-haired mermaid slides her gaze to Hazel. "We know, child."

I gulp. If they're calling Hazel a child, how old are they?

My voice breaks through the roaring of the waterfall. "You helped me the other night?" I ask more than state.

"Yes," she states matter-of-factly.

Her strong features and predatory stillness make my heart pound faster.

"And you're here because you know I have questions to ask you?"

A slight dip of her chin is the only response I get. I don't think she's blinked once since speaking.

"Will you answer my questions truthfully?" I ask hesitantly.

Those vibrant red eyes meet Hazel's. "You've taught her well, it seems."

Hazel's gulp is audible as she dips her chin.

"We do not take orders from Fae." The mermaid turns her gaze back to me. "Or has been humans," she says coldly.

These mermaids are nothing like the fairy tales my mother read to me as a child.

"We do, however, have two messages for you, Delilah," she says, the epitome of cool indifference.

As one, the mermaids speak, their voices coming together as if an enchanting song.

"When I starve, your soul will scream, adding melody to the song I weave."

The mermaids stop as the white-haired one swims closer, lowering her voice as if she's afraid of who might hear.

"I have no voice, but I have lots to teach. Your soul is my price, let me speak. Darkness enchanted is my tale."

Before I can say anything, the mermaids submerge, leaving as one.

I turn to Hazel, her face full of horror as she marches toward me. "We need to leave."

Walking through Hazel's cabin, I take a seat on the worn cushioned sofa. "What *was* that?" I ask as Hazel plops down beside me. "Were they playing a game?"

"The mermaids give riddles for their visions. For pure enjoyment or secrecy, I have no idea."

"So, we have to figure out the riddles?" I ask, dumbfounded. "Why can't they just be normal and tell us?" I throw my hands in the air. "I didn't even get to ask any questions!"

The questions keep piling up with every passing day, all going unanswered.

How am I in a Fae body? Why are some Fae trapped in the human lands? Why are Fae stuck here? Can the Fae help overrule the human king?

I massage my temples as a headache pounds against my skull.

"That, I do not have an answer for," she drawls.

Standing, I search for pen and paper. "Let me write it down before I forget what they said."

"I don't think I'll ever forget the sound of all of them speaking at once," she says, a shiver wracking her body.

I grimace in return. "Ominous doesn't begin to describe what that felt like."

Chewing my lip, I reread the first riddle over and over until my eyes begin to glaze.

"I think the biggest hint in the first riddle is *weave*. Not a lot of things weave," I murmur.

"Weave can be lots of things. Hair, flight pattern, streams, nests...Honestly the list could go on."

Sitting forward, I assess both riddles. "The first riddle has to lead us to the second...or at least I hope it does," I mutter.

"I can't think about it anymore. My head is going to explode!"

Sighing, I place the pen and paper down. "Tell me about the gremlins and tree folk."

Hazel grimaces as she retrieves a white leather-bound book from the bookshelf, placing it on the coffee table in front of us. Taking a seat beside me on the couch once more, she turns the pages, stopping on a picture of a small scaly creature.

My eyes widen as I stare at the drawing of a gremlin. Its green ears are shaped like bat wings, and its red eyes glow as if the burning depths of hell are within them. The body is shaped like a lizard, the underbelly a soft yellow color, its hands and feet clawed with talons.

"It's horrifying! Are those—"

"Teeth around its eyelids? Yes."

I shiver as I look at the row of teeth lining its eyes, matching those in its mouth. Its face is truly one created in nightmares.

"They run wild in the forests with no moral compass. They're the most trickster creatures you'll ever meet and the most violent." She snorts. "They give fire breathers a run for their money."

I look over the various drawings of gremlins. "Do they have powers?"

"No, hence the violence." Hazel turns the pages, landing on an image of a large tree.

I frown. "It looks like a regular tree."

"Look closer."

I lean forward, scanning the drawing from top to bottom. It looks as normal as any other tree in a forest, with its large trunk, various branches reaching out in all directions, leaves—

I suck in a breath. Its eyes are closed yet there's no mistaking the face that's subtly hidden in the grooves and bark lines.

"The tree folk are essentially harmless, but they hate it when Fae step on their roots or land on their tree trunks. They'll snatch you up and hold you for enjoyment until it gets sick of your whining."

A boom of laughter explodes out of my chest, my belly tightening and burning in pain at how hard I laugh. Easton's fear about being snatched up by trees comes back to me.

"He was right. They do snatch you."

# Chapter Fourteen

Crossing the small wooden bridge out the front of Hazel's cabin, we head toward a clearing in the forest to practice magic, secluded enough to not draw any attention, while also large enough that I don't burn the whole forest down.

On the way here, Hazel taught me how to run using Fae speed, opening up my senses, allowing the heightened gifts to overtake my body while I explored how they work. I used all my Fae strength to push off my feet, my legs seemingly knowing how to do the rest. I think I'd outrun Creseda's gallop. Not only was I fast but strong; no matter how far we ran my lungs didn't tire. I was barely breaking a sweat by the time we reached the clearing. I dare say I could have continued for hours.

Standing in the middle of the forest floor, I use my heightened sight to focus on Hazel a few feet in front of me. She said it was to give me space, yet I have an inkling it's because she doesn't want me to accidentally incinerate her.

"Emotions are what drive magic?" I ask, my voice mingling with the chirping birds around us.

"No, emotions trigger magic. You should never learn to access your magic through emotions. Your magic will become uncontrollable if you do." Hazel pulls a seed out of her pocket. Holding it in her palm, a small sunflower begins to grow. "Control is the most important element in using magic. Without it"—the sunflower in her hand grows so large it explodes, yellow petals and black seeds raining down around us—"you're a ticking time bomb."

"I take it control is our first lesson?" I drawl sarcastically.

Hazel dusts the flower petals off her clothes. "You need to learn to access it first, but yes." Hazel lifts her eyes to mine, widening her stance. "Okay, close your eyes."

I arch a brow, hesitant to where this is going.

Hazel huffs out a laugh. "Just close your eyes."

I mirror Hazel's stance, spreading my feet shoulder width apart as I close my eyes.

"I want you to breathe in for four counts and breathe out for four counts."

I'd think she was joking if I didn't hear her start to count. Following Hazel's instructions, I listen to her soft whimsical voice as I breath in deeply and out slowly, following her counts of four.

Hazel's calming voice guides me. "Starting from your chest, I want you to scan your body."

*Is she serious?*

I crack open one eye, only to find Hazel's stern gaze on mine. I snap my eye shut.

*She's serious.*

"Magic is a part of you. You need to know where it is and what it feels like to access it." Hazel pauses, her tone awestruck. "It feels like a crackle of energy, a force of life on its own yet the very essence of yourself."

I smirk. "That's very poetic of you."

"Just shut up and look for it."

Taking a deep breath, I relax deeper into my body, my taut muscles loosening as my breathing grounds me, calms me. My body grows heavier with each breath I take. I start from the top, scanning the differences in my senses, the way I can hear Hazel's steady heartbeat, feel the wind brush along my pointed ears, smell the difference in the flowers around me—jasmine, lavender, and lilac. I continue down my body, noticing the steady beat of my pulse, my chest as it slowly rises and falls. My muscles as strong as steel, strength coursing throughout my body like never before. I reach my feet, feeling the heaviness of my boots, the leather dragging me down, keeping me rooted to the earth.

But nothing crackles or zips through me. I frown, opening my eyes to Hazel's hopeful expression. "Besides the sharper senses, I didn't feel any energy. I just feel stronger."

Hazel's brows furrow before she claps her hands. "Okay, next tactic."

What feels like hours later, after trying different exercises, I fall back onto the grass, spreading my arms beside me as I groan. "Nothing!"

I turn my head to Hazel, who's just as frustrated as I am as she lies beside me, biting her lip as she thinks.

"If I didn't almost burn us alive the other night, I would think I have no magic."

Hazel giggles, her shoulders rustling the brown leaves spread beneath her.

"Perhaps it's different because the pendant turned my body into Fae when I crossed the border?" I muse.

"I doubt it. I don't know why you changed from human to

Fae, but you don't inherit a Fae body without magic. It doesn't work that way," Hazel says simply.

I don't dare explore the thoughts infiltrating my mind about what that could mean. I can worry about that later. For now, I need to focus on accessing the magic.

I sit up, turning my body to face Hazel. "Let's try another exercise."

She sighs. "We've tried them all."

I lower my eyes, focusing on the tiny insects crawling through the grass around me.

Hazel's face pulls into a grimace. "There is one thing we haven't tried." She sits up, mimicking my position, our knees perpendicular. "Think about Easton."

My head rears back. "You told me not to use my emotions," I say anxiously.

"You don't know what it feels like inside you. I'm only asking you to do this once, to get the feel for where your magic resides inside of you."

Trepidation fills me, the memories of Easton hovering at the side, waiting to bombard my mind.

Hazel's voice is gentle as she speaks. "The only time your magic has flared is when it's about Easton."

Dread coils in my gut. I know exactly which moments and memories she's asking me to think about. "Can we try another breathing exercise?"

"I'll be here to guide you through it this time. I won't push you, not about this, but nothing else is working."

Swallowing the ball lodged in my throat, I nod.

I know Hazel's right; we've been here for hours with no luck. If I want to tap into my magic again, I have to use my emotional drive. Taking a deep breath I close my eyes, dropping that invisible barrier in my mind. I allow the memories and feelings surrounding Easton to bombard me. The heartbreaking moment I turned to find my world had been destroyed, taken from me. Red hot rage burns through me, filling my veins, pulsing, itching for the need to escape. To fight.

My eyes fly open as my body ignites.

Hazel's eyes spark in front of me, and through them, I see my own eyes glowing red. "There it is." She sits up straighter. "Focus all your attention on your body. What does it feel like?"

"Rage," I spit. "I'm full of rage, like an inferno."

"Scan your body. Where is it coming from?" she asks.

"My heart," I pant.

The heat inside me is burning so hot it makes sweat drip down the nape of my neck.

"No. That's your emotions, the memory. Don't focus on that." Hazel's voice is stern. "What does your body feel like?"

I open my mouth to disagree, when I feel it answer for me.

A spark, as if to say hello.

I look within myself, scanning my body from head to toe until I feel it, pulsing and crackling. It peeks one eye open as if it was asleep.

"It's below my heart, near my sternum." I turn my head to the side, more feline than human, as I study it. "It's strange. I feel the familiarity…as if it's a part of me."

"It is a part of you," Hazel confirms. "You control it. It does not control you." Hazel's voice hardens. "Control it like a well. You choose how much you take, how deep it goes, and how you use it."

"A well," I whisper.

Hazel smiles encouragingly. "Magic is creation; use your

imagination. Picture a small flame burning from your fingertip."

I go within myself, imagining the sleepy magic as a well.

I see it full of pure white magic as I lean in and take a small drop in my hands. Cupping the power in my palm, I picture a small flame beginning to burn, flowing from my palm to the tip of my fingers.

Warmth dances along my hand, sizzling as it spreads throughout my fingers.

Opening my eyes, I watch in amazement, my heart leaping with joy. A tingling sensation flows down my arms and all ten fingers alight, twinkling with fire. I can feel the warmth on my hands, yet the fire doesn't burn my skin.

I cheer in delight, wiggling my fingers between Hazel and me. "I did it!"

Hazel whoops with joy. "Finally!"

A smile spreads across my face as I make the flames disappear and reappear. "It feels incredible," I breathe.

"Okay, next thing is protection." Hazel grabs a stick, drawing a circle in the dirt around me, creating a bubble. "Every Fae must learn a protection shield. It's our instinct to protect ourselves and the ones we care about. We can be extremely territorial." She smirks, placing her hands on her hips. "We don't need you feeling defensive and blowing people into smithereens on instinct. We need to make your first instinct to shield instead of attack."

I shake my head. "I would never attack innocent people."

Hazel points her finger at me. "You haven't felt the terri-torial instincts yet, just you wait." Hazel widens her stance. "Imagine what you can form. What does protection look like to you?"

Easton's face flashes through my mind. Fire engulfs my hands.

"No, not a memory. We're not using emotions anymore. Use your imagination," Hazel repeats warmly.

Taking a deep breath, I think about protection. "A metal shield."

Hazel dips her chin. "Good. How does the shield protect you?"

"It's impenetrable."

Hazel smiles. "Now imagine an invisible shield surrounding you."

My mouth gapes open. "You say it like it's easy!"

"It is easy. You just made your fingers turn into mini campfires," she teases.

I roll my eyes, shaking out my hands. I breathe in deeply, picturing a round shield surrounding me. On my next exhale, I feel the magic leave me, consume me. Nothing's changed, yet I can feel the difference, as if I'm cocooned by my own power.

Hazel steps closer, lifting her index finger to poke me when it stops midair, the tip of her finger turning flat and white as it touches an invisible wall.

"See? Easy." She smiles. "You can put protection shields around anyone and anything."

My breath leaves me.

I did it.

Before I can celebrate, Hazel's finger comes flying at me, poking my shoulder as my protection shield drops. The magic surrounding me flickers in and out as if it's a dwindling candle.

Hazel winces as she takes a step back. "It'll take time to strengthen your magic. It's like a muscle. The more you use it, the more it grows."

"More training for me, I guess," I mumble as I walk over to my waterskin.

# Chapter Fifteen

I circle Hazel, stepping in to correct her posture and stance with each movement she makes. The wooden staff in her hand never drops, her eyes as hard as steel as she hones all her focus and rage into the movements. I began training Hazel this morning, starting off with various defense, offense, and striking positions, making sure she learns the basics of footwork and balance before moving onto anything else.

Hazel wipes the back of her hand across her forehead as sweat drips down her skin. She thought it was ridiculous that simple fighting stances could make a person perspire. That led to the awkward conversation that although she's Fae and has heightened strength, some of her muscles are weak. Especially as she moves through the new movements, muscles she hasn't used before are coming to life.

Her legs quiver and shake as she flattens the soles of her feet, balancing with her toes and bending her knees as she prepares her body to attack and defend at a moment's notice.

Once her arms begin to shake from holding the staff after an hour, I decide to call it. "Okay, that's enough for today.

It'll take time for your muscles to remember the positions but you're doing well."

Hazel lowers the staff, grabbing her waterskin. "My god, that's taxing. I never knew balancing could be so difficult."

I follow Hazel, joining her as I drink my own water. "It's not so much the balancing as it is the muscle use."

Hazel dips her chin. "I need lunch before we begin our magic training. We need to replenish our energy before we start."

I pick up the staff and swords I brought outside, thankful that one of the bags I grabbed from the carriage that night contained weapons. "Sounds good to me."

"How long have you been training?" Hazel asks suddenly.

I shrug before carrying our supplies to the cabin. "Since I was seven."

Hazel's brows pull down low. "Why so young?"

I swallow, my throat suddenly dry. "I wanted to be strong."

Hazel's eyes soften. I didn't reveal the details of my father's treatment, but Hazel isn't stupid; she knows Easton's murder wasn't the only incident.

"What's Aloriah like now in the human lands?" Hazel asks softly.

I dump the training equipment beside my cot, breathing out a long sigh. "Horrible. The laws are ridiculous. No matter your age or sickness, the people are required to do manual labor. People are starving and homeless. There's no freedom, no joy, no life—not one worth living."

"Is that why you left?" Hazel asks, strolling through the kitchen.

"Yes and no. When I found the Fae in the In-between, I was hoping I could find the remaining Fae. The Fae and humans lived in peace for centuries, so I thought someone could help." I wash my hands beside Hazel before moving on to prepare lunch. "Speaking of, did you have loved ones in the human lands?"

Hazel places various vegetables on the worktop bench, passing me knives as she speaks. "No, however, I had many friends that lost loved ones. With the time that has passed, they're all gone now."

Sadness simmers in my gut.

Not only did the Fae lose their freedom, but they lost the ones they loved on the other side. Lost precious time with them, something they'll never be able to get back. To think that the very thing Fae are gifted—time—was played against them.

I awake the next morning to pure silence. I've become so attuned to the sounds of pans clanging and Hazel's chipper voice singing in the morning that the silence raises my internal alarm bells. I slide out of bed, searching the cabin, only to find it empty. Hastily tugging on my training clothes, I walk outside.

I'm past the sprouting tomatoes when my Fae hearing picks up on sniffling in the distance. Without second-guessing myself I follow it, crossing the river's wooden bridge, heading north. The sniffles grow louder with each step I take. The forest path gives way to a small swimming hole, surrounded by white, purple, blue, and pink flowers. A sob rings throughout the space, the guttural sound so full of pain even the birds leave the area, abandoning treetops as they fly for safety.

Dragging my sword from behind my back, I clench the

silver pommel in my grip as I crouch, wading through the grass surrounding the swimming hole as I search for Hazel.

Another sob chokes out, and I spot a piece of white material peeking through the tall blades of grass. Walking closer, I realize no one's harming Hazel, not physically at least.

A curved boulder sits above her head, the name *Luna* inscribed in the middle with an array of flowers and different colored crystals placed along the top of the headstone. Hazel is clutching a gray stuffed teddy bear to her chest, tears running down her cheek until sliding off onto the bear.

Kneeling beside Hazel, I gently place my hand on her shoulder. "Hazel?"

Her broken voice cleaves my heart in two. "It's her birthday today. I continue living while my daughter barely made it to seven years old."

With nothing to say to fix a grieving mother, I sit in silence with her as she breaks down. Each sob more gut wrenching than the last, making quiet tears roll down my cheeks.

It isn't until what feels like an hour later—after Hazel's shoulders rise and fall slowly, her breaths deepen, and the tears on her cheeks have dried—do I finally speak.

"Do you want to honor her today? Do all her favorite things?"

Hazel shakes her head adamantly. "No, it's not right without her. It feels like a piece of myself is missing and I can't bear the weight of her not being here, especially not today."

"You could tell me about her, all your favorite memories," I whisper.

Hazel blubbers as she chuckles. "She would love the attention."

"Then that's what we'll do."

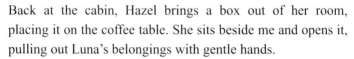

Back at the cabin, Hazel brings a box out of her room, placing it on the coffee table. She sits beside me and opens it, pulling out Luna's belongings with gentle hands.

Hazel's shoulders slump as she removes a small pink fleece coat, hugging it to her chest. "It was just the two of us when Luna came into my life. Luna's father wasn't my mate. He had no obligation to stay and raise her. I never saw him after I told him I was with a child, and I was glad for it when she came into this world. My whole life changed. She was adorable, with giant blue eyes, strawberry blonde hair and the longest black eyelashes I had ever seen."

Hazel pulls out a one-piece sunflower bathing suit. "Luna was an essence Fae, with earth magic from myself and water from her father. She was obsessed with water, would swim in it until her hands and feet turned into little prunes. I had to bribe her with pancakes to drag her out of it." She giggles sadly. "I buried her at the swimming hole because it was her favorite spot to go to."

Hazel's silent for a moment before looking into the box. It isn't until she pulls out an empty glass jar with a honey label that her face lights up. "When she was around four, she went through a stage of being obsessed with honey, asking for it at all times during the day. I didn't understand why honey made her so happy until I found her sitting in the garden near a big puddle of honey. A small squirrel came up and started nibbling on it." Hazel smiles yet it's full of sadness and long-ing. "She would sit out there for hours, squealing and laughing away. Watching animal after animal come to eat her honey."

Hazel turns toward me on the couch, bringing a knee up

and propping her chin on her fist. "She'd say hello to anything that crossed her path. Ants, insects, birds, all types of creatures and Fae. It never mattered what they looked like, nothing scared her. She would even say hello to the ground goblins, saying that they're just cranky because they need to smile more." Hazel's laugh is deep and full of love.

I chuckle along with her. "I like how she viewed the world."

Hazel leans toward the box. With each item, she tells me a story about Luna. Slowly, a small part of pain is replaced with happiness as she shares a part of her daughter with me.

# Chapter Sixteen

The next night I'm in the kitchen helping Hazel cook, chopping vegetables as we assess the mermaid's riddles. This has become our nightly routine since we encountered them last week. I can just imagine the white-haired mermaid's smug face watching us as we struggle to find the answer to what she perceives as a simple sentence.

I groan. "Why must they be so cunning?"

We've deduced that the first riddle is about an animal; the weave leads nowhere when it's about an item.

"In the mermaid's defense, we're eternal beings…We get bored over the years."

I shrug. "I still think it's about spiders."

"It would be too generalized if it was a spider. Spiders live in almost every habitat; they wouldn't make it that hard." She adds, "I think it's a type of bird. There's seven bird species that 'weave' nests."

I shake my head. "My gut's telling me spiders."

Hazel's boisterous laugh fills the kitchen. "You and your gut."

"My gut has gotten me very far in life, thank you very much." I chirp.

Hazel returns to the open fire as I mull over the riddle, the first line repeating in my mind like a song.

*When I starve, your soul will scream.*

"What if were focusing on the wrong part of the riddle?" I mumble. I stop cutting vegetables, placing the knife down. I turn to Hazel. "Do any creatures eat souls?"

"No creature in this world. The Fae lands use pure, divine magic." Hazel takes the vegetables I cut and places them into the pan on top of the fire. "We may have morally gray creatures but none that would inflict harm like that."

I lower my voice as my face twists. "What if it's not from the Fae lands?"

Hazel stops stirring the food, pausing mid-movement. I start to worry that I've overstepped or upset Hazel at the mention of the otherworldly beasts when she spins around.

"I have a book!" she exclaims, rushing to her room.

"Why do you have a demon book?" I call out.

Hazel returns moments later with a worn, brown book. "I wanted to learn everything about the creature that took Luna from me. It...didn't bring me peace," she says distractedly, placing the book in front of me. "Look for any creatures that eat souls, gain power from screams, weave, and or starve their prey," she says, returning to cooking dinner.

I grimace. "I'll pass on dinner now."

Opening the book, I read through each graphic detail about demonic creatures, thanking my lucky stars I haven't eaten since lunch.

"I've found it," I breathe.

Hazel sits up on the couch next to me, dropping the cotton material she had been sewing. "It's a demon?"

I nod, reading the title over and over as my heart thumps wildly. "It's called a soul eater," I whisper.

Hazel begins swearing expletives. "What exactly is it?"

I pick up the book, reading out loud. "'Soul eater, half-woman, half-spider, lures men into her web. She spends her days weaving, traveling far and wide for her next meal.'" I gulp. "'Using the top half of her female body, the soul eater lures attractive men into her path of spider webs. The soul eater delights in manipulating her prey, marveling at their torment, then slowly sucking the life out of them. The screams of the dying, bringing her pleasure,'" I finish, closing the book as I'm no longer able to look at the words.

All the color drains from Hazel's face. "Should we be relieved that the mermaids are sending us on a mission where the demon only enjoys eating men's souls or should we still be terrified?"

"I think the better question is, are they sending us on a fool's mission?"

Hazel leaves, returning with two cups of tea, her hands trembling as she passes me mine.

"We can't go into this with a false sense of security that she only eats the souls of men," I add, grimacing at the thought of a human-sized spider eating me.

"I agree, it would be stupid to think we're safe around it." Hazel shakes her head. "How could anyone possibly trap a gigantic spider?"

"I don't think we can trap it traditionally." Opening the demonology book I flip back to the soul eater's page. "It's half-spider. We should use its own weaknesses against it."

Hazel looks dumbfounded. "You know what spiders' weaknesses are?"

"One summer, the palace was infested with spiders." I shiver thinking about it. "I absolutely despise the hairy creatures, so I made my room spider-free using everything they hate."

Hazel giggles. "Of course you did."

I flail my hands in front of me. "I didn't want to wake up with one on my face!"

"Okay, spider expert, what do they hate?" she teases.

I lift my chin. "Mock me all you want but I never had a single spider in my room that summer," I quip. "They hate the smell of citrus fruits, won't go anywhere near them, and white vinegar kills them." I add smugly, "This spider might be the size of your cabin, but its legs will still be its weakest point."

Hazel's lips tug into a grin. "Impressive."

"Thank you very much," I say, taking a mock bow.

Hazel chuckles, her humor dying as she winces. "In all seriousness, I don't think a few fruits and vinegar will deter this thing."

"No, it won't." A smile plays on my lips. "But they will make it avoid certain areas, and it'll unknowingly walk right where we want her."

# Chapter Seventeen

My cheeks hurt from smiling so wide. My hair is a knotted mess as the wind slams into us while Hazel carries me. Flying over the top of the Earth Court woods, we pass mountaintops, meadows, streams, rivers, and endless green forests as we scout for the soul eater. I was hoping to have seen the Earth Court city from above, yet Hazel made a good point—the soul eater would hide in a dense forest, not near a bustling city filled with enough Fae to kill her. I'm surprised we haven't come across a single Fae though; I suppose with some earth Fae being able to shapeshift into an animal form, I wouldn't have known if I passed another one.

I know I should be looking below for the soul eater, but Hazel's been flying for hours and I can't help but savor the freedom I feel. I pray that while I'm here, I'll have a chance to see if I have wings, that Hazel can teach me how to transform and fly.

I'm daydreaming what it would feel like to have stunning wings when Hazel drops. I let out a squeak as Hazel's hold on me tightens. I'm surprised she's not exhausted yet, from not only flying but carrying me for hours.

I open my mouth to ask what made her drop into the tree line when the sight before me answers my question. A gray and white texture shimmers in the distance, the sun making it sparkle.

A sickening chill runs down my spine.

*Webs.*

Large, trailing webs cover the trees in front of us for what appears to be miles.

"Oh my god," Hazel exclaims.

"I think it may be larger than we thought," I whisper.

"Are you sure we should do this?" Hazel asks hesitantly, as she flies over the long trail of iridescent spider silk.

I nod. "We have to. The mermaids saw this, and wherever the soul eater leads us to will answer our questions."

Hazel takes a deep breath. "Hold on."

She shoots up, higher than before, flying so high the canopy trees below look like small ants. It isn't until we're far enough in front of the soul eater's webs that she won't detect us, by sight or scent, does Hazel drop through a small opening in the forest canopy. Gently landing, she places me on the ground, my legs wobbling after being in the air for hours. I shake my head, trying to clear the fog before we rummage through our bags, pulling out our waterskins filled with white vinegar. Hazel hands me one of the bags containing cut citrus fruit.

"We need to be as quick as possible," she breathes.

Wasting no time, Hazel and I take off in opposite directions at lightning speed. The trees fly past me in a blur. I barely register the snapping of branches beneath my boots as I sprint in a zig-zag pattern, my arms splayed beside me as I run. One hand sprays white vinegar while the other drops fruit. Hazel does the same, creating a wide berth for the soul eater to travel within. We change bottles as they empty until we reach a small round clearing in the woods. As if something was once burnt here, no trees grow in the circle. The only thing it contains is dead, brown grass while the lively forest surrounds it.

I meet Hazel in the middle, barely panting thanks to my new Fae strength and speed.

I smile at the thought. "How'd you do?"

Hazel holds out her bags. "Empty."

I nod, looking around for a place for Hazel to hide. "I think you should fly above; we don't know how good her senses are and there's no point hiding in one of the trees because she clearly climbs them all," I say, flailing a hand in the direction of the mile-long spider silk.

Hazel pulls her head back. "I'm not leaving you alone with that thing."

"If anything happens to me, I need at least one person to know. That way, you can go get help." I shake my head. "I mean no harm when I say this, but we've only just begun training. I have years of training with the newly added ability of a Fae body."

Hazel's voice softens. "I have magic."

I shake my head adamantly. "No. I refuse for anything to happen to you."

"Delilah, I'm a willing participant," she presses.

*So was Easton.*

Hazel must see the pain flash across my eyes, because she huffs, but relents. "The second something goes wrong I'm dropping down." Her jaw clenches. "I refuse to sit by."

I understand why Hazel wants to stay; it's the same reason as why I want her to leave.

I swallow. "You can fly overhead to make sure it's alone and signal me if anything seems amiss."

My spine straightens as the atmosphere in the forest changes, turning silent. A horrid energy swirls around us.

Hazel wraps her arms around me, squeezing tightly. "Please be careful," she whispers.

"I'll do my best."

Hazel steps back, spreading her wings. I raise my protection shield, feeling as Hazel does the same, before she takes off skyward.

Every free moment I've had, I've been practicing protection shields, both around myself and other objects. Now, my protection shield doesn't flicker or die; instead, it holds strong, as if made of steel.

Walking to the farthest point in the circle, I lean against a tree, unsheathing the small blade at my hip and begin cleaning my nails. I don't have to wait long. Only a few minutes have passed before the otherworldly wrongness of energy slithers around my shield, probing, questioning my presence.

A dark shadow falls over the forest in front of me.

Long raven black legs are the first thing I see, the feet tipped with clawed talons that dig into the mossy earth as it crawls into the circle. The spider's large body is shaped like a heart, the size of it as big as I am, the width wider than the tree trunk against my back.

I crane my neck to the upper half of a gorgeous female. Porcelain white skin, large breasts, round sparkling dark eyes, and chestnut brown hair greets me. The wicked smile on its face is purely ravenous as the soul cater's eyes widen, turning into large black pits.

I wonder if the mermaids have sent me to my death.

A sensual laugh leaves its mouth, the sound making my

stomach fill with dread. "You smell divine," it purrs, its dark voice skittering down my spine.

I make my face a perfect mask of boredom, dropping my voice to a sensuous husky tone. "Thank you, gorgeous."

Delight fills its features as eight legs crawl closer to me. "I love it when they're feisty. The begging gets boring sometimes."

I roll my eyes. "Men are babies."

"My tales precede me. Fascinating." It cocks its head to the side, smirking. "Why don't you drop that precious shield for me?"

I smirk back, folding my trembling hands behind my forearms. "Show me yours and I'll show you mine," I purr.

Its bewitching chuckle is so loud the leaves around us rustle.

"Feisty indeed," it taunts, standing in the middle of the circle. "What do you want to know, Fae?"

I arch my brow. Interesting indeed. "Where did you come from?" I ask. Perhaps the origin of the otherworldly beasts will lead us to the answers of what happened that dreadful night one hundred and forty-eight years ago.

Its chin tilts down, its eyes sparking with delight. "If I told you that, I'd have to kill you," it breathes. Cocking her head, her smile spreads wide. "In fact, I think I will."

Before I can blink it lunges, all eight gangly hairy legs flying across the field for me, curving in preparation to capture me. Its clawed talon aims straight for my throat.

I fling myself to the ground, sliding on my back leg as I unsheathe my blade, lifting it above my head. The underbelly of the soul eater flies above me. My blade plunges into its gut, the speed of its lunge doing half the work for me as I drag my blade, splitting her open.

My blade is halfway through her stomach when one of the

soul eater's legs knocks my head to the side. Pain sears through my pounding skull as stars shoot into my vision. I don't dare stop and wait for my vision to repair. Jumping to a standing position, its pure instinct that has the long blade strapped to my back in my hand as I step forward and strike. Right as two of her legs swipe for me, my blade connects before they crumble to the ground. Black blood oozes down my sword as the soul eater shrieks, the very sound not of this world.

Her eyes go wholly black, rage like no other filling them as she lunges for me once more. I spin, the spare dagger in my hand flying as I do, meeting its mark in her neck. Before she can react, I'm spinning again. Standing behind the soul eater now, I jump, both my feet landing on its hideous back-side. I plunge my blade into her human body. The sword slicing clean through her heart. I fling myself back, landing on my back as I drag my sword with me. The soul eater's body drops to the ground, its chest unmoving as black blood gushes out of it beside me on the dead grass. Gagging at the putrid smell.

Whatever the mermaids wanted me to see or find is obviously useless considering our riddle and source just tried to kill me. *Perhaps they were sending me to my doom.* She didn't go down without a fight, that's for sure. I lift myself up onto my elbows and pant, giving myself a moment to catch my breath. I'm so focused on coming to terms with the fact the soul eater was real and indeed didn't only eat men that I don't hear anyone land behind me.

A dark sensuous chuckle fills the space around me, the sound sending a warm tingle through my spine and goose-bumps down my arms. I stand, whirling around to find the most beautiful male I've ever laid eyes on. He's nowhere near me and yet the mere sight of him sends electricity through my body. Sensual grace oozes out of him as he leans against an oak tree, his feet crossed in front of him. I do a slow sweep, watching as his muscles bulge, straining his clothes. He's wearing black tailored pants and a white dress shirt. The top buttons are undone, the sleeves rolled up, showing off his muscular forearms. He should look ridiculous wearing a suit in the forest, yet it somehow suits him.

Reaching his face, I'm stunned into silence. He truly is the most beautiful man I have ever seen. Strong jawline, raven black hair, and a stunning smirk that makes deep dimples appear on his cheeks. His sapphire blue eyes twinkle at me with mischief. Not to mention how large his frame is; he looks to be almost a foot taller than me.

His sensual husky voice sings to a part of my soul. "Like what you see, Angel?" he purrs.

Another round of goosebumps run down my skin, electricity buzzing throughout my body by the sheer act of hearing him speak.

Why does his voice sound so familiar? I swear I've—

He juts his chin toward the dead soul eater. "Very entertaining," he muses.

I click my tongue. "I'm delighted to hear you enjoy swordplay."

"Oh no." He places a palm over his heart. "It seems I missed out on all the fun; I arrived just in time to watch you murder my friend."

My face blanches. "Your friend?"

His head turns, eyes calculating. "Have you got something against spiders, Angel?"

I'm utterly lost for words as I stare at his sapphire eyes sparkling with amusement.

I open my mouth to speak…gods knows what to him,

when feet land behind me a moment before Hazel rushes in front of me, apologizing profusely.

"We mean no harm, Your Majesty. We had no idea the soul eater was a part of your cavalry." Hazel winces on the last word. "It was an honest mistake, King."

A phantom bucket of cold water pours over my senses. The warmth he brought me earlier leaves me entirely at the word *king*. My eyes turn cold and detached.

His brows furrow as he notices my sudden distaste. With his attention still on me, he asks casually, "How did you find it?"

Hazel takes a small step in front of me, partially blocking my body. "We flew around the Earth Court until we found the spider silk." Her tone is strong, yet there's no mistaking her fidgeting for nerves.

He smirks, turning his head to look at Hazel. "And why were you looking for it?"

Hazel's gulp is audible. "That's personal, Your Majesty."

He moves to take a single step, no further than his shoe leaving the ground, does my protection shield snap around Hazel. His eyes widen, the humor and playfulness draining from his face entirely. In an instant he stumbles back, as if I physically struck him.

His eyes widen, voice wavering as he says, "You have access to your full powers."

Hazel turns to me, her brows furrowing as white light encases us. My entire body tingles as I float through the light.

One moment we're standing in the middle of a forest clearing with the soul eater's mutilated corpse behind me, and the next my feet are on white tiles in a hallway.

"What the fuck was that?" I snap.

Hazel's eyes widen. She yanks on my hand, scolding me like a child. "Delilah!"

The beautiful man is standing in front of us, humor dancing in his eyes once more as he smirks at me. "You're welcome," he purrs.

I scoff. "For what? Nearly blinding us?"

Hazel squeezes my hand again in warning, but I'm too riled up to tamp down my feelings.

He's a king, they're all corrupt and hateful. I would know best.

"The queen has spies everywhere. This is the safest space to talk freely." He waves a lazy hand around the room.

I take my time looking around, taking the opportunity to calm my breathing and get a hold of my temper.

The room appears to be a foyer designed with marble tiles, and white walls painted with intricate gold details that line the windows and columns. The setting sun touches my face as the golden pink hue shines through the glass floor-to-ceiling windows behind the stranger.

I have to hand it to him, it's beautiful. My heart skips a beat when I focus on the man once more. He looks like a beautiful dark god as the light shines behind him.

Hazel's anxious voice drags my attention back. "Forgive her. She's…um, strong-willed."

I ignore Hazel's apology, my attention solely on the king before me.

"How do we know you're not one of the queen's spies?" My tone drops, seeping with ice. "Your Majesty." I try not to spit the words at him, yet from the small furrow in his brows and Hazel's gasp of shock, I believe I was unsuccessful.

"I never lie." He sounds genuinely insulted.

I roll my eyes. "I'm going to need a lot more than just your word."

Before I can finish speaking, my breath hitches.

Memories flash through my mind, none of them my own. No, these belong to the stranger standing before me.

Quick enough to understand yet not long enough to dwell, each flitting memory is at a different location—some in the forest, various in this very room, a coastal city, and others in a study. Yet all the memories come to the same conclusion—he's secretly trying to figure out what has been happening to the Fae over the years. Fae throughout the courts have been going missing and slowly dying.

By the look on Hazel's face, he must have shown her the same snippets of memories.

I take a steadying breath, knowing exactly where the disappearing Fae went to.

"Believe me now, Angel?" he drawls coldly.

I narrow my eyes at him. That name…

"What business did you have with the soul eater?" he asks. Sliding his hands into his pockets, the epitome of calm and collected.

I cross my arms over my chest. "What business did you have with it?" I parrot, earning me a nudge in the ribs from Hazel.

"You can either tell me or I can watch for myself." He grins deviously.

I narrow my eyes at him. "You wouldn't dare."

His grin spreads wider as his eyes shine, his deep sensual voice floating through my mind.

*Oh, but I would.*

My eyes are wild as I snap, "Get out of my head!"

Hazel takes a step forward, her hands up in surrender. "We'll tell you everything!"

"Hazel!"

"We need him for information," she whisper-yells.

I'm so focused on Hazel that I forget the most important thing I need to keep hidden from this man.

"You were a human," he murmurs, his head cocking to the side as he studies me.

Fear like no other fills me. I open my mouth to speak but nothing comes out. I can't lie, he saw for himself my miserable life.

"Are you going to turn us over to the queen?" Hazel asks hesitantly.

The king before us straightens his head, fixing his impeccable clothing as he takes a step toward us. "No. I do, however, have a proposition."

I roll my eyes. Of course he does.

Hazel answers before I can. "What do you propose?"

"We seem to be working for the same cause, each having useful information the other needs. I propose we work together."

*Hell no,* I'm about to protest, when Hazel blurts, "Deal."

"What?" I snap. Grabbing Hazel's arm I whisper, "He will betray us the second he gets a chance. He's only looking out for himself and his best interests, whatever the hell those are."

And for all I know, the memories he showed me could be his imagination. You can never trust a king. No matter what kind of mask they portray to you.

The cocky bastard smirks at me.

"Delightful! This ordeal has been wonderfully entertaining; however, I'm parched. Let's discuss matters over dinner," he muses.

He strides directly to me, not slowing his pace until the tip of his leather boots touch my own. Bending, he lowers his face to mine. I'm transfixed as his soft lips brush the shell of my ear, sending goosebumps down my arms.

"My name's Knox. However, I do delight in hearing you call me a cocky bastard," he purrs.

My eyes widen as Hazel giggles beside me. Traitor.

*He can hear my thoughts?*

Knox straightens, adjusting his shirt before striding forward, leaving me with no choice but to follow him and Hazel.

I groan internally. I don't want to work with this asshole.

"I might be an asshole, Delilah, but I'm the only asshole that can help you," he calls over his shoulder.

"Get out of my head," I growl.

# Chapter Eighteen

Walking through French doors, I'm greeted with the most beautiful dining room I have ever encountered. In the center of the room sits a twelve-seated dining set, and French doors to my right lead to a terrace overlooking the stunning sea below. The ocean breeze flutters through the room, filling my senses with salt water and fresh air. The house we're in must be situated on top of the cliff face.

Knox takes a seat at the head of the table. I can't take my eyes off the glowing sunset descending over the ocean as Hazel takes a seat, her back toward the water. Pulling out a chair, I take a seat across from Hazel. The arrogant bastard seated to my left doesn't move as the doors behind him open. Two Fae women enter, their arms laden with dishes as they scurry into the room, gently placing them on the dining room table.

An assortment of spices fills the room, the aroma so delicious it makes my mouth water. I say a quiet thank you to the women, a small smile playing on their lips as they float out of the room, their long hair appearing to twinkle as they leave. As if the very stars of the night reside in their raven hair.

Knox's deep sensuous voice fills the room. "How did you get past the entrapment spell?"

I slide my gaze to the door the women just vacated; can we talk about such things here?

Knox's eyes narrow. "I trust my people with my life."

I keep my mouth shut, clutching my hands in my lap so tightly my knuckles turn white. It's all good and well that he trusts his people, yet I don't trust him. All kings lie and deceive.

Pain blares through my shin as a boot connects with it under the table. Gritting my teeth, I glower at Hazel as she gives me a tight-lipped smile.

"Delilah," she whispers.

I take a sip of my water, my throat suddenly dry. "A crystal pendant that had an unveiling spell cast to it centuries ago," I relent.

Knox's brow quirks. "How did you get a hold of such a thing?"

"My mother gave it to me," I answer flatly.

"Ah, I see."

How much did he see in my mind? My cheeks heat, embarrassment coating my tongue at the thought of someone so confident and powerful watching me get beaten.

"Fae have been getting kidnapped for decades, more so now than ever before. The ones you saw in your land were almost certainly the ones taken from here," Knox explains, his powerful arms reaching forward to serve himself dinner, Hazel and I doing the same.

Knox slides his sapphire eyes to mine. "They've also been dying. Those who had little magic to begin with one hundred and forty-eight years ago die as their magic vanishes over time."

Color leaches from Hazel's face as her body freezes, her hand wrapped around a spoonful of steamed green vegetables halting midair.

Knox lowers his knife and fork, resting his arms on the table as he leans forward. "You didn't know about magic vanishing? Have you not felt it yourself?"

"I thought it was the grief," Hazel croaks.

Fae magic has been slowly dwindling? That explains Knox's utter shock when I used the protection shield around Hazel. I have access to full powers while others are slowly dying. It feels eerily similar to how I felt at the palace, knowing I was alive while others died at the hands of my father.

"What exactly do we have to offer you that you think you need?" I ask, breaking the silent tension.

I cut a piece of pork. The second the food touches my tongue, my eyes widen. I thought Hazel's food was delicious, but this is divine. My taste buds combust as the spices dance along my tongue, salivating over the richness of the food. I have never tasted anything so heavenly.

Knox's husky voice captures my attention. "Our chances of breaking the entrapment spell have been diminishing each day that we lose our magic. I'd need you to break the spell once we find its origin. It appears you're the only Fae with access to their full power."

I steel my spine. "Why is magic vanishing?"

A muscle ticks in his jaw. "No one knows. It started when the entrapment spell was cast over the Fae lands."

"Has the queen searched for answers?" Hazel asks warily.

Knox picks up his glass of wine, stirring the red liquid. "Supposedly."

"Information for information, no holding back. That was the deal," I say, pointing my fork at him. His dark rumble of a chuckle fills the room. I try to tamp down the tingle it sends down my spine. I fail miserably.

"Yes, I suppose it was," Knox drawls, clearing his throat. "I believe the queen likes this current arrangement of power."

Hazel picks up her glass of water, her brows pulling low as she glances to Knox. "Are you not in reign? I thought you were all of age now."

Knox leans back in his seat, crossing a powerful thigh over his knee. "She's an old stubborn Fae, claiming the current system works in everyone's favor as she looks for the lost Fae and a resolution for the dying. Yet it's been decades and it's only getting worse."

"Is she behind it?" I ask, making Hazel's jaw drop open.

Knox, however, is unaffected by my blunt question. "No, I believe she doesn't want to rule as a democracy again."

That's not surprising, someone in power wanting more power.

"What did you want with the soul eater?" I ask, trying not to moan as I place a piece of sautéed potato in my mouth.

Knox's eyes dip to my mouth as I eat. "I was tracking it for weeks, hoping it would lead me to where the others came from."

"There's more than one soul eater?" I ask, horrified.

"No, but she turned up at the same time the others did. I've been trying to track them all, hoping it would lead to answers as to how they continue to get into this world and past the entrapment spell." He clenches his jaw, flitting his gaze between Hazel and me. "No matter how many other-worldly beasts you kill, they keep coming back. No one understands how or why." His eyes harden, pain flashing for a moment before vanishing entirely, his cool demeanor returning.

The room falls silent for a moment before Knox turns, placing all his attention on me. "What was your business with the soul eater?"

I lean forward, ignoring his question as I let my curiosity win. "Why was its blood black?"

Knox's brow rises as he leans back. "The soul eater is a demonic creature. Those who are not from this world or possess magic that isn't pure have the undesired effect of black blood. Their very essence rots their blood." Before I can speak, Knox leans forward, his eyes never leaving mine as his voice lowers, deepening to the point of making my stomach take flight with butterflies. "Your business now."

I flail my hand around my head. "I'm sure you've already seen."

His face sobers. "I'd rather hear it from you," he says sincerely.

My traitorous cheeks heat. Stupid, useless hormones. They must be heightened also.

My swallow is audible, making Hazel snicker. "The mermaids gave me two riddles, and the first led to the soul eater." Leaning back in the chair, I pick up my water. I declined the wine offered, needing a clear mind being in another royal court. "However, the hideous thing tried to slash my throat before I could ask any real questions or barter with it."

The corner of Knox's mouth tips into a smirk. "Perhaps the mermaids gave you that riddle to lead you to me."

Of course he would think it's all about him. This man is nothing but a cocky bastard.

"That's what I'm starting to believe," Hazel chimes in, making me swivel unbelieving eyes to her.

Hazel's words only make Knox's grin widen, his dimples popping out. "The second riddle?"

I clamp my mouth shut, uncertainty coursing through me. Hazel recites the second riddle, answering for me. She seems to be doing that a lot. "I have no voice, but I have lots to teach. Your soul is my price, let me speak. Darkness enchanted is my tale."

"A book of dark magic," Knox says flatly.

Hazel and I look at each other as we burst into a fit of laughter. It's comical how silly I feel that we didn't put it together ourselves.

"Yes, I suppose it is," I murmur.

Knox's eyes dip to my mouth as I laugh, a dazzling smile spreading across his face. It only adds to his sinful beauty.

"Who are the small Fae in the glass bottles?" I ask.

The second the word leaves my mouth, memories of that day come back to me, flashing through my mind as Knox watches me descend into the room to find shelves full of tiny Fae trapped in glass bottles.

His eyes shutter closed as the memory leaves my mind.

"Those would be pixies. They've gone nearly extinct over the years, and the small handful that's left are in hiding. The only magic they possess is protection from magic. They're immune to it."

I lower my eyes as sadness fills me once more. No one deserves to be held as a slave, let alone confined to a jar for experiments.

"Where's your court?" Hazel asks, changing the topic.

Knox returns to his food. "They're all out on their own scouting missions, trying to find where the beasts are getting in."

I gaze at him sideways. "Have you found anything?"

Knox leans back in his chair. "Not where they come from.

All we've gathered is that there's an array of different creatures, some like the soul eater who prefer to be alone, while others travel in packs."

"That's unsettling." Hazel frowns.

My heart stumbles at the reminder of Luna.

"Perhaps we should look for who's taking the Fae. Someone must cross the threshold to place them in the human lands," I offer.

"I agree," Knox says, shocking me.

I'm so used to being told to stay quiet and never offer an opinion it takes me a moment to recover.

"Maybe they're getting in through the same way the beasts are," Hazel counters. "We would be killing two birds with one stone if we continue searching for both."

"We'll look for who's transporting the Fae and search for the dark magic book. My court is currently tracking the beasts." Knox swirls his wine. "Have you got any ideas as to which book the mermaids are hinting to?"

"We didn't get too far on the second riddle," I mumble.

"I didn't even know there was such a thing," Hazel says.

I frown. "Dark magic?"

Knox answers for Hazel. "The Fae lands practice divine magic, which is pure. Dark magic was banned a millennia ago."

"Great, so the mermaids are sending us on a hunting mission for something that doesn't exist," I drawl sarcastically.

"Oh, it exists. Something has to exist for it to be banished."

I roll my eyes. "Do you have to be so dramatic and cryptic?"

Knox's dark chuckle rumbles around his wine glass. "It's hidden, Delilah."

My name falling from his lips makes my stomach feel warm… I kill that warmth.

After dinner finishes, an uncomfortable silence fills the dining room. My hands tap my thigh involuntarily, forcing me to sit on them to stop the fidgeting.

"How exactly do we get back to the cabin?" I ask.

Knox's head snaps to mine. "You're not going back there."

I open my mouth to protest, but Knox cuts me off. "You killed the soul eater. Other beasts will be roaming the forest to know who did. They're selfish creatures but they don't like their own being murdered."

"Hazel has wards around her house," I protest, turning to face her.

Hazel's skin has turned bone white, her eyes distant as fear fills them and in that moment, I know we're not returning to the cabin.

Knox must sense the change in her too.

"I have the strongest wards in Azalea, Hazel. Nothing gets in or out without my approval," he says softly.

*Azalea—the city of Essence Court.* My gaze roams around the room.

Hazel doesn't respond, too far gone into her own mind as her memories assault her.

I gently take her hand. "Come on," I whisper. Pulling her up to stand, I wrap an arm around her shoulder. "Can you please show us to our rooms?" I ask as nicely as I can, not wanting to fight when Hazel is so distraught at the thought of those beasts in her home. The very beasts she ran to the cabin to get away from.

"What about Luna's things?" Hazel whispers, her chin wobbling. "I can't lose those, Delilah."

"I'll go get them and bring them here," I offer.

"You most certainly will not," Knox declares.

I snap my head to him, narrowing my eyes.

*Do not upset her further.*

Knox's gaze slides to Hazel, shuddering at her pale face and small figure trembling in my arms, making his resolve falter.

"The guest rooms are this way," he announces as he strides out of the room.

Hazel and I follow Knox up three floors of staircases. Turning right, we walk down a long hallway as Knox points to the farthest door at the end. "That's my personal bedroom. My court sleeps at the other end of the hall, a level below. Hazel, you can stay in this room," he says, opening the door in front of him. He points to the door across the hall. "You can stay in the adjacent room, Delilah."

Knox slides his hands into his pockets as Hazel and I enter her room. It's nearly as large as my room back at the palace. A large bed that could fit at least four people comfortably sits in the center, chandeliers with flickering flames dangle from the ceiling, and sitting chairs frame the open window, overlooking what appears to be the back garden. To the right, an open archway leads to a bathing suite and dressing room.

I stroll behind Hazel as she takes a stiff seat on the bed. "I'll be back with your things as soon as possible."

Hazel dips her chin once, her eyes glazed as her mind takes her far away.

I frown as I leave her, worry making my chest squeeze tightly. Did I make the right decision in dragging her into this mess? Hazel has suffered enough; she chose to be alone for this very reason.

A warm hand suddenly encompasses mine, sending a jolt of electricity through my arm. I quickly yank my hand away. "What on the goddesses' green earth are you doing?" I hiss at Knox.

He shrugs. "You can't fly or teleport. I'm simply escorting you."

Is that what that was earlier? Teleporting?

"You didn't hold my hand last time," I say, tilting my head back to peer at him.

"I had more power last time," he drawls, a small smile curving his lips.

*Bullshit. This man has been teasing and pushing my buttons since the moment those turquoise eyes landed on me.*

Screw playing nice. "Bullshit."

Knox's deep laugh makes my toes curl. "You're utterly adorable when you argue with yourself in your mind."

I grit my teeth, about to snap profanities at him when his hand encompasses my own again. My jaw clenches as white light surrounds us, Knox's warm hand never leaving mine as we teleport to the cabin.

When my feet connect with the floor once more, I stumble back, wrenching my hand away.

"I'll just be a moment," I mumble. Leaving him standing in Hazel's living room, I search for Luna's things. Returning moments later with Luna's box and a bag full of Hazel's clothing in my arms, I stop short, finding Knox seated on my cot, holding Easton's clothing in his large hands.

Without a conscious thought, my gums tighten, pain searing throughout my mouth as my teeth grow involuntarily. My canines flare, the sharp point curving as they snap down. "Drop it," I growl.

Knox drops the clothing, standing quickly as he holds his palms up. "I meant no disrespect."

Energy falls over me, washing me with calm sincerity. A phantom hand strokes my arm as if to say sorry.

My canines retract. "Did—did you just send me your energy?" I stutter.

"You were two seconds away from ripping my head off. Of course I did."

An apology is on the tip of my tongue before my pride makes me swallow it. I didn't mean to snarl like a wild animal, yet seeing his hands on Easton's clothes…

He smirks. "No apologies necessary, Angel."

The guilt I was feeling moments ago evaporates entirely. "Stop doing that!"

"Put up a mental shield and I will," he purrs.

I make a mental note to get Hazel to teach me how to—

"I'll teach you." Knox shrugs.

I roll my eyes. "You're exasperating."

A smile tugs at the corner of his lips. "Some call me persistent."

I refuse to acknowledge that I said those very words to Hazel. I also ignore the tingling feeling his teasing invokes in me. Moving forward, I set down all of Hazel and Luna's belongings at his feet. Gently packing Easton's belongings into the bag, I move my own items to the pile I've created.

Knox bites back a smile. "Are you sure you have everything?"

Clicking my tongue, I hold out my palm. "At your nearest convenience, Your Highness."

He doesn't take my hand, instead sliding his own in his pockets. "Do you have an issue with my title Delilah?" His voice is caged, protective.

I narrow my eyes. "If you go into my mind, I will slice your favorite part of yourself and shove it down your throat."

Knox turns his head to the side, utterly unfazed by my threat. White light surrounds us as he places his hand on my arm. He doesn't utter a single word as he teleports us back to his house.

In the hallway once more, Knox removes his hand from my arm. "Goodnight, Angel," he whispers before retreating into his room.

Without letting myself think about Knox's dramatic farewell, I pick up Hazel's belongings and enter her room, only to find her curled in a ball on top of the sheets, sniffling. I gently place Luna's belongings beside her. "I got everything, including clothes for yourself."

"Thank you," she whispers as she sits up.

I leave her to rifle through the box and enter my own temporary room.

The ocean's breeze hits me first, the sea salt calming my tense muscles as it surrounds my senses. Directly across from me are black doors, the night sky twinkling above the ocean. Despite being atop a large cliff, I have my Fae hearing to thank for being able to hear the rolling waves and the crash as it hits the sandy shore.

A large king-sized bed sits in the center of the room to my right. I run my hand over the sheets to find its fitted with white silk, the smooth texture greeting my fingertips as I place my bags down on the futon at the end of the bed. To the left of the French doors is a vanity area, and beside that, the open archway leads to a walk-in closet and a glorious bathing room. I stroll through it, my boots squeaking on the marbled tiles as I survey the room.

A large porcelain sink area sits directly in front of me, a clawfoot bathtub resting in the center of the room, so large at least three Fae could sit in it comfortably. A large circular window on the far-right wall overlooks the ocean. I could have a bath while staring at the sea.

I sigh as I enter the bedroom again. I loved Hazel's cabin, but it will be amazing to sleep in more than one position on a small cot. Lying flat on my back, I spread my arms and legs out wide like a starfish as the mattress sinks, my body melting into the buttery soft linens.

Turning my head to the left, I see I missed a wide bookcase near the door. I pray to any god that will hear me that I'll be able to find a decent book somewhere. Something tells me I'll need the escape at the end of my days.

Dragging myself from bed, I get dressed for sleep, pulling Easton's white cotton shirt over my head, then crawl back into the silk sheets.

Lying in bed, I can't help but think that I've left one palace only to end up in another.

# Chapter Nineteen

I awake to the sound of waves crashing as the sun shines through the balcony doors, the sea breeze flowing into the room through the crack I left open last night. I sit up, stretching my limbs, marveling at how comfortably I slept. I grew accustomed to Hazel's cot, so much so the other side of the bed is completely untouched.

My stomach rumbles, making me drag myself out of bed. My bare feet pad across the plush white carpet as I change into my fighting leathers. I'm unsure of what's to come today and I want to feel prepared.

Strolling across the hall to Hazel's room, I knock twice, my gaze sliding down the hall to Knox's room. It's utterly silent in the halls, no guards to be seen or heard on the level.

The hinges squeak as Hazel pulls open the door. She still looks a bit ill, yet the color has returned to her freckle-covered cheeks.

"Are you hungry?" I ask softly.

"Starving! I was too nervous to eat a proper meal last night," she exclaims.

I offer my elbow. "Let's go find some breakfast."

We walk the same halls as last night, retracing our steps to the dining room. I freeze when I find Knox seated at the head of the dining table, drinking what smells to be coffee and reading a book. I'm not stunned to find the owner of this house seated in his own dining chair.

Knox is wearing similar clothes to yesterday. Tailored black pants, creamy white dress shirt, the sleeves rolled to his biceps, showing off his tan skin. The top buttons are undone once more, revealing the start of his hard planes and collarbones.

It's not that he's impeccably dressed again that's shocked me either—quite the opposite.

It's the purely ravenous heat I find sizzling in his eyes as he stares at me.

The corner of his mouth turns up, satisfaction ringing throughout his smug face as he watches me. "Morning, Angel." He doesn't wait for a response. He simply addresses Hazel, already sitting beside him to his left. "Hazel, sleep well?"

"You have the most comfortable mattress I've ever slept on," she chirps, serving herself food.

I swallow the lump that's formed in my throat, taking the same seat as last night. I sit beside Knox, ignoring the hole he's searing into the side of my head as I look at the array of food lining the table. Buttered croissants, eggs, sausages, pastries, pancakes…How many people are eating here this morning? This is an outrageous amount of food for three people.

Knox leans forward, plucking a croissant. "I didn't know what you like to eat, so I asked the kitchen to make everything."

I chastise my traitorous heart for starting to beat faster

from his considerate actions. Not trusting myself to speak, I place eggs, toast, and bacon on my plate.

I clear my throat. "That's very kind of you. Thank you."

Hazel places pancakes on her plate. My eyes sadden. I wonder if the last time she ate them was with Luna.

Changing the subject to distract Hazel, I say, "What's on the agenda for today?"

Knox takes a sip of coffee, his movements graceful. "I have business in Azalea. When I return, we can start with magic lessons."

"What sort of business?"

"It doesn't concern you," Knox dismisses.

I grit my teeth. He's already beginning to hide things. "Does it concern the demonic creatures or missing Fae?"

Knox turns his head to the side. "Yes, not in the matter you think, though."

"Information for information, remember?" I say sweetly, pointing my knife at him. "I'll join you," I declare, cutting into a slice of bacon.

Hazel leans toward Knox. "When she gets that look in her eyes, just agree to whatever she says. You'll get nowhere with her."

I gasp. "Hazel!"

"It's true!" she protests, splaying her hands in front of her.

"Yes, she does seem to be stubborn, doesn't she?" he murmurs to Hazel, while his eyes lock on mine.

I narrow my own in return. "I'm sitting right here."

Knox takes a slow slip of coffee, then grins. "If you wish. We can work on magic when we return."

"Why can't Hazel continue teaching me?"

"You have essence magic. I figured the King of Essence would be more helpful," he drawls.

Hazel's jaw drops open. "Well, that answers a lot of questions."

I'm more confused than ever. "Essence magic needs to have more than one elemental power. I only have fire."

Hazel shakes her head. "You cloaked us that day in the garden. That comes from water magic." Guilt fills her eyes. "I was distraught that day, I forgot. I'm sorry."

"Hazel, it's okay," I whisper.

"You also have air power," Knox chimes in.

"How?" I demand.

"You can hear me when I speak into your mind. You can do the same to me if you allow me to teach you," he says smugly.

Hazel shakes her head in astonishment. I open and close my mouth, utterly speechless, flailing around like a fish out of water. "You spoke into Hazel's mind. You showed her the images as well."

Knox crosses his powerful arms over his chest. "I intended to do that...I didn't intend for you to hear me the other times."

"You say rude comments into people's minds without them knowing?"

Knox throws his head back, his boisterous laugh sending electricity throughout my body.

Damn him and damn my body for reacting.

He simply shrugs. "It passes the time and keeps me polite."

I roll my eyes. "This is absurd...What other powers do I possess?"

Which is the wrong thing to say as his eyes spark with delight, a smile spreading across his lips. "We'll find out this afternoon," he purrs.

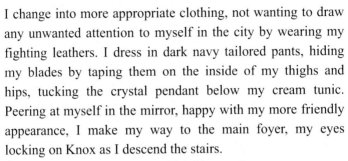

I change into more appropriate clothing, not wanting to draw any unwanted attention to myself in the city by wearing my fighting leathers. I dress in dark navy tailored pants, hiding my blades by taping them on the inside of my thighs and hips, tucking the crystal pendant below my cream tunic. Peering at myself in the mirror, happy with my more friendly appearance, I make my way to the main foyer, my eyes locking on Knox as I descend the stairs.

It's truly unfair how beautiful this man is.

"Shall we?" he drawls.

I ignore his question, instead looking around the foyer. Hazel's missing and there appears to be no guards posted in the foyer either. "Where's Hazel? Is she not coming?"

Knox shakes his head. "She wanted to stay back."

I frown. Why didn't she tell me herself?

"Why don't you have guards posted around the house?" I ask.

Knox stops dead in his tracks before he turns, his face guarded. "Why do you ask?"

I cross my arms over my chest. "Considering you're meant to be a king, I figured you'd have more guards posted around the halls."

Knox cocks his head to the side as he slides his hands into his pockets. "How do you know there aren't any in this very room?"

With his taunt, I snap my back up straight, clenching my hands to stop from looking around the room. I refuse to give Knox the satisfaction.

*I can't believe I didn't think about cloaked guards.*

I lift my chin, refusing to let him get under my skin. "Very well, continue."

Walking to the front door, Knox's lips spread into a heart stopping smile. "Welcome to Azalea."

As the steel doors fly open, I have no words to describe the beauty that greets me.

The house we're in sits atop the highest point of a cliff. Gardens full of life spread across the front of the grounds, leading to a wrought iron gate.

Looking over Azalea I finally find my breath again.

An array of different colored buildings line the cliff's face, surrounding the ocean. When low sounds from the streets below float toward us, I tuck my hair behind my ears, focusing on the music, cheers, voices, and laughter. My eyes burn, tears forming at the happiness I feel emanating from the city. I look toward the rich, aqua blue ocean, the exact same color of Knox's eyes. People are splashing around playing, others flying around the coastal city.

Turning to Knox, I find him watching me, his eyes shining with an emotion I can't decipher.

"It's beautiful," I breathe.

"Are you ready to explore?" he asks softly.

"Yes."

Knox opens his arms to fly us down to the city.

I have to be in his arms...

He sees my hesitancy. "I'm not going to harm you," he says defensively.

Except I'm not worried he's going to drop me. I'm worried about how I'll react to him being so close. I take a deep breath, knowing it's either this or walk for hours to reach the main streets.

I dip my head once, giving Knox my consent.

His strong muscular arms wrap around me, lifting me

gently into his chest. I feel the erratic thumping of his heart-beat against my shoulder as his warmth surrounds me, soothing my nerves.

I haven't felt this comfortable around a male since...*Easton*.

The thought makes any warmth I felt completely disap-pear as Knox takes off flying over the city. Swooping low and high above the buildings, I try to enjoy the flight and the city before me, yet the more happiness I hear, the sadder I feel.

The one thing in the world Easton deserved to see is this —a city of happiness.

I'm so consumed with my thoughts I barely register Knox landing on a busy street until my feet hit the cobblestone path. Vendors line the roads and vines snake around the multi-colored buildings. Hundreds of Fae are walking the street, some going to and from stores, others sitting in restau-rant verandas listening to the live music playing on the streets.

"I have never seen a city so joyous," I croak.

Knox studies my face for a moment. Placing his palm on my lower back, he leads me forward. "There's a house I have to visit before my meeting."

We walk through the streets for ten minutes, up and down alleyways and residential streets lined with beautiful houses of all various shapes and colors. I try my hardest to focus on everything, yet all the colors seem to blur as grief drags me down.

We reach the house Knox needs to visit, a small quaint yellow house surrounded by a short picket fence. Knox taps twice on the door, fidgeting as he waits, adjusting his impec-cable suit. It's the first time I've seen him appear to be nervous. A small woman answers the door. She's older than the Fae I've seen. Her skin is more weathered, her hair peppered with gray. Her face is red and blotchy as she looks from me to Knox.

"Christy, this is my dear friend, Delilah. I hope you don't mind that I've brought her here today," Knox says gently.

*Dear friend?*

Christy pushes her door open further. "That's all right." Christy looks to me when she says, "Please excuse the mess; we haven't had much time lately—"

"Oh, no problem at all!" I insist.

Stepping through the wooden door, the inside of the house is a completely different energy to what the front emanates. All the curtains are drawn, and small candles are lit around the space, yet it doesn't help the darkness that covers the room. Papers and maps litter every surface.

"Have you received any news?" Christy asks, hope lining her eyes.

Knox slides his hands into his pockets. "I'm sorry, Christy. I have good news and bad news."

Her entire face drops, tears forming in her chocolate eyes as her chin wobbles. "Is she dead?"

My chest constricts, my heart sinking to my stomach.

Why did he bring me here?

Knox gently takes her hands. "No," he affirms. "She's alive, but we don't know how to get to her."

Christy looks from Knox to me, her brows pulling low. "Where is she?"

Christy's eyes go vacant, Knox's own never leaving hers as he goes into her mind. In the next moment, she falls to her knees, sobbing. I instantly rush forward to hold her, my heart breaking at the sound of her cries, but Knox is faster than I am. He bends in front of her, whispering soothing words of comfort. "She's alive, Christy. She's unharmed."

Tears roll down my cheeks. I turn away to wipe my eyes.

When I look back, Knox has moved Christy to the couch and he—

Oxygen evades me as I stare at the image before me.

The King of Essence is *kneeling* before his people. My father would rather die than ever kneel before our people.

"I'm working on how to release them all. I haven't spoken to anyone about this because I don't know how long it will take to get to them." He lowers his head, catching her eyes. "I just wanted you to know that she's alive."

"Thank you," Christy says between sobs.

My chest constricts, making it harder to breathe.

I leave the room, no longer wanting to intrude on such a private moment.

Standing on the front pathway, it isn't long before Knox exits the house, joining me.

"Why did you bring me inside?" I rasp.

"You insisted on coming," he states coldly.

I grit my teeth, waiting for the real explanation.

Knox sighs, strolling forward. I follow him as he speaks. "I saw Christy's daughter at the compound in your memory. Because of you, Christy now knows her daughter is alive. I thought you would want to know you were a part of something good." His tone is still cold, yet I swear his eyes have softened.

I nod, not wanting to talk any further about the topic at hand. I can feel my resolve slipping on my emotions and the last thing I want to do is break down in front of this man.

"I'm going for a walk by the ocean."

"I have a meeting I have to attend to in town."

I start to back away. "Okay, just let me know when you're done." I turn my back on him, walking as fast as I can toward the ocean.

Praying I can outrun my feelings.

*Easton should be here.*

It's that one thought that keeps repeating on a loop in my mind that makes me break.

Sitting on a rock on the water's edge, with no one in sight to see me, my resolve completely crumbles as sobs wrack my body. I hug my knees to my chest, failing miserably to keep it all in.

I don't understand why he isn't here. We were so close to the boat; my mind can't make sense of it. Part of me believes he's back at the palace waiting for me to return, yet my heart knows he's truly gone.

Easton was everything good in this world. He was kind, caring, loyal, and fair. Like when he would sneak me dough-nuts if I had a bad day. When he'd rock me to sleep on the nights my father beat me. He loved everyone and brought so much joy to my life that it's horrendous that, in return, he died because of me.

Easton died.

Easton is *dead.*

The words clang through me, knocking me back as if someone physically struck me. That horrible word makes nausea fill my throat. I lean to the side as I vomit, no longer able to hold back the bile. My chest heaves, my heart beating so fast I'm afraid I'll pass out as my arms and legs begin to shake.

The wave of unending sadness and pain crashing into my chest makes it harder to breathe. I'm crying so hard I can't see through my tears, not noticing as someone approaches.

A warm hand lands on my back, making me jump.

Fear courses through me, making me blindly react. A

wave of gold power erupts out of me, the same power I used against my father.

Before it can hit the person in front of me, it's swallowed up by an invisible force.

I lift my head in horror. Knox.

Dread lines my stomach, bile burning my throat once more as I realize I just tried to attack the king.

Knox kneels beside me. "Delilah, what's wrong?" he asks, his voice holding a hint of concern. He pays no attention to my puke, also ignoring the fact that I tried to blast him with my power.

The sight of Knox kneeling on the ground beside my puke undoes me. I shoot out my hand, trying to stop him. "Go away," I wheeze.

Knox ignores my pleas. Instead, he simply scoops me up and takes off, flying us back to the house.

I try to focus on calming my breathing, praying that I don't vomit again, yet I can't get the picture of Easton's lifeless eyes out of my mind. The image of his body, unmoving on the ground, overtakes everything in front of me. I see nothing but the moment my father killed Easton, as if it's playing on a loop.

Boots tread on tiles, moving up and down as if we're walking up stairs. All movements around me pause as a knock fills the empty space. Then I hear Hazel gasp and I'm moved again, unseeing as Easton's body crumples before me in my mind, his blood on my hands as it oozes into my clothes. Sweat trickles down my back, making everything I'm seeing in my mind as real as the day it happened.

Knox's voice echoes throughout the room, his husky drawl making the images pause.

"Can you please help her into the bath? I think it will calm her down."

Blinking rapidly, my eyes adjust to the bright room to see we're in Hazel's bathroom. Knox sets me on the side of the tub, the sound of rushing water joins my panting. I claw at the tub, holding onto the porcelain so tight my fingers begin to turn numb, my nails cracking.

Mortification makes my cheeks heat.

Oh gods. He saw me kneeling over my own puke, crying.

My breathing begins to wheeze as the panic crawls its way further into my chest, burying down so tightly I know it won't go away any time soon.

So, I do what I do best.

"Leave," I croak.

I don't dare lift my head. I can't see the disgust in his eyes. I don't need the added embarrassment.

His footsteps retreat. Once the door closes, I enter the bath, not caring for my clothes as the sound of my sobs fill the room and Hazel strokes my hair.

Hushed whispers and muffled voices pull me from sleep, my head pounding so roughly I don't dare open my eyes. I can feel silk sheets below me. Running my finger through the fabric, I notice I'm in my nightwear. Who carried me to bed?

The muffled whispers begin to clear, and my hearing picks up on Knox and Hazel's voices.

"What did you say to her?" Hazel hisses.

"I didn't say anything! I found her like that."

Sleep tries to drag me under as Hazel fires something back. But the next words that leave Knox's mouth snap open my bleary eyes.

"Who's Easton?" he growls.

I thought he saw it in my mind. I thought he saw everything in my mind.

"That's not my story to tell," Hazel insists.

"Is he her mate? Did he hurt her?"

"No, you buffoon. They don't have mates in the human lands."

"You know what I mean, Hazel. Did he hurt her?"

"Stop growling at me like a wild animal! No, they weren't together and no, he didn't hurt her. That's the only thing I'll tell you," she snaps.

A small sigh of relief floats from my lips that she didn't tell him. I don't want him to know about Easton; he doesn't deserve to know. I don't want fake sympathy from a royal. Not when the very thing that took Easton away from me was someone who was meant to protect his people. A king.

I close my eyes, fresh tears pooling, spilling down my cheek as sleep pulls me under once more.

# Chapter Twenty

I awake the next morning before the sun rises. Still feeling drained and emotionally wrung out from yesterday's outburst, I rub my eyes with the heel of my palms. If Easton were here, he'd be giving me hell over missing training, so I honor him the only way I know how to right now. I drag myself out of bed and change into my fighting leathers.

Leaving my room, I tiptoe as to not wake the enhanced hearing Faes in the house.

Downstairs, I search for the training room. Knox is too muscular to not train; he'll have a training room somewhere in this house.

As I look around, I start to realize I don't need to sneak around. Knox is so informal, I haven't seen a singular guard in any hall, not now or since we've arrived. The only time I've seen guards is when I step outside and the only time I've spotted servants was the first night I had dinner here.

Never mind the guards, the house itself is informal.

Although it isn't a palace or a castle, Knox's house is ginormous, being three stories tall filled with endless rooms.

Looking through hall after hall, room after room, I finally descend to the lower ground floor, finding the training room that overlooks the back garden. I open the doors, breathing deeply as I inhale the scents of nature around me, letting it soothe and calm me.

Walking back inside, my gaze roams the room.

The far-right side wall is covered with swords, knives, staffs, and weapons. Training mats line the floor in the center, and seats and benches are scattered around the room. Standing in the center mat I begin training, executing the motions of Easton's latest workout regime he created. My heart burns with pain as I train by myself for the first time in my life.

After returning to my room for a much-needed bath, I dress myself for the day, mentally preparing myself for the embarrassment that's about to ensue. I can't believe Knox saw me like that. My cheeks heat as I swear expletives, chastising my body for already showing the signs of my mortification.

I run through scenarios in my mind of how I can smooth this over breakfast, but coming up with nothing, I decide to completely avoid all talks of yesterday and pretend it never happened. Nodding to myself, I plaster on a fake smile and make my way to the dining room.

Walking through the French doors, I avoid Hazel and Knox's eyes. "Good morning," I chirp. Rushing forward, I lower myself into the same seat as yesterday, praying no one notices my trembling hands as I serve myself breakfast. "Can we start those magic lessons today?" I ask, keeping my gaze locked on my toast.

Knox's deep gravelly voice floats over me. "Of course."

"I'm going to head into town today and search the archives in the library. I'm hoping there's a section of history written about dark magic," Hazel chimes in.

I sigh with relief that the attention is off me, successfully avoiding all conversations of yesterday.

Knox clears his throat; I watch in my peripheral as he crosses a powerful leg over his thigh.

"I'd use a different name checking in. I don't want the queen to get a whiff of what we're searching for and come knocking on my door," Knox explains.

Hazel pours syrup over her pancakes. "Anything in particular I should be searching for?"

"Anything to do with dark magic. I don't want to limit our searches and miss anything important."

Hazel dips her head. "I'll go when you two are training."

"Sounds good," I mumble.

This is the first time I've seen Knox in anything other than a suit. Knox stands several feet from me in the back garden, wearing a tight-fitted white shirt and black training pants. The fabric strains across his chest, his muscles bunching with each movement. I divert my eyes before he can see the spark of heat that courses through me at the sight of him.

Knox brought me to the far back of the garden, the house sitting to my left. It looks magical as it sits at the very peak of the hill, painted white with gray brickwork. A large oak tree towers over the area a few hundred yards away, and white daisies fill the space, complementing the sight of Knox's home. We're standing in the widest part of the yard. I dare say he brought us all the way out here in fear that I would incinerate the lovely flowerbed we passed along the way.

Knox's voice draws my attention. "What has Hazel taught you so far?"

"We touched on protection shields and control." Lowering my eyes to my feet, the nerves coursing through me make me fidget. "I have a problem with power outbursts from my emotions," I mutter.

"You didn't grow up with magic. It's only natural that it's harder to control at the moment," he says smoothly.

His statement eases my embarrassment. Lifting my eyes, I find a small smile playing on his lips.

"That makes sense. How do we figure out what powers I possess?"

"We need to work on your instincts first before adding any more power to the mix. When you're afraid, your first instinct should be to shield and assess. Currently your first reaction is to attack."

I dip my chin. "Hazel already covered this."

Before I can respond, a water-shaped arrow forms in front of me, flying so fast I barely see it coming before it barrels into my stomach, knocking the air from me. I crash to the floor, my stomach drenched as I sit up sputtering.

"You asshole!" I yell.

Knox cocks his head. "Clearly your lesson with Hazel didn't work." Knox slides his hands into his pockets as he strolls forward. "You need to start using your Fae senses to their full extent. If you were, you would have seen that coming and shielded." A faint smile tugs on his lips.

The smug bastard finds this amusing.

I grit my teeth. "I don't know how to do that."

"Yes, you do. You're the one currently blocking half of it."

"Half?" I yelp.

"Let go, Delilah," he says simply as another arrow of water forms beside him, without so much as lifting a finger.

I open my mouth to speak when the arrow flies for me. I instinctively throw out a hand, shock coursing through me as fire erupts, colliding with the water arrow until it's nothing but sizzling steam.

"Great. Now do that with a shield instead," Knox states flatly.

Already, another arrow barrels for me. I instinctively send out a fire ball that collides with it again.

"At least give me a moment to recover!" I snap.

Another water arrow rushes for my head this time.

"Instinct, remember? There isn't meant to be a thought process," he drawls.

He's enjoying this.

I grit my teeth, swearing up a storm as the water hits me in the face, turning me into a drowned rat.

"I'd say more like a raccoon," Knox drawls lazily.

My mouth gapes open. This stupid smug bastard—

Another water arrow hits me in the face, knocking me on my ass once more.

Irritation coils in my gut. Without moving a muscle, I watch as a fire ball flies for Knox. I sit up scrambling to apologize when it halts midair, turning to ash as it collides with his protection shield.

"Try again. I've got all day," he purrs.

That's how training for the next two hours goes.

Knox stares me down, smirking as he taunts me, throwing water arrow after water arrow, yelling about instincts and shields and *blah, blah, blah*. I tuned him out after the first hour, finding his voice no longer sexy but a nuisance.

I'm grateful that he's teaching me. However, I don't appreciate being soaked head to toe while a smug male stands there as dry as a desert.

I'm about to give up, reaching my quota of being pummeled with water. Opening my eyes, I see another arrow a second from hitting me again. Before I can think or move, I snap myself into a bubble. The water arrow hits an invisible shield, as if it's collided with glass. The water drips down my protection shield.

I throw my arms in the air, cheering profusely. "I did it! I put up a protection shield on instinct!"

Knox bursts out laughing, his head thrown back and smile carefree. The sound makes butterflies take flight in my stomach.

I frown. I liked it better when he was annoying me. At least then my hormones disappeared.

Humor dances in his eyes. "Great, now do that a thousand times more and we're done."

I narrow my eyes, irritation spiking again. I don't feel like being pummeled any longer. Challenge sparks in Knox's eyes, and before he can send another arrow of water, I erupt. All the irritation and anger over being a punching bag for the last two hours rises to the surface, filling my veins as my magic awakens inside of me.

It appears it's also done being pummeled.

I smile so wide my cheeks burn. In slow motion, a wave begins to form over Knox's head. With half a thought I have it slamming on top of him, drenching him completely. My magic seemingly knows exactly how I wanted to exact my revenge on Knox.

*I truly have water magic.*

I burst out laughing as Knox emerges, shock lining his features as he wipes water out of his eyes.

Slowly sweeping the entire length of his body, my laughter dies completely. I didn't think this through. Knox's white shirt is entirely see-through now that it's wet, clinging to every inch of skin on his glorious chest and stomach. My mouth starts to water, goosebumps running down my arms at the sight of him.

Whatever Knox does to train is working for his benefit. His cut muscles ripple with each breath he takes. I've never seen someone so fit before and I've trained with men my entire life.

My heart hammers as heat coils in my stomach.

"You were looking a little warm. Thought you might like to cool down," I croak, not as smoothly as I intended.

Turning away, I rush for the back door, trying to get away from him as fast as possible. I'm about to walk up the patio stairs when I smack directly into a muscular chest, bouncing off it with an *oomph*. Knox catches my arms before I fall, his large hands steadying me.

His eyes narrow. "Where are you going?"

"I mastered it. We're done for the day," I say flatly, refusing to acknowledge the way his hands on my skin make me feel.

He arches a brow. "Giving up so soon?"

I roll my eyes. "Don't goad me, I'm not a child."

"I wouldn't have to goad you if you didn't give up."

I throw my hands in the air. "I'm not giving up!" Frustration bounces through me. "I'm done with water. I'm soaked."

"We'll work on your mental shields then, considering yours are constantly lowered," he croons.

My cheeks heat at the possibility of him hearing the thoughts swirling around my mind. I swallow my pride and stare into his eyes, making myself smirk. "Brilliant idea. This nosey asshole keeps peeping into mine," I say, sickeningly sweet.

I walk away, not daring to see if Knox bought the false bravado I'm presenting.

Nothing can ever happen between us. I refuse to be with anyone like my father, and all kings are corrupt. The thought sobers me, washing away any sexual attraction I felt moments ago from staring at his ridiculously cut body.

Taking a seat on one of the many chairs spread across the patio, I clear my mind before twisting to face Knox. "How do you put up a mental shield? Is it similar to a protection shield?"

Knox takes a seat across from me, stretching out to let his clothes dry in the sun.

"Yes. Magic is creation, mind magic especially. You picture a gate, wall, or shield around your mind. No cracks or holes for anyone to slither into," he says smoothly.

"That seems rather easy."

Knox shrugs. "The creation is simple. Holding the protection shield itself is what's difficult."

I close my eyes, picturing a white brick wall covered in vines and pink flowers. I walk the perimeter of the wall, my hand dragging behind me, feeling the smooth texture as I check for any holes or cracks. I imagine it's peaceful and free of harm from others.

*No one can hurt me here. No one can touch me.*

Opening my eyes, I find Knox's sapphire ones studying mine.

"Ready?" he asks, his indifferent demeanor back.

I nod, preparing for a mental assault. His eyes narrow on mine, and I wonder when he's going to begin. I turn my head to the side as I wait.

"Did you hear that?"

I blink. "No, did you say something?"

"First try. Impressive," he says coolly.

My spine straightens. "Wait, I did it?"

"You must be more imaginative than you think. We'll use your imagination to help in the magic lessons," he states, standing.

"That's it?" I ask, shocked.

He made me practice the protection shield for hours, and now we're only practicing mental shields once?

Standing, we leave puddles of water on the tiled floors as I follow Knox inside.

"That's it for now." He turns to face me. His expression has changed—more distant, closed off.

What the hell pissed him off?

Knox places his hands in his wet pockets, his posture oozing confidence and power. "It'll take time getting used to having a mental shield. Over time, it should become second nature for you and you won't have to think about it to have it up." Dismissing our lesson, he turns away, walking up the staircase toward his room. "I'll see you at dinner."

# Chapter Twenty-One

"How was it going into town?" I ask Hazel nervously.

Yesterday would have been the first time Hazel had gone into a town since isolating herself in her cabin after Luna passed. I can't begin to imagine how she felt; I had anxiety just thinking about if she was okay or not.

Hazel bites her lower lip. "Honestly? It felt overwhelming at first, being around so many people after decades at the cabin." She's silent for a moment as we descend the stairs. "But it was good, I needed the push," she says, a smile turning up the corner of her lips.

I breathe a sigh of relief. "That's good. I'm happy for you."

Hazel begins to tell me about everything she saw in the library. Apparently, it's the second largest library in the Fae lands and was magnificent. High ceilings, beautiful architecture, art, and endless amounts of levels holding every type of book you could ever think of.

She looks around the hallway. "I snuck some romance books in also," she whispers.

I throw my head back on a laugh. "When you're finished with them, I want to have a read," I whisper back, stepping into Knox's study.

The room is ginormous for a study, housing a wooden desk in front of the floor-to-ceiling windows that overlook the back garden. Two armchairs sit adjacent to the desk, multiple bookshelves cover the walls, and a small sitting area is nestled in the right-hand corner, in front of a fireplace.

Knox's deep rumble fills the space. "What do you want to read?"

My cheeks heat thinking about the type of romance books Hazel has handed to me over the past few weeks. Picturing the beautiful wall around my mind, I snap my mental shield up. "Nothing that would interest you," I say, lifting my chin.

I walk toward the seating area Knox is currently lounging in. Three two-seated leather sofas create a U-shaped arrangement. In the middle, the large black stainless steel table is filled with stacks of worn books.

I lift my brows. "You truly weren't exaggerating with the number of books you found."

Hazel plops down on the couch perpendicular to Knox, leaving me on the middle sofa. Taking a seat, I lean forward and take a pile of books, Knox and Hazel doing the same.

Hazel dumps the pile next to her before picking the top one up. "It'll take us days to get through these. There's several more at the library, but I didn't want to take them all at once and raise suspicion. We'll go through these and swap whatever we don't need for new ones."

"What exactly should we be looking for? These all contain dark magic," I murmur.

I open the cover of the first book on my pile to see demonic creatures. *More monsters, lovely.*

"Anything to do with spell work, entrapment, and magic

dissolving," Knox answers, already reading a book from his stack beside him. His brows are pulled low in concentration as he leans back, crossing his muscular leg over his knee.

Sighing, I steel my stomach and begin.

I never knew there was a vast range of creatures when it came to magic. It feels as though it was just yesterday that I was sitting in my room with Easton reading about Fae, mermaids, and dragons. These creatures, however, are on a different level, from a different world.

Beasts with predatory senses, that kill Fae for sport, their black as night color allowing them to camouflage. Siphons, magic eaters, soul eaters. The more I read, the more I begin to feel ill. Each page holds the description of a demonic creature, explaining in graphic detail how they prefer to hunt, kill, or torture their prey.

Phookas come from a race of demonic goblins, with the body of a man and the head of a goat. Its long, curved antlers and white milky eyes are the definition of nightmares. A phookas's specialty is manipulation and deception, taking on different forms of animals to lure humans and Faes before turning into its true form and eating their entire body.

I turn the page, absolutely disgusted by the next two demonic creatures written.

Skinwalkers, another creature that hunts through manipulation. Skinwalkers have the ability to take on any form—human, Fae, animal—luring their victims through cries and pleas for help. As their prey gets close they capture their targets, skinning them alive to wear their skin.

I shudder, feeling my lunch start to rise.

The next page informs me that Wendigos were once Fae that transformed into a demonic creature after becoming a cannibal. I snap the book shut. Swallowing the bile that burns my throat, I take slow, deep breaths through my nose.

"Are you okay?" Hazel asks.

I hold up the closed book in my hand, not opening my eyes until the nausea subsides. "Demonic creatures, more graphic than the book in your cabin," I say as an explanation.

I open my eyes in time to see Hazel shudder.

I set the book down and pick up another, planning to come back to the demonic creatures when I have no food in my stomach.

Knox's voice surrounds me, calming the churning in my gut. "There used to be several libraries in the mountains of the Fae lands. The priestesses and keepers believed the sacred mountains would protect the history stored in the books." He places his book on the coffee table, leaning his elbows on his knees. "They've been closed for over a century, being as it took too long to reach and was utterly inconvenient."

Hazel sets the book she's reading in her lap, sitting forward. "You think they've hidden the dark magic books in the old libraries?"

Knox dips his chin. "The libraries are completely abandoned. No one goes near them anymore. What better place to hide something than in plain sight?"

"That seems too easy," I cut in.

Knox turns his head to me, his sapphire eyes searing mine. "It would most likely be veiled." He juts his chin to my chest, a smirk playing on his lips, making his dimple pop out. "Luckily, we know someone who possesses an unveiling pendant."

"It's worth a shot. So far there's no mention of black magic entrapment spells or where they could have possibly hidden such a thing," Hazel chimes in.

"Okay, Knox and I will go tomorrow," I declare.

Hazel's lips twitch as she tries to hold in a laugh while Knox's eyebrows shoot up into his hairline.

I raise my own brows. "What?"

"Nothing," they both mutter under their breath before going back to reading their books. After several moments, I can't hold in my curiosity any longer.

"Priestesses?" I haven't read anything about priestesses.

Knox's gaze lifts to mine. "Yes."

When he doesn't continue, I gape at him. "That's it? Just a yes? Where's my history lesson?"

Hazel and Knox burst into a fit of laughter.

"Would you like a history lesson on the priestesses, Delilah?" Knox teases.

I tamp down my irritation. "Yes," I state flatly.

Hazel's shoulders shake on a silent laugh as she returns to her book.

"The priestesses have no elemental power. They believe in a higher being that connects all types of life forces, and worship it with the cycles of the moon. They conduct all their spiritual rituals in the Fae lands such as mating ceremonies, sermons, rituals, and court celebrations. They're also trusted with knowledge and wisdom, so they run the libraries."

I frown. "Why can't we ask a priestess about all of this?" I ask, waving my hand to the piles of demon and dark magic books littering Knox's study.

Knox shakes his head. "They serve to protect the Fae lands. They would turn us over to the queen if they knew we were inquiring about such things."

With my curiosity answered, I turn back to my pile of books. "Thank you," I mutter.

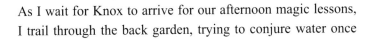

As I wait for Knox to arrive for our afternoon magic lessons, I trail through the back garden, trying to conjure water once more. Since dousing Knox in a wave yesterday I haven't been able to tap into it.

Taking a deep breath, I close my eyes, muttering to myself about imagination. I picture a lake within me—calm, steady, and full of water. I kneel before it, cupping my palms together to take a small handful of water, letting it flow between my fingers. I imagine it flowing into a beautiful delicate rose and will the magic within me to listen, to move with me. To become one with me.

Opening my eyes, I jump with joy as the bubble of water in my palm forms into a rose. Turning to check that no one can see me, I resume creating more shapes. Within a split second, I have the rose in front of me blossoming into a sunflower, then a butterfly, and finally a blade. I burst out giggling as I make it fly around the garden as if a ghost is running with a knife.

Letting the water knife disappear, I start to wonder if I can do the same with fire, but instead of a knife, an arrow. With Knox and I soon traveling into the mountains to search for the abandoned library, flying fire arrows would be useful if we encounter any demonic creatures. A slithering shudder runs through my body as skinwalkers and wendigos come to mind. I need to master fire arrows.

Walking deeper into the garden, where no trees or flowers could catch on fire, I imagine an array of fire arrows in a satchel. Then focusing on the area before me, I build a bullseye target out of water.

Willing my senses to open further, I focus my eyes on the bullseye.

Once again making the magic link with my mind as one, I watch in awe as a fire arrow whizzes past my head, flying in a deadly straight precision for the target. I whoop and leap with joy as it hits the water, the fire arrow sizzling in the target's center.

Magic truly is limited only by imagination.

Leaves crunch behind me as Knox's husky drawl makes me jump.

"Don't forget energy and iron."

I place a hand over my heart. "Were you an assassin in your past life? My gods, you nearly gave me a heart attack!"

Knox bites back a smile. "An assassin?"

I roll my eyes, ignoring him. "What do you mean magic is limited by energy and iron?"

Knox releases his hands from his pockets. He strolls toward me, every movement screaming power and grace.

"Everyone's power has a limit. The amount of magic you possess determines how powerful you are." He stops in front of me. "You need to figure out the depth of your power to know how much of it to use or reserve. Magic will do you no good if you let it out all at once."

Knox's eyes search mine as they sparkle in the afternoon light. "When you use magic, it uses a lot of your energy, meaning you need to eat and sleep to replenish it."

I quirk a brow. "Like hibernating?"

Knox bites the inside of his cheek. "How much magic you have depends on how long it takes to replenish. If I used all my power in, say, a day, it would take me three or four to fully be replenished."

My eyes widen. "You have that much power?"

Knox's smirk is my only response.

*Cocky bastard.*

His eyes spark with delight.

"Get out of my head," I growl.

His grin is purely wicked. "Make me."

I slam my mental shield down, half hoping it squishes whatever part of him that's in there.

"What about iron?"

Knox shrugs. "What about it?"

"Don't be coy; you said magic is limited by iron. How?"

"Everything Mother Earth creates must have a weakness, and the Faes' is iron. Making our magic entirely useless if shackled."

I cock my head. "It only takes iron to make a Fae's magic disappear?"

Knox's lips flatten into a tight line as he dips his chin.

"When are we leaving for the library?" I ask, changing the topic.

"Tonight," he answers smoothly.

"Okay, and what are we working on today?"

A water arrow flies into my protection shield before slowly trickling down the invisible force.

"You have to do better than that," I say with a grin.

Knox chuckles darkly. "You've been working on your shield."

I make a fire arrow appear beside his head and smirk. "Amongst other things."

# Chapter Twenty-Two

I exit my bedroom wearing fighting leathers to find Hazel has on the same clothes from dinner, anxiously wringing her hands as she stands in the middle of her door's threshold.

"You don't have to come if you don't want to," I say softly.

Hazel's body deflates, the tension visibly leaving her body. "I think I'll stay here and go through more books."

Knox's bedroom door opens, his large frame filling the hall as he stalks toward us, wearing his own fighting leathers. "That would be a great help," he says kindly.

Hazel steps forward, wrapping her arms around me in a tight embrace. "Please be careful," she whispers in my ear.

"I promise."

Stepping out of the embrace Hazel turns to Knox, her eyes hardening. "You may be a king but if you let anything happen to her, I'll kill you myself."

My eyes widen in shock. I bite my lip, trying to hold back my laughter at this tiny, delicate creature threatening a six-foot-five beast of a Fae.

Knox has the faintest smile on his lips. "I'll look after her."

Hazel searches his eyes for a moment before nodding. "Good." Stepping back, she leaves in the direction of Knox's study. "Don't wake me when you return," she calls over her shoulder.

Knox and I stand in silence for a moment. I turn to make a joke when Knox spins on his heel. "Don't even start," he growls, marching down the stairs.

I can't help the laugh that bursts out of me.

Still giggling over the image of Hazel scolding Knox, I join him in the foyer to find his own lips twitching.

"Can we teleport?"

He smirks, turning toward the back garden. "Unfortunately, there's wards placed over the libraries against teleporting, so we'll have to fly." He stops on the grass and slides his hands into his pockets. "Will that be an issue for you?"

"No," I blurt. "Whenever you're ready," I say, flailing my hand between us.

I hold in my sigh as Knox's large, iridescent black wings flutter open.

I wasn't paying attention the last time he flew; I didn't get to explore his wings. They're magnificent. I have the urge to run my fingers down them when I remember what Hazel said about wing touching to be intimate.

I swallow my suddenly dry throat. Pulling my eyes away from his majestic wings to his face, my gaze snags on his pulse, thumping rapidly at the side of his neck.

"As you wish," he croons.

Taking a step forward, he lays his palm on my back, sliding it around my shoulder blades before he bends, cupping my legs as he hauls me to his chest. I refuse to look at him as my heart goes haywire with the close proximity. I can feel every single muscle in his chest, my body turning to liquid against the rock-hard warmth.

Why does he have to be attractive? Why can't he look like a toad?

Knox clears his throat, his voice deeper than usual. "Ready?"

"Mhmm," I hum, my voice failing me.

Knox pushes off, flying into the night sky. He flies faster than Hazel and somehow smoother. The air still rips through my hair, yet I feel steady, calm in his arms. I can't help the smile that spreads across my cheeks. Tilting my head back, I look up at the night sky as we soar over Azalea, letting the stars and the moon sing to a part of my soul.

After flying for what feels like hours, Knox lands gracefully in the dense woods, setting me down before he hastily takes a step away from me. I'm about to thank him for flying when I notice his body is stiff, jaw clenched and face cold.

Before I can voice my question, Knox turns away. "Follow me."

I ignore his shitty mood as I make sure my protection and mental shields are raised as we walk through the mountaintop woods. Going undetected, we tread through non-traveled paths, avoiding twigs and branches as they try to dig and cut into my skin.

I'm wondering if I should voice the question about poison ivy when I slam into Knox's back, an *oomph* flying out of me as Knox throws his arms behind him, catching me with effortless precision.

Does he have eyes in the back of his head?

"What do you see, Delilah?" he asks, deadly calm.

Moving around his large frame I come to stand beside him, frowning when I do. "A rundown dome building, why?"

"I see absolutely nothing but woods."

I place a palm over my chest, finding my pendant pulsing with warmth. "It's veiled. Who would veil it? I thought you said it was abandoned."

"It should be abandoned. It hasn't been mentioned in any court meetings," he mutters. "Give me the pendant." He holds out his hand.

"Absolutely not," I snap.

Knox rolls his eyes. "I'm not arguing with you on this. We don't know who veiled it or if there's someone in there. If something attacks you, I can't go in and help."

I shrug. "Sucks for you then," I say, walking off.

I don't trust him, not with this information. This could all be an elaborate ploy to get the information for himself. For all I know, he could have veiled it himself. I wouldn't put it past a king.

A dark shadowed hand wraps around my own, yanking me back.

"Delilah."

I snap my head to Knox, my canines flaring as I growl, "Let go of me."

"You're not going in there alone."

"You're not in charge of me. You're not my king," I sneer.

*I have free will. I have freedom.*

I will never be somebody's puppet again.

Knox's eyes roam my face, searching my eyes. A moment later the shadowed hand drops. "Can you keep your mental shield open? So I can see for myself?" he asks coolly, placing his hands in his pocket as he leans against a tree.

"Fine," I snap, leaving him in the woods.

The further I walk, the more my irritation morphs into trepidation as the building looms before me. It's several stories high, with cracked and missing glass panels lining the outskirts of the dome building. My boots thump on the brick walkway that curves around an overgrown garden before the building. I think back to that first day in Hazel's garden, when the otherworldly beast flew above us. I had been so terrified I cloaked myself. I let the steps become a drum, calming my heartbeat as I dive deeper within myself. Picturing my very molecules distorting, transforming my being until I'm nothing. Walking up the cracked steps to the building's entryway, I cloak myself, going wholly invisible.

Magic slithers around me, probing my physical shields.

Not bothering to turn around, I roll my eyes. *I did it on purpose, Knox.*

Reading my mind, the energy retracts. I could have sworn I even felt it sigh in relief.

Ascending the final cobbled steps, dirt and debris crack beneath my leather boots. Pushing open the large arched wooden doors, they creak in response. I pause on the threshold, opening my senses to listen for any sound of movement. When nothing scuttles, scratches, or hisses, I continue inside.

The inside of the library was crafted into a spiral, the halls curving around one another. Peering over the railing, the levels of the library continue down until the shadows swallow it whole, the bottom shrouded in complete darkness. Down the curved walkway, I pass endless bookcases strewn about. Some broken, smashed, or fallen on their side, but all of them empty. There's no books on the first story, and as I descend level after level, I find it completely empty safe for the bookcases and dusty study rooms.

Eleven stories of forgotten wood.

It isn't until I return to the main level about to leave that I pause. All these old buildings have basement levels, like my family's vault.

I search for any hidden staircases, checking behind desks, picking up fallen bookcases, and even knocking on walls to see if there's a hidden entry point, yet I find nothing. Dejected, I walk back to the main doors. Passing through cracked archways and old study rooms, I stroll through the main reception area where a large oval-shaped desk sits. This must have been where the priestesses had people check in.

My curiosity piques, and I round the desk, inspecting the old books filled with names on the desk top. I start reading through the books, moving slowly down the length of the desk, when the floorboard beneath my feet creaks. I jump, shuffling my feet on and off the floorboard. Bending, I lift the dusty checkered rug that covers the hardwood floor to find a small, circular knob and the outline of a square.

Pulling the silver knob with all my strength, it lifts with a loud creak. Dust fills the air around me, making me cough as I wave my hand, trying to get the dust to settle. It reveals a small set of wooden stairs.

The stairs creak and hiss, bending beneath the weight of my body as I descend the old rickety boards. The space is utterly pitch black. Holding out my hand in front of me, I set flames alight on my fingertips. Still being invisible, all anyone would see is five separate flames glowing in the dark.

I lift my head from the flames before me, only to stumble backward.

The walls are covered in ancient drawings, runes and pictures etched into every inch and crevice of the stone hall. No space has been left free or untouched. I walk the short corridor looking at every single image on the wall, making sure Knox sees everything. Images of a human skull dripping with blood, stick figures with elongated ears fighting against a nameless, faceless shadow. Oval mirrors and severed wings scatter the walls. Large oak trees, the trunks spinning around themselves until they flourish, spreading branches far and wide. Buildings being built and ruined are surrounded by scattered bodies indicating the dead. The etchings stop completely once I reach the end of the hallway, a lone book-case sits against the wall, the small three-level shelf full of books.

The moment I lay eyes on the bookcase, the energy in the room shifts, making the temperature drop drastically. The books feel wrong, beckoning my name, and yet their essence screams for me to run and hide.

I give myself no time to think. Snatching as many as I can, I dump them all in the large brown sack Knox gave me earlier, filling it to the brim with every last book from the shelf. The more books I take the colder the room gets, and by the time the last book is off the shelf, my breath clouds in front of me.

Swinging the sack over my shoulder, I run as fast as I can, no longer wanting to be anywhere near this secret corridor alone. The energy feels disturbed, as if something awoke and knows I'm taking what doesn't belong to me.

Running down the cobbled path, I see Knox by the nearest tree pacing.

It feels as if someone's watching me, their eyes searing into my back. I open my mouth to tell Knox exactly that when a deadly roar erupts around us.

Knox twists his face to me, his eyes wide in horror.

Before I can blink, I'm in his arms, the sack of books in his hands as he flies above the woods in a zig-zag motion.

"What was that?" I whisper.

"I have no idea and I don't want to find out," he breathes.

He tightens his hold on me, flying faster as another roar pierces the sky and the mountain below.

"Did you feel it too?" I ask quietly, as if whatever awoke in the library can still hear me.

Knox's Adam's apple bobs as he swallows. "Yes."

White light encompasses us midair. Tightening my hold around Knox's neck, I hold on for dear life as Knox teleports and flies, jumping between space and time within the Fae lands. What would have been several hours' worth of flying turns into only half an hour. I'd question Knox on why he forced me to be in his arms while he flew for hours to the library, yet by the stiffness in his body, I think better of it.

Landing in Knox's back garden, I can't shake the feeling of wrongness that emanates from the books as he sets it down between our feet. "I don't think we should leave them in the study."

"I don't either." Sighing, Knox picks up the sack again, making my magic retract. Knox shivers. "I'll put it in the backyard cellar. Whatever residual magic is clinging to the books is horrid."

I take a step away. "I need to bathe and wash off whatever it is. It feels like it's crawling all over my skin."

Knox's eyes snap to mine, concern flashing in them. "Are you okay?"

"Yes, it just feels…wrong. I want to wash it off."

"I'll place a concealment spell around them. No magic can get out of the room," he says, carrying the sack further into the garden.

I stand there watching him until he disappears around the side of the house before I head inside. Walking into my bathing suite, I've never felt more grateful for a bath.

# Chapter Twenty-Three

W hen Hazel and I enter the dining room the next morning, breakfast is already served, with Knox lounging in his usual seat, sipping coffee while food overflows his plate.

I take my own seat, noting that the breakfast food served this morning consists of mine and Hazel's favorites—nothing else. I make a mental note to go to the kitchen today and thank the workers for the wonderful food. With the servants concealing themselves, I haven't been able to thank anyone.

I fill my plate with eggs, bacon, sausages, and toast, feeling famished after last night's experience. The constant use of magic—holding the protection shield, concealing myself, and lighting embers of fire—used a good chunk of my energy, so much so that even though I was rattled from the experience I slept like the dead.

I wonder how much power I truly have if that made me tired. Will I truly be able to break the entrapment spell when the time comes?

"What happened last night?" Hazel asks, biting into a forkful of pancakes.

"We found a hidden trap door; the room was full of all these intricate drawings and at the end of the corridor were books all containing dark magic and demons." I shiver thinking about the room. "It felt as if something awoke when I took the books."

Knox places his coffee down. "Someone placed a guarding spell around the room and whoever did knows the books were taken." He picks up his cutlery, cutting into a slice of bacon. "We must be careful in handling the books. There's residual dark magic clinging to them."

Hazel's brows furrow. "Is that even possible? After all this time?"

"I felt it for myself." Knox takes a bite of his food, his brows drawing into concentration. "I think the drawings on the walls tell a story. I haven't seen etchings like them before."

"Can I see?" Hazel asks, placing her fork down.

Hazel's eyes glaze over while Knox continues eating, as if transferring memories is a mundane task.

"What was that?" she breathes once her eyes clear.

"We should see if any of the Fae history books contain similar storytelling," Knox murmurs.

"It looked like—"

The dining room doors fly open, cutting off my speech. Knox is standing at the back of my chair in an instant, his protection shield snapping around Hazel and I.

I look past his large frame. In the doorway stands a small Fae male, his chest heaving and hair wild as if he's been running for hours.

"What happened, Hugo?" Knox rumbles.

The young man gulps. "Fae were taken again last night, sir."

Knox's entire body goes taut; his shoulders stiffen as the

corner of his jaw clenches. His voice a dark rumble of rage as he asks, "How many?"

Hugo, who must be Knox's messenger, blanches. "Thirty," he croaks.

Knox doesn't move. The whole palace falls quiet—birds stop chirping, dishes stop rattling. Even the hidden servants around the house pause, as if they feel the shift in the air.

My heart sinks. Turning to Hazel, I see her horrified expression mirrors my own.

"Thirty," Knox breathes, running a hand through his hair. "That's the most that's ever been taken in one night. How on earth…?" His voice sounds utterly broken as anguish flashes through his sapphire eyes.

And in that moment, I realize with utter clarity that he is nothing like my father at all. He truly does care for his people. My father wouldn't bat an eye at thirty people going missing; he'd simply raise his glass in a toast, celebrating.

Guilt rushes to my stomach and something eerily similar to shame. I misjudged Knox, projecting my feelings of my father onto him. When I looked at Knox, all I saw was my father and Easton's lifeless body on the ground. As unfair as that is to Knox, I couldn't help it. Knox's title alone makes my internal hackles rise.

Knox's deep exhale snaps me out of my thoughts. "Can you show me where they were taken?"

Hugo's cheeks redden. "Yes, sir. Whenever you're ready."

Knox's pain-filled sapphire eyes find mine. "Do you mind if I show you what I see? I want to speak to the families."

I nod, my eyes softening. "Of course. I'll stay with Hazel."

Knox doesn't utter another word as he follows Hugo out of the dining room door.

Turning to Hazel, I declare, "We need to go through the books."

Hazel and I spent the entire day pouring over every inch of the library books in Knox's study. When the sun begins to fade in the afternoon, I snap the book in my hand shut, irritation coursing through me after another day of no answers.

None of the books Hazel and I read today held any information as to where dark magic books are located, let alone anything about entrapment spells large enough to hold an entire race. After the horrible presence we felt in the library, Knox suggested we hold off on going near the books for a few days. The only thing we can stay positive about is that some of the dark magic books weren't destroyed when they were banned.

I look toward the clock mounted on the wall to my left, chiming across the room.

Knox hasn't returned to the house since his departure this morning and I hate to admit it, but as each hour passes, I become more restless and jittery. Anxiety pulses through me, my thoughts telling me that something has happened to him. I tell myself that's ridiculous, Knox can handle himself just fine…yet my anxiety has a mind of its own.

No longer able to sit still as my heart beats wildly in my chest, I pace around the room.

"I don't think I can read another word of this horrific demonology crap," I declare.

Hazel sighs, closing the book in her hands. "Me neither."

"Can you teach me more about magic?" I pause behind Hazel's chair. "I want to see if I have earth magic."

A smile spreads across her cheeks. "Of course!"

Exiting Knox's study, we leave the books strewn about as they are, not bothering to tidy them up as we'll have to continue sorting through them later.

My boots squeak in the tiled hallway as we walk through the house to the back garden. Hazel passes the spot in the garden I usually practice magic with Knox, heading straight for the outhouse shed in the far-right corner. Hazel has no qualms about entering the shed, rummaging through its contents of yard tools, pots, plants, seeds, and soil.

Emerging with an empty bucket, soil packets, seeds, and small hand shovels, Hazel inspects the garden until she finds an open sun-streaked spot. Kneeling, she dumps the items on the ground, arranging them to form a line.

I take a seat beside her, watching as she begins pouring soil into the black bucket. Once it reaches halfway, she drops a single seed into the bucket, adding another layer of soil. Clapping her hands together, she dusts off the dirt.

"Grow a flower," she chirps.

I sputter out a laugh. "I don't know the first thing about gardening and flowers, let alone growing one."

Hazel picks up the bucket, placing it closer to me. "You don't need to know what type of flower, plant, or herb it is. You simply have to find the life force within, send your magic toward it, and help it flourish. If you have earth magic, the seed will start to grow the second your magic connects with its life force," she explains.

Everything else with magic has been about imagination. If I don't have to picture what the flower looks like each step of the way as it develops, I should be fine.

Shaking out my hands, I lay my palms on either side of the bucket, then submerge myself into my power. Picturing myself dipping into my well of magic, I send a small portion of it out, feeling around the bucket. It brushes against the damp soil, grounding my very essence as I float in my magic well. My magic pauses as it finds the seed, swirling around it as it assesses and probes, trying to find a way in.

A warmth glows inside of the seed, a small kernel of life.

I will my magic to flow inside of it, becoming one with it. I feel the moment it connects, my magic flaring, pouring into the seed. I flutter my eyes open, watching as a small green stalk flourishes from the damp soil, growing tall and strong.

A white rose blossoms before me.

A smile spreads on my own face as I stare at Hazel. "I did it."

Hazel claps her hands, her eyes shining bright as she stares at the rose. "This is going to be so much fun teaching you earth magic!" she exclaims with excitement. "The things you can do!"

Knox never showed for our afternoon magic lesson. I don't blame him. Thirty missing Fae are more pressing matters.

Hazel and I walk through the dining room later that evening. We waited two hours before deciding to eat without Knox; it felt rude to eat his food without him being present.

The moment I take my seat, food suddenly appears on the dining table before me. I yelp, scraping my chair back in a rush to stand while Hazel throws her head back on a laugh.

"You should have seen your face!"

"I apologize for not being used to food appearing out of thin air!" I sputter, making Hazel's laugh grow.

"Sit down." She chuckles. "This is standard in the court palaces."

I hesitantly take my seat. "The servants have been placing the food on the table by hand before this."

Hazel smiles slyly. "They were being kind to you, letting you get used to the different formalities of how the Fae work."

My eyes widen. "Why would they do that? I don't need any special treatment."

"Knox asked them."

"Why on earth would he do that?" I snap.

Hazel rolls her eyes, muttering under her breath, "I wonder why."

"Why? Is it protocol for them to not place the food on the table themselves? Does Knox not allow them in the room?" I ask, my anger rising at the thought.

"God no!" Hazel exclaims. "Most servants have shadow magic. They're very introverted Fae and prefer it this way."

My jaw drops. "They were in the room when the food appeared?"

Hazel nods, her lips twitching.

"They saw my outburst?" I yelp.

Hazel covers her mouth with her hand, failing miserably to contain her laughter. "Yes."

I throw my napkin at her. "You're horrible!"

"If the roles were reversed, you'd tease me endlessly."

I lift my chin. *Point taken.*

We both giggle as we fill our plates with lamb, creamy mashed potatoes, and vegetables.

"How are you doing with everything?" I ask, waving my hand around the room.

She cuts a piece of lamb, pushing her food around her plate. "It was an adjustment at first but I like it. I miss my home, but I have a purpose here and something to accomplish. It feels nice to be needed again…" She trails off.

"I'd apologize for turning your life upside down, but it's

been nice having a friend," I say softly in return, opening myself up.

"I think we both needed it," she murmurs.

I dip my chin, changing the subject before my heart gets buried with sadness and grief. "How many books do we have left to go through?"

Hazel swallows. "Around twenty, give or take."

"Is there any more to check out in the library?" I ask.

"Fifteen or so," Hazel says. "So how are your magic lessons going with Knox?" she asks, the picture of cool indifference.

I narrow my eyes. "Just fine, why?"

Hazel shrugs, keeping her eyes glued to her plate. "He's very handsome."

I cough, choking on a green bean. I quickly recover, taking a sip of my water. "If you say so." *Deny, deny, deny.*

Hazel finally looks at me, her eyes searching mine. "So there's nothing going on?"

I sputter. "Going on? Are you insane? He's a Fae king."

Hazel cocks her head. "That's not a denial. And what's wrong with being a king?"

I ignore her last question. Cutting up my food I bite into a small piece of lamb, nearly choking for the second time tonight as the dining room doors fly open.

"Sorry to startle you ladies," Knox purrs as he strolls into the room.

He's freshly bathed, his short tousled black hair wet and styled back. His soapy, pinewood scent fills my nose. I squelch the sigh that wants to escape, ignoring how my anxiety evaporated the moment he entered the room.

Knox takes his usual seat, filling up his plate. "I have good news. Whoever took the Fae left their scent. It's faint, yet trackable." Knox slides mischief-filled eyes to mine.

"Care to join me? I can teach you how to track with your new senses."

I'm so used to being cut out of information and being told I could never do anything at the palace that I have to tell my stupid heart not to be excited at being included. This is part of the bargain. Simply the deal we made.

I twirl the napkin in my lap. "I know how to track and hunt."

Knox's brows rise, delight filling his eyes. "Great, we leave tonight."

I'm dressed in my fighting leathers and armed to the teeth in weapons as I squat beside Knox, looking into the pitch-black darkness of vast forest before me. We tracked the disgusting smell the beasts left behind. The scent was eerily similar to the soul eater's, with the odor of a rotting corpse. It led us from rooftop to rooftop through Azalea before finally descending into the forest, heading northward.

"How did it get past the wards around the city?"

A muscle ticks in Knox's jaw. "I would love to know." Clearing his throat, Knox changes the subject. "Send your magic out, see if you feel anything dwelling in the forest."

"I don't know how to do that," I confess.

Knox leans closer to me, speaking barely above a whisper. If I didn't have Fae hearing I wouldn't be able to hear him at all. "Close your eyes." Goosebumps prickle my arms, but I follow his instructions, letting his voice guide me. "Cast a small part of your magic toward the woods. Tell me what you feel."

I do as he says, letting a slip of my power out, imagining that I'm physically searching the forest. Joy fills my heart as my magic glides over different energies pulsing throughout the grounds. Trees, birds, rabbits, and even a small family of foxes. Nothing feels out of the ordinary, my magic distinguishing the energetic feel.

Awestruck at what my magic is capable of, what I'm capable of, I smile.

How extraordinary, to have a gift that can feel the magic of life itself.

"I don't feel anything wrong," I breathe. "I can sense animals, yet they're from these lands. I feel their sense of security and calm."

Knox watches me, the hint of a smile playing on his lips.

"Good, let's go," he announces, warmth encompassing my hand as he grabs it, teleporting us.

I stumble before righting myself as my feet land on the dense forest floor. "You have to teach me that," I whisper.

"I'll add it to the lesson plan," he says before strolling away.

I'm too shocked to speak. He plans our lessons? Warmth fills my chest before I squelch it, tamping down on the ridiculous notion that Knox cares.

Eyes, ears, and shields on full alert, we follow the scent of the beasts, the smell of fear mingling beside the rotting beasts' scent.

We walk for miles in silence, barely disturbing the forest floor as we do, not wanting to be detected. Knox blows our scents in an opposite direction. We pass sleeping foxes, ravines, ponds, bird nests, and endless amounts of trees until I'm officially lost, having no idea where I am. I could have sworn we've even walked around in a circle. Each tree begins to blend into one. Hearing running water again, I'm about to voice my concerns that we're going nowhere when I hear the difference in the water pattern.

It's large, the largest volume of water we've come across yet. The further we walk, the louder the water becomes, deafening to the point I have to tamp down on my hearing as my ears throb.

Passing lines of trees, Knox starts to slow, a curse leaving his mouth as he stops dead.

I come up beside his broad frame, seeing a gorgeous waterfall below us.

If we walked to the left and followed the cliff's edge, we'd collide with the stream that flows down the waterfall into a swimming hole. I'm about to comment on its beauty when my senses pick up on what's made Knox tense.

The scent is gone.

"They went into the water," Knox growls.

Before I can respond, I'm in Knox's arms, airborne as he flies back to his house.

Irritation pulses off his body in waves. If I hadn't flown with him before I would say his body being taut is normal, yet I know it's not.

Every day we take one step closer to finding answers only to be led to a complete dead end.

With no words to comfort, I stay silent the whole flight back.

Knox and I walk down the hallway to our rooms. Hazel bursts out of hers, hope filling her eyes until she sees our own dejected expressions. Hazel's face falls as I say, "It was a dead end."

"I've gone through every single book; I haven't found any more leads," Hazel adds hopelessly.

"We need to go through the books we found in the abandoned library," I whisper.

We've been holding off on going near them due to the dark magic clinging to them. Everyone felt hesitant about touching them; now, we have no other choice.

Knox nods. "Tomorrow. For now, we need to rest. It's been a long day." He sighs, retreating into his room.

"He's been doing this for years without any answers. I can't imagine how that feels over time," Hazel whispers.

I nod my agreement as memories fill my mind, each containing my father. I don't voice that I know what it feels like to wake up every day to live out the same horrible pattern. Luckily, I only endured it for twenty-two years, but Knox has been living like this for over a hundred.

Saying goodnight to Hazel, I enter my room, bypassing the bed and heading straight into the bathing suite. I need to settle myself after thinking about my past, and the only way I know how to is a bath.

I unstrap the swords and various knives attached to me, dumping them on the ground to be cleaned later, then peel off my fighting leathers.

Hissing as I enter the steaming water, I can't stop the onslaught of memories that arise of my father and his beatings. Nothing can stop them from pouring out once the lid to the box has been cracked open, so I sit there in the porcelain tub as memory after memory assaults my mind and soul. Tears rolls down my cheeks, and I wonder if the memories will ever disappear.

One day, I pray I will never remember any of it.

# Chapter Twenty-Four

Hazel and I walk beside each other, following Knox through the back gardens. We pass gorgeous flowerbeds and a fountain decorated with statues of angels before Knox stops in front of an underground cellar door.

He turns to us, sliding his hands into his pockets as a force snaps around us. "I've put a shield around all three of us. We can touch the books, but any power that's lingering can't penetrate the shield. If you feel dizzy, lightheaded, or nauseous we stop immediately."

Knox uses both hands to pry open the wooden door, revealing a small set of stairs. We venture down a damp passageway, water dripping as mold clings to the walls. Stopping in front of a metal door, Knox places his palm on the cellar, purple light shining beneath his hand as a click sounds a moment before Knox pushes it open. The sack of books sit in the center of the otherwise empty room.

Wasting no time, we begin combing through the books. The faster we get through this, the better. The dark magic can't touch us, yet its presence can still be felt, making the hairs on the back of my neck stand on end.

I grab a flimsy black leather book from the sack, taking a seat on the floor, the cold seeping through my clothes. I'm horrified to read its contents. "This one talks about sacrificial rituals in exchange for power," I whisper.

Hazel's wary voice fills the room. "This covers devil worshipping rituals."

I wrinkle my nose in disgust that anyone would practice this type of magic.

"There's spells on how to conjure demons to your realm," she whispers.

Knox leans over, slowly taking the book from Hazel. "Let's swap books," he mumbles.

Hazel gives Knox a small smile of appreciation as I continue reading mine, each page more disturbing than the one before.

"It says that if you sacrifice a soul, you'll receive dark magic in exchange." I whisper.

My statement makes the room drop in temperature. Both Knox and Hazel look at me with grimaces plastered on their faces.

"It what?" Knox asks warily. I pass him the book so he can read it himself.

"No wonder they banned black magic," he states.

When he hands the book back, my fingers brush his skin, making the hairs on the back of my neck stand up for an entirely different reason.

"Who banned dark magic?" I ask.

Knox clears his throat, his voice deeper than usual. "The archangels, centuries ago."

The book in my hand drops. "You have archangels?"

Hazel shakes her head. "They're extinct."

I frown. "How?"

Knox leans back on his hands, his lean legs stretching out before him. "There were only seven to begin with, and sadly, they were destroyed in battle. They died heroes defending these very shores."

"That's heartbreaking."

With nothing more to say, everyone resumes their tasks. The rest of the book only contains an absurd number of rituals and spells one can cast to receive dark magic.

I set the book aside, then pluck up another one.

This one is as horrific as the last, containing different forms of manipulation and mind control spells. I'm disgusted that anyone would practice this corrupted version of the beautiful magic I've grown to learn and love each day. The thought of someone taking something so pure and tainting it with something this evil makes me queasy.

"I think I've found something," Knox murmurs.

Hazel and I put down our books. Feeling the heaviness lift from my chest, I'm thankful for the interruption.

Knox hands me his book, his fingers grazing mine once more as he says, "Witches used to practice black magic. They have ritual sites in their lands and territory."

I give the book back instantly. "I trust your word; I don't want to touch any more books."

His brows pull low. "Do you feel the magic?"

"No but it feels heavy, as if a weight is pressing on my chest when I touch them."

Knox stands, separating the unread books from the ones we've read. "We're done for the day," he states flatly.

"We need to go through them all," I protest.

"Not in one day. It's too much. Besides, we now know about the witches. Perhaps they kept some of their books."

I have no reason to argue with that; the books are awful to be around.

Hazel walks out without us. "Don't have to tell me twice!"

Once we exit, I stand to the side as Knox locks the vault, the heaviness in my chest lessening with each step I take away from the cellar. I take a deep breath as we step outside into the garden, my lungs feeling free as I inhale the crisp fresh air.

Knox places his palm on the wooden door, the purple light shining beneath his palm once more.

I cock my head to the side as I study the light. "What type of magic is that?"

"It's a binding spell. You and Hazel have access to it. All you'd need to do is send your power through the door."

A customized binding spell. That certainly works better than a lock.

"When do you want to go to the witches' territory?" I ask.

"We should go today before the sun sets." He slides his hands in his pockets. "Fae are forbidden from entering the witches' territory after nightfall."

Joining Hazel in the garden, we fall into step beside each other. "Why?"

"Witches and Fae have a long-lasting feud. Without the treaty that was made centuries ago, it would be a blood bath every day," he says casually.

"Witches are horrible. Their hatred has been passed from generation to generation, so they're born hating Fae," Hazel adds.

"There are rules to the treaty. A witch cannot harm a Fae and vice versa. However, if one party does, the treaty is broken, and it becomes free rein. The witches desperately want Fae to make the first move in ending the treaty, so they purposefully goad Fae and push your buttons." His voice is flat, the tick in his jaw the only indication that he doesn't like the witches.

"So they're cruel, wickedly manipulative creatures?" I state flatly, earning a wince from Hazel and a chin dip from Knox.

I shrug. I've lived with a manipulative beast my entire life, I can handle the witches. My father used every chance he could to torment and push me; I've practically made ignoring manipulation an art form.

I walk through the back doors, turning to find Knox studying me, his eyes hard as steel as his jaw clenches over and over.

"What?" I ask, frowning.

"We'll leave in an hour," he states, stalking off.

"Did I say something insulting?" I ask Hazel.

Hazel shakes her head, her gaze on Knox's retreating form. "I don't think it was that," she mumbles, walking off in the direction of the study.

I throw my hands in the air. Why is everyone in this land so dramatic and cryptic?

I stalk up the stairs, needing another bath.

Knox is waiting for me in the foyer an hour later, a hesitant Hazel beside him.

"You don't want to come with us?" I ask softly.

"I don't want to go anywhere near the witches," she says, shaking her head. "I can do more here, going through the books."

I think Hazel has a hard time with anything involving the beasts that killed her daughter. Every time Knox and I leave to investigate the creatures, she's a nervous wreck over the idea of coming face-to-face with them, witches included.

I can't say that I blame her.

"If they're as horrible as you say, I understand," I say with a smile.

Hazel moves through the foyer, pausing in the doorway of the study hall. She takes a deep breath, scanning the room to make sure no prying eyes or ears are around before she says, "The entrapment spell was created with black magic. Divine magic doesn't create anything so horrid, not on a scale this large. I think it's a good idea to at least understand how dark magic works in order to break it."

"Whatever you can find will be worthwhile. The more information we can gather, the better," Knox says smoothly.

Hazel's lips spread into a smile. "I'll keep researching."

"Remember, don't take their words personally," Knox says after he teleports us to the border of the witches' territory. We walk the rest of the way on foot. Apparently another one of the witches' rules, Fae cannot teleport or fly in their lands.

I roll my eyes. "I remember, Knox." I trudge further in front of him. "I also remember when you told me at your home and again on the flight here."

Knox falls into step beside me, striding through the mud with ease. "Forgive me if I don't trust your short temper."

I stumble on a gasp. "I don't have a temper!"

Knox ignores my protests, knowing it will only irritate me further. Distracting myself from the tense silence, I look around.

The witches' territory is vastly different from Azalea and the Earth Court, made entirely of wetlands. The grass is submerged underwater, the tips of it floating and bobbing with the water's current. And if not wading through water, you're sloshing through mud, making me feel like a waddling duck.

"How's that temper going?" Knox smirks.

I purse my lips. "Just fine, thank you," I say sweetly.

Knox somehow knows how to push all of my buttons. When I'm around him, I can't help but get riled up. He'd be more likely to set me off than the witches.

Perhaps it's how my new Fae body processes emotions—

*I highly doubt it, Angel.*

I whip my head to Knox, narrowing my eyes as I snap my mental shield up.

"You don't want to give the witches any more ammunition, do you?" he drawls.

"Can they read minds?"

Knox's deep chuckle sends goosebumps down my arms. "No."

I mutter expletives at him, holding up a vulgar gesture as I stomp forward through the mud. I retract my earlier thought. It's not my emotions, it's just Knox.

Knox's humor fades in an instant. His spine straightens as his face becomes a cool mask of indifference. Coming to a stop, Knox slides his hands in his pockets. The portrait image of a calm, unbothered king.

"Hello, beautiful. Care to show yourself?" he purrs into the empty wetlands.

Knox isn't silly or stupid. I follow his lead, reinforcing my mental and protective shields as I relax my posture.

"Who's your little friend, Knoxy?" a nasally female voice coos.

I don't dare try to find where the voice came from. These witches like playing games, and I refuse to be someone's mouse.

"Why don't you come and find out for yourself?" Knox drones.

Darkness swirls ten feet from us, transforming from a swirling black mass into a shadowy female figure. Once her face appears, I have to bite the inside of my cheek to stop the wince from showing on my face.

Porcelain white skin and eyes as black as coal face me. The stunning features would look beautiful on anyone else who didn't possess such cruelty in their eyes. It's as if she's been grimacing all her life, her face stuck in a permanent scowl.

The witch sniffs in my direction. "She smells of human filth. You've stepped down from the usual whores you keep company," she spits.

"Jealous, are we, Stella?" Knox tilts his head to the side in such a predatory gesture I have to hold in my shock.

"Never, pretty boy," she coos.

Knox begins to slowly pace, as if the conversation bores him to death. He stops slightly in front of me. I move around him. I don't need to be coddled.

Stella's eyes spark at my movement, her voice grating down my ears. "This one has a brain of her own. How delightful."

I make my face wholly blank, giving nothing away.

"What a shame she comes with so much baggage. She's a pest to those around her." Sniffing the air once more, her eyes spark. "And a murderer. I'm pleasantly surprised."

My heart lurches, yet when I check my mental shields, I find them intact. I don't understand. If she can't read my mind how does she know that I blame myself for Easton and my people?

"At least she has a soul," Knox drawls, clicking his tongue. "Can we get on with this? I have more pressing matters to attend to."

Stella sneers. "Name your price, king."

A purple bag of coins land at her feet, splashing mud on her black robes.

"Gold for entrance to the burial."

Delight shines in her otherwise dead eyes as she bends to snatch the gold coins. "Remember, you touch one of us, dead or alive, and the treaty is off."

Knox places a warm palm on my lower back, guiding me as he walks away. "I understand, Stella."

Stella's eyes snap to mine, her horrid lips lifting into a wicked smile. "Another loved one added to the list. How horrible that you'll lose her too," she sing-songs, turning into shadows once more before disappearing entirely.

Knox's hand tenses on my back. Without a second thought, I reach behind me and take his hand in mine, giving it a slight squeeze before dropping it.

They truly do love to play with your mind and emotions.

"How do you know Stella well enough to barter with her?"

Knox slides his gaze to mine. "A king should always be aware of his enemies."

I stare into his eyes, the strength in his posture and the confidence he oozes as he walks. It's breathtaking being near someone so sure of themselves.

We trek through the muddy grass, past endless wetlands, until we reach the only spot in the land that has feasible grass. Dead, leafless trees create a barrier around the graveyard that's haphazardly lined with hundreds of boulders, signaling the fallen witches.

Life around us seems to pause, as if asking us why we're disturbing such a thing.

Ignoring the ancient energy simmering around the land, Knox and I circle the perimeter, looking for any sign of the old ritual site. Passing row upon row of boulders marking dead witches, I read the names. On the farthest side of the burial ground, I find debris scattered everywhere—crumbled stone, broken pillars, and cracked concrete. The broken debris looks over the entirety of the burial site, and two large dead oak trees stand on opposite ends of the rubble, almost as if they're protecting and shielding the area.

Bending, I sift through the scattered pieces, until an ice-cold shiver wracks my body. "Kn—"

He's kneeling beside me before I can get the rest of his name out. Knox starts to inspect the other pieces scattered around. Turning over shards of concrete, I find runes in all different forms, shapes, and sizes. Pentagrams, spirals, moons, pentacles, stars, and triangles. This is where the witches practiced dark magic. In their burial site, as an offering to the dark gods.

When dark magic was banned, the Fae must have destroyed the altar, making it unusable. But why keep the debris of the ruined altar here after all these years?

Perhaps in memory? Or…do they still practice?

When both of us come up empty-handed, not finding any dark magic books, Knox strides to my side and whispers in my ear, "We should go."

Happy to be leaving such a dark space, I stand. We don't run into any more witches as we exit the wastelands, a small victory in itself as the sun starts to set, turning the sky a lovely pale pink hue.

On the outskirts of the witches' territory, I turn to Knox. "Are they still practicing?" I whisper.

"I highly doubt it, why?"

I chew my lip; it's ingrained in my mind to not go against a king's opinion or word. It's going to take time for me to understand I can speak my mind freely with Knox. I haven't witnessed any cruelty on Knox's part to his workers or his people—quite the opposite.

Yet I know how deceitful people can be.

When my father was younger, he was believed to be a fair king, beloved by many. Nobody would have ever believed that he beat his own daughter and wife. Yet over the years as he enforced more laws and crueler consequences, the mask he wore dropped. He no longer needs to wear it, not when there's nobody to overrule him.

I take a steadying breath to calm my nerves. "Why would they leave the altar there after all these years? It still has residual energy."

"From what I've read, dark magic leaks into the very ground where spells are cast. That would explain the residual energy."

"Do you think they left the altar ruins as a tribute to the old magic they practiced?"

He turns his head to the side. "You don't?" he asks softly.

I shrug. "Looks can be deceiving."

I'm looking at Knox's gorgeous face, waiting for him to speak, when suddenly I'm falling. The wind is knocked from me as my back slams into the ground. Moments earlier I was peering at turquoise eyes and now I'm looking up at the darkening sky and canopy of trees as pain sears through my stomach and shoulder.

Unending, blinding pain.

I try to suck in a breath to no avail.

In a daze, I turn my head to the side. Knox's face has turned feral, his canines flaring as a roar pierces the air around us, his power erupts with the guttural sound, snapping me out of my haze.

I look down to find an arrow embedded in the right side of my stomach and another in my shoulder, crimson blood pouring from both wounds. I drag myself into a seated position against the tree trunk, wincing with each movement. The arrowheads grate against my very bones.

In front of me, Knox holds two long swords dripping with black blood as he guts and slices beasts. Three already lie dead, disembodied on the forest floor. The creatures are as black as shadows, their eyes a hollow pit of hell. Not a single piece of hair is to be found on their leathery skin. Two small slits mar their face where a nose should be, and their mouths are lined with row after row of sharp teeth. The creatures—shaped as a human with two legs and two arms and a hunched back—are terrifying to come face-to-face with.

Four surround Knox, hissing and slithering their pointed snake tongues. I unsheathe my blade and try to stand, yet each movement wracks my body with blinding pain, making nausea swirl in my gut.

The ringing in my ears starts to fade, replaced by the sounds of the beasts. Their sniveling voices make the hairs on the back of my neck stand.

"You'll pay for this, King," the demon spits. "What a delightful taste she will be."

"I've been dreaming of her blood the second we got her scent," another sneers.

"The girl was the price, yet I don't think she will mind if we bring your head," one demon snarls before all four pounce.

A scream of warning leaves my lips, only to die the second Knox moves.

Knox is a whirlwind of steel and power as he unleashes himself upon the demonic beasts. Where one hand strikes with his sword, the other throws daggers, each one hitting their mark with deadly precision as his magic blasts them. Holding off the beasts with blasts of fire, shadows capture their gangly limbs while others seem to suffocate, clawing at their necks until his blade strikes them so brutally their heads fly off, their bodies slumping to the ground.

Each kill is as deadly as the last.

My head begins to swirl, dizziness wracking my body as the forest spins around me. Knox's powerful form blurs into two versions as he sheathes his swords behind his back.

I didn't see him with swords before. Where did they come from?

"I got you, you're okay," Knox soothes, bending as he wraps his arms around me, cradling me to his chest. The movement makes me grunt in pain.

His beautiful black wings blossom, beating wildly as he takes off into the night sky, flying faster than ever before.

Stars flash in my vision, the edges blurring.

"Don't tell Hazel," I croak before darkness consumes me.

Heat encompasses my body, so warm it stings.

I can hear a faint voice in the distance, yet I can't focus on anything right now. It feels as if I'm floating, my body tingling while fuzz fills my head.

*Am I flying?*

A faraway voice seems to grow closer. It sounds beautiful, deep and sensual. I know that voice.

I use all my strength to roll my head to the side, sliding on what feels like porcelain. My eyes connect with Knox's. His mouth is moving but I don't understand what he's saying.

*Angel.*

My body jolts at the voice intruding my mind, making water splash around me.

"What do you feel, Delilah?"

I blink. I heard the words, but nothing is making sense. It feels as if my mind is full of air and everything that enters flies out.

*Angel, what do you feel?*

The dark grumbling voice appears once more.

It stays this time, as if my mind welcomes the voice. Holds onto it, cherishes it.

"Water," I croak.

Understanding dawns through me.

I sit up as I float back to my body, my sensations returning to me as pain spears throughout my body. Hissing, I look down to find I'm seated in the bath, fully clothed save for the holes in my shirt where the arrows were only moments before.

Knox's voice captures my attention. He's kneeling beside the tub, his eyes wary and guarded. Standing, he grabs two fresh towels, holding them out in front of him. "I removed the arrows and healed you, but your muscles will be sore for a day or two. I had to wash the rest of the poison off you."

I stand on wobbly limbs, feeling weak as my clothes try to drag me down. I step out of the tub, splashing water everywhere as I take the towel from Knox and wrap it around myself.

"I don't understand. I had my shield up... How did the arrow get through?" I rasp.

Knox steps back, leaning against the vanity counter. The

veins in his arms bulge as he fists the counter. "They were tracking you. Whoever sent them also gave them poison to lace the arrows. It went right through your shield."

I furrow my brows. "Why would someone send those horrible creatures after me?"

Knox rubs a hand down his face. "I have no idea."

The creatures' horrifying features flash through my mind. "What were they?"

"Demon hounds. They walk like humans, but they're known for their tracking abilities."

"Are they dead?" I whisper.

"For now. We can't put it past whoever sent them to not send more," Knox grumbles.

"You can't tell Hazel they're hunting me."

Silence fills the bathroom.

Drying my clothes with the towel, I peer at Knox, finding his sapphire eyes burning a hole into me.

"I don't appreciate lying," he states coldly.

"I brought her into this mess. I'm not having her worried sick every time I step out that door." I throw the towel into the wash hamper. "If she asks, we'll tell her…Just don't actively tell her." I lock my eyes with his hard gaze. "Please."

Knox is silent for so long I wonder if he heard me at all. When he speaks, he ignores my pleas. "We'll start training together. Combine your current training with magic so you can use both if you're ever under attack again."

I nod, walking past Knox and pull out Easton's shirt to sleep in. My voice is hoarse as I say over my shoulder, "Thank you."

"I promised Hazel," Knox grumbles as he leaves the room.

Of course. Hazel's promise. That's why he went feral. He

needs me alive to help his people. That's the only reason why I'm here in his house.

I change into Easton's shirt, thankful for the lingering scent clinging to the material as it soothes the ache in my heart. I drag myself into bed, collapsing into a pitiful sleep, the faces of demon hounds chasing me in my dreams.

# Chapter Twenty-Five

**K**nox keeps my promise, striding into the study the next day. Hazel appears oblivious to what happened last night as she talks animatedly with her hands. "There's more books! The ones we found in the abandoned library are part of a set."

Knox stands behind the couch, his hands on his hips. "You think it's someone's personal collection?"

Hazel nods vigorously, pacing in front of the wooden desk. "They're all mismatched. Some are volume three, others one and six...Six books about how to manipulate demonic creatures!"

"It could be random," Knox considers. "The priestesses could have confiscated them from various Fae."

Taking a seat on the sofa in front of the fire, I add my own thoughts. "What if a spell was cast to watch over the books because it's someone's personal collection? They could have separated the series of books to make it appear as if they were placed at random."

"Someone orchestrated this entire horrific ordeal all those years ago, and with the number of demonic creatures that roam the courts along with the missing Fae…They're still using dark magic." Hazel lowers her voice. "It's no longer just an entrapment spell."

"You can't return to the library. The priestesses might already be suspicious of the books you've taken, and we can't draw any more attention." Knox meets my gaze. "Considering someone sent those demon hounds after me, I'd say we're getting a little too close to finding how the spell was cast."

I breathe a sigh of relief at his white lie.

The last thing I need is to make Hazel worry. I don't want to burden her any further.

"I still have five books to read in the cellar. None contain entrapment spells but they hold information on how black magic works. That'll be helpful to destroy it when the time comes," Hazel says, finally taking a seat in front of the fire.

"Any hints as to where the other books could be hidden?" I ask.

"Other than the witches' altar, nothing so far," Hazel says solemnly.

Silence descends around the room, each of us thinking about different locations as to where the remaining dark magic books could be.

"What if the books were burned?" I ask.

Hopelessness fills my chest. We might be running around searching for a book that may no longer exist. The mermaid's first riddle turned out to be true, yet what if this is an elaborate game to them?

"They can't be," Hazel says confidently.

Knox's eyes grow wide with surprise as he reads her mind.

"They're all connected; if one burns, the others in the set

die too." Knox shakes his head. "No wonder dark magic is clinging to the books. The books themselves are dark magic."

I lift my brows as I lean forward. "You're saying dark magic is sitting on this property right now?"

Hazel winces. "Yes."

"You knew and didn't tell us?" I ask in disbelief.

Hazel's head shoots up, her eyes clouding with worry. "I knew the moment you realized they were dark magic themselves, you would tell me to stop. I didn't want to be coddled."

I blink. I don't mean to coddle her, I just don't want her to get hurt, especially because I'm the one who dragged her into this situation. Hazel has suffered enough pain as it is—she doesn't deserve more.

However, Hazel is right. She's a grown woman. "I'm sorry," I say softly, sincerity lacing my words.

She waves a hand in the air, dismissing my apologies. "It's fine, but what you can tell me is what *really* happened last night."

I open my mouth. Not knowing what to say, I close it again.

"You're wincing more than usual, and you didn't train this morning." She grins. "Call it intuition."

A surprised chuckle escapes me. Knox stands beside the sofa, staring at Hazel with an impressed spark in his eyes.

"Perhaps you should be a spy, Hazel," he drawls.

Hazel shrugs. "Too much drama."

"I got hit by two arrows, but I'm fine now," I blurt, recoiling when Hazel's head snaps toward me, her red hair flying across her face. "They weren't tracking Knox...They were tracking me."

Hazel's mouth pops open, fear flashing across her ocean blue eyes before they harden. "I'm glad you're okay. Don't keep anything from me from now on," she demands, giving me the same stare down she gave Knox earlier.

I lift my hand in the air. "I promise."

Raising a brow, she turns to Knox. "Now that that's settled, where do we go from here?"

"I'm going to track the remaining demon hounds tomorrow, see if they lead me to who's ordering them to hunt Delilah," Knox says.

"I'm coming with you." I cut him off before he can argue. "I can take care of myself."

His brow arches. *Can you?*

I narrow my eyes in return. *Yes.*

"I'll be more prepared this time. Besides, I'm not letting you go alone," I say flatly. My heart pinches at the memory of Knox surrounded by the demon hounds.

"I'm one of the most powerful Fae in this kingdom." His grin is pure arrogance. "It would take a lot more than a few demon hounds to take me down."

I shrug. "Great, then you can enjoy my delightful company."

"More demon books for me," Hazel says, a small shiver wracking her body. "They truly are horrendous creatures."

Yes, and whoever is sending them into these lands is more disturbed than they are.

Widening my stance, I prepare for the assault. All afternoon Knox has been training me, teaching me how to combine my sword and defense training with magic. Where my sword strikes, my magic protects, and when magic attacks, my training instincts defend.

I must admit, my morning training sessions have been

slower than usual, taking me more time to adjust to my new body than I thought. I'm stronger, faster, and can see moves coming before an opponent does thanks to my sharp senses. My body has had to adjust to the faster, more violent movements it can produce.

Knox says combining them will be more lethal than relying solely on my magic. I could burn myself out and have to rely solely on my past training or be in a compromised position where magic isn't available.

I can't let my magic become a crutch.

Locking my gaze on Knox's sapphire eyes, I lift my hands, awaiting his assault. I've tried making the first move countless times in the past few hours, to no avail. He's been training far longer than I have, his techniques sharper, more focused and far deadlier.

His right foot moves, and then he's lunging forward, his sword swiping for my arm. I spin before his sword connects, rolling into a crouch. I swing my leg out, knocking Knox off his feet. I strike before he can, thrusting with my right hand, my sword barely an inch from his heart.

I soak up the shock that lines his features. "I win," I purr.

A grin tugs at his lips. In a flash, the sword is knocked from my hand, his own flying across the grass, as his legs wrap around my waist. Rolling, he takes me to the ground and pins his knee into my back.

"Arrogance gets you nowhere," he growls.

I groan, shoving him off my back as I mutter curses under my breath. Walking away, I take a break, drinking from my water.

"I think we need to work on your mental blocks," Knox says casually before drinking from his own waterskin.

"I don't have mental blocks."

Knox chuckles. "You most certainly do."

I fist my hands on my hips. "What mental blocks do I supposedly have?"

"You tired yourself out the other night at the library. You have a lot more power than simple cloaking magic."

He tips his head back as he takes another drink, the sun shining on his tan skin as water runs down his chin, over his exposed neck. His Adam's apple bobs as he swallows.

I suddenly need a lot more water.

Knox wipes his mouth with the back of his hand. "You've put up a mental block, you're not fully accessing your power."

"How would you know if I have more power?" I ask defensively.

Knox shrugs. "I can feel it."

I chuckle. "You can feel it?" I ask dubiously. When I see that he isn't laughing, my own humor dies. "How?"

"You sometimes, unknowingly, send your magic toward me."

I slam my mouth shut. How did I not know I was doing that?

"I—"

I have no words.

"Why are you afraid of magic?"

I blink. "I'm not afraid of magic."

Knox's eyes flatten. *Really?*

I'm not consciously afraid of magic. I love everything there is to do with magic and I love these lands. If you take away the beasts and entrapment spell, it's a beautiful place to live in. I would love to—

Knox clicks his tongue. "You don't want to get attached."

The smug bastard needs to stop invading my mind.

"My mental shields are up. How the hell did you read my mind?"

His lips twitch as he takes a step back. "I didn't, but I love to be proved right."

I glare at him. "You insufferable bastard!"

Knox walks off, chuckling. Turning, his face grows serious. "No matter where you end up, Delilah, the magic and Fae body aren't going anywhere."

My heart begins to race. Even if I end up going back to the human lands, back to my people…my father will kill me on sight the moment he sees me with elongated ears and magic. My father and his abuse appears to have wiggled into my head further than I thought. I shake the thoughts of my father away.

"How do I access my full powers?" I demand.

Knox crosses the grass and slowly leans in, the warmth of his breath tickling my cheek as his lips brush the shell of my ear. His dark rumbling voice makes my stomach fill with liquid heat. "Accept it, Angel," he whispers.

I grit my teeth at the shiver that runs down my spine.

"Accept what?" I ask, taking a step back, needing as much distance from him as possible.

Knox takes a deep breath, his jaw clenching before he relaxes his body, settling into cool indifference as he slides his hands in his pockets. "Whatever it is that you're afraid of feeling."

I'm afraid of getting comfortable in this world knowing I'll have to go back the second the entrapment spell lifts. I never want to go back to that palace; it was only home because Easton was there. I think I'd kill my father if I ever saw him again.

My breathing picks up, my chest rising and falling faster as my thoughts spiral out of control, making fire build inside of me.

"What are you afraid of, Delilah?" Knox pushes.

His voice sends the thoughts in my mind into overdrive, each fear flooding my mind.

I'm afraid of losing the people I love, afraid of getting close to anyone in case they get taken away from me again, afraid of what it will feel like to return to the palace without Easton. I'm afraid of what my father will do to me now that Easton is gone.

I have no one to shield me from my father anymore.

Fire erupts.

My eyes burn as fire explodes around me, shooting out of my hands and encompassing my entire body, yet the heat doesn't harm me.

Knox's icy air brushes against my flames, soothing them before they turn his garden to ash.

"There she is," Knox breathes, taking a step forward. "Show me the gold magic."

His voice is like a command. A soothing golden light envelopes me, replacing the fire. This power feels different from the flames, more serene.

"Interesting," Knox murmurs, walking around me.

His magic probes mine, as if to say hello. Involuntarily, my magic strokes up against his, as if it's a cat.

"What power is this?" I ask.

Knox's brows furrow as he stops in front of me. "That…I don't know."

My jaw goes slack. "How do you not know?"

My panic makes my magic flare in response. Light pulses around us before Knox's power strokes a tendril down my back, the black shadow containing his essence soothing me and my magic.

I squirm away. "Stop that," I hiss.

Knox shrugs. "It works, and I don't feel like finding out what power you possess by being incinerated with it."

I smirk, spreading the gold light toward him. "Scared, Knox?"

My power slams into an invisible shield, so strong it makes me stumble backward from the force of it.

"Not for a second, Angel," he purrs.

My magic retracts as he drops the protection shield.

"Can you create shadows?" he asks curiously.

"Where do the shadows come from? What element?"

"Fire. From the light and darkness created in the embers of a flame."

I close my eyes, imagining long black talons creeping from behind me. I flutter open my eyelids to see swirls of darkness have consumed me. I send them scattering for Knox with half a thought.

I click my tongue. "Apparently."

As the magic builds inside of me, I imagine water flowing through me, calming me, washing away the magic I let escape. The shadows dissolve entirely. It feels easier this time, as if I'm able to access my magic faster. Knox was right —I was blocking it.

"You truly are an essence Fae," he says in awe.

Wicked delight shines in those beautiful sapphire eyes. With that look, I begin to tentatively back away, getting no further than two steps before a vine slithers up my right leg, halting my movements completely.

"Do you have earth magic?" He smirks.

The smug bastard thinks he's found something I don't have; little does he know Hazel already helped me tap into my earth magic.

Quicker than Knox can blink, two long green vines shoot out of the earth, wrapping around his hands and feet. His eyes widen before a burst of shocked laughter falls from his lips.

I use my own magic to unravel Knox's vine from my leg.

Stalking toward him, I stop so close my shoes touch the tip of his.

He's making magic fun for me instead of something to fear. I squelch the tenderness that arises from his kindness.

"Have any more tricks? Your Highness," I teasingly add.

He leans his head down, whispering in my ear, "Your wish is my command."

My vines around him wholly disappear before he snakes his arms around my waist, his wings exploding behind him. He takes off into the sky so quickly I yelp. Wrapping my legs around his waist and my arms around his neck, I cling to him for dear life. His pulse thumps rapidly against my forearms. With nowhere to look but those sapphire eyes filled with an emotion I can't decipher, I concede that Knox wins this round and possibly every future round. Considering if this is his power after it's been dwindling for nearly one hundred and fifty years, I'd be terrified to go against him at his full strength. What a sight that would be.

Electricity hums through my body. Feeling every inch of his glorious body makes liquid heat pool in my stomach.

"You win," I breathe, not daring to break eye contact.

A slow grin spreads across his lips, making him even more gorgeous. "That's what I thought," he says roughly.

Flying us back down to the garden, Knox gently sets me on my feet, my body instantly cooling at the loss of contact.

My heart's beating so fast I'm afraid Knox can hear it. "I'll see you at dinner," I rasp, leaving Knox alone in the garden.

I kill the feelings he's eliciting in my body, shoving it into a box and throwing away the key.

Stupid, useless hormones.

# Chapter Twenty-Six

Hazel bounces into my room later that afternoon, wearing a floral summer dress. Placing down the romance book I was reading, I sit up, whistling as she stands at the end of my bed. She twirls to make the dress flutter around her shins.

"You look amazing," I say, earning a beaming smile from Hazel.

"I'm glad you think so." Clapping her hands, she starts rummaging through my clothes in my dressing room. "We're going out to dinner tonight! Knox is going to give us a tour of Azalea."

My heart stops for a second before picking up once more.

The last time I went into Azalea, I had a panic attack. I barely got to enjoy the beautiful city because I was so over-come with sadness and grief over Easton. He wouldn't want that, for me to cower away from such an experience. He would tell me to stop acting like a fool, to smile and enjoy everything. Sliding out of bed, I decide I'm going not only for myself but for Easton.

I walk into my dressing room, finding Hazel frowning at my clothes. "Did they offend you?" I chuckle.

Hazel waves her hand to the small handful of clothes hanging up. "You have no dresses."

I shrug. "I didn't pack for fancy evenings."

Hazel rolls her eyes before grabbing my hand and dragging me out of my room. "You can borrow something of mine."

"Why do I need to get dressed up?" I ask.

"Because we need to have fun. Everything has been so serious lately, it's about time we let our hair down."

I don't protest. It is true. Everyone's mood has been dejected lately, the black magic book we need to find and the missing Fae being a dark storm cloud hanging over everyone's head.

Hazel drags me into her dressing room, which feels like I'm crossing through a rainbow. She wears her personality; all her clothes are extremely vibrant colors.

Hazel pulls out a red dress, shoving it into my chest as she marches me into the bathroom. "Hurry up and get changed," she demands.

I mock salute. "Okay, boss."

The dress is significantly shorter on me considering I'm seven inches taller than Hazel. It has a low neckline, and the silky fabric cups my chest tightly, pushing the swell of my breasts higher. The material hugs my torso, then flares out at my hips, making the silk swish around the top of my thighs.

When I walk out of the bathroom, Hazel's eyes widen as a smile spreads across her lips. Mimicking my early behavior, she whistles. "Damn, that looks so much better on you."

I must admit, it's a stunning dress. "You don't think it's too short?" I ask.

She shakes her head as she stands from the futon at the

end of her bed. "No, it's the perfect length. Shows off your long legs." Hazel starts rummaging through her shoes in her dressing room. Looking from her feet to my own, she huffs. "I don't think we're the same size."

I wave my hand in the air. "It's okay, I can wear my own."

Hazel follows me back into my room as I throw on shin-length boots. Hazel sits on the end of my bed while I run a comb through my wavy dark brown hair at the vanity.

"How was training with Knox this afternoon?" she asks casually.

Too casually.

I look at her through the mirror. "Good. He showed me how to access more power. Why?"

She shrugs. "I was just…wondering if anything fun happened."

I narrow my eyes, watching as she fidgets with her fingers. "Spit it out."

"I think you need to open your heart," she blurts.

I cackle. "I most certainly do not." Spinning in my chair, I face Hazel, cutting her off before she can continue with more nonsense. "There's nothing going on. The only reason we tolerate each other is because of the bargain."

Hazel clicks he tongue. "If you say so."

I do say so. I refuse to believe anything else.

Because all of this is temporary.

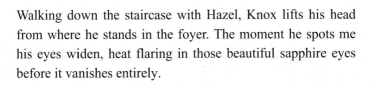

Walking down the staircase with Hazel, Knox lifts his head from where he stands in the foyer. The moment he spots me his eyes widen, heat flaring in those beautiful sapphire eyes before it vanishes entirely.

Knox clears his throat, putting his hands in his pockets. "Ready?"

No sooner than we agree, white light encompasses everything around us before the twinkling stars of the night sky and sounds of the ocean waves surround us.

Hazel looks completely unaffected by the sudden teleporting. I, however, would appreciate a warning next time. It always leaves me feeling wobbly after.

We're standing at the top of a hill, the street below lit up with crackling fire lanterns hanging overhead. Lively upbeat music floats through the bustling street as people sing, laugh, and dance right there on the street.

Warmth fills my heart at how much happiness floods the streets. There is still joy to be found in the darkest of times, no matter how small. Knox, Hazel, and I head down into the streets. Every person we pass smiles wide, beaming at Knox and saying hello. He returns their kindness with a genuine smile of his own, wishing people a good evening, his words full of sincerity and, dare I say, love toward his people. It isn't a mask at all, I can feel it. Perhaps there can be good kings.

Only time will tell.

We pass bustling fashion stores, taverns, and restaurants full of chatter and music before stopping before a small white building, red flowers dangling from the ivory vines on the brick wall. Walking into the low-lit restaurant, calm washes through me. The tables are covered in white cloths, candles provide a soft glow around the room, and the smell emanating from the kitchen makes my mouth salivate.

We make it no further than two steps inside before a small woman rushes out from behind the kitchen door, straight into Knox's arms. Wrinkles line her eyes and mouth, her ageing skin glowing in the candlelight. I wonder how old she is.

The woman squeezes him. Pulling back, Knox leans down so she can place both her palms on his cheeks. I think they're about to have a cute moment—that thought dies the moment her mouth opens.

"You haven't been here in almost a month, young man!" she scolds.

Hazel and I chuckle. This woman is even shorter than Hazel, seeing her reprimand someone as tall, built, and powerful as Knox is hilarious. He seems to have a pattern of being scolded by tiny females.

Knox turns his head, his eyes connecting with mine. He knows exactly why we're laughing.

His voice holds a hint of humor. "I know, Mia, I'm terribly sorry."

She squishes his cheeks together before releasing him, shaking her finger. "You will eat everything I serve you. You're too skinny."

Pink blossoms across Knox's cheeks as he adverts his gaze.

My laughter dies when Mia turns her focus on Hazel and me. We both straighten our shoulders; she might be small but her energy commands respect. Mia's brow arches. "Are you going to introduce me to your new friends, Knox?"

Knox's lips twitch as he splays his hand to the side. "This is Delilah and Hazel."

Hazel and I say hello, trepidation coating our words.

Despite her height difference, Mia somehow looks down her nose at us. "Do you eat?"

"Plenty," I breathe, Hazel mimicking me.

A loud burst of laughter erupts from Mia. Clicking her tongue, she grabs our hands, leading us to a table in the back. With a view of the ocean, the moon and stars shine brightly overhead.

"Great! You will love everything," she demands.

Mia seats me in the middle, directly overlooking the ocean as Hazel sits to my left. Knox joining us to my right.

"How long have you known my Knox?" she asks once we're seated. We're almost at eye level now that I'm sitting.

"Not long, only a few weeks." I smile. "How long have you two known each other?"

By the look of horror on Knox's face, I know I've asked the right question. I bite my lip to keep from laughing.

A pinch in my thigh jolts me. I narrow my eyes at Knox, kicking him under the table.

"I've known Knox since the day he was born." Mia's smile drops, her eyes hardening. "His parents used to bring him here every Sunday for dinner."

Now I feel like a bitch.

This is supposed to be a joy-filled dinner and I've managed to direct the conversation to Knox's dead parents.

Knox saves me from trying to come up with a reply. "Whatever you feel like cooking for us, Mia, we'll eat it all," he offers with a warm smile.

Mia pats Knox on the shoulder with a tight smile. "Coming right up."

Guilt wracks my body as I look at Knox. His entire body is tight, eyes guarded as he stares out the window.

"Mia seems lovely." I smile.

Knox pulls himself away from wherever he went. "She's a character. You have nothing on her threats," he says, visibly shivering at the thought.

I smirk. "What do some of her threats entail?"

Knox lifts his chin. "I don't need to give you two any more ammunition."

Hazel and I chuckle at that, mischief flashing in our eyes.

"Where are the best shops in Azalea?" Hazel asks, squirming with excitement.

"There's a street not too far from here. It has the best clothes in all the courts if you ask me. I can take you there after dinner."

"I'll go during the day. Something tells me that I'm going to have trouble walking after all the food Mia serves us."

Hazel's assumption pulls a chuckle out of Knox, his shoulders finally loosening.

"Yes, that would be wise," he murmurs.

No sooner than Knox has spoken do two servers approach our table, their arms laden with an array of different plates. My mouth waters as the smell hits me, different herbs and spices caressing my nose.

The servers begin to fill our table plate by plate.

Chicken, lamb, roast, mashed potatoes, stir fry noodles, sautéed vegetables, freshly herbed bread, and pasta. Knox thanks the waiters as Hazel and I sit shell-shocked, both our jaws hanging open.

"I don't even know where to begin," I whisper. "It all smells incredible."

"Don't think, just eat. It's the only way you'll get through it," Knox says seriously.

Following his lead, I place herbed chicken, mashed potatoes, bread, and pasta onto my large plate. Taking a bite of the creamy pasta, I can't stop the moan that escapes me.

Knox's eyes widen as they snap to my mouth. He drags his gaze away, his swallow audible.

"This is the best food I've ever eaten," I state, not pausing to breathe before I shove another forkful of creamy pasta into my mouth.

Hazel chuckles. "You say that about everything you eat, but I agree, this is the best."

"What's your favorite food?" Knox asks, scooping mashed potatoes onto his fork.

I don't have to think before I answer. "Doughnuts," I say dreamily.

Remembering the last time I ate doughnuts with Easton in my room brings a small smile to my face.

Hazel chokes. "Really? I thought it would be something more lavish than dough."

I point my fork at her. "Don't you dare mock doughnuts."

"Have you always liked them?" Knox asks.

"Like them? I *love* them," I say on a wide smile. "When I was a child, Annie snuck it into my room one night to cheer me up. I've been hooked ever since."

Moving onto the vegetables, I notice Knox staring at me in my peripheral, his face a blank mask yet his eyes are swimming with questions. I've never spoken about anyone from my supposed home.

Instead of voicing those questions, he says, "My court will be arriving in two weeks."

"Are you excited to see them?" Hazel asks.

Knox's lips tug into a grin. "It will be much louder with them around but yes."

Trepidation settles in my stomach. Will Knox's court be as bad, if not worse, than the sniveling snakes infesting my father's court? I bite my cheek, pushing food around my plate with my fork. "What's your court like?" I ask hesitantly.

Knox studies me for a moment, choosing his words carefully. "They're all very big personalities, but for the most part, we work great together. Nevertheless, we butt heads at times."

I frown in disbelief. "Your court disagrees with you over your decisions?"

He cocks his head, his eyes sharpening. "They have a say in important matters, yes."

I mull his words over in my head, wondering if it's truly possible for a king to allow his court the freedom to speak their mind and opinions.

Hazel's assumption wasn't wrong. I feel as if my stomach is about to burst, my body sluggish as we exit the restaurant, entering the busy street of Azalea once more.

"I have to pick up a package from a store. It's not too far. Perhaps we can walk the food off," Knox muses.

Hazel grimaces. "I'd have to walk for a week to do that."

I throw my head back on a laugh, the sound mingling with those of the people of Azalea.

*It truly is an amazing city.*

I've never in my life seen such a vibrant sight. Where the sectors at home were dull and cold, Azalea flourishes. The beautifully tailored clothes in Essence Court colors—turquoise and sage—alight the streets. Dresses and jewels adorn the people, and the rich smells of spices drift through the air as we pass by restaurants. My favorite sight is the people dancing in the street, children running and playing with their elemental powers. A young blonde-haired girl rushes past, bubbles of water forming into butterflies flapping around her head as she squeals in delight.

Knox stops before a one-story red brick building, the glass window case housing various swords and knives to show off the swordsmanship's work. A small bell jingles overhead as Knox steps through the door. An old weathered man appears from the back and greets him with a wide grin.

As they embrace, talking about Knox's order, I browse the room.

Passing aisle after aisle of weapons, each one crafted with care and creativity, I pause in front of a table, my eyes swimming with tears. I peer down at a stunning sword displayed on top of a black cloth.

A dragon curving around the hilt of the sword makes my breath hitch.

It's designed with so much detail I'd swear it was real, its scaly limbs and sharp teeth sparkling as the candlelight bounces off the steel. Its mouth is open in a roar, pointing directly down the sword, as if whoever you strike, the dragon will eat.

Easton would have loved this, begged for it even. I couldn't imagine a more perfect sword for him. I pick it up gently, running the tip of my finger over the dragon's body. But reading the price tag, my heart sinks. I place it down, taking in every intricate detail as to not forget it.

Pinewood surrounds me before Knox's voice brushes my senses. "Ready?"

I step back, leaving the sword behind. "Yes."

The next morning, I awake to find the dragon pommel sword sitting on my futon.

A smile spreads across my face. My heart fluttering at Knox's kindness.

I pick up the sword, cherishing the gift that honors Easton.

# Chapter Twenty-Seven

W ith my new dragon sword strapped to my back I enter the foyer, searching for Knox. We're tracking the demon hounds today. Whenever the image of those creatures enters my mind, ice skitters down my spine. Earlier this morning after describing the beasts to Hazel, she showed Knox and me the demon hound description in the demonology book of creatures.

The demon hounds travel and hunt in packs, each pack having a leader. They don't possess any magic, yet their senses—especially their smell—are as sharp as a Fae's. Their strength comes from being immune to our divine magic from the dark magic coursing through their blood. While you can cut off their airway or hold them down with shadows and ward them off with fire, it won't kill them, only delay. Besides beheading them, the only weakness they possess is angelic magic. Knox informed me that no one has possessed angelic magic since before the angels were extinct, around the same time dark magic was banished.

Although, it was only the seven archangels that possessed the angelic magic. With the archangels not being able to reproduce and pass on their lineage, it was believed to be that they were a gift from Mother Gaia herself, to protect the Fae lands from the very creatures we stand against today.

With that in mind, every blade I own is currently strapped to my body.

I'm leaning against the center table when Knox enters the foyer. He's dressed impeccably as always in his black fighting leathers, armed to the teeth with swords. Pushing off the table, I encompass us in a silence shield thanks to Knox teaching me in our earlier magic lesson. "Could we ask the other court royals if they know what happened to the dark magic books?"

Knox flashes a fake smile. "Hello, Delilah, I'm great today, thank you for asking."

I roll my eyes. "I just saw you at lunch several hours ago. We don't need to say any fake pleasantries."

Come to think of it, we've never done the fake pleasantries.

He mock pouts, placing a hand over his heart. "You wound me, Delilah."

"No, I wound your ego."

I stare at him, waiting for the answer to my question. When only silence greets me, I cross my arms over my chest. "Knox," I say irritably.

"Delilah," he mimics, crossing his own arms. His biceps flex and bunch with the movement.

We have a stare down. I don't crack or break. That stubborn part of me keeps my gaze locked on his.

"Hazel was right about the face you pull," he mutters under his breath before letting out a long sigh. "No, we can't trust them. Many are in the queen's pockets, sucking up to her for any scrap of power. They'll turn us over to the queen for asking such things."

I place my hand on my hip. "That wasn't very difficult, was it?"

Knox ignores me, striding to the back door. "Let's go before we lose any more sunlight."

That was the other thing Hazel found. The demon hounds are impossible to see at night. With their shadows and leathery black skin, it would be impossible to track them without a source of light.

Trailing after Knox, I notice his body is tense. I don't pry; if something's bothering him, he can tell me, otherwise it's none of my business. A lot of my beatings from my father came from asking too many questions. I learned a long time ago to keep my curiosity to myself, regardless of if its concern.

Knox pauses in the garden, holding out his hand to me.

I slowly step forward, sliding my hand in his, feeling the rough calluses tickle my skin. White light surrounds us, wind pulling my hair this way and that a moment before my feet connect with the forest floor.

Whichever way I look, all I see are endless trees. The dense forest smell assaults my senses. We must be near the witches' border because I can smell the damp moss.

Knox's back is taut, face hard as granite as we walk silently, avoiding anything that will make a sound. Letting my senses take over, I listen to the flaps of small birds' wings, trees rustling, and critters crawling. We continue for hours like this.

If I was still a human, I wouldn't have felt it—the energy shift in the air. It's as subtle as a pin dropping.

Knox blows our scent in the opposite direction, then pauses.

I force myself to open my senses fully, allowing the Fae

body to take control as I calm my breathing and pay attention to the change in the forest.

Animals are no longer around us, hiding or deserting the area completely. I can't hear or feel them. Even the trees seem to hold their breath, right as a putrid smell fills the air. My canines flare. *Demon hounds.*

I can hear their sniveling voices and slithering tongues in the distance. They're not trying to be silent; they don't care if they're seen or heard. They're acting like they own the forest.

I lean closer to Knox, sliding my hand in his palm. Knox whips his head to me, confusion swimming in his eyes before understanding smooths his furrowed brows. A gentle energy flows through me, zipping up my arms and legs as I make Knox and I wholly disappear from the eyes of the forest. I don't know how to make someone disappear without being physically connected, so Knox has to shut up and deal with holding my hand.

We approach their atrocious scent, careful to not disturb our surroundings until the next demon hounds' conversation makes Knox freeze.

"She wants them alive," it sneers.

Growls of protest break out. "I want a piece of the king," another spits.

"You'll enjoy it more if it lasts longer," it hisses.

My hand instinctively tightens in Knox's, but his returning squeeze does nothing to soothe the anxiety rushing through my chest at the thought of being taken and held captive by a pack of these creatures. The torture they would inflict would break even the strongest of Faes.

The demon hounds discuss how they plan to pick us apart piece by piece for enjoyment. Despite my gut telling me to run we get closer, silent as night as we creep around a large oak tree. No more than a hundred feet from where we stand are six demon hounds, black shadows swirling around their leathery skin.

"I want the bitch. Her blood smelt pure," one purrs. "Her screams would be like a melody—"

"Speak of the devil," another snarls.

As one, the demons separate in different directions, their sniffing fills the forest air. They're hunting us, not aware that we're already hunting them.

I inch toward the one who claims to love the smell of my blood, until Knox yanks me back hard, shaking his head. I narrow my eyes at him. With his mouth on my ear, speaking so quietly I barely register it, he whispers, "Wait for it."

Leaning my back against his chest, I wait, but there's nothing.

A gentle brush of a finger down my ear raises goosebumps on my arms.

*Listen and feel.*

Listening to his soft purr in my mind I take a steadying breath and focus.

The forest went silent the moment the demon hounds arrived, making it easier to feel them. I don't need to send my power out to find them. It feels wrong with them here, as if they're disturbing the very essence of the forest's pure energy.

I feel more than hear one moving directly toward us.

I unsheathe the blade strapped to my back, widening my feet as I prepare myself.

Swirls of shadow are the first thing I see, followed by leathery black fingers clawing the tree in front of me. Its pointed, razor blade claws scratching the bark as it slices down.

"Delilah," it sings.

My body stills at its gut-wrenching voice.

They're caging us in.

Deadly calm washes over me. I refuse to let these creatures win. Keeping my hand in Knox's, I open my mind to him.

*Teleport us.*

Within a blink of an eye we vanish, moving through light and time before standing on the forest floor once more. Instead of being in front of the demon, we're behind it.

Its leathery back is hunched, its smooth black head tilted to the side as it slowly slithers around the tree.

The hound freezes the moment I drop Knox's hand and uncloak myself, turning to face me, bearing the rows of endless sharp teeth in a smile. Crimson blood drips from its fangs.

I mimic its stare, my smile serpentine.

Before the hound can move, green vines snap its hands and feet to the tree trunk. My blade rests on its neck as I shove all my strength into it.

"I hear you like the smell of me," I croon.

Its face slackens, rage burning through those depthless black pits of hell it has for eyes.

I cock my head. "What's the matter? Don't like being held against your will?" When all the creature does is bare its teeth at me, I roll my eyes. "See, this is how it's going to go. You either tell me who sent you, or you never walk through this forest again."

The hound blinks.

One.

Two.

Three.

"That's fine, I'll just ask someone from your pack."

"I'll come back for you, bitch," it sneers.

My grin widens as it thrashes below me. "I plan on it."

I drag my blade across its neck, black blood oozing down the silver as its body slumps to the floor. The hound is never going to speak. We need to track them instead of caging them.

My confidence is short-lived as a branch snaps behind me.

I spin around to find Knox gone. Where he should be stands another hound, uncontrolled rage making it physically shake before it explodes. "You're dead!" it roars.

The hound lunges, clawed talons making to rip out my arms but I see it coming and he's not quick enough to see the blade in my hand. I duck, and with its left side exposed, I lunge, dragging my blade against its skin. It cries out in rage as black blood oozes from its ribs. Before it can blink, I'm moving behind it again. With my dragon sword I slash a clean cut across its Achilles heel. The sound of its shrieks fill the air, the horrible sound grating my eardrums. I strike again before it begins to fall to the ground, my blade meeting the black leathery flesh across its throat. Its head lolls to the ground, black blood covering the forest floor, joining that of its friend's.

I wipe my blade on the nearest tree, the smell emanating from their corpses so foul I gag.

Feeling power ripple at my back I turn, finding Knox leaning against a tree.

"I was wondering when you were going to come out and play," he purrs.

I lift a brow. "You testing me?"

He shrugs. "Perhaps." The smirk Knox gives me is purely ravenous. "Ready to run, Angel?"

A roar of outrage fills the forest as the demon hounds smell their dead.

Knox and I take off, running as fast as the wind.

Trees fly past me, the forest turning into a green blur. The hounds' snapping jaws at my heels make me run faster. I follow Knox as he maneuvers in a zig-zag pattern between trees before he cuts me off, heading east. I hear the rushing of water in the distance. We push ourselves faster, the other-worldly energy close behind. The drop of a cliff looms in the distance, nearing closer when Knox drops back suddenly. I twist my head, not daring to slow as the hounds gain on us.

My eyes widen as Knox barrels straight for me. His arms circle my waist as he slams into my body, throwing us both off the cliffs edge.

Free falling for the rushing water below, I watch the blue sky get further and further away, waiting for Knox to expand his wings and fly. But he never does. I take a deep breath, locking my entire body, readying it for the assault as we hit the water.

The impact makes my bones scream, feeling as if a boulder hit me. Knox tightens his arms around me, pulling my back fully to his chest as he holds me.

I wait for my chest to squeeze in protest of needing air, yet it never comes. Awe fills me as Knox siphons air into my lungs. My body relaxes into his, my muscles softening, easing into the planes of his hard chest.

Knox starts to swim, not up but behind. Dragging us further into the water, the flow of the waterfall pelts the surface above us. The roaring gets louder before it begins to fade. Knox pulls us up, and I take in deep gulps of air once we breach the surface. Darkness surrounds us, the roar of the waterfall at my back, the water drops splashing me.

We're behind the waterfall.

My eyes lift to Knox to find his sapphire ones already on me, always watching. We silently stare at each other, not daring to speak in case we alert the hounds.

I open my mind, a tiny crack in my wall.

*They hate water,* he explains.

I bite my lip to stop the laugh inside me from escaping. Knox's humor mirrors my own in his beautiful eyes.

After treading water for what feels like hours, my body is weak and wobbly as Knox and I emerge from the swimming hole. My feet and hands have turned to prunes, and my white t-shirt is completely see-through as it clings to my skin.

I hold onto the slippery rocks, not trusting my shaky legs as I exit the water.

No hounds are to be felt or heard for miles. I'm so focused on sensing them that the power that erupts behind me knocks me to the ground, a phantom shadow catching my fall before my face smashes into the rock.

I turn to Knox, his lower half submerged in the water hole, his chest rising and falling rapidly. Rage I've never seen in him before clouds his eyes. His fists are clenched so tight they're shaking.

"Who did that to you?" he asks, deadly quiet.

My brows furrow in confusion. "What are you talking about?"

His rage pulses around us, making fear stuff itself down my throat.

He's terrifying when he's angry. I've never seen him lay a hand on anyone unless they're attacking him. *You haven't known him long enough,* I remind myself, and that thought makes anxiety churn in my stomach.

"Who did that to you?" he growls again.

He's not looking at me directly; no, his gaze is locked onto the side of my stomach.

My blood turns to ice, freezing me entirely.

I open my mouth to say something, yet my own voice leaves me. Knox doesn't take his eyes off my side, his gaze so fiercely strong I peer down at myself.

Rigged white lines start from the side of my stomach and snake around my back. I stopped counting how many lines of scars my father left after slicing me open. I've never looked at my back in the mirror out of fear, but I know small round circles pepper the jagged cuts. Those would be courtesy of the iron fire poker my father used to burn me. The image of what my back potentially looks like sends bile into my throat. I don't ever want to see the permanent damage my father inflicted on me. The ramifications of his words and actions are felt every day, and the fact there's physical proof of my unworthiness in my father's eyes kills me.

Shame and embarrassment coat my tongue, propelling me into action.

Knox is still staring at me when I turn. Ignoring him and the eyes I can feel burning a hole into my back, I exit the water, only to smack into a wall of muscle.

Knox's hands fly out to stop me from falling. I rip my arms out of his grip as if his touch burned me.

"Don't touch me," I snap.

My words make Knox stumble back.

He lowers his voice, yet it doesn't contain the rage still simmering in his eyes. "*Who did that to you?*" he demands.

"What does it matter?" I snap. "It has nothing to do with you!"

He lifts his brows, astonishment and shock flashing in his eyes before determined anger takes over again. "So help me gods, Delilah, you will tell me who did that to you, or I'll find out for myself."

Unease slithers down my spine. I don't want him to see those memories. I don't want him to look at me as weak.

The bastard stands there waiting for an answer. I know he'll go into my mind if I don't tell him. Which feels like a violation in itself.

"My father," I spit through gritted teeth.

Not wanting to see his reaction, I lower my eyes to my sopping wet shoes. "Take us back," I say flatly.

He's silent for so long I begin to wonder if he teleported away. I'm sure he's waiting for me to make eye contact with him, but I refuse to. He's not the only one feeling angry at this moment.

He had no right to push me.

"Is he still alive?" he asks, his voice dripping with ice.

I grit my teeth. "Yes."

"Good," he growls.

Before I can respond his warm hand takes mine. White light surrounds us as the wind rips at our wet clothes. The second my feet connect with white marble tiles, I storm away, locking the door to my room.

I pace as rage burns inside me. I'm only here because of the stupid bargain. What happened to me before doesn't concern him. Knox only needs me alive so I can use my power to break the entrapment spell, then he will be done with me.

A small part of me protests the idea that Knox will be done with me the second he gets what he wants, but the majority of me expects it. It's what a king would do, after all.

I silence the small voice in my mind that questions why he was so enraged.

# Chapter Twenty-Eight

L ast night wasn't my proudest moment.
I sulked like a child, yet I couldn't stop the irritation that sparked in me every time I tried to get out of bed. Knox pushing me yesterday opened a part of me I've been shoving so deeply inside of myself that once it came to the surface, it exploded.

I told Hazel I wasn't feeling well and needed to rest. Being the amazing woman that she is, she brought a plate of food for me upstairs. I thanked her profusely and when I started devouring my food, I think she understood that my refusal to leave my room had more to do with the dark broody Fae downstairs than an upset stomach.

I don't like being pushed, regardless of if I needed it or not. I don't like the feeling of my inner boundaries being crossed. I was so violated growing up, having every single one of my physical and emotional boundaries destroyed by my father that my inner walls became a sanctuary to protect me and Knox just demolished one yesterday, making me withdraw while I rebuilt it brick for brick.

Groaning, I throw my arm over my eyes and roll over. My

knee collides with something on my bed. I jolt up, rubbing my eyes as I stare at the black box wrapped with a white ribbon. I frown as I pull the box toward me. I didn't hear anyone come into my room.

Unwrapping the white ribbon, my mouth drops open as I lift the lid.

It's a box full of doughnuts, filled to the brim with various flavors and colors. The smell alone makes my mouth water.

Tears line my eyes. He remembered.

The only two people who ever brought me doughnuts were Annie and Easton.

*Easton would have done the exact same thing as Knox last night.* The thought makes me pause. Am I being too hard on him? Now that I've calmed down, I can acknowledge that his rage wasn't directed at me; it was toward what happened to me.

Regardless, he pushed me too hard yesterday.

I sigh, taking an iced pink doughnut and flop back, nestling myself into the silk pillows. I moan as the flavor erupts in my mouth, my eyes rolling into the back of my head. The doughnuts I ate as a human don't compare to how delicious they taste now. I'm shoving another in my mouth when there's a light tap on the door.

"Come in," I mumble around a mouthful of glazed goodness.

I freeze when Knox strolls in. I thought it would be Hazel coming to check on me for the hundredth time.

Knox sucks in a breath as heat flashes in his eyes. He clears his throat, ripping his gaze away, looking anywhere but at me.

I frown as I look down at myself. Confusion swirling before clarity strikes and I gasp. In my doughnut haze I forgot that the only thing I'm wearing is a thin white satin shirt—

which is transparent. My nipples are poking through, saluting Knox.

I snatch the sheet, covering myself as Knox clears his throat again. "I thought you were Hazel," I murmur.

He looks back, the heat that was there moments before gone entirely. "I see you found the doughnuts," he says smoothly, leaning against the door frame.

I take a deep breath as he crosses his arms over his chest, his muscles flexing as he does. My heart begins to race as my cheeks heat. "They're delicious…Thank you."

Knox dips his chin before closing the door and taking a seat on the white-cushioned futon at the end of my bed. He scans me from head to toe—for what, I have no clue.

"My court will be arriving soon. I was wondering what parts you want me to reveal to them."

I blink. That's…awfully considerate of him.

"I don't think you're able to explain what we need to without the full story," I say slowly.

"There's ways around that if there's something you're not comfortable with them knowing."

I'm utterly shocked that someone of his power and status is asking me what I'm comfortable with. It's completely unnatural to me.

I swallow past my dry throat. "You can tell them that I was human and how the pendant gave me access to this land. They might know why I turned into a Fae."

"If that's what you want."

I stare into his warm eyes, my mouth moving before I can stop it. "I don't want them to know about my life as a human princess," I blurt.

Dealing with one grumpy Fae is enough. I don't need anyone else knowing about my horrible life. I don't need the pity or the embarrassment.

Knox's features slacken, his face draining of all color. I cock my head, confused by his reaction before it finally dawns on me.

He didn't see in my memories why I lived in the palace. Knox had no idea who has been sleeping in his guest room. That realization—that I'm the heir to the human lands, that the one who beat me was not only my father but the King of Aloriah—lights in his eyes.

Knox snaps upright as he clenches his fists. "The king is your father," he growls.

My breathing quickens, coming out in shallow pants.

At my erratic breathing, he turns away and takes a deep breath. "My anger isn't toward you, Delilah," he says gutturally.

"I know that, but my body doesn't," I whisper.

When he faces me, his body is more relaxed. I can feel the tension surrounding him but he's putting it at bay, for me.

"Do you want to talk about it?" he asks softly.

"Absolutely not," I snap.

Rearranging myself so I'm cocooned by pillows, my breathing starts to slow, returning to normal as I look into Knox's calm eyes. "How did you not see that he was my father?" I ask. Knox read my mind that first day we met. He saw that I was human.

Knox clicks his tongue. "There seems to be a part of your memory that's locked."

"This changes nothing," I breathe.

"It changes everything, Angel."

I narrow my eyes. "How?"

He leans back on his forearms, his large frame and presence filling the room. He looks like an absolute god.

Screw him for being so attractive.

"For starters, I can't kill him without starting a war," he drawls calmly.

His knowing smirk at catching me ogling him doesn't deter me from his words.

"You will do no such thing," I demand.

He rolls his eyes, as if this is a mundane conversation. "Fine, you can kill him."

"No one is killing him."

Knox looks at me so intently it makes me feel as if he can see right through me and my fear. Despite his teasing tone, I know he isn't joking. The murderous rage he had in his eyes yesterday told me that if my father turned up on his doorstep, he would kill him in a heartbeat for what he did to me.

I would hate to be around him if he found out the true extent of my father's harm.

"Does this change our deal?" I ask.

He cocks his head to the side. "Not at all."

I breathe a sigh of relief. "Good."

Working to free the Fae is what's been keeping me going. If I had to leave and go back home, without having helped anyone and without resources for my own people, I think I would completely break.

Knox stands. "I like your company too much," he murmurs over his shoulder as he walks out.

I snap my head toward the closed door, his admission stunning me. He likes my company? I thought he only tolerated me for my magic…

An involuntary smile creeps over my lips.

# Chapter Twenty-Nine

"Teach me how to teleport," I say by way of greeting as Knox strolls down the steps to the back garden.

"Aiming to achieve great things today, are we?"

I roll my eyes. "Don't tease me, I want to teleport."

Knox stops in front of me. A tight-fitted black shirt stretches across the planes of his chest. "Not many can," he says simply.

I frown. I thought everyone could teleport. Now that I think about it, Hazel has never done it, but I assumed it was by choice because she adores flying.

"It depends on how much power you possess. It's a gift in itself," Knox explains.

"How far can you teleport?" I ask.

"Not far. You can move in small bursts. The farthest I can go is from one end of Azalea to the other. It's extremely taxing energy-wise. That's why I prefer to fly. Saves more power."

Interesting. "How do you teleport while flying?" I ask.

"It's simple." He shrugs.

I wave my hand around us. "Show me."

Knox disappears before a tap on my shoulder makes me yelp. Now behind me, Knox's infuriating face grins down at me.

"I didn't mean literally."

That only makes his smile widen. "I know."

Groaning, I run a hand down my face. "Knox."

"Yes, Angel?" he purrs.

"Teach me how to teleport," I grit out.

Why is he being so insufferable today?

His eyes glitter with amusement, his lips tugging into a grin. "As you wish."

Before I can move, water pummels me, and arrows from all directions target me as Knox teleports from one end of the garden to the other. I grit my teeth as I shield myself, groaning when he breaks through it with a split-second thought. I start jumping side to side, trying to dodge the arrows to no avail. It isn't until they start hitting my face do I snap and vanish.

It's an eerily similar feeling to flying, yet instead of the sky, I'm surrounded by white light. A small crack breaks through the surrounding white, a sliver of earth, a peek of where I want to go.

I can see Knox's outline, and focusing on the area behind him, time and air stretches around me. My feet once again land on the plush grass as if nothing happened.

I kick the back of his knees, trying to make him kneel, but he's too quick. He spins, yanking my arm as he tumbles to the ground, taking me with him. I land on top of his chest with a grunt.

Knox's boisterous laugh floats between us, his chest shaking with the force, jostling me side to side.

"Insufferable cocky bastard," I grit through my teeth.

My words only make Knox laugh harder. I go to scramble off his chest when my eyes widen. Suddenly, I'm aware of how we're lying. I'm completely sprawled on top of him, every intimate part of myself aligned with his. Knox realizes my position at the same time, his laughter dying in an instant. I lift my gaze, focusing on the fountain at the far end of the garden. One moment I'm lying on Knox and in the next moment, I'm standing in front of the fountain.

My head spins as my body adjusts to teleporting.

When I turn, Knox has composed himself, standing as he dusts off blades of grass from his clothes. I stroll back toward him. "Is that all for today?" I ask calmly, feeling anything but.

Knox's eyes harden. "I think we've covered enough," he states, walking back toward the house.

I groan. He truly has the worst mood swings I've ever encountered.

Knox and I enter through into the foyer when the front doors blast open before us.

I freeze, watching as four incredibly handsome and large Fae men stroll through the room, a small Fae woman leading them. The men are all nearly as tall as Knox, their own bodies crafted by muscles. They all burst through the room with energy and life, smiling and laughing.

I watch in slow motion, horror filling my stomach as the female flings herself into Knox's arms, Knox catching her seamlessly as they embrace. My skin itches as my heart sinks, something eerily similar to rage burning through me. The feeling intensifies the longer I stare at their close proximity, and I hate myself for it.

Hazel's knowing face breaks through my vision as she enters the foyer from the study. I snap myself out of it, taking in the other four males that apparently have been watching me as I make a fool out of myself. Heat fills my cheeks.

This is ridiculous. I need to stop acting like a child. I join Hazel, needing comfort from someone I know, certainly not to get away from the apparent love birds.

Knox's smile falters as his bright sapphire eyes meet mine, making me feel worse. He never openly flirted with me —he just has a teasing personality. I have absolutely nothing to be jealous about.

I plaster on the fakest smile I have ever worn, praying that he can't see through it.

Knox welcomes each of the Fae males with pats on the back, his face beaming at seeing his friends. Turning to face Hazel and me, Knox gestures to us. His deep smile accompanied by his dimples. "This is Hazel and Delilah."

"We have a lot to catch up on it seems," a long blond-haired Fae male drawls.

"Indeed," Knox says. Stepping into the middle of the group, a wide grin, accompanied by his dimples, spreads across his cheeks. "This is my court, my family."

A dark-haired male steps forward, his tousled locks resting at his jawline. His roguish face and strong bone structure make his amber eyes stand out as they sear into Hazel and me while he smirks. "Are you going to introduce us, Knox?"

Knox's eyes are on me, assessing, before he turns back to the group, waving his hand at the wolfish Fae that stepped forward. "This is Lenox. Ignore majority of the things he says," Knox drones, making a show of ignoring Lenox's protests.

The others in the group laugh at his grumbles. The blond-haired Fae male steps forward, his hazel eyes less friendly.

"This is Nolan," Knox introduces.

When I turn to Nolan, he's already staring me down, his hazel eyes unflinching.

Knox draws my attention to the two males at the back. The moment they step forward my heart drops. Twins.

They're twins yet entirely different, the Fae version of yin and yang. One is covered in various black tattoos, a set of tattooed wings spanning the front of his neck, with black wavy hair curling around the tips of his ears and green eyes. It's not that their faces are identical that surprises me; it's that the other one looks eerily similar to Easton. He's clean cut with short ash brown hair, golden tan skin, and forest green eyes. He smiles at me and it's filled with genuine warmth —kindness.

That smile steals the breath from me.

Knox introduces them as Axel and Ace. I can't stop staring at Ace, but I have to shake myself out of it. If I keep looking at him and his welcoming expression, I'll cry. Turning to Knox, I see the question in his eyes at my unusual reaction, yet he doesn't say anything. Instead, he gestures to the woman. Her straight black hair, with red streaks through-out, rests above her shoulders. She's stunning, with honey-toned skin, round brown eyes, and pouty lips. She smiles at Hazel and me. "I'm Harlow." She cocks her head to the side as a devious smile spreads across her lips. "Knox's unofficial sister."

My head snaps to Knox.

*I'm an idiot.*

A giant, hormone-crazed idiot.

Hazel looks between Knox and Harlow. "Unofficial?" she questions.

I breathe a sigh of relief, thankful that Hazel asked the question. I don't think I can speak right now, unless it's to call myself stupid. Gazing at Knox and Harlow, they look nothing alike. They couldn't even pass as distant relatives.

"Knox took me in as a family member when we met," Harlow says dismissively, as if it's not important at all.

Lenox scoffs, a wolfish grin on his lips. "He's the only one that could tolerate you."

"Yet he kept you as a pet," she taunts, making the men in the room burst into laughter as Lenox mutters vulgar words under his breath.

"Are you going to tell us what the hell happened while we were away?" Nolan asks, the most unwelcoming of them all.

Knox sighs. "Short version, Delilah is from the human lands, and we're working together to free the entrapment spell," he says casually, adjusting his shirt.

Hazel and I freeze as the air in the room shifts. No one's laughing or teasing anymore.

Nolan stalks toward me, his face twisting into a sneer. "And you believed such a story?"

"Nolan, back down," Axel demands, frowning at his behavior.

Hazel stays rooted to the spot. I, however, back up with each step Nolan takes. He ignores Axel and keeps coming. He's shorter than Knox yet far more intimidating.

"She's probably the queen's spy and you've gone and told her everything," he barks.

I flinch at his outburst.

No sooner do my shoulders lift does a body appear in front of me, the scent of pinewood surrounding me, soothing me.

"Back the fuck off," Knox growls.

I don't dare move. I don't care if that makes me a coward. I'm not getting in the middle of a pissing contest with two grown Fae men.

"We'll discuss everything over dinner. You're welcome to join if you lose the piss-poor attitude," Knox snaps.

I haven't heard Knox use such a commanding voice before.

I don't see whether Nolan backs away, as my view is engulfed by the taut muscles of Knox's back.

The foyer remains silent for a moment. I look to Hazel who's eyeing Nolan, assessing. The tension in the room dissipates as several footsteps echo throughout the foyer, retreating into the dining room.

Without a word, Knox follows his court.

In the dining room, Knox is at his usual seat. Mine and Hazel's spots sit vacant. Axel and Ace sit to my right, while Harlow, Nolan, and Lenox are beside Hazel on her side of the table. Food appears once we're all seated, more than I've ever seen on one table. And that's saying something considering the spread at Mia's.

Knox's court wastes no time digging into it all as if they've been starved for weeks.

Lenox groans. "I missed this so fucking much."

Harlow rolls her eyes. "What? Does the princess not like the food on the road?"

Lenox's gaze sweeps Harlow from top to bottom. "Says the one with freshly washed and styled hair…Did the forest do that for you, Low?"

Harlow clicks her tongue as she throws her red-streaked hair over her shoulder. "Unlike you, I prefer to be clean. I don't lick myself like a dog."

Snickers ring out around the table. Even Hazel bites her lip, trying to hold her laughter in.

My palms are clammy as I serve myself seasoned roast and vegetables.

"How did you get through the border?" Axel's deep voice asks beside me, the darker half of Easton's doppelgänger.

His words halt all other conversations around the table.

I swallow through the dryness of my throat. "A pendant my mother gave me was cast with an unveiling spell. I walked right through." I stare at Axel; his appearance is intimidating, yet I don't feel afraid in his presence.

"When did you transform?" he asks, taking a sip of his wine.

"As I crossed over."

"Fitting that the first person to be able to enter these lands since the spell was cast is a human who suddenly turned into a Fae," Nolan grits out, his neck turning stark red against his light blond hair.

All eyes are on me now. Anxiety pulses through my body, my heart beating so fast it makes me feel like I've just gotten back from training.

Hazel narrows her eyes at Nolan, a slight sneer on her lips as she says, "I found her in a rowboat tied to my dock—" Hazel looks to Knox for confirmation to reveal the rest. At his shallow nod, she continues, "Delilah was brought to me by the mermaids."

That silences everyone.

Harlow whistles, breaking the silence. "Damn, this shit gets more interesting by the second."

"They gave Delilah riddles to complete. She found the first, which led to me, and the second we're still working on," Knox explains.

I focus on my plate as Knox catches everyone up on what's happened over the past several weeks. When he finishes, nobody has a teasing remark or joke to break the ice.

"How do we know that her story is true?" Nolan asks from across the table.

Harlow openly frowns while Lenox shakes his head in disgust.

"I read her mind, Nolan, that's how," Knox says, his voice as cold as death.

Nolan turns to me, surprise flashing in his eyes before he lowers his gaze. His Adam's apple bobs as he swallows. Hazel-colored eyes lift to mine, his face sheepish as he says, "I apologize. The queen has spies everywhere, and it's unheard of anyone passing through the border."

Not the best apology I've heard, yet I don't feel like being scrutinized by him again. "I understand," I say, returning to my food.

It feels weird to me that not only am I sitting in a court meeting and speaking, but that I'm eating dinner with them. It's so different from how my father operated at the palace that it makes me fidgety.

"The entrapment spell was truly cast with dark magic?" Harlow asks.

Knox nods. "Unfortunately, yes. How did the scouting mission go?"

Harlow swirls her glass as she speaks. "The queen's guards have been dwindling. Nobody knows where they've disappeared to."

Lenox leans forward. "There were reports of the aerial legion acting out."

Knox lowers his wine glass. "In what way?"

"The beasts refuse to fly near the northern end of the island," Axel chimes in.

The memory of Creseda refusing to go near the In-between floats through my mind, along with the numerous times the animals in the forest vanished when a demonic creature was near. Perhaps animals can sense not only the demonic creatures but the dark magic they possess. I look around the room as they all cut each other off to offer their thoughts on why that could be. I bite my lip, wondering if I can—

*We're not formal here, Angel. If you have an idea you're encouraged to speak.*

I look over at Knox. His eyes are on me, not paying attention to his court in the slightest.

"What did you say, Delilah?" he asks casually, taking a sip of wine.

*Bastard.*

All eyes turn to me again.

Squaring my shoulders, I offer, "Perhaps the animals sense the demons and their dark magic. When the demonic creatures were present, it's as if they all vanish entirely."

Knox nods. "We'll go to the aerial legion after the Eclipse Ball," he says roughly.

Harlow claps her hands. "I've got the most stunning dress—"

"You say that every year," Lenox mumbles

Harlow narrows her eyes. "And I have the best dress every year."

"If you say so," Lenox sing-songs, lifting his fork to his mouth.

"Excuse me for not taking fashion advice from the man who wore the same shirt for a year," she taunts.

Ace spews his wine across the dining table, wetting Lenox and Nolan in the process. Everyone around the table bursts into a fit of laughter.

"You said that was just a rumor!" Ace blurts.

"They're a loud bunch but you'll get used to them," Axel whispers beside me.

I turn to him with a small smile of appreciation. Besides speaking about court matters, Axel hasn't talked much throughout dinner. His brother seems to be the chatty one of the two. If it isn't about work Axel appears to remain silent.

Lenox's scoffing draws me across the table.

"It is a rumor," he grumbles, wiping wine off his shirt.

"What's the Eclipse Ball?" I ask, wondering if it's indeed the same ball all the royals were murdered at, and if so, why they would still celebrate considering what happened.

Harlow gasps. "Are you depriving her of the Eclipse Ball?" she whines to Knox.

Knox rolls his eyes. "No, Harlow."

"Thank the heavens." Focusing all her attention on me, she explains, "It's an annual masked ball. Everyone is required to come, and it's amazing." She leans forward, placing her forearms on the table. "It's held during the yearly eclipse. Twenty-four hours of darkness and more than half the time is spent partying…amongst other activities."

I turn to Hazel. "Are you going?" I ask.

Hazel beams. "This year I am."

"I'll take you shopping." Harlow winks, flicking her red-streaked hair.

Hazel rolls her eyes. "Good luck. I've been trying to take her shopping for weeks."

Delight shines in Harlow's eyes. "Challenge accepted!"

Knox rests his head in his hands. "Are you finished?"

Harlow waves her hand in the air. "Continue with talk of those pesky little things."

Lenox chuckles. "I'd hardly call dragons *little*."

My head snaps up, my heart pounding at the word. "Dragons?"

"Dragons and griffins make up the aerial legion," Ace chimes in. "I have a beautiful white griffin. He stays on the island when I travel."

*They're alive, Easton.*

Lenox must take my silence for fear, smirking at me from across the table. "Scared of dragons?" he teases.

"I'm sitting at a table with you, aren't I?" I say, taking a sip of my water.

Lenox howls with laughter as he turns to Knox. "I like her."

Knox's head falls into his palm, his shoulders shaking on a silent chuckle.

"You like anything that's female and moves," Harlow quips.

"At least I have a heart," Lenox mocks, making Harlow roll her eyes.

"We've been through this, sweetie... I'm only half-witch." She cocks her head. "Do you need a moment to understand?"

"You're a witch?" I blurt. "But you're nice."

"On a good day," Lenox mutters.

Harlow points a long red-manicured nail at me. "Half-witch." She winks. "I have fire and shadow magic."

Knox interrupts. "Harlow is my spy."

Taking in her stunning looks, I can see how men would underestimate her. A slow smile spreads across her face as crackling embers of fire and shadow swirl around her.

Oh, they most certainly would underestimate her.

I open my mouth to ask why she doesn't live with them, only for Harlow to cut me off. "They abandoned me. The bitches couldn't deal with a half-breed Fae."

That's why Knox took her in...She had no one.

"Lenox is my third-in-command," Knox cuts in, changing the subject.

Lenox's eyes alight with red fire. "Don't forget warrior—"

"Of course, because being a warrior is *oh so highly* important," Harlow quips.

Knox cuts off their bickering. "Born warriors' senses are more enhanced than a Fae's. They're built to weather through wars."

"Do you have to be born a warrior to join?" I ask.

"No, anyone can join. Although those who are born warriors move up in the ranks quicker."

"I'm the commander of Knox's armies," Nolan says around his fork.

That doesn't surprise me at all.

I know he apologized, but he didn't leave a good first impression on me, and it'll take a lot more than a half-assed apology to feel comfortable around him.

"Who do the warriors serve?"

"Aloriah. The royals of each court have their own personal army, people serving them from their own court lands. However, the warriors from the Fire Court serve to protect Aloriah as a whole."

I turn my gaze to the silent Fae beside me. "Where do you fit in here?"

"Axel is my second in command," Knox explains.

"What powers do you possess?" I ask him.

"Air and Earth," Axel replies casually, the wing tattoo on his neck bunching as his Adam's apple bobs.

"What court are you from, Hazel?" Ace asks softly.

"Earth," she states proudly.

I look over in time to see Ace give Hazel a gorgeous smile, making her cheeks heat. Oh, I am *so* going to tease her over this after all the nonsense she gives me about Knox.

Ace beams. "I'm Earth and Water."

That's interesting. How do identical twins end up with

different powers? I slide my gaze to Hazel, catching a flash of pain in her eyes. Oh.

Ace has the same powers as Luna.

Knox's deep husky voice drags my gaze away. "Ace is my emissary."

Now that makes sense. Ace is the friendliest of all the males. I can see him spreading peace throughout a group; he's too loveable to be angry at.

"Do you all live here?" I ask.

Knox said his court lived at the other end of the hall a level below us, but it doesn't seem like the house is big enough for all their personalities.

Harlow shudders. "God no. Too much testosterone. I live in an apartment by the ocean."

"The twins and Lenox live in the house," Knox cuts in smoothly.

Nolan's quiet when he speaks, sadness coating his words. "I live in my mother and sister's house."

"Who should go to the aerial legion?" Axel chimes in.

I frown at Axel's sudden change in conversation, my eyes glued to Nolan's face as sadness lines his eyes.

"You and Ace. I need Lenox and Harlow to scout for the demonic hounds." Knox addresses me. "Delilah, care to join us?"

Everyone at the table besides Hazel stares at me, waiting for my answer.

Is this a test to them? To see if I'll truly help them?

"Of course," I reply smoothly.

Hazel chimes in, taking her eyes off Ace, "I'll continue sorting through the dark magic books. I have three more to go."

Knox nods, ending the discussion of work.

Harlow and Lenox waste no time as they begin taunting each other.

Bubbles of water float in front of me as I lay in the clawfoot tub, practicing my water magic. I tried going to sleep hours ago but was unable to shut my mind off. The more time I spend with Knox and the more I get to know him, the more my body seems to want him. Reacting before my mind can shut down the involuntary responses.

For heaven's sake, I was jealous at the thought of Knox having a lover. Knox is nothing but a flirt, but apparently his flirting has confused my hormones.

Perhaps being in a Fae body heightens your emotions… After all, everything else is heightened. I certainly never used to feel hot and bothered while training with men.

Groaning, I slide my head under the water.

Knox is the least of my worries and shouldn't be consuming my thoughts. So what if my body is attracted to him? Who wouldn't be? The man's practically a walking sex god, and my body is simply enjoying the sight.

I run my hands through my hair as I breach the water.

I need to have full concentration on the tasks at hand. So many lives depend on it, yet here I am obsessing over why I felt jealous over Knox. I can't be distracted by his charm or good looks; I need to focus on learning magic, finding the dark magic book, helping my people and the trapped Fae.

I can make a difference here. I can help.

This is all temporary…I simply need to focus.

# Chapter Thirty

"Where's Hazel?" Knox asks, leaning against my bedroom door.

Putting down the sword I was cleaning, I look at him through the vanity mirror. "She's started working on the books already."

Knox scans me from head to toe. "I can't give you any lessons today."

"Oh, okay."

I'm shocked to feel disappointment flutter through me. I've come to enjoy our lessons in the garden. Such a silly notion to get attached to them—I know better than that.

Knox kicks off the door, striding toward me. "I have to go with Nolan to the warrior island and smooth a few things over," he explains.

I give him a small smile. "No problem."

As Knox stands there staring at me, not saying anything, butterflies take flight in my stomach, my nerves making me want to fill the silence.

"What's the warrior island?" I ask.

"It's an island off the coast of Fire and Air Court. It's

where all of Aloriah's warriors are sent to train. They live there for several years until they graduate from a trainee to a full-fledged warrior."

I turn back to my dragon pommel sword, cleaning the silver with oil. "That sounds fascinating."

"Delilah, I—"

"Knox!" Nolan blares from somewhere in the house.

Knox's shoulders stiffen. He looks at me for a moment before walking to the door. "I'll see you later this evening," he calls over his shoulder.

After training for two hours, bathing while practicing water magic, and walking around Knox's house aimlessly, I think it's safe to say that I'm antsy today. If I stop moving, I'll begin analyzing why I'm so fidgety and nervous, and if I do that, I'll have to admit to myself why I miss Knox's company.

Exactly like I am right now.

I've been sitting in Knox's library trying to read the same paragraph for thirty minutes, yet my mind won't let me relax. Slamming the book shut, I leap to my feet and head for the back garden. Just because Knox isn't here doesn't mean I shouldn't be practicing magic; I don't need him to run through simple exercises.

The moment I walk outside, I pause. Ace and Lenox are shirtless, dueling with swords and magic. Where one swipes with a sword the other strikes with a fire or air shield, alternating between magic and weapons to defend and attack.

They haven't noticed my presence yet and with a single thought, I cloak myself.

I take a seat on the last of the veranda steps, placing my

feet on the soft grass, marveling at how precise the men's techniques are. They each run through various moves, trying to outdo the other, yet nobody is getting in any victory hits. My focus is drawn toward Ace, watching him move in black fighting leathers. He smiles each time after nearly striking Lenox, reminding me of Easton.

If he were still here, the twins would look like triplets.

Shaking myself out of my thoughts I uncloak myself. Leaning back on the steps I clap, laughter bubbling from me when the men jolt. Good to know that even the Fae can be scared.

"Holy shit," Lenox exclaims. Lifting his sword, he points to me, a wolfish grin on his face. "Just for that, you're tapping in."

I smile internally. He doesn't think I can fight.

Rising, I slouch my shoulders, wringing my hands. "I did some training at home. Obviously not at this level though."

Lenox rolls his shoulders. "That's fine, everyone starts somewhere."

Ace eyes me curiously as he passes me his sword.

I make a show of concentrating on entering a defensive position, shuffling my foot this way and that, as if I rarely place my hips and feet in the position. I raise my sword, loosening my wrist as I stare into Lenox's amber eyes.

Lenox lunges, his right foot stepping forward as he tries to strike my side. With his fire shield covering his front, his left is vulnerable. I grin as I whirl, spinning around to lunge forward, striking his open side. Surprise flares in Lenox's eyes as he tries to right himself, but too late.

Crouching, I roll forward so fast Lenox doesn't see me coming. I use all my strength to knock his legs out from under him. The moment his back connects with the grass, my blade is poised at his neck, an arrow of flame hovering above his heart.

My smile is serpentine as I peer down at him. "I win."

Ace bursts out laughing behind me. "I can't believe you fell for that crap, Lenox."

Outrage fills Lenox's expression. "You knew?"

"Who do you think was making all that noise in the training room this morning?"

Lenox shakes his head, muttering expletives under his breath.

I offer him my hand. "Regardless of your deceit, that was impressive," Lenox admits as he stands.

I smile. "I would love for you to train me," I say to Lenox.

Lenox's mouth hangs open, his eyes widening.

I realize it's highly inappropriate of me to ask. Just because Knox is teaching me magic doesn't mean his court owes me anything. If I had asked my father's court at home for any help I would have been yelled at for hours and whipped. They wouldn't help me even if I was on fire.

"Sorry, I shouldn't have asked," I rush on.

Lenox runs his fingers through his dark hair. "No, it's all right. I'm just—you seem to be able to hold your own. Clearly." He chuckles.

"I've had some trouble adjusting to the enhanced…abilities. After watching you two, I know there's more to learn."

Lenox beams. "I'd love to."

That was surprisingly easy. I smile back. "Amazing!"

"What time do you train?" he asks, crossing his arms over his chest.

"Usually in the mornings before my lessons with Knox."

Ace frowns. "Where is Knox? Aren't you meant to train soon?"

"He's with Nolan at the warrior island," Lenox answers for me.

"We can teach you instead," Ace offers, his kind eyes sparking with excitement.

*Why is everyone so kind here?*

It should make me feel welcome, but it's so unusual that anyone in a court who isn't Annie or Easton would show kindness to me. It makes me feel uneasy, as if I'm a burden.

"I already intruded on your—"

"We should teach her how to fly," Ace says to Lenox, completely ignoring my protests.

That gets my attention. "I don't have wings," I point out.

"Yes you do," they say in unison.

"Knox gave us a rundown of your magic," Ace explains, a warm smile on his lips. "You have too much power not to have wings. You just don't know how to make them appear yet."

I blink. "Are you telling me that I have wings inside of me that I just…haven't found yet?"

"It's unheard of for a Fae to possess as much magic as you do and not have wings," Lenox cuts in.

Knox said something similar to me, yet my mind can't process the idea of ginormous wings hiding somewhere within me.

"Well, where the hell are they and what do they feel like?"

"It's a form of shifting. You transform yourself," Ace explains.

"Transform," I state flatly.

Lenox crosses his arms over his chest. "Yes, you have to completely accept your Fae form."

When all I do is look at Lenox blankly, Ace chimes in

with his own explanation. "It feels like going from ninety percent Fae to one hundred percent Fae."

I shake my head. "Still not understanding how I make wings flourish from my back."

Lenox chuckles. "What makes you access your powers in the first place?"

I shrug. "I just use my imagination."

"So imagine you have wings," he says, as if it's the easiest thing in the world.

I look between Lenox and Ace's serious expression, making a mental note to never let them teach me about magic. They're horrible at explaining.

I take a step back. There's no harm in trying. Worst case, I become their entertainment for ten minutes. Taking a deep breath, I try to picture wings, imagining there's a small opening in my back where they're tucked away safely. Knox's gorgeous face floats in my mind, his beautiful black wings blooming to life at his back.

Diving deep within myself, I find my well of magic. Instead of it looking at me with a sleepy eye like it did that first day in the forest with Hazel, it's fully awake and ready to play. I dip my toes into the well, slowly submerging my entire body inside. It should feel like swimming in water, yet it feels like floating on a cloud. Iridescent white light surrounds me, swirling and twinkling with different colors as I move. I tilt my head back, letting my magic surround me, pulse through me, become me.

Lenox and Ace gasp before I feel the shift. A sudden weight is on my back, trying to drag me down. Shifting my stance and back muscles to accommodate the new weight, I open my eyes. On a deep exhalation, wings spread across my back, the shadow in front of me outlining my body with large wings to confirm what I'm feeling.

*I have wings.*

Ace falls back on his ass at the same time Lenox stumbles backward, more gracefully than Ace's outright tumble. They both start swearing in unison, and my internal panic alights. I turn to see what's behind me, the added weight of the wings making me slower than usual. My peripheral vision picks up a golden glow, but I can't get a good look. They're both staring at me with open mouths. I don't think they're even breathing.

I frown. "Did I do it wrong?"

Ace tries to speak. Nothing but mumbling nonsense comes out. Lenox is worse, his entire face stark white.

"Someone explain why you're both freaking out!" I blurt.

"They...your...They're gold," Lenox stutters.

"Are they not supposed to be gold?" I ask, confused.

Ace slowly shakes his head, his mouth opening and closing as he tries to speak.

A white light flashes in the garden before Knox suddenly appears in front of me, his eyes wide and full of shock while Nolan trails behind him, frowning deeply at my wings. Knox couldn't have come back at a better time, as if he could feel my distress.

"Can someone tell me why you're all looking at me like I have three heads?"

"Nobody has gold wings," Ace breathes, awe coating his every word.

I have never been more confused in my life. I turn to Knox for confirmation, finding his eyes locked behind me on my wings. "It's impossible."

I throw my hands in the air. "You're not making any sense!" I snap.

"The only creatures that have gold wings are griffins and angels," Knox murmurs.

My brows furrow. "Are you trying to tell me that I have angel wings?"

"No, they've been extinct for centuries." He shakes his head. "The angel wings were different than the Faes'. They were feathered. Yours are the same material as ours, but gold."

A feeling of familiarity washes over me—serenity.

My frown deepens. "Then why do I have gold wings?"

A smile spreads across Knox's face. "I have no idea, but they're beautiful."

My cheeks heat. He didn't call me beautiful, he called my *wings* beautiful. It feels the same nonetheless.

"They shimmer," Ace whispers in awe.

Snapping out of the trance Knox's declaration put me in, I slam my wings closed, the weight of them knocking together, making me stumble. I tuck that part of myself back into the deep well of magic. Ignoring the men's whines and protests, I head back inside.

I have to see them for myself, without all the eyes on me.

Standing in front of the bathroom mirror, I prepare myself for what I'm about to see. Seeing my elongated ears every time I passed my reflection took some time to adjust to, but accepting wings seems like an entirely different thing.

I immerse within myself, to the part that contains and holds my magic. I fully submerge myself, letting the magic become me.

Peering at myself in the mirror as iridescent gold wings flutter across my back will be a memory I cherish as long as I live.

My breath leaves me on a gasp. Covering my hand over

my mouth, I can't stop staring. I twist to both sides, looking at them from every direction.

As the gold wings spread to their full width, I find they're longer than my arm length. When I move, the leathery gold skin glows, twinkling where the sun shines through the window. They're slightly different from the others' wings. Where theirs slope at the top, mine curve to a point. The color starts off light at my torso, so bright it's almost white, then darkens as it travels upward, the tips of the wings so dark it's almost yellow.

I'm about to try and flap them when my bedroom door opens. In the next moment, Knox strolls through my bathroom, leaning against the door. He crosses one ankle over the other, sliding his hands in his pockets. He looks as amazed as I am.

"You truly don't know why they're gold?" I ask.

"I wish I had an answer for you. They're truly magnificent." He slides his sapphire eyes to mine. "I apologize if we made you uncomfortable. It isn't every day someone has gold wings. Forgive us for being curious."

I shrug. "I wanted to see them for myself."

Knox stares at me intently, his eyes heating. I look away, not daring to read into it.

His husky voice caresses my spine as it echoes through the bathroom. "Getting them out is one thing. Leaning to fly is another thing entirely."

"I figured. They're surprisingly heavy," I say, earning a dark chuckle from Knox. The sound sends goosebumps scattering down my arms.

The bathroom suddenly feels extremely small for two people to occupy. Retracting my wings, I edge past Knox, pinewood surrounding me as I take a seat on the futon at the end of my bed. "How exactly does one learn to fly?"

Knox twists his body to face mine, the heat I saw earlier gone. "We can work on that lesson later. I actually came to warn you."

I blink. "Warn me?"

"Harlow is on her way up here, and she's decided to make it her mission to take you shopping. Good luck saying no to her."

I internally chastise myself. Of course he wouldn't follow me up here to check on me. He just wanted to give a polite warning to a friend—*are we friends*? I think the lack of human decency in the palace back home has damaged me so thoroughly I have to overthink whether someone is truly a friend or not. How pathetically sad.

"I'm looking forward to going shopping actually," I say.

I don't mention the issue that I have no money. I don't want him to think I want anything from him besides our deal to work with each other.

I plan to look at many stunning dresses, picture them in my mind and how beautiful it would be to wear them, and then pretend to not find anything I like with a smile on my face.

"That's great news. I can't be bothered to bargain with anyone today," Harlow announces as she saunters into my room.

Speak of the devil and she appears.

Harlow looks stunning in tight-fitted leather pants and a cropped navy shirt.

"I'll leave you to it," Knox says.

"Tell Hazel we'll be down in a moment!" Harlow calls out.

My gaze trails Knox as he strides out of the room, his large frame oozing sensual confidence. His arms sway beside his torso, the protruding veins making his muscles appear even more—

"Are you done ogling him?" Harlow croons.

My eyes widen. Shooting up, I walk past her. "Don't be ridiculous," I snap.

Harlow's sultry laugh follows me all the way down to the foyer.

"You look absolutely beautiful, Hazel," I say in awe. Hazel stands in front of Harlow and I in a gorgeous emerald green floor-length dress. The material hugs her curves in all the right places. She looks like a bombshell with the split running down her thigh, showing off her legs.

Harlow whistles. "God damn."

"It's not too much?" Hazel asks nervously.

Harlow and I shake our heads profusely. "Gods no, it's perfect."

"Ace will love it," Harlow says flippantly as she rifles through the racks of dresses.

I guess I'm not the only one who's caught onto the teasing smiles and blushes coming from the two of them.

Hazel's eyes widen, the tips of her ears turning red.

"What about this one?" Harlow asks me, holding up a silver floor-length dress.

I shake my head even as my heart cries out in protest. "Not my thing."

Harlow rolls her eyes. "Nothing is your *thing*."

This has been the routine for every store. Harlow shows me numerous dresses I pretend to not be dying to try on and she gets irritated. I think Harlow and Hazel have forgotten that I come from the human lands and have no money.

I certainly haven't.

Without Hazel and Knox, I probably would have died by now.

"We've gone into every decent store, and you still haven't found anything you like!" Hazel protests, backing up Harlow.

"I'll come look for something tomorrow before the ball."

Harlow deadpans, "All the stores will be shut. Nothing is open during the eclipse."

Shit.

"I'll just wear one of Hazel's dresses," I blurt. They both wince in unison. I roll my eyes. "You're both acting like it's the end of the world. It's just a ball."

"An extraordinary ball," Harlow mutters.

"I'll find something to wear, I promise," I say, smiling.

Hazel looks at me quizzically before moving on to pay for the dress she picked out while Harlow assesses me like I've grown another head.

Walking out of the store, I wait for them to join me. It's peak dinnertime and the streets are nearly deserted. Everyone is apparently already prepared for the eclipse tomorrow or at home starting the celebrations early. The only thing to keep me company are the twinkling embers of fires dangling overhead, the salty breeze from the ocean, and the night sky shining down on me.

I've never felt this peaceful in a city before. Come to think of it, I don't think I've ever felt this peaceful. Besides my time with Easton and Annie, there was never a moment where I walked around the palace and thought, *what a beautiful place to call home.*

Standing in a silent street in Azalea, my chest feels warm, my heart safe, screaming for me to stay.

A bell chimes overhead as Harlow struts out of the store. I've yet to see her walk another way. Hazel joins us a moment later, a white bag dangling from her hand, her emerald green dress inside.

Walking beside the girls, I voice the question that's been nagging me for days. "If the Queen of Air is the only one in power, why do the other courts have their titles of king and queen?"

Hazel shrugs. "I was raised with the courts having kings and queens. That's how I view them."

Harlow chimes in, "It's respect. No matter what the Queen of Air says, the courts view the heirs as kings and queens. I know everyone in Azalea looks to Knox as their king. It has nothing to do with power and everything to do with loyalty and respect."

I lower my gaze to the ground, Harlow's explanation stunning me.

My people would spit on my father if it didn't mean they'd be executed. Respect and loyalty have been lost in our lands since before I was born.

Harlow chuckles to herself. "Even the Air Court residents don't agree with the old hag."

Hazel gasps. "You can't call her a hag!"

Harlow simply waves her hand, dismissing Hazel. "I can call her what I see fit. She's old and still views the royal families as children. It's preposterous."

I frown. "When will the courts be reinstated to rule as a democracy again?"

Harlow rolls her eyes. "Probably not until the queen kicks the bucket."

"You can't say things like that!" Hazel snaps.

Harlow raises a brow, turning in a circle she splays her arms. "Who's here to tell her?"

"She has spies everywhere," Hazel whisper-yells.

I look between the two of them. "Why does she have spies?"

Harlow rolls her eyes. "She believes they'll help her find out who cast the entrapment spell."

"Clearly it's not working," I mutter.

# Chapter Thirty-One

Once we return to Knox's home against Harlow's protests to continue searching for a dress, she surprisingly drops the matter of what I'm going to wear. Which is a relief because I was running out of excuses to give her.

After changing into more comfortable clothes for dinner I'm seated in my usual spot next to Knox and Axel, as Lenox and Harlow bicker. I've come to realize that this is their usual thing, teasing and taunting each other until one of them snaps. If I didn't know any better, I would say it's their form of fore-play, yet Harlow insists that she only views the men in Knox's court as brothers.

"Planning to disappear again this Eclipse Ball, Harlow?" Lenox grins.

"Wouldn't you like to know?"

Lenox shovels food into his mouth. "Believe me, I've heard."

"The rest of us haven't and we'd like to keep our appetites," Nolan grumbles.

Perhaps that's why he's so grumpy—he's constantly in the middle of their bickering.

Lenox snorts. "Like you haven't done half the shit she's done."

"With the same women," Harlow coos.

Lenox's grin is feral. "With the tally of men and women you have on your belt, I'd say more."

My gaze meets Hazel's, both of our lips twitching as we try not to laugh.

"I'd rather not hear about your sexual indiscretions, Lenox." Knox swirls his wine. "Again."

"When does the ball start?" I ask.

Harlow rolls her eyes. "Not until the evening. The first half of the day is spent on rituals." She snickers. "They act like they're so holy—"

"They are holy," Nolan argues.

Harlow narrows her eyes at him. "They're not better than anyone else just because they wear robes and preach to the stars."

"Does everyone attend the ceremonies?" I cut in.

Knox shakes his head. "It's more for the priestesses. They honor the lunar cycle; eclipses are seen to be cherished."

I must admit, I'm excited for the lunar eclipse. I've never experienced anything like it.

"Why don't the human lands experience the yearly eclipse?" I ask.

"Magic," Harlow sing-songs.

Knox's jaw clenches. "The priestesses believe that it's the moon goddess's gift to the Fae, to those who preach to her."

"You don't believe that?" I ask.

The entire table goes deadly silent. No one dares move or speak. Even Hazel's eyes widen at the energy shift. Is it improper to ask what one believes?

Knox isn't looking at me anymore. His eyes burn a hole into his plate. "Not anymore," he says coldly.

Harlow's overly chipper voice rings throughout the room. "I say screw the priestesses. The ball is the best part. Eclipses are meant to be spent dancing, drinking, and fucking."

"Preaching to the choir." Lenox grins.

I choke on my water. I still haven't drunk any wine here, wanting to keep a clear head at all times, but maybe at the ball I can let loose and have one or two.

Harlow groans at me. "Please don't tell me you're still a virgin."

Knox snaps his head toward her, baring his canines. "Harlow."

My cheeks heat. I'm not a virgin, far from it. I've had lovers over the years, but it's openly frowned upon in the palace to talk about the topic freely.

"Is everyone in the courts as open as you?" I ask, my voice higher than usual.

"No one's as open as Harlow," Lenox quips.

Harlow ignores him, waving her fork at me. "Well, have you?"

Dark, rumbling power ripples through the room.

"Don't coddle me," I snap at Knox. "If this is how most Fae talk, I might as well get accustomed to it." I turn to Harlow. "I've had lovers."

*None that were any good*, I don't add. The majority of the time, I just lay there, wishing for it to hurry up and be over. I've never felt the spark that the books I read tell me I should feel, and it certainly isn't the experience I've read in those books either. To say my past lovers were lackluster is an understatement.

Knox's entire body has stiffened. My stomach sinks as I realize I've just barked at a king. A powerful Fae king nonetheless. I don't know what it is about Knox, but he pushes all my buttons, bringing me out of my shell that my father conditioned me to stay in. "I'm sorry, I shouldn't have snapped," I rush out.

Knox raises a hand to silence me, his words guttural as if he has to force them out. "I misread. I apologize."

"Well, that's good. The ball will be more interesting now," Harlow continues.

I grimace. "These escapades aren't happening on the ballroom floor, are they?"

The table bursts out with laughter, every one of them giggling at my words. Even Axel chokes on a laugh. Knox is silently chuckling, which is much better than the intense version of him a moment before.

"No, sweetheart, it's not a sex club," Harlow drawls.

I look to Hazel, relieved that I'm not the only one going red in the face.

I enter my room after dinner, happy to be alone so I can soak in the tub. Instead, I walk through the door to find a large black box tied with a white ribbon sitting on the end of my bed. Did Knox get me more doughnuts?

Picking up the box, I slowly peel the ribbon off, gasping as it falls opens.

It's a dress.

A stunning gold dress, the same shade as my wings.

Tears well in my eyes at how beautiful it is. I rush into my changing room, slipping it on and standing in front of the mirror, taking in every intricate detail.

The dress is floor length, the bodice cupping my breasts and cinching my waist before flaring out at my hips. The ballgown skirt material is thick and heavy, the gold fabric flowing around my lower body as it swishes from side to side. A small slit down the side reveals my leg as I walk. Starting at the side of my chest, three gold chains dangle on each exposed arm, then wrap around my upper forearms to my back. The gold material glints and sparkles as the candle-light hits it.

Happiness fills my heart at the gesture.

I can't believe Knox bought me a dress.

# Chapter Thirty-Two

I awake to darkness and starlight. Stretching my limbs in bed, excitement fills me. There were no festivities, celebrations, or traditions at the palace. To be here, witnessing and experiencing such a tradition is a gift in itself.

It feels different to be wide awake as darkness surrounds the lands.

Rushing to get dressed and start the festivities, I don't notice the booming of laughter in the house until I descend the stairs. I follow the sounds of laughter and glasses clinking into the large sitting room.

A smile lights my face as I see Hazel smiling and giggling as she sits beside Ace. Perhaps I didn't drag her to her doom after all.

It looks like mostly everyone is inebriated. Axel is the most relaxed I've ever seen him, Ace's eyes are bleary and red, Harlow won't stop grinning, and Lenox is outright drunk. Even Nolan is smiling and laughing. The only person that's unaccounted for is Knox.

"Delilah!" Lenox jumps up, crashing into my side as he

wraps his arm around my shoulder. "We've been waiting for you," he slurs.

I turn my face away. "Your breath could stop a dragon. My gods, how much have you had?"

Lenox gives me a wobbly grin. "The right amount."

I chuckle. Disentangling myself, I take a seat next to Axel, purely because he looks the most sober out of the bunch.

Looking around the room I can't help but notice who's missing.

"He disappears during the day before the ball starts. He'll be back later," Axel whispers.

"Oh, I wasn't wondering where he was," I lie.

Axel lifts his brows, amusement filling his green eyes. Note to self—you can't lie to a Fae. They pick up on everything.

Axel leans in further, lowering his voice. "Today is the anniversary of his parents' death."

My heart sinks—of course.

With everyone's excitement about the ball later tonight I completely forgot about what happened all those years ago to Knox. I don't know the specifics; he's never brought it up—or his parents, for that matter. I only know what Hazel told me those very first days we met.

Axel pulls back, focusing on his friends and their drunk mumblings.

"Shut your fat mouth!" Harlow yells.

Lenox raises his hands in protest. "All I'm saying is that your technique could use a little work."

Harlow arches an incredulous brow. "My *technique*?"

Lenox sways as he sits on the couch. "You're a little sloppy with—"

Harlow disappears. Perhaps Lenox pushed a nerve, and she didn't—

I scream so hoarse my voice cracks. A giant black panther with glowing red eyes appears out of thin air, roaring at Lenox. He falls off the couch, clutching his stomach as he howls with laughter. *Why is everyone laughing?*

The panther disappears, only to be replaced by Harlow. She sits where Lenox just was, her smile ravenous.

"You should have seen your face!" Lenox sputters.

I sit there, unable to move. "What the fuck was that?" I snap. My outburst doesn't get me answers. No, they all start laughing harder.

Hazel takes pity on me. "Harlow is a shapeshifter," she says between giggles.

"I know that now," I grumble.

Harlow offers me wine as a peace offering, but I decline. I don't want to be drunk the whole time and forget my first Eclipse Ball; I want to at least experience a part of it sober. I try explaining that to Harlow yet she's too drunk to make sense of anything, which only proves my point.

She waves her glass around, sloshing wine all over the floor. "The eclipse is meant to be spent drunk."

"Not everyone wants to be as inebriated as you, Harlow," Lenox slurs.

"Coming from the man that's seeing two of everything."

"Three," he chirps proudly.

Nolan chuckles. "You two are insufferable."

"I, my dear, am a pure delight," Harlow teases. "Lenox just has a big head."

Lenox's mouth drops open. "My head is proportionate to my body!"

The room fills with howls of laughter, my own making my

cheeks burn. My chest feels lighter, freer as I sit with everyone. My stomach begins to ache from laughing so much it burns, especially when Lenox demands for us to measure his head.

Later that evening, I stand in front of the mirror studying myself. I've applied small amounts of gray makeup around my eyes and a rosy tint to my lips. Nothing too drastic, as the dress speaks for itself, but the eye makeup does make my ice blue eyes sparkle.

My nerves are going haywire; not only has everyone praised this event for days but I'm about to see every Fae that lives in these lands—those that attend the ball, that is. What if they can tell I'm not truly Fae, that I was once human? Will they laugh at me? Spit on me with distaste?

I shake my clammy hands out at my sides, trying to dispel the nerves. It feels like a million pins are pricking my chest.

My bedroom door opens and I turn, the end of my gold dress swirling as I do.

Hazel doesn't initially notice my distress, her eyes focused on the dress. She gasps, covering her mouth with a hand. "You look beautiful!" Her head slowly lifts to mine. "Where did you get—Delilah, what's wrong?"

"Are they going to be able to tell?" I wheeze. "That I'm not truly Fae?"

Hazel's eyes soften. "No, sweetie, you *are* Fae."

"I don't feel like one. I feel like this is all an elaborate dream."

Hazel takes my hands in hers. "I know it feels odd, and it will take you time to come to terms with it. I don't know how, and I wish I could give you those answers, but you are Fae," she says softly.

I nod, not truly believing the words. "You're right, I'm being silly."

She tugs my hand. "No, you're not being silly. It's practically a new body." Hazel takes a step back, a reassuring smile on her face. "Let's just focus on having fun tonight. All our problems will still be there for us tomorrow."

"You're right," I say sheepishly.

I've never been able to explain the anxiety that infiltrates my mind and chest. It feels as if it's always there, but I've gotten so accustomed to it that I've learned to either ignore it or embrace it being with me.

I pick up my mask, placing it over my face. The intricate gold mask covers my face from my eyebrows to the bridge of my nose, making my blue eyes sparkle against the gold tone.

As I follow Hazel down the stairs, we turn the bend to see everyone waiting in the foyer, dressed immaculately, yet I only have eyes for one.

My breath leaves me entirely. I thought it would be impossible, yet he looks even more gorgeous than usual. Knox's raven black hair is styled back, dressed in a tailored black suit tailored to fit his powerful body perfectly. A gold bow rests on his throat, an identical mask to mine in his hands.

My heart pounds for another reason entirely.

*We're matching.*

The second my heel connects with the foyer tiles, Knox lifts his eyes to mine. His gaze slowly sweeps me from top to bottom, and when he reaches my face, his eyes are blazing with heat. My stomach clenches.

Whistles ring out around the room, pulling my attention away from Knox.

"Now that's a dress." Harlow grins, making me blush. She's wearing a stunning red floor-length dress that hugs every inch of her skin, highlighting her beautiful curves. A flame red mask covers half her face.

The rest of the men are wearing tailored suits colored to their chosen element, their masks matching. Ace walks up to Hazel, a green mask dangling from his hands as he lowers his head, whispering in her ear. A smile plays on his lips as Hazel blushes profusely, her own smile mirroring Ace's.

Harlow claps her hands together. "Let's get drunk, bitches!"

"Already ahead of you," Lenox chirps proudly.

Once everyone crosses the front door threshold, they disappear. I assume no one wants to fly and ruin their clothes.

I'm about to follow when Knox steps in front of me, his eyes piercing mine as he offers his hand. I don't dare look away as I glide my hand into his warm one, electricity flying up my arm as we touch. The last thing I see before white light encompasses us is his gorgeous face, beaming down at me with a smile so beautiful liquid heat pools in my stomach.

My feet land on the ground once more, but this time, endless chatter surrounds me. Thousands of Fae in various masks and clothes line the street. The array of vast clothing is exquisite, from ballgowns to skintight clothing, different colored suits, and the matching masks decorated to suit their elemental magic.

I'm standing on a cobbled driveway, and when I turn, I come face-to-face with a brick castle, two towers framing either side. It's one of the oldest buildings I've seen, yet its age doesn't hinder its beauty—it only enhances it. The brick-work and detail on the large and imposing building is magnif-icent, weathering through the years and standing strong. Lanterns line the walkway to an arched front door, its black wood sanded to perfection.

Everything is perfectly styled and upkeep, yet I can't help

but notice the water fountain situated in the middle of the driveway has been left in despair. The seven archangels long forgotten, mold and dirt clinging to the otherwise beautiful statues.

The energy surrounding us is palpable, everyone's excitement buzzing in the air as the night's stars shine upon us. The moon is completely covered in darkness, its outer ridges glowing faintly as if to say, *I'm here*. It's exquisite to see, that something so beautiful, shrouded and hidden by darkness, can still shine bright.

The Fae around us notice Knox and his court. They start cheering, moving aside to clear a path to the entrance. Knox smiles at those who say hello.

I walk behind Axel, Harlow, Ace, and Hazel as they stride through the doors, Knox trailing behind me. Lenox and Nolan are probably already inside. At the front entrance, a petite woman stands in the threshold holding a clipboard as she scribbles down names of attendees on the paper attached. Her dark-as-night hair is slicked back into a tight ponytail, her dark navy gown flowing to the floor.

Knox appears in front of me before I can reach her. His husky voice floats through my mind.

*Cloak yourself.*

The command in his voice is jarring enough that he doesn't have to ask me twice. Everyone around me is so invested in their own experience that no one notices when I disappear. I stick close to Knox as he stops before the woman.

He lifts his chin as the woman gives him a small curtsy. "Prince Knox."

Prince, not king.

Knox lifts his chin higher as he stares the woman down. "Emmalyn."

Without another word, Knox walks inside. I don't reveal

myself until we've passed the front door. Grabbing Knox's arm, I drag him to the side, into the shadows, as other attendees pass us.

"Why did I have to cloak myself?" I whisper.

Knox leans against the wall, shrouding me from those who pass us. He speaks so quietly I have to lean forward into his warmth to hear him. "I don't want the Queen of Air to know about you and how you got here. I don't know what she'd do with you."

I blink. "Emmalyn's the Queen of Air?"

Knox shakes his head. "Her second, and her best spy."

That explains why she called him prince and not king.

Knox pushes off the wall. "Enough about that. Enjoy your time, Delilah."

Trailing behind Knox through the entryway, a smile spreads across my face. Large doesn't begin to describe the sheer size of the ballroom. You could fit Knox's entire estate in here. The walls are painted black, embers of fire twinkling in crystal chandeliers on the ceiling, surrounding the circle skylight window. In the direct center of the skylight is a view of the eclipse. Round tables circle the outer skirts of the room, leaving a wide berth for those who wish to dance. Each table is adorned with ten gold seats, white tulips and various candles are placed beautifully as the centerpieces.

Music blares all around us. Multiple live bands and singers play in unison, set up in each corner of the room. Servers in all black, wearing moon-styled masks, walk around the room, serving endless amounts of wine and food. Several trays pass by me stacked with glasses of red and white wine and an array of skewers. The aroma of lamb, roast, and chicken makes my mouth salivate.

Hazel and Harlow come to my side. Taking my arms, they drag me to the center of the room where everyone is dancing, smiles spreading across their face. The music pulses through my veins, taking over my entire body, urging me to move, to join, to celebrate. I lose myself in the music, letting it overtake my body, giving it what it wants. Happiness explodes within me, making me smile so wide my cheeks start to ache.

Harlow stops a server as he walks past, taking three glasses of red wine. I don't protest or say no this time. Taking a sip from the crystal glass, my chest vibrates as I moan. Everything is better in a Fae body, wine included. The rich flavor dances on my tongue, soothing my muscles instantly. My mind buzzes as the strong liquid runs havoc through my veins. All my nerves evaporate as I completely surrender myself to the experience. I dance until my feet hurt and drink until I no longer feel them.

The music overtakes everyone in the room, as if the instruments and those playing them have put magic into the very melodies they weave. It feels like we've been dancing for hours when I look up to see where the men have disappeared to.

I spot Ace first, standing next to a male I've never seen before. His companion's hands move a thousand miles an hour as he speaks, yet Ace only has eyes for Hazel as she dances beside me. I've never seen her so carefree, as if the music commands her to let go too. Harlow is purely wicked as she dances, oozing sexuality.

Scanning the room as I dance, I'm about to give up searching when I spot him.

Only for my heart to be lodged in my throat.

Knox is smiling and dancing with a stunning woman in a black dress, her hands all over him, caressing his arms, his stomach. When she sinks her long manicured fingers through his hair, I feel red hot jealousy burn through me.

Of course he's with a stunning blonde Fae. Why would a

Fae king be interested in a human has-been? I was stupid to read into his kindness as flirting. I was nothing but entertainment to pass the time.

*Don't worry, Angel, I'll save a dance for you.*

Bile rises in my throat, my eyes burning as his deep voice floats through my mind. I slam my mental shields up.

Stupid. I feel utterly stupid.

Any happiness and joy I felt moments ago has completely evaded me. I turn away from Harlow and Hazel, not wanting to add to the embarrassment of Knox not only reading my mind but the girls seeing me cry over him. Navigating through the throng of happy Fae dancing only adds salt to my already burning wounds.

I spot a dark hallway on the other side of the room, sighing in relief when I find it deserted. I don't care where I go, I just need to get out. I feel like I can't breathe.

My vision blurs as tears line my eyes, so much so I don't see the male that appears before me. I smack into his chest with a grunt, pinewood stuffing its way down my nose. I squeeze my eyes shut, refusing to let Knox see me cry. It's my own fault, my own damn fault that I read into things wrong. I step away until my back feels the bite of the cold brick wall.

"Careful, Angel, your feelings are showing."

I snap my eyes open. *How dare he.* Rage replaces the heartache as Knox peers down at me, nothing showing through his cold mask of indifference. *Perhaps it isn't a mask.*

He slowly leans forward, placing both of his hands against the wall beside my head, caging me in with his body. "Going somewhere?"

"Why the hell do you care?" I spit.

Knox clenches his jaw so hard I hear his teeth snap shut.

"I'm just a tool to free your world." I push against his

chest with all my strength, each word I spit at him enunciated with a shove. "Why. Do. You. Fucking. Care!"

Knox doesn't move an inch. All I succeed in doing is placing my hands on his warm chest. I rip my hands away as if I was burned. His eyes narrow as he glares at me. Fury pulses from him as if he can't contain it anymore. *Why the hell is he so irritated?*

"Because your thoughts are irritating," he growls.

"If you stopped invading my mind, you wouldn't be so irritated!"

He shakes his head in astonishment. "You truly don't see it."

"See what?" I say through gritted teeth.

"I'm giving you time, Delilah."

I fling my arms out beside me, all the fight leaving me. "Time for what?!"

"To grieve! To not hate me!" he snaps. His voice lowers as he continues, "You hated me when we met...*hated* me. You hate kings and you hated them even more after your father killed Easton." His eyes burn as he stares at me, his chest rising and falling rapidly. "You thought I was exactly like him."

I suck in a breath. *How does he know about Easton?* I open my mouth to protest that he's being ridiculous, but I can't. Everything he's saying is true. I did think he was like my father. That still doesn't explain—

"It explains everything," he spits vehemently.

I bite the inside of my cheek, looking at him, truly looking at his face, his open expression filled with pain. We're both breathing heavily, our chests rising and falling in tandem.

His voice is hoarse, as if he hasn't spoken in years. "Do you see now?"

*Yes and no.* It still doesn't answer what he was doing earlier with—

"She was touching me, and I was trying to move away. It was one-sided on her end," he cuts in, reading my thoughts again.

I narrow my eyes. "Then why taunt me?"

He shrugs. "Thought it was an opportunity to give you a shove."

I shake my head in bewilderment. This man is so—

"Charming?" He grins.

"My shields are up. How are you still in my head?"

"I don't know," he whispers.

"Liar," I breathe, my chest rising and falling faster with each passing second.

Knox parts his lips, the tip of his tongue darting out, licking his bottom lip. My stomach tightens in anticipation. I hate myself for it but I want him to kiss me and I hate him for being right.

Knox's eyes droop, his gaze turning predatory as heat blazes within them. "I'll be here waiting. Whenever you're ready," he whispers.

I lean forward instinctively, inviting and welcoming his touch as my body screams with electricity, begging for his touch. Knox lowers himself, dipping his head so close to mine the warmth of his breath brushes across my lips.

My eyes are closed when the music suddenly stops, along with every sound in the room. Voices stop cheering, people stop moving, even the air around us seems to pause, including Knox's body as he freezes above me. Fluttering my eyes open, I peer into his gorgeous face to find Knox completely gone, his blank face utterly devoid of the person I was speaking to moments before.

I duck under his arms, moving away from him as fast as I

can to the other side of the hall. Knox doesn't move, he stays frozen as he is, his arms propping him up against the wall. My heart is beating so fast it feels as if it's going to explode out of my chest. Approaching him, I lay my hand on his back. The second my fingertips connect with his taut muscles, I cover my mouth with my hand to stop the scream from escaping as Knox twists around. His face is drawn, eyes empty. Vacant of the person I've come to know.

Movement in the ballroom begins to pick up once more. At the same time, Knox lurches forward, completely unaware of my presence as he leaves the hallway. My gulp is audible as I anxiously follow him, stopping on the threshold, not daring to reveal myself as my gut screams for me to run.

I peek my head through the black curtains separating the hallway and ballroom, only allowing a sliver of my eye to look through. I press my hand over my mouth to stop any noises from escaping, fearing that even my breathing will alert someone of my presence.

My eyes are as wide as saucers. Every single Fae in the room has lined up, walking and turning in rhythm, facing one single wall as if they're a unit in an army. Rows upon rows of Fae fill the entirety of the ballroom. There's not an ounce of emotion or sign of life behind their eyes.

*They're moving like the trapped Fae in the human lands.*

I spot Hazel, Harlow, and Ace together in one line. Lenox, Nolan, and Axel are in another on the other side of the room. Knox stands in the line closest to the hallway. Despite the difference they're all facing away from me, waiting.

It's not long before I find out why.

Hundreds of guards march into the room. They're all wearing the same outfit, gray fighting leathers with a red swirling symbol on the sleeve. They seem to be as lifeless as the others, moving and marching in rhythm with the guards around them. As the guards begin to separate, I realize they're working in teams. As one moves forward, choosing a line of Fae, two guards trail behind, carrying a large black trunk. I watch in terror as each set of guards open the black trunk, revealing thousands of syringes.

They work effortlessly and smoothly as if it's not their first time.

In unison the guards pick up a syringe and a small bottle of vibrant orange liquid. Turning to the Fae at the front of the line, each guard injects the needle into the Faes' necks. Once the needle is out, the Fae walk to the back of the line.

My entire body shakes with terror while every Fae in the room is injected with the orange glowing liquid against their will.

Even after they've been injected, they don't return to normal. Their eyes remain a hollow vessel of what once used to hold life. My mind finally begins to process what I'm seeing—they're being mind controlled.

*Cloak yourself.*

The ethereal voice from Hazel's cabin has returned, the urgency in its voice making me snap out of shock. I don't look around to see where the voice came from, knowing I won't find answers. Without a second thought I heed the ethereal voices demand, making myself invisible, I shield myself and my scent.

I'm shaking so violently the curtain in front of me vibrates. Tears well in my eyes as I stand there, unable to do anything, as every person in the Fae lands is compelled.

# Chapter Thirty-Three

Once the last of the Fae are injected, the guards pack up their black trunks and leave just as quickly as they appeared. I hold my breath, praying as I wait for life to resume in these beautiful people's eyes. Just as quickly as their world stopped the music begins to play again, the Fae moving as if nothing ever happened.

Knox's body stiffens, his head swinging from side to side, scanning the room for me, confusion swirling in those gorgeous sapphire eyes.

I put all my focus on Knox, onto that beautiful mind I thought had disappeared. Repeating the same words over and over, I pray with every piece of my heart that he hears.

*We need to leave now. Act as normal as you can.*

My entire body heaves a sigh of relief as his deep sensuous voice floats through my mind. I have never been more grateful to hear him intrude my thoughts.

*What's wrong?*

*We all need to leave, now. Don't draw any attention to yourself.*

I watch in amazement as each one of Knox's court

members, including Hazel, pause for a moment. Whatever Knox tells them mind to mind works. They each find a different time to leave—some retreating to the bathroom, some going outside to dance, others finding refreshments. It takes no longer than ten minutes before Knox and I are the only two left.

Knox begins stumbling through the crowd for the hall-way, appearing to those who watch that he's nothing but a drunk. The moment he enters the hallway I open my mouth, but he quickly places his hand across it, stopping me from speaking. No sooner has his hand touched my lips are we disappearing into nothing but white light. I cling to Knox as we teleport back to his house, as the depth of what I just witnessed slams into my body.

The depravity of freedom these people have experienced for decades. Being violated not only physically but mentally, without their knowledge. My stomach rolls as bile churns through it, my throat burning with the threat of my stomach's contents coming up. Nobody deserves to be touched like that, to have their boundaries crossed. Their very self controlled unwillingly.

The moment my feet touch marble-tiled floors, all hell breaks loose. Knox's court stands in the foyer, each one of them as pissed as the other that Knox cut their celebrations short.

"What the fuck, Knox?" Lenox bellows.

Harlow's murderous gaze pierces Knox. "Are you trying to ruin—"

Harlow's protests die the second Knox raises his hand, gesturing everyone to be silent. He turns those sapphire eyes to me. "Show me."

I open my shield, a small gate in the beautiful sanctuary I built inside my mind.

Knox's entire body freezes, changing from wary to tense to outright trembling with rage. Wave after wave of his power leaks from him, each pulse more intense than the last. It doesn't harm anyone, yet his control completely snaps as his wings blast behind his back, the leash on his rage crumbling to nothing. He stumbles away from me—from what I showed him.

"Impossible," he breathes.

He scans me from head to toe as if he can see right through me, see the fear that paralyzed me the moment Knox disappeared and those guards entered the ballroom. He sees everything.

"Knox?" Axel asks, curiosity and trepidation lining his green eyes.

Knox turns to his court and shows them all mind to mind what happened tonight.

Harlow's face leaches of all color, Axel instinctively steps in front of Ace as he begins to tremble, Nolan is a shell of a person as shock mars his features, Lenox outright stumbles backward as if he was hit and Hazel… Loving, caring Hazel vomits right there in the foyer.

I lurch forward to help her, but Ace is quicker. He bends, holding her hair back as he rubs soothing strokes up and down her back. I don't know what power it is or who uses it, but with a simple click of fingers, the vomit and smell disappear.

"Everyone in the study, now," Knox demands.

One after the other, everyone suddenly sober from the memory Knox showed them, we silently file into the study. Knox lifts a silencing shield around the room. The second he shuts the door everyone explodes, talking over each other.

"Who the fuck is behind this?" Harlow bellows.

"How long has this been happening?" Hazel asks, her voice broken.

Nolan crosses his arms. "And why wasn't Delilah mind controlled?"

"Because she cloaked herself," Knox answers, his eyes narrowing. "No one knew she was there."

"My name wasn't on the entry list," I breathe.

"Trust issues much?" Harlow sneers.

"It's what's making our magic slowly dissipate, isn't it?" Lenox asks, rubbing the side of his neck where the needle was inserted.

Knox dips his head. "The orange liquid that was injected tonight is what the Fae in the In-between are being compelled to create."

I gasp. "It's the immunity from the pixies. That's why they're held separately. They're turning the pixies' immunity to magic into a potion for the Fae, making your own magic disappear."

My statement silences everyone, the temperature in the room dropping as Knox's power leaks throughout the room again.

Axel's eyes harden. "Did you notice the guards' attire?" Ace whips his head to his brother, their eyes connecting before Ace's mouth drops open. Knox's slow nod is his only answer.

"I've never seen that red emblem before. What is it?" I ask.

Knox turns to me, his next words making my heart stop. "The queen's personal guards. I suppose we know why they went missing."

Everyone freezes, utter shock silencing the room.

"The queen is behind this?" Harlow spits.

"We don't know that for sure," Nolan cuts in.

Harlow and Lenox, for once agreeing on something, shout at Nolan in unison. "Are you fucking kidding me?"

"He's right," Axel cuts in. "The queen's men went missing, she doesn't know where they went, and the queen wasn't present. No one but the missing guards were injecting the Fae."

"Either way, we need to proceed with caution," Knox says smoothly. He looks everything like a king should, protective and loyal to his people, once again the epitome of calm and collected, but I can feel him. I can see through it. It's a mask to keep everyone in the room calm while panic and fear run havoc through his mind.

"Everything is connected. Fae are trapped in the human lands creating potions that are injected into the Fae in this land. The Fae began going missing the day the entrapment spell was cast. Whoever is orchestrating the poisons created the entrapment spell," I chime in.

"The demonic beasts as well." Ace wraps an arm around Hazel. "They arrived the day the entrapment spell was cast."

Knox nods. "If we can track down where they come from, it could lead to whoever is letting them in."

"We've been trying to track them for years," Harlow says dejectedly.

"They've never wanted one of us alive before," I say softly.

Knox's body goes taut. I think he even stops breathing. "What are you suggesting, Delilah?" he asks calmly. Too calmly.

I swallow my nerves, steeling my spine. "You heard them in the woods that day. Whoever sent them wants me alive."

"No," Hazel blurts.

I turn to her horrified face, my heart twisting with guilt for being the one to put that fearful look in her eyes.

"Absolutely not!" she continues. "We have other leads to follow, like the aerial legion."

"And if that leads to nothing?" I ask gently.

"I'm not asking you to do this, Delilah. No one is," Knox cuts in.

"No, but we don't have many options at the moment," I say.

Nolan steps forward, crossing his arms. "I think Delilah should do it."

Of course he does. He hasn't trusted me since the moment his eyes landed on me.

Knox snaps his head to Nolan, murderous rage contorting his face. Axel leans forward in his chair, preparing to stand, his hands clenching the arms of his seat.

"Why?" Knox growls.

"She can lead us right to the doorstep of whoever is letting the beasts in," Nolan states flatly.

Knox's shoulders rise on a deep inhale. "We will follow our current leads before doing anything drastic."

Nolan's jaw hardens. "It's a waste of time. The two things we need are the dark magic book and the knowledge of who's behind it all. Delilah can solve the biggest problem."

Knox's face hardens, his voice deadly quiet. "In all the years you have known me, when have I ever put another Fae in harm's way?"

Nolan clicks his tongue. "She's not Fae."

His statement clangs through my mind.

I'm not Fae, not truly. I don't belong in this world, yet I don't belong in the human lands either. I belong nowhere. I'm not welcome anywhere.

*Don't ever say those words again, Angel.*

Knox's demanding growl snaps me out of my thoughts.

When I look up, Axel is looming over Nolan, standing between him and Knox.

"Quit it with the pissing contest," Harlow snaps. "We can revisit the idea after we've gone to the aerial legion."

"Whatever, but mark my words, it's a waste of time," Nolan sneers.

Watching Nolan storm from the room I can't help but think he's right.

I tap on Hazel's door, hearing her soft, "Come in." I enter to find her sitting on her bed, her face red and splotchy.

My heart tugs as I sit beside her. "Are you okay?"

A tear rolls down her cheek. "It sickens me that someone who's meant to protect their people could be the reason for Luna dying."

"We'll find whoever is doing this, Hazel," I whisper.

Hazel sniffles, whipping away her tears. "Let's talk about something else. I can't bear to think about it any longer." A smile tugs on her lips. "How's Knox?"

"He's fine," I say flippantly. Avoiding her eyes, I lean back into silk-covered pillows.

The bed dips as Hazel worms her way in front of me. "I saw you both disappear into the hallway."

The almost kiss that never happened. My heart catches at the memory. His promise to wait…I don't know how I feel about it. Even if Knox is a good person, it doesn't change the fact that when the time comes, I'll have to go back to help my own people.

To face not only my past but my father.

Can I open my heart to another person, knowing I'll have to leave? It'll be difficult enough as it is. I've already grown attached to Hazel and I'm finding it hard not to care for Knox's court as I get to know them.

The only good thing that came from tonight was that the kiss didn't happen. I would have kissed him if he leaned forward. It was a lapse in judgment; my resolve had crumbled temporarily. Nothing can ever happen between us. I'm a human princess and he's the King of Azalea, and when the spell is broken, I have to leave. We have to remain friends. I can ignore the feelings he invokes in my body—I have to.

"I needed fresh air. Knox thought something was wrong. He was simply checking on me, as friends do."

Hazel quirks a brow. "Friends?"

"Friends," I chirp.

Hazel looks at me dubiously but doesn't push me further.

# Chapter Thirty-Four

I lunge, only to be met with air. Turning, I find Lenox grinning at me. "You're going to have to do better than that," he croons.

A fire ball flies for me, only for me to put up a shield of water, the fire sizzling as it connects. I whirl, striking with my sword as my own fire arrows rain upon him. Lenox dodges each one, our swords clashing, my very bones shaking with the force as we spar. Sweat slides down my neck, clinging to my shirt as I pant.

"Forgive me if I'm wrong, but you haven't gotten a hit in either," I taunt.

Hazel's in the corner working on her abdominal muscles, surrounded by her own shield as our magic careens around the room.

I slide my gaze back to Lenox in time to see his sword raised. I bring my own up as I prepare for another fire arrow to assault my shield only for Lenox to freeze, his face draining of color. I open my senses, trying to pinpoint what caused the change in him, when I hear it. Hazel must have heard it too because, in synch, Lenox and I drop our swords,

Hazel standing from the workout mat, as we run out of the room.

Entering the front foyer, I see the harried messenger, Hugo, from a few weeks ago, looking just as frazzled as the last time I saw him.

Knox stands in front of him, deadly still, exhaustion and defeat swirling in his eyes. "How many this time?"

Hugo grimaces. "Twenty."

Knox's shoulders slump. "Thank you, Hugo."

The twins dash into the foyer with the same grim faces as our own. "We need to go to the aerial legion today, Knox," Axel says dejectedly.

Knox nods, muttering before he walks away, "I need a moment."

We all watch as he goes, my heart screaming for me to follow him, to comfort him. Instead, I keep my feet rooted to the tiles. I can't cross that boundary.

Everyone's already in fighting leathers, so we stay standing in the foyer as we wait for Knox to return.

"Are you coming with us, Hazel?" Ace asks softly, breaking the silence.

Hazel jerks her head up. "N-no, I'm going to stay back."

Ace's body visibly deflates, a sad smile on his lips as he dips his chin.

The sound of boots thumping against tiles makes us turn. Knox strolls down the stairs, looking nothing like the man who walked up them. His calm mask has slipped back into place. "Harlow, can you spy on the witches? See if they're involved?" Knox asks.

Harlow smirks, simmering with wicked delight. "You think they kidnapped the Fae?"

If the witches kidnapped the Fae, it would break the

treaty, allowing Harlow free rein on whatever revenge she's surely been plotting for decades.

"No, I think they might be working with whoever is doing this. They miss using dark magic; they wouldn't let the opportunity pass them," Knox answers smoothly.

Harlow clicks her tongue, practically skipping as she walks out the door. "It would be my pleasure."

The moment Harlow steps through the front door, she vanishes only to be replaced by a black hawk swoops low past the entrance, a cry ringing from its beak as it sails away.

Lenox snickers. "You realize she's going to shit on them right?"

Axel and Ace chuckle darkly. "I'd expect nothing less from her," Axel says.

"Lenox, I need you to go to the last sightings of the missing Fae. See if you can pick up on any tracks," Knox cuts in, returning the conversation to work.

Lenox mock salutes Knox, sauntering out of the house with a grin plastered to his face.

"I'm going to start working on an antidote," Hazel announces. "Now that we know how our magic is lessening, perhaps I can create a tonic to reverse the magic poisoning."

The corner of Knox's mouth tips into a smile. "That would be amazing. Thank you, Hazel."

Hazel beams as she exits the foyer.

"Good luck!" Ace blurts out, his cheeks reddening.

I can't help the smile that spreads across my face. They're both smitten, and Hazel deserves some happiness. Axel shoves his brother's shoulder, though genuine happiness fills his eyes. They both continue teasing each other as they exit the foyer, glorious black wings flourishing as they step through the front door.

"I'll meet you there," Knox calls over his shoulder.

The twins take off, airborne faster than I can blink as Knox strolls toward me, his tight black shirt stretching to accommodate his broad shoulders.

Does this man ever look unattractive?

He lifts his arm, offering his hand. "We have to fly to the island. It's too far to teleport," he says, his eyes sparking with mischief.

I curse myself for not being able to learn how to fly. Each time I try I land on my face, even though everyone makes it look effortlessly easy. Saying nothing and never breaking our gaze, I slide my hand into his waiting one, his very touch sending goosebumps down my arms. *This is going to be a long flight.*

Knox scoops me up, one arm under my knees as he wraps the other around my back, carrying me through the foyer and out the door as if I weigh nothing. He smirks down at me. "Ready, Angel?" he purrs. Knox doesn't wait for a response. Glorious black wings blast across his back a moment before he takes off into the bright sky.

I cling to Knox tighter than usual, laying my head on his chest, his warmth seeping into my bones. I tell myself it's because I'm afraid of flying over the ocean, yet that couldn't be further from the truth.

Wings, talons, claws, and feathers fill the sky as ginormous beasts fly around the island before us. The creatures, some leathery and others furry, change formations as they run through sky drills. Some fly alone, while others are in packs. Their roars fill my ears, the sound so loud it makes my bones shake. I understand why they keep them here, separate from the cities. They're so large their tails alone could destroy a building in seconds.

My breath leaves me entirely as a shadow falls over me. A dragon flies over our heads, its booming wings loud in my ears. The belly of the leathery black dragon is white. Its tail swishing from side to side as it soars, the sun gleaming off its barbed spikes. I gaze above me, to the one I know is always watching, always listening.

*Dragons are real, Easton.*

I watch in shock as the creature roars, a row of sharp teeth glinting as flames spit from its mouth.

*Fire-breathing dragons.*

Tears rim my eyes for what Easton would have loved and adored—despite their terrifying, scaly faces. The sharp teeth could rip limbs off even a Fae body with just a snap of its jaw.

My gaze follows the dragon as it aims for the island, which grows closer with each passing second. Two mountain peaks sit perpendicular to the other, connected by lower mountain trails, creating a natural half-moon barrier around the land. Warrior compounds are scattered throughout the island in the forest, the ocean shores a deep crystal blue.

Knox flies around the perimeter, swooping low as he soars over the canopy of trees. Below, I spot the roofs of houses for the beasts and the riders who live here.

As Knox lands beside the takeoff strip, a group of griffins launch into flight, their formation tight. The alarmingly ginormous lions with enlarged feathered wings like a bird are astounding to be near.

Knox gracefully sets me on my feet, and I right myself as my legs wobble from the hours-long ride. We meet up with the twins beside a one-story brick building. Neither one of them is speaking yet they're staring intently at each other, as if they're having a conversation that only the two of them can hear.

"The creatures are still refusing to fly near the northern side of the island," Axel says, turning to face Knox.

Knox's gaze roves around the landing strip. "I want to speak to the general before we head there."

"I'm going to see Zephyln," Ace says, pushing off the building.

"Can I come with you?" I ask. It's not every day I can meet a griffin or dragon up close. Besides, Knox will fill me in later on the information he gathers from the general.

Ace's eyes are warm as he smiles. "Of course!"

Trailing behind Ace, nerves and excitement buzz through my veins, making my skin feel electric. We walk across pebbled paths, passing rows upon rows of brick buildings. There must be at least over a hundred on the island. My magic is lively and awake, allowing me to sense which ones have creatures residing in them.

Ace veers off the path to the left, approaching a single-story building. He faces me. "He's friendly but he's also a beast. Treat him as if you would a dog. Let him sniff you and read your energy before you go near him."

I've never had a dog before. "Okay."

Ace unlocks the door, pausing before he pushes it open. "They smell fear, too, so be calm."

I take a deep breath as he opens the door. The smell of fresh grass washes over me, along with the smell of goat. I never want to find out why it smells like goat in a griffin stable.

Stepping into the room I find it's a living quarter. A two-seated sofa sits to my left, with a small kitchen set up against the right-side wall. A fireplace crackles with embers in front of the couch, and a twin-sized cot is placed against the far corner. Paying no attention to the living quarters and personal belongings lining the bed, Ace strolls to the door perpendicular to the one we just walked through. His lips turn up in anticipation of being reunited with his griffin.

Ace walks through the door, holding it open for me. I step through to see a grass enclosure. High metal fences line the perimeter, separating the griffins' enclosure on either side. I see nothing at first as Ace walks through the gate. He places his hands on his hips. "We can't do this every time, Zeph. You know I have to travel for work," he grumbles.

I bite my lip to hold in my laugh. It's the most human thing I've ever heard a Fae utter.

"I brought a friend for you," he sing-songs.

"Ace, why are—"

A griffin as tall as my head appears in front of me, its mouth open, canines glinting as it roars. I scream so loud my voice cracks as I fall back on my ass.

Ace throws his head back on a laugh as the griffin stops roaring. Turning, it lies down at Ace's feet, nudging his legs with its giant white furry head. "I'm going to remember that moment forever." Ace chuckles. Kneeling in the grass, he pets the griffin behind its ears, whispering to him as Zeph purrs.

I huff. "Are you kidding me?" I wave my hand at Zephlyn, "You couldn't warn me that he can be invisible?"

Surprisingly, Zeph turns his head to me, as if he can understand what I'm saying and found the encounter as hilarious as Ace did.

Ace's lips twitch. "Only a few can. It's extremely rare. Just come and say hi before you insult him."

Walking through the gate, I keep my eyes on Zeph who surprisingly does the same. He truly is huge. Just lying on the ground, he reaches my hips, his paws the size of my head.

The lion part is amazing enough, but the wings flourishing from Zeph's back only add to the magnificence of the creature. The wings are feathered and shaped like a bird's, slumping against the ground as he soaks up Ace's pats like a dog.

As I slowly approach, Zeph stops purring. I stay still as he stands to his full height. He stalks toward me, slowly, not taking his eyes off mine. My heart begins to thump so wildly I'm afraid it will explode out of my chest. I'm about to protest that perhaps this isn't a good idea when the griffin stops, slowly leaning in to sniff me and proceeding to huff out the air he inhaled. I drag my eyes up over his furry legs and long mane before finally reaching his blue eyes once more. I hold my breath. Zeph stares at me so intently I think he might be human; this creature understands everything.

They must be sentient beings.

I watch in awe as Zeph sits on his back legs, slowly tipping his head down in submission, an invitation to approach him. I tentatively reach out my hand, the tips of my fingers connecting with his fur. His white coat is shockingly soft, silky even. I bury my hand in the mane, and mimicking Ace's earlier movements, scratch behind his ear. My lips tug into a grin as Zeph begins to purr.

"He likes me!" I declare, earning a deep chuckle from Ace. He starts scratching Zeph's other ear, and the purring grows louder. "How long have you had him?"

"Nearly a hundred years," he says, smiling. "I was obsessed with dragons at first, always wanted one and came here to pick one. Yet the moment I saw Zeph, I knew he was my soul pair."

One hundred years…

"Are griffins long-lived like the Fae?"

Ace's smile grows wider as Zeph licks his hand. "Yes, and thank the heavens for it."

His happiness makes my own heart warm. Watching him with this creature, it's obvious that he loves Zeph dearly.

Ace's words from earlier come to mind. "What's a soul pair?" I ask.

"Some Fae have soul connections with animals, similar to a mate. But this connection is platonic whereas the mating bond is love."

I frown. "A…mating bond?"

"Every Fae has a mate. Usually when you meet, the mating bond snaps into place. It's like finding the other half of your soul. Your equal, true partner in life, and in most cases, your true love," he says dreamily.

"What do you mean usually?" I ask.

He grimaces, lowering his voice. "Mating bonds have become rare over the years. Now that we know the potions are making our magic slowly fade, it's as if the magic that connects the two souls has been blinded."

"That's horrible," I breathe. "Have any of you met your mate?"

Ace shakes his head. "None of us have. And for all we know, we could've already met them and we are just oblivious." Ace falls quiet, contemplative. I wonder if he's thinking about Hazel and if she's his mate. If their bond would have snapped into place the moment he laid eyes on her.

I wonder if Knox has met his mate, if he'll know who she is once the entrapment spell is broken.

The thought makes me queasy.

I change the topic, trying to draw Ace out of wherever his mind has taken him. "You remind me of my best friend, Easton," I whisper. "He loved dragons too. He was excited to find out if they were extinct or not."

"Was?" Ace asks.

My voice lowers, sadness coating my every word. "He died before he could enter the Fae lands."

"I'm sorry," Ace offers sincerely. "Do you want to tell me about him?"

I laugh, only for the sound to come out sadder than I meant. "Look in the mirror. You not only look alike, you have the same personality."

Ace's eyes widen. "Seriously?"

I nod, a small smile playing on my lips. "Seriously. You have the same eyes, hair, and facial features. You also have similar hearts. Easton's was full of love and kindness."

Ace studies me. "Did you love him?"

"I did, with all my heart," I whisper. "We used to say we were each other's platonic soulmates."

Ace's lips lift into a smile. "Well, I'm glad you got to see the dragons for him. Even if he's not here, he will always be in your heart."

I dip my chin, not daring to speak. The second I do, I know the dam within me will burst and I don't want to ruin this. This moment is for Easton. He would have been happy here.

"Let's go find Knox and Axel," Ace says, saying goodbye to Zeph.

I turn to follow Ace only to halt midstride.

Deep golden eyes are staring at me through the metal fence, the eyes belonging to a beautiful black griffin. It's smaller than Zeph, so it's either younger or female. It turns its head to the side, more feline than beast as I approach it.

"You're beautiful," I breathe. My heart gallops, happiness filling my chest as the griffin continues to stare so intently, I swear she's reading my own soul.

Ace must notice I'm not behind him any longer. Turning,

he leans against the fence and calls out, "She doesn't have a rider. She seems to be stubborn and hasn't chosen one yet."

The griffin slowly turns her head, piercing Ace with those golden eyes.

I chuckle. "I don't think she likes being called stubborn. Perhaps she doesn't want to settle for an ordinary rider." The griffin puffs air out of her snout, as if to say she agrees with me. I grin at Ace. "She just knows what she wants."

I keep our gazes locked. "I have to go, but it was delightful to meet you," I say with genuine warmth. She truly is beautiful. Her black coat is as dark as the night sky, and those bright golden honey eyes only enhance her beauty.

I cock my head to the side. She reminds me of Creseda.

No, she's certainly not stubborn; she's worthy of an incredible rider.

I feel her gaze on my back as I leave, until I disappear out of sight.

Strolling through the main landing area, Ace tenses beside me as we spot Knox and Axel standing next to an older male. All three of them look like they've swallowed a lemon as they scowl at each other. Yet it isn't the older gentleman that has Ace and I wary—it's the small woman looking down her nose at Knox.

Knox is tense, his entire body taut, jaw clenched and eyes hard as steel as Axel mirrors his stance, looking just as pissed off as Knox.

"Fuck," Ace mumbles under his breath.

"Why wasn't anyone informed?" Knox demands.

The older Fae spits. "Why do you think?"

"Settle," Emmalyn quips.

Knox narrows his gaze at her small figure. "Why are you here, Emmalyn? I thought you didn't do the queen's dirty work."

She clicks her tongue. "Same could be said for you, *Prince*. Very suspicious timing for you to arrive."

Axel crosses his arms over his chest. "Why would we take General Fortz's men, only to show up asking about them?"

Axel's logical reasoning only further agitates the pair. The older man has gray peppered hair, with small wrinkles around his eyes and mouth. He stands significantly shorter than the men around him. His neck turns red as he grits his teeth, spitting at Knox and Axel, "You all play games."

"General Fortz, I assure you my court, nor my people, took your riders," Knox says smoothly.

"Well someone did!" Fortz thunders.

My heart sinks. More Fae have been taken. Not just Fae from the cities, but guards and riders too.

A headache begins to form, a dull throb in my skull. There's so many unanswered questions and yet they keep piling up as the days go on.

"We'll look into it, General," Axel states.

"As is the queen," Emmalyn interjects, lifting her nose in the air.

General Fortz marches away, swearing profanities under his breath.

Emmalyn steels her spine as she turns to Knox, the move as smooth as a snake. "I suggest you return to Azalea, Knox. Worse things are happening in these lands. You shouldn't busy yourself with problems that aren't yours to be dealt with."

Before Knox can so much as swallow, Emmalyn vanishes into thin air, probably teleporting back to the queen to report on Knox. It's truly horrid how the queen won't let the royals be reinstated.

Knox and Axel turn, their grim faces unyielding.

"Is there some place we can talk?" Knox asks Ace calmly.

Ace looks around the area, at the hundreds of men walking around tending to their daily duties. He subtly shakes his head. They stand there for a moment, each one making eye contact, seemingly having an unvoiced conversation.

Axel and Ace spread their wings, flying high into the sky, without so much as uttering a word.

"Where are they—"

I yelp as Knox scoops me into his arms, plastering me to his chest. His wings spread wide, and we take off in the direction of Axel and Ace, who fly in sync with each other, moving as if they're one. We fly between the two mountain peaks, heading for the northern side of the island, where even the dragons and griffins refuse to fly. Once we pass the mountains, far enough away from the flying creatures and riders with Fae hearing, the men pause midair, hovering so perfectly they look as if they're standing on a cloud.

"None of this is a coincidence. Someone's preparing an army," Axel declares.

My entire body freezes, every muscle within me locking up tightly. Knox's thumb brushes back and forth on my leg, soothing.

"An army? For what?" I blurt, not able to hide the fear tinging my voice.

"Perhaps they're preparing to attack," Ace suggests.

Knox shakes his head. "Whoever is orchestrating this has had one hundred and forty-eight years to prepare. They would have attacked long ago if that was their plan."

"What's changed?" Axel asks no one in particular.

That I can answer. The only question I have confidence in answering.

"Me," I whisper.

The twins look toward me, not in disgust that I spoke, no. I only see kindness and patience as they wait for me to elaborate.

"I came into these lands when nobody else could, I found the hidden dark magic books, and I'm the only Fae that has access to their full magic, the only one that has the power to break the entrapment spell."

"You think they're preparing an army to attack you?" Ace asks, horrified.

"No, I think it's to stop whatever momentum we've started. We must be closer than we realize. Otherwise, they wouldn't have sent the demon hounds to track me down... alive," I add with a grimace.

Knox's chest vibrates as he speaks. "Delilah's right. We must be closer than we realize; we have something they want."

Axel and Ace look toward each other, exchanging another silent conversation with themselves.

"What is it?" Knox asks.

Ace outright shudders while Axel grimaces. "What if they *want* her?"

Knox's entire body stiffens. "You think they know she can break the spell?"

My heart stops dead. Of course it's my luck that I leave a home where I'm the target daily, only to end up in another place where I'm hunted once more.

I instinctively brush the tip of my finger down the hard planes of Knox's chest. He relaxes, yet not entirely.

Ace's eyes are full of horror as he says, "How would they know she has access to her full powers?"

"Can't you feel it? Knox felt it that day in the forest."

Knox shakes his head. "I can feel others' powers because of how strong my own is. It's a gift within itself."

"Could it have been the demon hounds?"

"No, they can't feel the depth of magic." He turns his gaze to the twins. "No one outside of my home knows that she has access to her full powers." Knox tightens his grip on me. "Let's discuss this when I can shield the room. For now, we need to scout the northern side of the island."

Axel and Ace dip their heads in unison, flying in front of Knox as we take off, deeper into the northern side of the island. Passing the twin peaks of the mountains, we keep to the outer ridges of the island. From above it appears calm and peaceful, nothing out of the ordinary. It isn't until we fly past caves embedded in the mountainside does an ancient force slither down my back, making my blood run cold.

"Do you feel it?" I whisper.

It feels wrong, utterly wrong, exactly like the demon hounds.

Knox's jaw clenches. "There's demonic beasts here."

I shake my head in disbelief. "How did they get on the island?"

"I don't know, but we're about to find out."

Knox falls, flying into a current that takes us lower, right to the cave system, Axel and Ace doing the same in front of us. Shields snap around us as I clutch Knox's arm, making us wholly invisible as tingles spread throughout my body. Axel and Ace fly ahead, above the cave system as to not alert whatever creature dwells inside. Knox, reading my mind, flies past them, spearing his magic throughout the tunnels as we move invisible to those around us. A shiver wracks his spine as he grimaces, banking so sharply I hold onto him for dear life as he aims for the lower edge jutting out of the cliff face.

The wind that assaults me as my feet touch the ground makes me cling to the rock. I look below, my knees trembling as I peer at the sheer drop to the ocean below. Rocks protrude like spikes in the water; if I fell, it wouldn't be a pleasant swim.

Knox's voice floats through my mind. Axel and Ace's eyes are on him too as he speaks to all of us, mind to mind.

*There are two creatures inside the middle lower cave. Axel, Ace, take the left to come up from behind. Delilah and I will enter through the front.*

I instinctively clutch the blade strapped to my hip, checking that everything is secure and ready, as creature after creature float through my mind, the possibilities of what we're about to face endless.

Before I can blink Knox's hand is in mine, the stone beneath my feet disappearing only to return as darkness surrounds us, the ocean at my back. I stand in the mouth of the damp cave, listening to the crackling embers of a fire before us.

My heart stops cold, fear pounding through me as two figures emerge. Standing two feet taller than Knox, the sheer size and muscle on the creatures instinctively makes me take a step back. With the body of a man, gray skin like a rotting corpse, claws for hands, and hooves for feet, I feel bile burn my throat. Their putrid smell makes my nose tingle as I stare at their wolf-like skull they have for a head, their black beady eyes unblinking.

A slithering tongue darts out, their eerie voices like nails scraping down chalkboard. "Hello, Princeling."

Knox seems completely unfazed as he slides his hands into his pockets, a smirk playing on his lips. "Wendigos.

How lovely. Cannibalism hit you in your later years, gentlemen?"

*Wendigo.*

Creatures that were once Fae, turned into these monsters as they traded pure magic for dark magic. Now I truly feel like I'm going to vomit.

"We've been waiting for you," one sneers.

Knox places his palm over his heart. "How touching, yet I'm afraid I don't dine with mutts. Please tell your owner I send my condolences."

The wendigo takes a step closer. "Condolences for what?" it spits.

Knox's smirk turns predatory. "For this."

Axel and Ace appear behind the two wendigos, their swords gutting the corpse-like bodies. Even with the dark magic running through their veins, their bodies take damage like any other Fae or human. They grunt, shrieking and squirming as the twins hold the swords in their abdomens.

Knox strides forward, the epitome of calm and collected as he stands before the enraged demons. "Care to tell me who you work for, gentlemen?" he asks casually.

One spits at his feet as the other sneers. "You'll get what's coming to you. You all will."

Knox tips his head to the side. "I don't believe I will." Before I can take a breath his hand is embedded in the wendigo's chest. Its eyes widen before Knox rips out its heart. When he pulls back his hand, his skin is covered in black blood as he clutches a decomposing heart.

The wendigo beside him roars so loudly my ears ring.

Knox shoves his clean hand into its chest cavity, pulling out another rotting heart. The wendigo slumps to the floor, crumbling next to its friend.

"They received orders from a mutt. They don't know

who's behind any of this. I saw it in their minds," Knox says as he drops the hearts as if they burned him. Darkness encompasses his hands, the shadows fading to reveal his hands clean once more.

"It's the only way they can truly die. Beheading doesn't work," Axel explains gently, coming to stand beside me.

I grimace. "That is absolutely horrid."

Knox turns to me, his own disgust marring his features. "Tell me about it. The entire inside of their body is like a rotted animal."

Ace's face is green as he stands beside us. "I'm so grateful I'm an emissary."

I'm about to laugh when power slithers down my spine, ancient and cold, wickedly cruel as it taunts me. I squirm away, my face dropping. "There's something else in the cave."

Knox spears his power out, his sapphire eyes sparking with delight. "They were protecting a dark magic book."

I snap my head to his. "How can you tell?"

"It's alive and feels exactly like the others in the cellar," Knox says, treading further into the cave.

I follow behind Axel and Ace as they flank Knox. The deeper we go the colder it gets, the musty cave walls dripping with water as we walk throughout the tunnel system. It isn't until we reach a dead end that we find it. A cold fire pit sits in the center, bed rolls surrounding the circle. The ground is littered with bones, the smell so putrid it makes everyone dry heave.

Knox leans forward, moving a pile of bones to reveal three books, each pulsing with dark magic as he picks them up. "The beasts are protecting hidden dark magic books. That's why they're scattered throughout Aloriah."

I take a step forward. "They're guarding the collection," I say in awe.

Axel opens his mouth to speak when a deafening roar shakes the walls of the cave. Turning wide-eyed to each other, no one wastes any time as we sprint through the tunnel, running as fast as we can to escape the cave. The light from outside begins to shine through, that very sunlight a beacon for our exit as Axel turns the corner. Only to fly back into the wall. Knox and Ace unsheathe their swords as five wendigos walk around the corner, each one quivering with rage as they pass their dead friends.

"Oh look, it's dinner," the middle one sneers. A moment before launching into an attack.

My hand shakes as I unsheathe the sword from my back. Spinning, I bring it down with every ounce of strength I have as a wendigo pounces for me. It digs its claws into my arms, ripping the skin beneath my fighting leathers, blood pools from the wound. The blade in my hand sings with the force of my strike as I bring it down clean through its head. Cracking the skull in two, its claws retract from my arm as it crumbles to the ground, twitching and spasming.

I don't care if it doesn't truly die. I just need time to get us out of here.

In front of me, Axel's on his feet, slashing and striking as two wendigos attack him. Ace cleaves them in half from behind, cutting them both through the abdomen in one fell swoop.

Knox's power blasts throughout the room as another wendigo lunges for me, this one taller, more muscular than the last. I run at it, falling to the ground as I slide beneath it, only to pop up behind and plunge my sword into its heart.

I lift my head at the sound of hooves behind me, from somewhere deeper within the cave system. "Knox." I don't dare take my eyes off the cave mouth. The stampede sounds like a war cry.

Knox appears beside me in a second. "We need to pull back. There's too many."

*Why isn't he teleporting us? Is he hurt?*

Axel and Ace withdraw their swords from the wendigos' hearts as we start to back out, only to be met with two wendigos at our backs. On the cave's cliff edge, dozens of wendigos round the corner, caging us in. Panic sinks its claws into my chest, their fury a palpable thing in the cave.

Before the wendigo can attack, a deafening roar pierces the sky. A black griffin sails past us, its mouth open, razor sharp teeth shining. It spreads its claws wide, banking in and ripping the wendigos off the ledge. They fall to their doom on the rocks.

My eyes widen as I realize it's the griffin from earlier, her deep honey golden eyes on mine as she flies back around. I grab Knox's hand and scream, "Jump!"

I propel myself backward, leaping off the cliff's edge, twisting my body as the wendigos' hands reach for me, their claws trying to sink into my skin. I land on the griffin's back as she loops back. I clutch her fur, clinging to the griffin for dear life as Axel, Ace, and Knox also leap off the cliff mouth, their beautiful wings blossoming seconds before the wendigo can snag them.

Panting, I throw my leg over her back and straddle her, whispering my gratitude in her ear.

Axel and Ace fly past us, hollering and whooping with joy as they praise the griffin. Knox comes up beside me, his eyes hardening as they lock on my arm. "Are you hurt?"

I peer down. The adrenaline coursing through my blood made me forget that one of them tried to tear my arms off.

But the skin on my arm is already starting to stitch together, dried blood caking the surrounding area. I didn't even feel it.

I never knew Fae could heal themselves subconsciously either.

"I'm okay," I whisper.

My hands tremble in the griffin's fur as we fly back to the aerial legion.

# Chapter Thirty-Five

After Knox talked to the commander about the wendigos on the island and I said goodbye to the gorgeous griffin, thanking it profusely for saving our lives, I'm in Knox's arms once more, the adrenaline long gone from earlier as fatigue wracks my body.

"That was eventful," I say flatly.

Knox's chest shakes on a laugh. "Just a tad."

I look him up and down, realizing we don't have the books. "Oh my god, where did—"

Knox cuts me off. "Axel has them."

I slump into his body. "Thank god that wasn't for nothing."

Knox chuckles, his deep rumble of a laugh making my lips twitch into a smile, until his face turns ashen, his body tensing. "Something's wrong."

Knox flies faster than ever before, reaching the house within minutes as he teleports and flies at the same time. He lands on the front pathway so quickly I bounce in his arms from the impact. Ace and Axel have their swords drawn as they land, Knox and I doing the same.

"The shields are down," Axel pants.

Knox's face leaches of color. "The island. It was a diversion to get us away from the house, to get me to use my power so I wouldn't feel the wards being destroyed."

My heart stops entirely.

Hazel.

A killing calm washes over me, everything around me sharpening as my senses sweep the area. My canines flare as I snap my gaze to the silent house. Ignoring Knox's shouts of protest, I run for the house as fast as I've ever run before, spearing out my magic as I do, praying that it finds Hazel.

The smell of blood shoves its way down my nose, so strong I can taste the metallic tang on my tongue. It isn't long before I find the source. As I run through the open front door I'm met with deadly silence. Bodies of Knox's guards pile along the floor, crimson blood pooling in every crack and crevice of the once white marble tiles.

Rage burns through me, hot searing fire, crackling in my veins as I take in the innocent lives butchered around me. I think I scream, yet I can't hear anything through the ringing in my ears. I run through hall after hall, opening doors as I go, my magic erupting around me as panic digs its claws deep within my heart.

I spear my power into every inch of the house, searching for Hazel.

*Please be alive, please be alive, please be alive.*

I'm running up the foyer stairs when I feel it—her energy, lightly pulsing. I spin so fast I nearly shove Ace down the stairs. I didn't even hear him behind me. Running through the house to the backyard, I scream in horror. Dead guards line every inch of the garden, dozens of Knox's men dead. Bile burns my throat as I splash through puddles of crimson blood, torn body parts, and lifeless eyes. I throw open the cellar door so strongly the door snaps off its hinges. I practically fly down the cellar stairs, my feet never touching a single one.

Shaking as I lay my palm on the door, purple light flaring beneath my hand before it clicks, I shove it open, rushing into the room only to stop cold. Hazel is curled in a ball in the far corner, a long sword dripping with black blood gripped in her hands so tightly her knuckles are white. Her soft floral dress is no longer yellow, but stained red.

I can't contain my sob as I fling myself toward her, tears of relief streaming down my face as her bloodshot eyes snap to mine. Hazel drops the sword in her hand, a cry leaving her lips as she focuses, seeing it's me. She's shaking so much I'm surprised I don't hear her bones rattle against one another.

"The books," she croaks. "The books."

"I don't care about the books," I say as I search for any injuries. The majority of the blood isn't her own, I can smell it, yet she has several deep gashes on her arms and legs.

Boots stomp down the cellar stairs, making Hazel flinch.

"It's the boys…It's the boys," I soothe, sweeping her hair back.

I hear a broken cry pierce the room before Axel's deep voice says, "She's okay, Ace."

I turn to see Ace shove Axel off him, lunging for us. He stops abruptly, his face dropping, eyes filling with pain. Knox comes up behind the twins, his own face grave and pale.

"The books," Hazel mutters again.

"I think she's in shock."

"No," she blurts. "The books."

I look around the room noticing that it's completely empty. I lift my widened eyes to Knox. "They came for the books."

"I hid them before they could find them. I wouldn't let

them have the books," Hazel whispers, her eyes glazing over again as her mind takes her far away.

I lean forward, kissing the top of her forehead when words fail me.

Ace's broken voice fills the room. "Hazel, do you want to go to your room?"

Hazel snaps her head up at the sound of his voice. Tears roll down her cheeks. As if the trance was broken Ace rushes forward, no longer in shock at the horrible sight. He slowly lifts her to his chest, Hazel's head settling in the crook of his neck.

"I need to heal her," Ace says softly as he leaves.

I stand by, feeling utterly useless as Ace carries Hazel up the cellar stairs.

"I'll go get the others," Axel says solemnly.

I drag my eyes to Knox, finding his face as white as a ghost, his eyes unseeing and hands shaking. Finding so many of his people dead, in his own home...

I gently lay my hand on his arm. "Knox?" He doesn't move, doesn't even flinch. Worry claws through me. I slide both my palms up his neck, gently cupping his face, forcing him to look at me. "Knox."

Silver lines his eyes as he slowly focuses on me. "My men...my friends..." he says brokenly. "I swore this would never happen again."

With nothing to say to soothe or comfort the loss he feels, I lift onto the tip of my toes, wrapping my arms around his neck. Knox's arms circle my waist in return, crushing me to him as he buries his face in the crook of my neck.

I'm sitting with Ace and Hazel in her room when Knox strolls past the open door, heading to his room down the hall. His clothes are splattered with mud and blood from burying his friends.

I don't know what sort of person it makes me, but I couldn't stomach seeing so many people dead, so many innocent people brutally murdered. If I had to see it again it would have utterly shattered a part of me. Guilt courses through me that Knox had to do it, that he had to bury his friends at all.

*I should have helped him.*

"He wanted to do it alone, Axel and Lenox too...as a goodbye," Ace whispers to me, reading the guilt wracking my body.

"It's not right," I croak.

"No, it's not," is Ace's only response.

We sit in silence, waiting for Hazel to emerge from the bathroom.

The house is full of sounds, bangs and clatters as the workers fix whatever was knocked over or broken. It's a small miracle that the servers got out unharmed; they had invisibility and shadow magic to thank for that. The guards hid those who didn't possess the magic...they died protecting their friends.

The bathroom door opens at the same time Axel strolls into the room, his steps unhurried and face drawn. Sadness lingers in every inch of his body as he stares at Ace, having another silent conversation between themselves. Without so much as uttering a word, Axel turns, his boots squeaking down the hallway as he retreats.

Ace turns to Hazel as she takes a stiff seat on the bed. "Hazel, can you come downstairs into the study?" He takes a shuddering breath. "Can you tell us what happened?"

Hazel stands, her hands quivering. "Yes, of course."

"If you're not ready to talk that's absolutely—"

"No, I need to tell you what happened," she cuts in.

Ace leads, walking in front of Hazel as I walk behind her, acting as her own personal shields.

The foyer has returned to normal. The dead guards, shattered glass, and pools of blood are gone, a lingering scent of lemon coating the air. My eyes burn as the image of the foyer not so long ago flashes through my mind. I blink rapidly, praying that my tears vanish and the image goes away.

Harlow sits up straighter in her chair as we enter the siting room. Hazel takes a seat with Ace on a two-seated sofa, leaving me to sit beside her in a single chair. Lenox's face is as drawn and solemn as the rest of them. Everyone here lost friends and family today.

Knox enters the room a moment later, sealing a silencing shield around us. He's freshly bathed, wearing clean clothes, yet he continues to rub his hands together behind his back as if he can't get the blood off them. "Can you show me what happened?" Knox asks Hazel gently.

She gives one quick dip of her chin before her eyes go vacant, glazed and unfocused.

Knox's jaw clenches, his hands balling into fists at his side. Hazel slumps back in the sofa as Knox transfers her memories to all of us.

### Hazel

*Walking through the foyer, I peer down at my feet, watching my yellow sundress twirl as I move when suddenly screams and shouts fill the house.*

*Two harried guards crash through the front door. "We're under attack! Everyone hide, now!"*

*Fear slithers through my body, my eyes widening as I run for the training room.*

*I will never be unprepared. Never again.*

*I pump my legs as fast as I can, my chest heaving as I reach the room. I rush to the far-side wall, grabbing as many knives as I can fit into my pockets, then draw the long sword from the middle shelf. My hand wraps around the hilt, and I loosen my wrist just as Delilah taught me. I pause as the smell of blood fills not only the training room but the entire house. Then the screams ensure.*

*Outside, dozens of guards in gray suits, red emblems attached to the sleeves, attack Knox's guards.*

*The backyard is covered in blood splatters within seconds, puddles of crimson forming as men fall dead on the grass. Their limbs chopped and butchered.*

*A dark shadow in my peripheral catches my eye. A large beast, its scaly leather skin rippling with shadows, heads toward the cellar door, flanked by five gray-suited guards.*

*"No," I rasp.*

*Invisible talons squeeze my chest as memories of Luna bombard my mind. The gashes slashed across her small torso, the smell of the beast clinging to her tiny body as her blood gushed into my arms. The horrid beast grasping my baby girl as it—*

*No.*

*I refuse to let these horrid beasts take any more from me.*

*Sprinting out of the training room, I run down the hall to the servants' stairwell, swinging the metal door open. Only to be met with lifeless eyes as three guards, dressed in that horrible gray uniform, walk through the threshold.*

*Before I can move, they lunge for me.*

*I scream as I swing my sword, sobs racking my body as I strike. Crimson blood leaks down my sword as I defend myself against those who used to be my own people, who were meant to protect and serve the very thing they're destroying today.*

*A heavy hand wraps around my arm, yanking me so hard my head snaps back with the force. I kick and scream as the man drags me down the stairs. I try to cut the back of his legs but another guard appears. In one fell swoop he slices my arm so deep I drop the sword as I scream. Dragging me to the bottom of the stairs, they kick the exit door open, sunlight shining through the dark hall. Frantically diving deep within my magic, roots sprout from the ground. Wrapping around the guards' neck, they strangle the very life out of them until their hands on me go slack, their jaws hanging open as they fall to the floor. I thank Mother Earth for saving me.*

*I unsheathe the swords strapped to their waists and run. I never stop. I don't dare look back at the carnage, the sounds of metal hitting metal. The screams of agony and the smell of tears and blood is enough for me to know that we've lost many today…too many.*

*I push my feet to go faster, begging the goddesses to listen to my prayers that they haven't taken the dark magic books, only to come to a skidding halt. The five guards that were flanking the beast pounce on me the moment I turn the corner, pinning my arms and legs to the ground as I thrash, roaring. Their nails bite into my skin, fresh blood trickling down my limbs. Darkness slides over my face. The beast. Its red glowing eyes peer down at me as it licks its lips, practically buzzing with anticipation as it hovers above me.*

*"What a pretty little thing you are. I think you'd be delightful entertainment in my bed," it croons.*

*My eyes widen, my magic blasting out of me with the force of my panic.*

*Thick vines sprout from the ground below me, so tall the guards can do nothing as they wrap around their bodies like snakes, suffocating and squeezing their necks so tightly their eyes bulge and pop out of their sockets. With my limbs now free, I scramble back, the beast shaking with rage as I kill his men. He slinks forward only to stop inches away from me, his eyes going wholly blank. The red glowing tinge moments before turns a milky white color, as if a light switch was turned off.*

*I don't dare wait to find out why. Standing on a sob, I sprint for the cellar. My fingers tremble against the door as purple light shines beneath my palm, and when I push open the door, my knees buckle at the sight of the books. I pick up every one, already shooting my power out into the garden, digging a hole so large, so deep, they'll never be able to get to it in time.*

*I sprint from the room, trembling and shaking as I run around the building to the hole I created. I don't second-guess myself as I drop them into the black pit. With the little power I have left, I cover the hole and run for my life. I pick up a fallen sword as I sprint into the cellar once again, clutching the blade to my chest as I curl myself into a ball in the corner.*

*Praying that I survive.*

Bile burns my throat, threatening to rise.

I place my hand over my mouth, swallowing profusely until it subsides. I know Hazel is strong, I truly do, yet seeing what she went through and knowing that I'm the one who brought her here...

My hand falls to my lap as ice coats my veins; they're all dead because of me. I was the one to bring Knox the information about the dark magic books, I was the one that found them in the library, and I was the one who brought them into the house.

Those guards and that horrendous beast killed all those innocent people because of me, because of the decision that led me here, my actions.

*Angel, this isn't your fault.*

He should hate me right now; he should hate me that I'm the reason his loved ones are dead.

Numbness spreads throughout my body, the couch beneath me disappearing as it feels like I'm floating. The coffee table before me blurs. Everything around me appears to not be my own sight. The words leaving people's mouths no longer reach my ears.

My heart leaves me once more.

I forgot how it felt; it's been such a long time since it's abandoned me. I can see everything, yet it doesn't appear to be my own. The hand resting in my lap feels foreign, as if I'm looking at someone else's body. My breathing turns so shallow and slow I wonder if I'm dying. Suffocating like those that Hazel wrapped her vines around. A hand touches the knee in front of me—I think it's my own, yet I can't feel the weight of it. Someone moves my head because suddenly I'm looking at sapphire eyes. Lips move, yet no sound leaves.

*Angel.*

The voice calls to me, to my heart.

I'm plummeting, falling so far, and I jolt as my heart returns to me. My body feels like my own once more.

"It's not your fault," Knox says gently.

I lift my heavy head to find the room empty, save for Knox kneeling in front of me.

When did everyone leave? How much time has passed? Where did my heart go?

"The monster who sent the beast and guards is responsible. Not you," he says vehemently.

No matter what he says, I know I'm partially to blame. Those innocent people died because of my actions. *I'm no better than my father.*

"Don't," he snarls.

I snap my gaze to Knox. His sapphire eyes blaze at me, my heart catching at the worry I find there.

He exhales slowly, his voice guttural as he says, "I need your help. I'm not strong enough to seal the wards around the house. Not if it could be shattered while my magic was occupied. I need you to seal them."

My mouth feels like cotton. "I don't know how to do that."

"I'll teach you."

It's the least I can do. For now, I have an insurmountable number of deaths hanging over my head.

"I'll do whatever I can to help," I breathe.

# Chapter Thirty-Six

Pain laces through my hand with each swing of my sword, yet I don't cower from it.

Instead, I welcome the pain. My mind won't shut off, won't stop flooding with images of Hazel being attacked and guards dying, each flitting image worse than the last. With each image comes my anxiety and the spiraling of my thoughts.

I did this. I brought her into this mess. I left her alone and she nearly died.

Hazel nearly died.

Knox's guards died.

Everyone around me is dying.

As each thought stabs my heart and assaults my mind, I strike harder. I don't remember when my blisters became raw, when my skin splits open, when the blood pools down my palm.

All I can see is Hazel covered in blood, the same deep crimson red of Easton's. I'm responsible for spilling both. I can't take it if another person dies because of me. I push my body harder, not stopping for anything, even as my lungs scream in pain. I lunge, my legs wobbling as my arms come up over my head. Flowing into a fighting sequence, my sword flies through the air. Turn, strike, start again, attacking the air as if it were my thoughts.

"Delilah." Knox's deep voice brushes a sensual finger down my spine.

I pause, my chest heaving as I try to get more air into my lungs. "I'm not in the mood, Knox," I say, gritting my teeth as I continue with my regime.

Suddenly Knox is standing in front of me, the sword no longer in my hands but clanging on the floor. I open my mouth to yell as he grips both of my forearms, his touch gentle yet firm.

"Delilah, why are you training in the middle of the night?"

I look into his sapphire eyes, seeing uneasiness and…concern?

My throat burns as I whisper, "I can't stop seeing it."

Knox stares at me intently; it's like he can see right through me. The pull I feel toward him grows inside me with every passing second.

He glides his hands down my arms, sending goosebumps along my skin, and takes my hand. "Come with me," he whispers.

"Where?"

He leans forward, slowly dragging his jaw against my own, brushing his lips against my ear. I bite my lip to stop the sigh from escaping, his touch soothing the ache in my heart.

"I promise it will make you feel better," he whispers.

I'm so mentally and physically exhausted I have no fight left in me to push him away, not right now. Not when I feel like my very heart is breaking.

I trail behind him, his hand still clutching mine as we

walk through the silent house to the front yard. He turns, gently scooping me into his arms as his wings flutter open, and takes off.

He flies for what feels like hours. The wind on my face, smell of crisp fresh air, and the night sky lull me to sleep at some point. Yet I don't think it was the flying that I have to thank for that. I think it's the man carrying me and the comfort he brings.

Warmth brushes against my ear as a soft voice whispers to me, "Delilah."

I flutter my eyes open. Dawn is fast approaching, the night sky fading to a deep navy blue. I blink rapidly, looking around as my mind begins to wake up, piecing together where I am. We're on top of a mountain peak, the twinkling city lights of Azalea shining up at us, the beautiful ocean surrounding the coastal town sparkling beneath the fading moon.

It looks like a dream.

I start to move forward, to be closer to the breathtaking view, when I notice I'm seated on a large rock boulder, two powerful male legs on either side of me.

I'm sitting between Knox's legs.

I begin to shift away, entirely alert to how close we're sitting when he wraps his arms around my waist, pulling me back flush against his chest. My traitorous body responds with a shiver, melting against his hard planes.

His voice is a deep husky rumble as he says, "Just pretend for a moment that you don't hate me."

"I don't hate you," I argue.

"I know. I just wanted to hear you say it," he says smugly.

I elbow his stomach, laughing with satisfaction as he grunts.

I lean back, allowing myself to soak in the intricate details of the sparkling city, the happiness that emanates from it. "How did you find this place? It's so peaceful."

"I snuck out of my room one night when I was a young boy. I loved flying and spent most nights in the sky. One night I had run myself ragged; this was the closest spot I could find to land."

"When did you get your wings?" I ask, my curiosity getting the better of me.

He groans. "A long time ago."

"How old are you?" I tease. Knox looks no older than his late twenties, yet so does Hazel. I've come to expect the Fae features to be misleading when it comes to their age.

Knox's arms tighten around me. "That, Angel, I cannot tell you."

I huff out a laugh. "Why not?"

"I don't want it going to your head."

I click my tongue. "You're insufferable."

How does he do it? He knows how to calm me, yet pushes every one of my buttons. I was punishing myself, my mind overruling me, and now I'm sitting with Knox laughing and smiling. Even with everything going on around us, my heart feels at peace when I'm with him.

"What do you dream about?" he asks suddenly.

"That's a strange question."

"Entertain me," he purrs.

I pause, considering his question. What do I dream of?

"Honestly, I've only dreamt of making the human lands a better place. To make the world a happier place." Knox can't see the smile that spreads across my lips. "That's why I've fallen in love with Azalea. It brought hope to my heart again, to see a city so full of life and joy."

"Why did you lose hope?" he asks quietly.

My smile dies. "My father began executing innocent people."

His body stiffens behind me. "He executes people?"

"Daily. He made a show of it, made it a law that the citizens must watch otherwise they'll be the ones up there the next day." My voice grows quiet. "The week I left, he murdered an entire sector. Eleven thousand people…gone in an instant."

"Why did you decide to leave then? He had murdered people before that."

His blunt words make my spine straighten. "Because I realized I couldn't help anyone. I had been freeing as many innocent people as I could for years. Yet, in the grand scheme of things, nothing truly changed."

"That's not true," he argues. "I know the people you freed wouldn't say what you did was worthless."

"No, they wouldn't," I whisper. "I crossed the border to help the trapped Fae in our lands. But a large part of me hoped that in doing so, the Fae would help the humans."

Knox places his chin on the top of my head. "You want to overrule your father."

"I just want my people to be happy and to live a life of freedom. A life worth living." My body starts to relax once more, melding into the hard planes of Knox's muscles. "That's not the only reason why I'm helping."

"No?" I can hear the shock in his voice.

"Your people deserve freedom as well, and in this situation I can actually do something. I have the power to help." I lower my voice, barely hearing my own words. "I'll never turn my back on people in need. I'm tired of seeing people suffer."

My admission silences us both, but it's true. At the beginning, I wanted the Fae to help my own people, yet over time, as I slowly fell in love with everything about this beautiful city and its people, I wanted to do this for them, to end their suffering.

"What do you dream of?" I shoot the question back at him, watching the sunrise as the golden hue illuminates the ocean.

Knox is silent for a moment, mulling over my question. When he speaks, his voice sings to me, calming me. "I want my people to be safe, for the family I've created to live a long happy life. That I myself will live it with them."

"Do you think you won't get that?"

I feel his shoulders shrug against my back. "Threats and danger come with being king. I'm not naive enough to think I'll never have enemies at my back."

"I hope you get to live the life you dream of. You deserve it."

He doesn't say anything, and I wonder if I've stunned him. The birds chirping and the distant crashing of waves below fill his silence.

"Why did you bring me here?" I suddenly ask.

Knox clears his throat. "I come here when I need to clear my head."

"Thank you," I whisper.

# Chapter Thirty-Seven

I t's been nearly a week since the attack in Knox's home and everybody is still roaming the halls as if they're half asleep. The blood of those lost stain the atmosphere. It isn't until later in the evening when everybody is in the sitting room does anyone speak of such things as demons.

"The witches aren't using black magic," Harlow declares as she saunters into the room.

Lenox leans back in his chair. "You're sure of it?"

"When am I ever wrong?"

Knox, sitting in the seat beside me, cuts Lenox off before he can jab at Harlow. "What makes you think they're not in on it?"

Harlow grimaces. "Their land is dying. They're spending all of their time trying to find out why."

I lean forward in my seat. "Is it because of the dark magic?"

"They don't know," Harlow says solemnly.

Knox slides his gaze to me. "Do you think it's connected?"

"Everything is connected at this point," Nolan mutters.

Ace grimaces. "It's true. Every problem leads back to what happened that night."

Knox falls silent, his jaw clenching as he leans back in the sofa.

Harlow plops down into a seat beside Nolan. "I'm going to scout other locations. I have a sinking feeling that the witches' territory isn't the only land being affected."

Knox rests his elbows on his knees. "We need to hunt down the demonic creatures." Knox's words silence the room, the tension in the air palpable. Knox lifts his sapphire eyes to his court. "We now know why the demonic creatures roam the courts. They're guarding dark magic books they've hidden."

Unfortunately, the ones the wendigos were hiding didn't contain any entrapment spells.

Harlow scoffs, her eyes narrowing. "There's hundreds of creatures and we're expected to not only go after them, but also find the books they're hiding?"

I clear my throat. "One of the books they're guarding contains the entrapment spell." I look around the room to Knox's court. "If we want to destroy the entrapment spell, we need the dark magic book that created it."

Lenox's face scrunches as if he sucked on a lemon. "We have to go after them all, don't we?"

Knox grimaces. "Unfortunately, yes."

Axel steps out of the shadows of the room. "When do you want us to start?"

"Tomorrow morning. Lenox, you'll patrol the aerial legion, and Nolan will go to the warrior island. Harlow, we need you in the Water Court."

Harlow's eyes blaze with excitement. "As you wish."

Knox's lips twitch as he looks between the twins. "Ace and Axel, you'll go to the Air Court."

Ace clears his throat, his eyes darting between Hazel's quiet form and Knox. "I'd like to stay behind in the Essence Court, if that's okay."

Knox's sapphire eyes consider Hazel, eyes glazed and unfocused. Hazel has been quiet since the attack. She says she's okay, snapping at everyone to stop fussing around her like an insolent child, yet in moments like these when she goes silent and her eyes get far away…you know she's not dealing with it well.

Knox dips his chin at Ace. "You can patrol Essence while Axel patrols the Air Court. Delilah and I will go to the Earth Court. We can reconvene in two days' time to switch patrols for Fire and Air."

Harlow leans back in her seat, crossing her arms as she smirks. "What exactly do we have permission to do?"

Knox deadpans, "You have free rein on the beasts, Harlow."

Harlow clicks her tongue. "Delightful."

The next morning, Knox and I are flying over Essence Court as we make our way to the Earth Court. Anticipation sizzles through my veins as we soar over forests, lakes, and villages, scouring for demonic creatures. Every demonic creature we encounter is one step closer to the dark magic book.

Lifting my head to the sky, I can't help but bathe in the sun, the warm glow making my skin tingle. I flutter my eyes open to find Knox's sapphire eyes on me, the beautiful blues holding an emotion I can't decipher.

"You're meant to be looking for demons."

"I only stopped for a moment." Lifting my brows, I quip, "Besides, my eyes weren't the only ones to wander."

A tick in Knox's jaw is my only response.

As I turn back to the view, I expect to see more forests, yet the sight I find knocks the air from my lungs.

It's the most gorgeous sight I've ever beheld.

A tree, so large it must be over ten stories high, stretches before me. Its large trunk twists and twirls around itself until flaring out at the top, its branches spreading far and wide as its leaves glow. Pulsing with white light, it shimmers and twinkles as we fly past as if to say hello. The tree shines as bright as a star. Not only is the fluorescent color of the tree capturing, the energy pulsing off it in waves is hypnotizing, enchanting even. As if it's beckoning for me to join it.

"What is that?" I breathe.

Knox's warm breath tickles my ear. "The Tree of Life."

I'm grateful I don't have to voice the question on the tip of my tongue as Knox flies around it once more, its enchanting appearance and energy singing to a part of my soul. As if begging me to go inside and take a look.

"The very life force that's connected to magic, to Fae and these lands," Knox whispers.

"That's where magic is from?" I ask in awe.

Knox dips his head lower, flying slower as he circles the tree. "It *is* magic."

I have never been so drawn to anything in my life, as if the tree is a magnet, pulling on my heart strings. My body physically tenses, locking up as Knox sails away from the tree. It isn't until we've crossed the Essence border into Earth Court does my body start to finally relax.

It feels strange to be back here, in the woods where it all began. How vastly different my life has changed in a mere few weeks. It's shocking what time can do to a person. It isn't until Knox lands in an open field, with shin-length blades of grass tickling my legs, do I get a strong sense of déjà vu.

My gaze lifts to the swimming hole mere feet from me. The feeling of a dozen eyes on my back, watching my every movement, makes me shiver.

Knox's deep voice pulls me to the present. "This is where the mermaids gave you the riddle?"

I nod toward the swimming hole. "The pod was waiting for me there."

"Hmm, interesting."

I don't look back at the swimming hole as I leave, trailing behind Knox as we search the woods. "Hazel told me that they don't usually help anyone. Is that true?"

Knox doesn't take his eyes off the forest. "Yes. They only give freely to those that can do something for them in return."

I blink. "But I didn't do anything for them in return."

"Hence why it's interesting."

"I just wonder if—"

I knock into the hard planes of Knox's back, his large hands reaching behind him to hold my own, squeezing tightly. He drags me with him as he crouches in the long blades of grass.

Devious chuckling fills the forest, the sound of life around us holding their breath as the manic laughter grows louder with each passing second. White light surrounds us, time and space stretching and bending as Knox teleports us. Knox doesn't let go of my hand until my feet are touching the ground once more.

"What was it?"

Knox visibly shivers. "Gremlins."

Memories from Hazel's cabin come rushing to mind, images of green scaly creatures with teeth lining their eyelids. The lizard-like creatures appear as if from nightmares.

"Are they that horrid?" I ask, shocked to witness even Knox shudder.

"I grew up hearing legends about the gremlins in the forest. I learned at a very early age to stay far away from them."

I bite my lip, trying to contain my laughter. "Are you afraid of small gremlins, Knox?"

He scoffs. "Don't be ridiculous. I'm one of the most powerful Fae in Aloriah."

"That's afraid of gremlins," I mutter under my breath.

"If you don't shut up and search for demonic creatures, I'll leave you here alone to fend for yourself. You won't be laughing after you meet one of them."

I can't tell whether he's joking or not, and not daring to find out, I snap my mouth shut. Falling silent, I trail behind Knox through the dense Earth Court forests.

Thunder cracks, the darkening blue of dusk fast approaching as light ruptures across the sky, rocking the ground beneath my feet. Knox and I run for cover as lightning strikes throughout the lands of Aloriah, water beginning to pour.

We've searched the forest for hours with no such luck in finding any demonic creatures. Fitting how when you don't want to run into them, they're everywhere and yet when you do, they're nowhere to be found.

"I can't fly in this," Knox calls through the hammering weather.

I tip my chin to the sky, the pounding rain pummeling my face. Thunder explodes above me so loud I squeal. I open my mouth to suggest teleporting when I think better of it. He's been using his magic all day today and yesterday with very little rest. If Knox could teleport, he would have already.

Knox wraps his large hand around my arm, pulling me as we take off into a sprint. Running through the torrential pour is something I'm grateful to have experienced. With chaos surrounding us, the calm it brings me is euphoric. As if a part inside of me has been unlocked, released from its cage, grateful for the permission to soar, experiencing joy as if a child once more.

A giggle escapes me as my left boot sinks into a puddle, splashing Knox in the process. I fling my arms to the side, tipping my head back and letting myself laugh freely, enjoying the moment. Allowing my body to sense the forest around me, allowing Knox's energy and magic to flow over me, guiding me through the dense trees.

When I open my eyes, Knox is staring at me, a smile playing on his lips. His eyes shine, sparking with joy, yet not for himself—for me.

My laughter ebbs and flows, slowly dying as Knox's pace turns unhurried and a small log cottage appears through a break in the trees. A wooden sign dangles in the front garden. *Tavern of the Wild.*

Knox and I remove our wet coats, shaking the water off before entering through the front door, the hinges squeaking as bells chime overhead. The smell of pine washes over my senses, and oddly enough, lemon. The small cottage area is filled with various art pieces all depicting the lands of Earth court. The stories and history of the traveled paths taken, along with the found treasures Mother Gaia gave the Fae as gifts.

A small woman sits behind a wooden desk, a set of swords laid out as she cleans them. When the woman's eyes connect with Knox, they widen before she stands upright, bowing her head in respect. "Your Highness, how can I offer my services?"

"We'll take two available rooms, please."

The woman's cheeks tint pink. "I apologize, Your Highness. We only have one availability. The storm washed everyone in."

Knox turns on his charm, his smile deepening, making the woman's cheeks darken. "No worries, we'll take whatever is available."

My throat tightens, belly pinching as heat pools in my core. *We're sharing a room.*

The woman nods before scrambling for the other side of the desk, her steps harried yet slow with age. When she returns, her wrinkled hands hold golden wings, the key attached to the center.

"Second floor, last door on your left," she says with a smile.

Knox and I say thank you before climbing the creaking wooden stairs. As we pass each room, I'm surprised to find the hall deadly silent, no noise coming from any of the rooms, until I remember this isn't any ordinary lodge. It's a lodge filled with magic and silencing shields.

Using the golden-winged keys, Knox enters the last door at the end of the hall. Number seven. Stepping through, I'm shocked to find that not only is it freezing in the room, with the howling wind weaving in through the cracks and crevices on the roof, but...there's only one bed. The door shuts behind me, sealing me inside, along with my haywire hormones.

I'm rooted to the floor when Knox begins to peel off his clothing. "What are you doing?" I ask incredulously.

Knox's gaze lifts to mine. "Getting ready for bed."

My eyes widen. "You don't have to be naked to do it!"

He quirks a brow as he strips off his shirt. "No, but I'd prefer not to be drenched."

I don't hear a word he says. My eyes are glued to his stomach; it's not like I haven't seen his muscles before, but I've never seen them wet…as we're alone in a bedroom.

The sight makes my mouth dry. "There's only one bed."

My breath hitches as Knox drags his pants down, standing in the small room with only black boxers on. "I'm very much aware, Delilah, I do have eyes."

My cheeks heat as he walks around to the double bed, all his glorious muscles bunching as he slides between the sheets. When everything is covered by the white material, I finally lift my eyes. Knox lies there with the smuggest expression I've ever seen.

I stand in the middle of the room, not knowing what to do until I croak, "Do you need to be half-naked? It's freezing in here."

A phantom wind blows through the room, snuffing out each lantern until I'm plunged into darkness, the only light being the lightning striking outside.

"Get in bed, Delilah."

I gulp, unsheathing my blades and wet clothes before inching toward the bed. Sliding onto the sheets, I lie on the very edge, refusing to touch him. If I touch him, I'll lose all control.

My mind is wired, running through a thousand thoughts. I can feel the heat emanating from his body, teasing me as I shake from the cold. This is going to be a horrible night's sleep.

Knox's voice sends a shiver down my spine. "You can warm yourself and the room you know."

"I-I don't know how to do that," I sputter.

I can practically hear his smirk. "Shame."

The sound of my teeth chattering fills the room. Is he making the room colder? The temperature has dropped significantly from when we first entered.

I grit my teeth. "Knox."

"Yes, Angel?" he purrs.

"I'm freezing. At least tell me how to warm the room."

He lets out a long sigh. "I don't feel like being your test subject…You could very well turn us into ash in your sleep."

I groan, sliding further under the thin sheet. *He's insufferable!*

The bed dips as his body moves closer. "What are you doing?" I snap

"Your teeth are annoying. I'm warming you up. That's what friends do."

He spits the word *friend* as his wings unfurl behind his back. A wing drops in front of me, cocooning us. I moan at the heat radiating from them and instinctively snuggle closer, stiffening when Knox lets out a deep groan, the sound making my core clench and pulse.

My eyes widen at what I've just done. I touched his wings. I fling myself back, only to bump into his bare chest.

"If you're about to complain about the arrangement, I suggest you shut your mouth."

I huff out a laugh, thankful that he doesn't comment on the wing touching. My teeth stop chattering as his chest slows and his breathing turns shallow. I close my eyes, trying to calm my body as every nerve ending lights on fire. Lying next to him after spending weeks avoiding how he makes me feel is absolute torture, and the more time I spend around Knox, the more my body screams to have him, to want him in any way I can. Gritting my teeth, I force my body and hormones to relax and pray for sleep to come.

A whimper leaves my mouth as I awake to Knox's front plastered to my back, his arms circled around my waist as he holds me, the hard length of him probing my backside. I don't know how it's possible, but I've woken more turned on than when I went to sleep. My underwear is wet, my core pulsing as goosebumps skitter down my body. My chest heaving at the feel of his hard length behind me.

Knox's hands twitch, one nestled between my breasts and the other under my head. His chest rises and falls against my back, and the puffs of his warm breath tickling my ear make me whimper. My hips instinctively swivel in small circles as Knox's length twitches from my sounds.

His hips grind against me, making my head fall back, my lips parting, a low moan escaping me. His hand squeezes my breast, pinching my sensitive nipples, then trails lower down my stomach to where I need him most. I part my legs to accommodate his hand when power blasts throughout the cottage. Knox's shields snap around us as he sits up, his wing covering me. I peek around Knox's wing as shouts and screams come from the hallway.

"How dare you do this to me, Xavier!"

"I think it's time to leave," Knox whispers.

Wordlessly we slide out of bed, the argument on the other side of the door penetrating our walls as we silently get dressed. I can't believe what we were about to do.

No matter how much time has passed, my cheeks remain tinted pink while I lie in Knox's arms as he flies over the

Earth Court back to Azalea. I haven't been able to look Knox in the eye since we left the small cottage several hours ago. Reading how embarrassed and uncomfortable I am, Knox decided to fly back to Azalea instead of continuing to scout for demonic creatures.

I'm not embarrassed over what could have potentially happened. I'm embarrassed that any time I look at Knox, my body ignites in flames from how much he physically affects me. One glance from him and I know my resolve will crumble instantly.

Keeping my eyes downcast on the Earth Court lands, I can practically feel Knox's thoughts running a thousand miles an hour. He also hasn't said a word to me since we left. I'm wondering how I can fix the situation when my eyes practically fly out of my head.

"STOP!"

Knox halts midair so forcibly he has to tighten his hold on me as I fly forward from the impact, as if we hit an invisible wall.

"What is it?"

I shake my head, unable to utter the words. "Land on the floor now," I croak.

The second his feet touch the forest floor, I practically throw myself out of his arms, my feet shooting off the ground as I run.

Knox's shouts and protests at my back chase me. My feet slide as I come to an abrupt stop, my knees buckling, taking me to the floor as a sob leaves my mouth. Knox's gasp behind me is the only sound in this desolate land. I lift my hands before me, watching ash flutter between my fingertips.

*No.*

Knox falls to his knees beside me, the air rushing from his lungs in one fell swoop. Silver lines his eyes as he shakes his head, his hands lying helplessly on his lap. We stare at the dying land before us, the lively color of the forest burning black as it turns to ash.

Exactly like my dream.

There is no fire, no one creating this. It's as if the very essence of what makes the forest magic come alive is dying.

*The Fae lands are dying.*

"I've seen this," I whisper.

Knox's eyes burn a hole into the side of my head. "When? Can it be fixed?"

I shake my head. "I saw it in my dreams. I dreamt of the Fae lands dying, that everything turned to ash."

"I don't understand any of this," he rasps.

"We need to break the entrapment spell."

# Chapter Thirty-Eight

Tossing and turning in bed, my thoughts won't shut off with all the unanswered questions running havoc in my mind. It's been over a week since we searched the courts and we haven't found any more books, let alone answers as to why parts of Aloriah are dying. Every day Knox's court scours the lands for demonic creatures, and every day they return to the house with dejected faces. It's as if all the demon creatures have completely disappeared, vanished overnight. We can't break the entrapment spell without the dark magic book it originated from, and we can't find it without the beasts. They've all gone into hiding. Every last one of them.

Only to be replaced by small patches of ash. Each day we find a new piece of land dying, the once colorful and lively forest dead, ash fluttering in its wake.

The possibility that I have to be taken by demonic hounds to help free everyone is becoming a real possibility as the days pass. Being one of the biggest reasons for my pitiful attempt to sleep.

Every lead we find turns into a dead end...We have nothing, absolutely nothing.

Groaning, I throw the covers off and drag myself out of bed. I know I won't get much sleep tonight; it's pointless to even try. Kneeling beside the futon at the end of my bed, I scan through the titles of books I stashed here that Hazel gave me. Selecting a romance book, I nestle myself into the pillows.

I'm halfway through reading the first page when I drop the book, fear pulsing through me so strong it feels as if I'm drowning in it. Yet it isn't my own. It feels—

Shadows and darkness blast through my room until I'm standing in nothing but a dark abyss. I know whose power that belongs to. I can feel the anguished fear and pain.

Not bothering to change, I blindly search for my fighting leathers, grabbing the first blade I find, I snatch the silver before running out.

I rush for the end of the hallway, surprised to find I'm the only one awake. Not bothering to wait for anyone, I blast through the door only for my face to be singed with heat.

Knox's entire room is shrouded in flames.

Instinct takes over. Before I can think water is flowing through my hands, putting out flames as I enter the room. Yet every time I extinguish one flame, another ignites. I can still feel Knox's panic, his fear and sadness pulsing throughout the room, but I can't see him anywhere.

Baring my teeth, I shield myself as I run through the flames, using my water to put them out as I go. Panic begins to consume me, making my throat tighten.

*Where is he, where is he, where is he?*

I fling my power out, searching, probing, sensing—

Feeling his essence thrash and struggle in the middle of the room I run for the area, finding him in the middle of the bed. Lunging across the large frame, I try to shield him from the fire only to find Knox panting in the flames as they engulf him.

This is Knox's own doing.

He's having a nightmare. That's why the fire has only spread so far as his bedroom.

Shielding every inch of my skin, I sit on top of him, pinning him down with my weight. Holding his firm shoulders, I jolt him with all my strength. "Knox!"

Nothing.

I enter his mind only to bounce off shields on fire. Everything is consumed by fire. "Knox!" I scream, shaking his body harder, pleading for him to wake up. Using my own fire, I make my flames dance with his, yet where his are screaming with pain, mine are singing a calm melody. "Knox it's a dream," I repeat like a mantra, panting it over and over.

Wings explode behind his back so fiercely the sudden movement jolts me. Fear like no other consumes me as the flames engulf his beautiful iridescent black wings. Without a second thought my canines flare, and I sink my teeth into the apex of his shoulder and neck. I pray the pain from this side will wake him up from the pain within his mind.

The flames around the room pause, assessing. I send my flames toward his own, caressing, soothing.

*Knox, it's a dream.*

His thrashing pauses as the flames slowly simmer. I retract my teeth, tasting him on my tongue, my heart roaring in response.

Knox's eyes snap wide open, his lips pale and face sunken as he breathes erratically.

"Knox, it's a dream," I repeat, my chest rising and falling in rhythm with his own.

As forcefully as they arrived the flames disappear, smoke

filling the air as his flames dissipate. His wings are still flared, yet the flames are gone, revealing his magnificent, *unharmed* wings.

"Angel," he croaks.

"Yes," I breathe.

He smirks. "Why are you straddling me?"

I gasp, realizing that I am indeed straddling him. Not only that but in my haste to rush here and help, I didn't change. I'm only wearing my silk pajama shirt and panties. Gritting my teeth, I whack his shoulder. "You're welcome."

I begin to slide off his body, but Knox wraps his arm around my waist, pulling me down flush against his chest. "Thank you," he whispers gutturally.

A deep sigh leaves me, the adrenaline wearing off as relief flows through my body.

"Do you want to talk about it?"

Knox exhales before sitting up, dragging me with him as he goes. I shimmy off his lap—he lets me this time—and sit next to him on the bed.

"Let me guess, flames?" he mutters. Knox runs a hand down his face, groaning at my nod. "Sorry, it's usually contained to my room."

I frown. "It was, but I felt it."

Sapphire eyes snap to mine. He searches my gaze, but for what, I'm not sure.

He clears his throat. "I always have them around this time of year." Knox's gaze lowers. "Did Hazel tell you what happened?"

My heart twists, aching for this more vulnerable side of Knox. "I'd rather hear it from you," I say, repeating his own words from when we met.

Knox's eyes look far away as his brows furrow, lips pinching. "My parents had me young for a Fae. We would have had hundreds—possibly a thousand years together. I always thought I would have that time with them." His voice cracks. "I came home late from the Eclipse Ball. I was out celebrating with friends…I knew something was wrong the moment I approached the gates. We had guards stationed there twenty-four seven, and when I got closer, I found that they were dead. Not only the gate guards but every single guard in the estate. It was horrible, seeing the people I grew up with, that I cared for and loved, taken from this earth in such a brutal way." His chest heaves as his eyes shutter closed. When he opens them again, they're pooled with tears.

My heart breaks for the pain etched across this gorgeous man's face and the sudden realization that he not only saw his grounds covered with his dead men once, but twice. His broken words from that day come back to me, punching a hole through my heart.

"By the time I reached their quarters, I knew what I would find. Yet seeing them…It was a shock. They were both so brutally tortured and murdered. The amount of blood in the room showed that whoever did it got off on it. They were healed repeatedly to drag out the murders. I vomited all over myself and the ground…To this day I have never seen anything like it," he whispers brokenly.

I lay my hand on his arm. "I am so deeply sorry."

Knox shrugs.

"No. Don't do that. Don't diminish your pain."

He finally lifts those gorgeous sapphire eyes to mine, lowering once more as he frowns. "Why are you crying?"

I place a hand on my cheek, finding wetness. I didn't realize I was crying. I feel embarrassed that I am but I can't help it. Nobody deserves to lose their loved ones in such a brutal way. "Because the world can be a horrible place," is my only response.

Knox stares at me intently for a few moments before he speaks.

"What happened to Easton?"

My body physically jolts at his words. "I'm sure you saw it in my mind."

His eyes soften. "I'd rather hear it from you."

I lower my gaze, allowing my heart to open this small fraction. A story for a story.

"Easton was my everything," I say on an exhale. "We met as children and were inseparable." My lips tug into a smile, remembering Easton as a little boy. "He was kind and caring. He had so much love to give others, it was like breathing fresh air for the first time." I fall quiet for a moment, building the courage to speak.

Knox pats the pillow beside him. Taking his invitation, I lean back into the silk pillows, the warmth of his arm seeping into my own as I stare at the ceiling.

"I loved him," I whisper. "Platonically, but I truly, deeply loved him for the person he was, and he loved me for me." I turn my head to find Knox already watching me. "Not that it matters, but Easton was gay. Even if he wasn't, the love we felt was different, two souls caring for the other." My lip begins to wobble. "Easton begged me every day to leave. He despised my father and wanted to run away. Sometimes he thought about taking me away in the middle of the night, despite my protests," I say on a broken laugh.

A tear falls down my cheek as I continue. "I had finally decided to leave, just for a few weeks, but Easton was ecstatic nevertheless. He never said it, but he hated the palace. He would have left a long time ago if it wasn't for me." My voice cracks as I say, "We were no more than ten minutes away from the rowboat when my father turned up."

I take a deep breath, squeezing my eyes closed as Easton's lifeless face flashes in my mind. "My father began to beat me, and Easton stepped in. It happened so fast…One moment Easton is standing behind me and the next my father slits his throat. He cut him so deeply he was dead before I turned around."

Tears roll freely down my face. Knox lifts his hand, gently brushing away my tears as I speak, his fingers sending electricity through my skin. "I broke that night. Some intricate part of me died. Seeing Easton's lifeless body hurt me so deeply…and seeing my father *smiling*…I snapped. Gold light surrounded us, and then he was on the ground unconscious."

Knox freezes, his brows pulling low. "Delilah, you had magic before you crossed the border."

My face matches his own confused expression. "No I didn't. I woke up as Fae."

Knox sits up. "That golden light was your own magic, the canines too," he says, looking at the memory in my mind.

"Why didn't you see that before?"

"Most of your memories with your father, including the one with Easton, are hidden, as if you've locked them away. If I opened them, you would have felt that pain and I didn't want to do that," he whispers gently.

"I dissociated when my father beat me," I admit.

He nods. "That's why they're locked away."

I bite my lip. "Why would I turn into a Fae in the human lands?" Knox looks at me, waiting patiently as my mind wraps around the unfathomable idea. "I was never truly human," I breathe.

Knox's eyes soften. "It appears not."

I groan, sliding down the bed until I'm lying flat on my back. "Add that to the pile of unanswered questions," I grumble.

Knox is silent for a moment before he asks, "Do you want to talk about your father?"

"Gods no. That conversation can be for another day."

Knox lies beside me. "Tell me the good parts about Easton, the happy memories."

My heart flutters at his request, a small smile tugging at the corner of my lips.

So I do. I tell him about every little moment I had with Easton, about all the good he brought into my life. We talk for hours, exchanging stories for stories, Knox telling me his own cherished memories of his family, until sleep and exhaustion drags both of us under.

# Chapter Thirty-Nine

"**R**eady to fly, Angel?" Knox calls from a few feet away. The sun shines behind him as we stand in the back garden, waiting to conduct our magic lesson for the afternoon.

Insufferable cocky bastard. "I hope I land on your face," I snap.

The moment I woke up determined to put space back between us, he woke up determined to smash the wall I created entirely.

He smirks. "You love my face too much to do that." He taps his lips with his index finger. "What is it that you say? Gorgeous, beautiful…the most handsome man you've ever seen?" His eyes shine with utter delight as I gasp.

"You're insufferable!"

He shrugs. "I know you don't truly mean that."

"Oh trust me, I do," I grit.

His smile is predatory as he stares me down. "You don't think I scent the change in you when you're pissed at me, Angel?"

My eyes blaze with fury. Knox woke up this morning,

took one look at me wrapped in his arms, in his bed, and chose pure violence.

He disappears, teleporting behind me, resting his lips on the shell of my ear. "No, Angel, I chose foreplay," he purrs.

A shiver wracks my body at his blunt words.

I spin, preparing to do anything and everything to shove him away, but he's gone already. I turn back to find him lounging in the garden seat, his powerful arms spread along the back of the bench. "Are you ready yet?" he drawls.

I cock my hip, crossing my arms. "Are you done playing games?"

He looks up at me beneath his thick lashes, eyes blazing. "Never."

My toes involuntarily curl. "Just shut up and show me."

"My pleasure," he croons, disappearing from thin air before I feel his breath on the back of my neck. "Open your wings."

I close my eyes and take a deep breath, Knox's presence making it hard to concentrate. Nevertheless, I immerse myself within my magic, becoming one with it. I shift my stance as my wings unfurl, trying to drag me down.

Knox places his hands on my hips. "Engage your core and back muscles to steady yourself."

He trails his hands up and down the side of my stomach as I listen to him. My core muscles aren't the only thing being engaged. My nerve endings spark to life, ready to combust at a moment's notice, my body screaming for his hands to trail lower.

Knox's touch never leaves me as he walks around me. Aligning his feet with my own, his wings blossom behind him. With barely a foot between us, my breathing turns shallow.

"Flutter your wings," he says softly.

The wind brushes my back as my wings open and close. Hazel wasn't wrong about their sensitivity. Every brush of air against them sends a jolt through my body, heightening the experience of my already electric flesh.

I grit my teeth, taking deep calming breaths.

Knox's cocky voice travels down my spine. "Something wrong, Delilah?"

"Nope. Everything is just fine," I chirp.

Knox takes a small step forward. Picking up my hands, he spreads my arms out beside me. His gaze never leaves mine as he drags his index fingers along my arms, traveling from the tips of my fingers to my shoulders. A shudder wracks my body as his featherlight touch trails down my chest, over the swell of my breasts, before he lays his palms flat against my ribs, stroking his thumb under my breasts. "Engage your back muscles as you pick up the pace," he whispers.

Muscles I've never used before burn as they work to accommodate the faster movement of my wings as they flap.

"Good girl," he purrs.

My nipples tighten painfully, my breasts growing heavier with each breath I take.

Knox's husky voice sets my stomach on fire. "Faster, Angel."

My eyes close on their own accord. How Knox has turned a lesson in flying to be such an erotic experience escapes me.

"Knox," I breathe.

He lowers himself to me, bringing his face so close to mine I feel his exhale brush against my lips. "Yes, Delilah?"

My eyes shoot open to see his are drooped, blazing with heat. I close my wings and take a step back, ignoring the way my toes curl at his guttural groan. I shake my head and turn for the house.

*This can't happen.*

"Where are you going?" he shouts.

"Lesson over," I call over my shoulder. Then I slam into a wall of rock-solid muscles. "Stop doing that!" I snap.

"Why are you still pushing me away?" he asks, the intensity in his gaze drying my mouth.

"I'm not. I need a break," I say flatly.

He cocks a brow. "Why?"

I flail my hands beside me. "Because flying uses new muscles and my back hurts."

"Try again."

I ball my hands into fists. Why is he pushing me on this? "I'm tired," I grit out.

"Wrong." He lowers his mouth to my ear. "I think you're struggling to cope with how wet I make you."

I gasp, shoving his chest with all my strength. "Stop it!"

Knox pushes forward, invading every inch of my space until I have to tilt my head back to see his face. "Give me one good reason why I should," he demands.

"You're fucking annoying," I spit.

"Delilah." He clenches his jaw, irritation coating every word. "You either tell me the reason to whatever this new problem is you seem to think we have, or I see for myself."

My self-control snaps.

"I'm princess of the human lands! You're a Fae king, it's too complicated, and there's too many consequences!" I scream in his face.

"Fuck your consequences," he growls, smashing his lips to mine.

The moment his soft lips touch mine I moan. Every reason as to why we shouldn't be doing this leaves my mind entirely as Knox slides his arms around my lower back, pulling me against his body. Every dip and hard ridge of his muscles press against my body. My nipples tighten, wetness pooling in my center when the large length of his hardness prods my stomach.

His tongue peeks out, stroking the seams of my lips, demanding to be let in. I part my mouth, welcoming him. Knox groans into my mouth, the vibrations traveling through my body as his tongue explores mine, tasting every inch, kissing me as if he never will again, savoring every stroke and taste.

His hands slide up my body, slowly teasing my sensitive skin as his fingers trail up my stomach, gliding over the swell of my breasts. I whimper when his thumb brushes my nipples, stroking small circles around the hard nubs. His hands continue up my neck and cup my cheeks.

My body is on fire. Nothing has ever felt like this before, and nothing compares. I place my hands on his hips, slipping my fingers under his shirt, the warmth of his skin seeping into my hands as I greedily feel every inch of muscle. His growl of appreciation vibrates into my mouth, traveling down my spine to my toes, turning my exploration frenzied.

I need more. I need to feel everything, see everything, taste every inch of him.

"Keep talking like that, Angel, and I'll take you right here where anyone can see," Knox growls.

My breath hitches, my core pulsing at his words.

Knox leans forward, nipping the shell of my ear. "I love hearing everything you want to do to me."

My chest heaves as I pull away, my body screaming in disapproval. It yearns, begs, to be worshipped by Knox. His sapphire eyes are so full of heat they look predatory.

My mind whirls, panic grasping me. No matter what happens, I still have to leave—

"One day at a time, Angel, we'll take it one day at a time," Knox says softly, reading my mind.

"Knox, get your ass inside!"

A shield snaps around us the second Lenox's voice booms across the yard.

I frown. "Why are you shielding us?"

Knox's grin is devious. "Scent."

My eyes widen. You can truly smell the change in a Fae? I thought it was a myth or the men were taunting and joking about it. My mouth drops opens when I realize all the times Knox had turned me on and I played it off...he knew the whole time.

Humor dances along every inch of his face. That's why he was so cocky all the time. He knew, he always knew how he affected me. I shake my head in bewilderment. "I still don't understand how you're getting past my mental shields," I find myself saying.

Knox looks at me intensely, gazing at me as if he can see right through me. "I think we'll find out soon," he murmurs.

"For fuck's sake...Knox!" Lenox shouts.

Knox slides his hands into his pockets, strolling for the back door. "This isn't over, Angel," he calls over his shoulder.

No, it isn't.

Whatever the hell this is.

"Do you and Axel have telepathy?" I ask Ace as we sit in front of the fire.

Lenox dragged Knox into his study the moment he stepped into the house, leaving Ace and I standing alone in the foyer. Ace offered to keep me company, joining me in the sitting room on the brown leather sofa as he helps me clean my swords.

Ace stumbles over a swipe before halting his movements, my question throwing him off guard. "I didn't realize we were being watched," he says defensively.

"I wasn't watching you on purpose," I rush out, placing my hand on his. "I didn't mean to intrude. I've just noticed that you tend to know what he's thinking and vice versa."

Ace's shoulders relax. "Sorry, we used to be..." He shakes his head. "Our telepathy was used against us when we were younger. We're very—"

"Protective of it?"

Ace nods sheepishly and picks up the sword again. "Yes, something like that."

I look over the back of the couch in the direction of Knox's study. They've been in there for over an hour now; I hope everything is okay. I turn back to Ace. "Do you mind telling me about the other courts?"

His eyes fill with excitement. "Of course, what do you want to know?"

I bite my lip. "Everything. I know there's five courts for the elements, each one housing a city, but what are they truly like?"

"Each city is styled in honor of the element. Air is all mountains and hills, the eastern side of the country getting the ocean's wind knocked into them. Earth is full of waterfalls, forests, and lands. Naturally, they have the best crops. Water is magnificent, with canals and rivers running throughout the city, and the Fire Court is a warrior's playground. They're all very hot-headed," he mutters, smiling to himself.

I pick up another sword, wiping oil down the silver. "What are their kings and queens like?"

"They all dealt with their grief over what happened differently. It shaped all of them, most for the better and some for the worse."

I frown. "In what way?"

Ace lifts his head, pausing his movements. "Some of the ruling families became hateful. I don't think they knew how to deal with their grief, so they started taking it out on those around them." Ace's voice hardens. "It's selfish, making your city, your people, pay for something they didn't do."

Ice fills my veins. "What are they doing to their people?"

Cold forest green eyes lock with mine. "Some courts' ruling royals want to reinstate old barbaric laws."

I arch a brow. "Such as?"

"They want to reestablish class lines with the lesser Fae," he says, rage that I've never seen in him before contorting his face.

"Why would they want to do such a thing?" I breathe.

"Power," he says simply.

Of course, it always comes down to power. The only royal I've come across that isn't power hungry is…Knox. "Is there any chance of that happening?"

He shakes his head. "Not with everything else that's going on."

Axel strolls into the room wearing his fighting leathers, pulling our attention away. "Where's Knox and Lenox?"

Ace waves his hand to the door "Lenox dragged him into the study."

Axel plops down into the single sofa in front of me, crossing his powerful legs at the knees. "Hazel was asking for you," he says casually, his gaze locked on Ace.

Ace's head snaps up. "Where is she?" he asks, already standing.

"In the cellar." Axel grins.

Ace doesn't utter another word to his twin as he rushes out of the room. I can't help but chuckle.

Axel picks up the sword Ace deserted and begins cleaning it.

"Oh, you don't have to."

He simply shrugs, the epitome of unfazed. "I don't mind."

I resume cleaning mine, both of us working silently as we wipe down the blades. I'm surprised I feel so comfortable around him. In the past, silent and intimidating men have made my internal alarm bells go off, accompanied by an overwhelming need to avoid them at all costs. Yet I don't feel that way around Axel. He seems silent and closed off for a whole other reason, other than it being an intimidation tactic. He's constantly alert, assessing and taking in his surroundings, as if he's waiting for a fight and needs to protect himself at a moment's notice.

"How did you meet Knox?" I ask, breaking the silence.

Axel doesn't lift his head from the sword as he speaks. "On the streets of Azalea when we were boys. My mother was in and out of our lives until one day she didn't return, leaving Ace and I to fend for ourselves."

I try to hide my shock, not only to the horrors of his childhood but that he's opening up to me at all. "That's awful."

"She was a horrible person," he states coldly. "When she was high, she found enjoyment in making me her punching bag and when she wasn't high, she was out on the streets searching for her next fix."

Bile churns in my stomach. That's why he's so protective of Ace even after all these years; Axel grew up protecting him, shielding him from the horrors of their so-called mother. Perhaps that's why I feel safe around him, subconsciously knowing we were similar, that he would never do to others what was done to us.

Trepidation runs through me. "Why are you telling me all of this?"

Axel lifts his head, vibrant green eyes piercing mine. "Because I know why you're finding it difficult to not get attached and comfortable with people."

Panic sinks its claws into my chest, an invisible hand squeezing until it burns. Do they all know? Is that why they're kind to me? Out of pity?

"Did Knox tell you?" I ask calmly, feeling anything but.

"No, I can see the signs."

I blink. "Do they all know?"

"No, that's your story to share if you wish," he replies gently, staring at me for a moment before adding, "Ace doesn't know either. He was more sheltered from my mother, so he doesn't know what that part feels like...not to the full extent."

My heart breaks at his admission, my earlier thoughts confirmed.

Axel got the brute force of his mother's fists to save his brother from ever feeling that type of pain. The confusion, hurt, and betrayal of someone you love making you feel so worthless, as if you're nothing.

I lean forward, placing my hand on his forearm, feeling his muscles tense before relaxing. "Thank you for sharing yours with me," I whisper.

Axel dips his chin, picking up the sword, retreating into his mind once more.

I'm about to leave the sitting room when Harlow, Ace, and Hazel storm through the back door, their chests heaving frantically. "We know how the spell was created," Hazel wheezes.

My mouth falls open, utter shock zipping through my body. Knox appears in front of me, facing the others, as if he could sense the change in the air. The spark of hope that they've found, an opportunity for redemption.

Axel rises from his seat, his eyes guarded as he faces his brother.

"What the fuck? At least tell me what's happening before you disappear into thin air!" Lenox shouts, barging through the sitting room door. He stops the moment he takes in all our expressions. "Someone better start talking," he mutters.

"We know how the spell was created," Hazel repeats.

The energy in the room sparks—with hope.

"How?" Knox asks.

Hazel opens her mouth only to slam it shut, casting a wary glance at Ace.

Ace steps forward, grimacing as he says, "Sacrifice."

Knox's body goes still as death, his hands clenching at his sides so tightly his knuckles turn white.

"We still need the original spell book that the caster used, but now we know what type of dark magic was performed and how it created something so large," Hazel rushes on.

Harlow cuts in, saving Hazel from being the one to break Knox's heart. "They used the energy of the king and queens' murders as a conduit to power the spell," she says in disgust.

My entire body goes numb.

Knox's family was brutally murdered—sacrificed—*for a spell.*

I'm thankful I haven't eaten dinner, otherwise I would have vomited right then. I turn to Knox, finding his face full of agony, his features twisting in pain.

"That's not all." Ace winces, making Axel's body go rigid. "The demonic creatures aren't being let in through the barrier like how Delilah was…They're being summoned."

"The reason why they keep coming back is because they can't be killed in this world. The moment they die, they return to where they came from and whoever is doing this just summons them again," Harlow explains.

The beasts truly aren't from this world.

Lenox's face is deathly pale as he mutters, "Holy shit."

Everyone stands around the sitting room, utterly speechless. I don't think Knox is even breathing as he says, "Did you find anything else?"

Pain fills Ace's eyes. "That's all."

Knox leaves the room without another word, his entire body locked tight, his hands clenching and unclenching at his side. My body screams to try and fix this, soothe him in whatever way I can, to make the horrible pain he feels disappear. I start to follow after him when a large hand catches my bicep. "Give him a moment," Axel murmurs.

Axel has known Knox longer than I have; he'd know best. I take a step back, despite my heart crying out otherwise.

"We need to continue tracking the beasts, try and lure them out of whatever hole they crawled into," Lenox states, rage morphing his features.

"We will," Harlow says adamantly.

"I need to update Nolan," Lenox mutters before leaving, his shoulders slouched. I swear I see silver lining his eyes before he disappears from the room.

Everyone disperses, nobody having an appetite for dinner.

Anguish races through me, deep and utter sorrow, so crippling it takes my breath away. The only other time I felt this type of pain was...when I lost Easton. But it's not my pain I'm feeling. Without second-guessing myself, I head straight up the stairs and down the hall.

Not bothering to knock, I open the door. My gaze doesn't linger on the room long. I find Knox sitting on the futon at the end of his bed, slouched over his knees, a glass tumbler of what smells to be whiskey dangling from his hands.

My heart pinches.

He doesn't move as I approach. Kneeling before him, I see the utter devastation on his face as silent tears roll down his cheeks. I take the tumbler out of his hand, placing it beside me on the floor. Sliding my hands up his neck, I tilt his head, making those pain-filled eyes connect with mine. "What do you need?" I whisper, my thumbs stroking his cheeks, catching the tears that escape.

"You," he whispers brokenly. "I just need you."

My heart cracks at his vulnerable admission.

Climbing onto his lap, I wrap my arms around his neck, stroking my fingers through the soft strands of his hair as he buries his head into the crook of my neck.

We stay like that for hours, as he mourns the loss of his parents all over again.

# Chapter Forty

I wake up exhilarated from my dream. Rushing from bed, I throw on my fighting leathers and knives in a haste, as elation rushes through my veins. Dawn is hours away; I should be asleep, yet my dream had other plans.

After consoling Knox for hours, he seemed to come around, returning to his normal teasing and flirting. Yet I could tell the pain still simmered within, trying to drag him down. I knew Knox could read my thoughts, so I allowed him to roam freely. I didn't want our first time to be after a revelation that caused him such pain. I didn't want to become an emotional crutch, or to be a distraction. I can't say no to him, especially after that kiss, and if he truly pushed me, I wouldn't have stopped him, so he kindly set me into my own bed for the night, returning to his after a toe-curling kiss.

Next time, I won't be able to say no to him. I can't continue pushing him away as my body screams every moment of the day for what it wants. I've decided that even though I have to leave when all of this is over and say good-bye, it's okay. I can cherish my time here, the friendships I've made, this city, and I can cherish Knox—for whatever time we have left together.

I barrel down the hallway toward Knox.

I can't believe I didn't think of it sooner.

Not caring with pleasantries, I storm through Knox's bedroom door, waking him with a jolt. His raven black hair is for once not perfectly styled, except even his tousled bed hair looks divine. He sits up in bed, revealing his stunning bare chest.

I scan his room; I was in such a rush to leave it this morning, and it was encased in darkness and flames the previous night, that I never truly looked around. It's larger than mine, almost twice the size. It houses a seating area, with white-cushioned couches in front of a crackling fireplace. Rows upon rows of bookshelves line the wall beside it. An open archway leads to what appears to be his dressing and bathing suite. A small bar cart sits behind the couch, various wine and whiskey glasses atop it. His bed is the largest I've ever seen, and now I know, also the most comfortable.

I rip my gaze away from Knox's glorious naked chest, completely ignoring him as I walk past into his dressing room. Knox's sleepy drawl follows me as I rummage through his clothes. "I love you in my room, Angel, but care to explain to me what you're doing?"

A shiver runs down my spine at his deep husky voice. It's so thick it makes liquid heat pool in my stomach. I chastise my body—not right now, this is not the time, there are more important things to deal with. I walk out of his dressing room, his clothes and weapons ladening my arms. I dump them on the bed, placing my hands on my hips. "Get dressed," I demand.

Knox's head pulls back in shock before his lips widen into a grin. "Playing a different type of game are we, Angel?"

"You can deal with your own issues later. Get dressed."

He cocks a brow. "The next time I do, you'll be under me." His smile turns predatory. "Or on top, whichever makes you scream the loudest."

My eyes widen, cheeks heating. "Get dressed!"

Knox chuckles as he slides out of bed, my eyes widening for another reason entirely. He's only wearing boxers, white boxers, that do absolutely nothing to hide the glorious package hidden behind the material. My stomach clenches as I watch him get changed.

"Are you going to tell me what we're doing or are you going to continue fantasizing about what my cock will feel like inside you?" he drawls casually.

I suck in a breath. Knox has taken away all pretenses about his intentions. No longer is he pretending not to be interested, only his blunt desire and need come out of his mouth now.

"I had a dream," I blurt.

Knox straps his twin swords across his back, waiting for me to continue, no judgment on his face, just pure openness.

"We need to track where the beasts are being summoned from and where they're hiding the dark magic books, correct?"

"Correct."

"It would take weeks to track down where they're all hiding…" I trail off.

Knox walks into the bathroom. I hear water splash before he walks back out with a toothbrush in his mouth. "Go on."

"Griffins won't fly near land where demonic creatures reside. If we fly with a griffin, we'll know where they're located without even having to land."

Knox's eyes widen before he walks back into the bathroom. When he returns he doesn't stop until he's a hair's breadth away, leaning down to place a gentle kiss on my fore-head. "Brilliant idea."

I smile sheepishly. It's going to take time for me to accept being openly praised for speaking about court matters. Even after all these weeks it still feels abnormal. My father's words and beatings are something I'll never be able to shake.

I lift my chin. "I want to ride the black griffin."

Knox's lips spread into a grin. "I'll fly us there."

Knox stops into his study to write a note for the others, explaining where we're going but not why. Knox also gives his court orders for the day. He keeps Ace from resuming his usual duties, allowing him to remain close to Hazel. I find it sweet that he knows Ace still won't leave Hazel here alone, giving him the task of helping her with the potion antidote.

Taking off into the night sky, I lay my head on Knox's chest, letting his steady heartbeat calm my senses.

Landing at the aerial legion hours later at sunrise is an eerie feeling. Not only can you sense the creatures and riders asleep, but it feels as if the island itself hasn't awoken.

Knox and I tiptoe through the compound. The black griffin doesn't have a permanent rider, so technically we're not stealing her, but by the quiet way Knox navigates the area, we're probably breaking some sort of protocol.

The minute I walk into the enclosure, the beautiful black griffin locks those golden eyes on mine. She rushes over, bouncing with energy. I can't stop the giggle that escapes me, happiness filling my heart that she's excited to see me.

I pat her behind her ears, her soft feline purr making my heart melt. I know the moment Knox walks through the gate because she snaps her head to him, her eyes sharpening. "This is Knox," I whisper.

She juts out her snout, sniffing once, twice, before turning her head away.

I laugh. "I don't think you got the approval."

A chuckle slips from Knox's mouth as he comes up beside me. "Perhaps she's jealous."

"Are you jealous?" I ask her.

She drags her head to mine, her eyes flat, as if to say, *Really?*

I roll my eyes. "We need your help today. Care for another ride?" If I told myself months ago that I would not only be having a conversation with a griffin but that the griffin would understand me, I would have thought I lost my mind. She lowers her head in submission. I stroke her ears in return, as a thank you. "We really need to give you a name," I mutter to myself.

Knox leaves the pen, returning with saddle equipment. His sapphire eyes sparkle as he stares at me, yet it's not heat that I find in his eyes, but something akin to endearment.

We fly for hours, scouring Earth Court lands without seeing a single demonic creature. At least all this empty time allowed me to think up a name for the griffin. Aurora. I think it suits her strong feline personality.

As we're passing over endless sand dunes, I see a city glinting in the distance. Knox's voice floats through my mind a second later.

*We'll stop here for lunch. The griffin needs a break.*

The city looms before us, the intricate details of Ornx, the Fire Court's main city, greeting us. Buildings upon buildings line the streets, some small while others tower over the land. It's beautiful and yet nothing like Azalea. The city is fast-paced, dry as stone, with no colors beside red and black as Fae rush to and from buildings. Hundreds walk the streets as they go about their day. I don't hear lively music playing from the streets. Instead, I hear boots, endless stomping of boots. Almost every male and female Fae wear matching black and red clothing.

Warriors.

A city of warriors.

Knox flies in front of me, signaling Aurora to follow. She's kept her distance from him the entire journey, albeit listening to his directional commands, yet nothing else. If I didn't know any better, I'd say she's distrustful of men.

Knox lands on the only large patch of grass in the vast city, a designated area for riders' companions. Aurora lands on all fours, strolling to a corner. I dismount her, stretching my sore, stiff legs as Knox appears with a bucket of water, carrots, and by the smell of it, goat carcass. Aurora stares Knox down, watching his hands as he slowly places the bucket of water and food in front of her.

"Are the riders cruel to the animals?" I ask, frowning at her distrust.

"Not usually, but some people get around the system," Knox answers, earning a huff from Aurora.

I stroke behind her ears, wondering what her story is and my heart breaking that she can't tell me. "We'll be back after lunch," I say, giving one last pat on her fluffy head before I trail off after Knox, Aurora digging into her food without another glance.

We approach an old, shackled building, debris lining the steps. Entering the bar isn't any better. It's a seedy tavern, flickering candles placed haphazardly around the room, my boots sticking to the floor as we walk past people milling about drunk.

Why on earth are we eating here?

"I don't trust leaving Aurora here alone, and this is the only spot large enough for her to rest," Knox whispers as we take a seat in a red-lined booth.

At least the smell of food is half decent, although the true test will be in eight hours' time of whether we get food poisoning or not.

"What can I get for you folks?" a squeaky voice asks beside me.

I turn to find a small man peering up at us. His wide smile stretches across more than half of his diamond-shaped face. His enormous round brown eyes appear to glow in the dark lighting, and his round nose twitches as he sniffles. He's wearing an adorable checkered green shirt with matching green pants, and a faded worn brown hat upon his head, the tips of his large ears flaring from underneath it.

A house brownie.

"What's the best thing to eat here?" Knox asks.

The brownie scratches his head, his eyes looking up at the ceiling as he mulls over the question. "Honestly, go with the stew. It's the safest option."

I chuckle.

"We'll have two of those and water please."

The brownie snaps his fingers, scuttling away. "On it!"

"He is the most adorable creature I've ever seen," I whisper once he's disappeared behind the tavern kitchen doors.

"I think Aurora would be offended."

"Aurora is beautiful and strong; she'd hate being called adorable."

Knox's lips twitch. "Very true."

"Why do you think she's so distrustful of men?" I ask.

Knox leans his forearms on the table. "She could have been a wild griffin. Most of the aerial legion is bred and raised on the island, yet sometimes we find wild ones flying." He cocks his head. "I can find out for you if you like."

"Please."

I look around the room to make sure no unwanted ears are listening, but most everyone is either swaying or passed out drunk. No one is paying us a lick of attention. "It's as if the demons have disappeared entirely. We should have come across one by now," I whisper.

Knox nods. "We should be encountering at least ten a day on scouting missions. They've taken over the forests and woods for decades and now they're suddenly gone. It's unusual."

I grimace. "It makes me nervous."

Knox mirrors my expression. "We should be more on guard and tread lightly as we search the remaining courts."

I rub my temples as a headache begins to form.

Knox places his hand on my knee. "We'll figure it out."

"I have this horrible feeling that we're running out of time."

Knox's lips flatten, not voicing that he feels the same way.

The top of the brownie's hat appears over the table, his brown hands placing two pots of stew and two glass bottles of water on the table. "Let me know if you need anything else!" he chirps, the top of his hat disappearing between tables.

I chuckle as I pull my bowl of stew toward me. It surprisingly smells delicious. I try a small heaping, my stomach grumbling at its emptiness. Knox and I look at each other in unison, both wearing expressions of delighted shock. "It's actually good," I whisper.

"I just hope it stays down," he grumbles.

We scarf down our food and water, renewed energy warming my body.

Knox lays five gold coins on the bar bench in front of the brownie. I smile when his eyes go wide as he snatches the coins. "Thank you," he squeaks.

Knox returns the warm smile. "Is there a bathroom?"

"Down the hall, second door on the left," the brownie chirps, his eyes glued to his new coins.

"I'll meet you out back," Knox whispers in my ear, strolling for the hallway.

I exit the tavern door, squinting as the sun beats down my face, needing a moment to adjust from the dark tavern. As I head down the crumbling stairs my heart stops cold, the sounds of snarling whimpers and laughter reaching my ears.

Aurora.

She's backed into the corner of the yard, five Fae men hollering and cheering as they whip her with a tree branch. They all sway from side to side, absolutely drunk. The sound of the thick tree branch hitting Aurora and her cry of pain makes me snap out of my haze.

My canines flare on a growl. "Back the fuck off."

Aurora's fear-filled eyes find mine, making my heart burn and guilt lace my body. The men pay me no attention. One steps forward, lifting the branch to bring it down on Aurora again. I don't let it get that far.

I fling my hand out, fire erupting as it flies for the tree branch, turning it to ash and burning the man's hand. "I said, back the fuck off!" I roar. Fierce protectiveness rushes through my body, screaming for me to harm them like they've harmed her.

The men turn to me, their faces full of rage that I interrupted their entertainment. They're all stocky and tall, wearing leather fighting clothes. Just what we need—shitty warriors who don't care about innocent lives. The thought makes my body burn, fire erupting from my fingertips.

"What did you just say to me?" the leader of the men sneers, swaying forward.

The group of pathetic drunks follow his lead as they storm up to me. My relief of their attention off Aurora is short-lived as they quickly surround me, caging me in a circle.

Channeling my courage, I cock my head at the one who spoke to me. "Do you get off on torturing? Do you need someone to scream in order to feel anything below the waist?"

*I can't believe I said that.*

I'm never one to start anything, never with a group of drunk men, let alone Fae. Yet I couldn't stop the words, my anger controlling my tongue.

Disgust ripples across his face as he bares his teeth. "How fucking dare you disrespect a city warrior." No sooner does he spit the words does his palm connect with my cheek, my head flying back with the force. But it's what he says that make my ears ring, not the slap.

*Disrespect.*

The word clangs through my mind. That horrible word my father spat at me daily, screamed at me, as his boot came down on my ribs. I hate myself for it, utterly hate myself in that moment, as my entire body freezes. Every ounce of fight I felt coursing through me moments earlier disappears. My heart abandoning me once more, until I'm nothing but an empty doll, just as my father created me to be. My vision blurs as they close in on me. I feel nothing, absolutely nothing. I swear I can hear Aurora's roar in the distance, yet nothing is making sense. My mind can't process what's happening around me.

Pinewood fills my nose, my eyes shuttering closed as it soothes me, comforts me.

My heart sings one word over and over, as it starts to float back toward me.

*Safe. Safe. Safe.*

I blink rapidly as my body starts to tingle, the numbness wearing off.

"If you breathe in her direction again, I'll murder you without so much as blinking," Knox growls.

The icy rage in his voice snaps me out of my trance completely, slamming back into my own body.

"You're not our king," the drunk seethes.

"I may not be your king," Knox spits, "but mark my words. If you lay a finger on one of my own ever again, I will hunt you down and kill you."

Knox's entire body trembles with the force of restraining himself and his anger.

The drunk man must truly be stupid because he takes a step forward, sealing his and his friend's fate. The second his foot lifts off the ground, power blasts around the area, knocking every single drunk Fae surrounding us to the ground, rendering them unconscious, without Knox so much as blinking. It never touches me or Aurora.

Knox takes my hand, pulling me to where Aurora is crouched in the corner, blood trickling down her side from where they whipped her. Her fearful eyes look between Knox and I, her small whimper of pain spurs me into action. Kneeling before her, I stroke her soft ears, snout, and head as I apologize profusely for leaving her alone out here.

"Can you heal her?" I ask Knox, my voice shaking.

He takes one step toward Aurora, but she bristles at the movement.

I stroke her soothingly. "He's going to heal you. I promise he won't hurt you."

Aurora stares at him so intently I'm about to ask Knox to teach me how to heal when she lowers her head in submission and acceptance of his help.

Knox slowly approaches her. Aurora flinches when he lays his hand gently over her open wound, stroking her unharmed coat with his free hand as his other begins to work. Blue light shines between his fingers, pouring his magic into the wound. I watch in awe as the wound begins to heal, the skin stitching together until there's only dried blood and a thick white scar marring her skin.

I place a gentle kiss on her forehead, apologizing over and over for letting her down. She huffs into my shirt, as if to tell me to get a grip. "Perhaps we need to face our fear of intimidating men together," I whisper, for her ears only. My words earn me a small spark of understanding in her eyes.

"She's going to be okay. Luckily she has a thick coat of fur and skin. It was only a surface-level wound," Knox murmurs to me.

I nod. "Do you still want to fly?" I ask Aurora.

I swear she rolls her eyes at me for asking such a stupid question. She may have fear, yet that doesn't diminish her strength. The thought sears hope into my heart, hope for myself.

Knox huffs. "I'll be damned."

"What?"

Knox cocks his head, staring intently at the griffin. A spark of surprise flashes across his features. "You two are each other's soul pair."

I frown. "How do you know?"

I'm not the only one searching for answers. Aurora looks at me with questioning eyes, wondering if Knox's statement rings true.

Knox takes a step closer, coming to stand behind me. "I can feel it."

Perhaps I can too. Peering into Aurora's golden eyes, my heart grows the longer I stare at her. My love for her unending.

Aurora is my soul pair.

*Easton would have loved this.*

I huff out a laugh. "Okay, let's get out of this dump."

"Do you want to go home?" Knox asks gently.

I look at him, his open face, the warmth and kindness in his eyes shining from his heart, and I realize that my earlier thoughts are true. He is the definition of safety. Being around Knox makes me feel safe.

I mount Aurora, patting her fur as I get settled into the saddle. "No, we have a job to do today. Let's scout the other courts." With new conviction in my voice, I lean forward, whispering to Aurora, "Let's go."

After hours of flying, scouring Fire Court lands, it isn't until the sun has set and we're returning to Azalea does Aurora react. We're flying straight toward Azalea, Knox at my back, when Aurora banks, taking a left turn so sharp I yelp, grabbing onto the reins to stop myself from plummeting to the ground.

Knox lands on the saddle behind me, his front plastered to my back. "What is it?"

"I don't know, she just banked on her own."

Knox reaches around me, taking control of the reins and

trying to steer Aurora back onto course, yet she ignores him, outright refusing to listen to his commands. She takes off in the opposite direction.

"She's showing us. See? She's circling the same area," he says in awe.

I lean forward, whispering into Aurora's ear, "Show me what you see."

It isn't until I place my hand in Knox's, the other buried in Aurora's fur, my body tingling as I make us invisible, does Aurora descend lower, flying over the treetops. I feel it before I see it, the wrongness emanating from the forest below. My magic withdraws, shrinking away from it, as it screams for me to run, to hide.

I look below, seeing nothing but forest, trees, and—

There are dozens of guards posted around a tree so large it would tower over the buildings in Ornx. Knox's sudden sharp inhale tells me he sees them too. Their uniforms match those from the night the Fae were injected at the ball, the same guards who murdered Knox's men, the red emblem patched onto the gray sleeve. Dozens stand around the tree trunk, none of them moving or speaking, completely lifeless.

My breastbone heats, pulsing as we near the guards. I shove my hand in my shirt, pulling out the pendant at my neck, its faint white glow illuminating my face. "Something's veiled. My pendant is glowing," I whisper.

Aurora keeps her slow pace around the area, letting us assess it from all angles. My stomach drops as the tree trunk opens. It's not a real tree—the inside of it is black, hollowed out and rotten. An underground tunnel. The four guards standing at the base of it step aside, allowing a pack of sniveling demon hounds to pass through the tree trunk.

Where the hell did they come from?

I turn to Knox, moving as fast as I can to take the pendant

off myself and hang it over his neck. His body tenses behind mine, his hands tightening around my waist. With the veiling pendant off my neck, all I can see are the lifeless guards standing watch around the tree. My heart sinks to my stomach; this is going to make it harder to steal the book they're guarding.

Knox and I continue to circle the tree, taking turns wearing the pendant, noting every detail we can. Wordlessly, I take Aurora's reins, gently tugging to the right, indicating for her to take us back to Azalea. Knox and I are silent the entire ride. There are no words for what we've uncovered.

After insisting that Aurora stays on Knox's grounds in the old stables, albeit it didn't take too much convincing on Knox's part, we enter the house. Everyone's already waiting in the sitting room. The moment he closes the door, the silencing shield snaps around the room, making everyone stand to attention.

"We found the compound where the beasts are hiding."

"Holy fucking shit," Lenox mutters.

Harlow flicks her hand in his direction. "Not now, you idiot."

Lenox throws his hands in the air. "This is huge! I'm allowed to have a moment to freak out!"

Axel rolls his eyes. "Both of you shut up."

As serious as the situation is, humor softens Knox's eyes at their exchange. "As much as we've missed you today, Lenox, finding the compound seems to have been the easier task."

Lenox frowns. "Where is it?"

"It's more of a *what* is it question," I mumble.

Knox strolls through the room, plopping down into the two-seat sofa, his eyes on mine as he waits for me to join him. I've sat much closer to him in the past, so I don't know why my heart is thumping wildly at the idea of sitting next to him on a couch. For heaven's sake, he was plastered to my back no more than an hour ago. Chastising myself, I perch next to him, his thigh grazing mine.

"It's veiled. We could only see it with Delilah's pendant," Knox says.

"Still not seeing the problem," Lenox mutters.

"It's underground. The only entry and exit point is through an old, rotted tree trunk, guarded by thirty of the queen's guards, who appear to not be present mentally."

The room falls silent.

Lenox's brows furrow, his eyes downcast. Axel's face is in his palm, his expression mirroring the deep concentration of Lenox's. I pick up the glass in front of me, needing some wine after the long day. I take a sip, and over the rim, I lock eyes with Harlow and sputter. Her smile is so devilish it makes me laugh.

"Of course you're getting a kick out of this."

Harlow loves every type of challenge thrown her way. I think that's why she verbally spares with Lenox; he dishes it out as much as she does. She flicks her red-streaked hair over her shoulder. "We've had the same measly tracking duties for decades. Of course I'm delighted to finally know where our enemy sleeps," she croons.

I chuckle. Looking around the room, I frown when I notice who isn't present. "Where's Nolan?"

Axel leans back in his chair, swirling the amber liquid in his glass. "There's apparently an issue in the legion camp that has grown out of control. He's gone to sort it out for the next few days."

Knox frowns. "I didn't hear about any problems."

"Because you weren't here," Lenox drawls flatly.

Axel drops his head into his hands. "No shit. He means he hasn't heard of any issues within the camps prior to this."

"I knew that, I'm not stupid," Lenox mumbles into his glass.

Harlow coos, "Aw, poor baby. Did the big bad man hurt your feelings?"

"Jealous that I can feel?" Lenox quips.

Harlow clicks her tongue. "Come up with something original."

On the other side of the room, Hazel giggles. I'm glad to see her color has fully returned to her face. She seems to be back to normal as she sits beside Ace.

Knox lays his arm behind the sofa, his fingers twirling the ends of my hair. "Can we get back to more pressing matters, or should we leave you two to bicker like children?"

Lenox and Harlow snap their mouths closed. Everyone abandons their drinks as Knox has food brought to the room, devouring whatever they can get their hands on to sober up as we discuss a plan to get into the compound. We sit in that room until midnight, discussing every course of action on how to steal the dark magic book that doomed them all one hundred and forty-eight years ago. We don't know if it's there for sure, but they wouldn't build an entire compound, surrounded by beasts and warriors, if it wasn't guarding something important. Everyone agrees that our best chance of finding the dark magic book lays within the walls they've masked as a tree.

# Chapter Forty-One

I flop into bed and nearly melt into the silk pillows, my body languid after hours of discussing a plan of action. I picked up a book as I entered, only planning to read a few pages to switch my mind off what's sure to be another long day tomorrow, yet I can't seem to put it down. My exhilaration over each page has made my exhaustion take a back seat. I've just turned to a particularly steamy page when my bedroom door opens and closes. Knox casually leans his shoulder against the wall, still dressed impeccably from earlier. His white shirt isn't wrinkled in the slightest, the rolled-up sleeves make his tan forearms stand out, while his black tailored pants hide his powerful legs.

"Come to tuck me into bed, have we?"

"Are you certain about tomorrow's plan?" Knox asks, ignoring my sarcasm.

I roll my eyes. Knox and Hazel spent the majority of the meeting earlier protesting my plan, flinging haphazard ideas out to replace my own. Yet they fell on deaf ears; my idea is the best plan we have, regardless of the risks. "Absolutely."

A muscle ticks in his jaw. "Someone else can go in your place."

"No they can't. I'm the only one who can go," I say flatly. He opens his mouth, but I cut him off. "I'm going forward with it. I'm capable of holding my own."

He pushes off the wall, stopping in front of my bed. "I know you are; I don't doubt your skills or your magic training. I doubt all the possible variables that could go wrong."

"That's why we discussed exit strategies and backup plans in great lengths."

"I know that but—"

"No buts. We're doing this."

I watch his face and his body language for any sign of irritation that I'm putting my foot down on this, finding nothing but worry in his eyes. His statement holds true that people can speak freely in his court. No matter how many times Knox has said that my thoughts and opinions are welcomed, my mind can't seem to comprehend it. It goes against the very belief my father ingrained in me. The control he has around my mind is nauseating.

Knox assesses me right back. Whatever he searches for he must find because he puts the worry behind him, lowering his eyes to the book in my hands. "What are you reading?" he asks smoothly.

My cheeks heat. "Romance."

"Anything interesting?" he asks innocently.

Either he's an incredible liar or this man has no idea that I'm reading toe-curling scenes. "Nope," I chirp.

He cocks his head. "Mind if I join you?"

"Yes, I do actually."

He rolls his eyes. "I won't judge you for what you like to read."

"I know that—"

"Read to me," he demands.

I stare into his sapphire eyes, my own sparking with delight. We haven't had a moment alone since he kissed me, breaking the last of my resolve. My body has been buzzing with need and anticipation ever since. Knowing I could have him but not finding time has made me not only want him but need him…I want Knox to feel as desperate for me as I am for him. Perhaps this will snap his self-control. I grin. "As you wish."

I don't dare read the page out loud in a house full of Fae hearing. I glance down and begin to read, knowing he can see and hear everything in my mind. I couldn't have been on a better page even if I planned it. I get no further than two sentences before Knox's wings blast behind him, power rippling throughout the room as his eyes ignite with heat.

Stopping mid-sentence, I smirk at him from where I lie sprawled on top of the bed. "Something wrong?" I ask innocently, batting my eyelashes.

"Do you enjoy teasing me, Angel?" The heat in his eyes and the deep purr of his voice make my stomach clench. I've just started a war with someone I can't win against. Knox knows this, perhaps I knew it as well, teasing him to get his hands on me. His eyes spark with delight as he kneels on the edge of the bed, his imposing body towering over mine. "Do you want me to touch you, Delilah?"

My breath lodges in my throat. My shirt suddenly feels to be too much, the silk brushing my sensitive skin, setting my nerve endings on fire. Knox crawls toward me, and it is the most sensuous thing I have ever seen, watching a powerful, six-foot-five male on his hands and knees for me. He sits back on his heels, placing his hands on my ankles. Slowly, he pries my legs apart, until the only thing that's in the way are my thin sleep shorts. I gasp as Knox drags me down the bed, his knees knocking into my inner thighs. Placing one hand beside my head he leans over me, his chest rising and falling as fast as my own as he lowers his head. His lips brush the shell of my ear, sending shivers racing through my body.

"I said, do you want me to touch you?"

I nod vigorously, my lips parting in anticipation.

"Say it," he growls.

"Touch me," I pant.

Knox smashes his lips to mine, kissing me as if he's starved. He doesn't have to ask this time. Knox groans into my mouth as his tongue strokes mine, the sound sending a jolt of electricity to my clit. I wrap my legs around his waist as his hands slide down my outer thigh. Cupping my ass he lifts me, both of us moaning the second his hard cock touches my wet center through the fabric. My stomach clenches as he begins kneading my ass, moving my hips back and forth as he grinds me into his hard length.

*I need to touch him.*

The thought sends my hands into action. I fist his shirt, pulling with all my strength until the buttons pop, scattering all over the floor. He lets go of me before quickly taking my own shirt and lifting it over my head. Knox growls as my breasts spring free. Not a moment later is his mouth on me, sucking my nipple into his mouth as his hand kneads and teases the bud of the other.

The pressure inside me begins to build, tension spiraling inside my core as I rock my hips, needing friction, begging for friction. I run my hands through his hair, yanking his head closer to my chest, needing more. Needing everything. I have never felt so hot in my life, so frenzied to have someone buried inside of me.

Knox's hand leaves my breast, trailing slowly down my

stomach, brushing his fingertips from side to side on the edge of my sleep shorts. "Tell me what you need, Angel," he whispers.

"Touch me," I beg.

His hand dips between my legs inside my shorts. Not wasting any time, his fingers enter me in one slow stroke, his thumb circling my clit. I buck wildly, panting as I cling to him.

"You're so fucking wet," he groans, lifting his head to mine as he devours my mouth, his tongue stroking me in equal rhythm with his fingers. He slides his hand up my back, his callouses raking over the dips and scars, and takes a fistful of hair. He tugs my head back, his lips hovering over mine as he pants, "Tell me what you want. Let me hear your pretty mouth say it."

"I want you." My hips grind wildly on his hand.

Knox's canines flare, scraping the shell of my ear and trailing down my neck, making me clench around his fingers. "Say the words, Angel," he purrs.

"Make me come."

I throw my head back on a scream as his canines sink into the crook of my neck. My orgasm explodes, my body convulsing around his fingers as stars shoot into my vision.

The last shred of control Knox was clinging to completely snaps as I come around his fingers. Growling like a wild animal, he slips out his hand from between my legs and flings me down, ripping my shorts off faster than I can blink. His own pants follow.

I sit up as fast as I can. Taking over, I drag his boxer briefs down, whimpering when his length springs free. He is utterly glorious. I wrap my hands around his velvet-wrapped steel, relishing at the feel of his hardness pulsing in my hands.

He's so large I'm worried about the fit between us, yet I can't seem to care as I stroke him. He throws his head back, the veins in his neck straining as his hips buck on a deep groan.

The pressure begins to build inside of me again as he thrusts himself into my hand, his stomach muscles rippling and bunching. He brings his head back, and the sight of me near his cock makes his eyes turn feral. He pushes me down onto my back, spreading my legs wide as he lowers himself. Every glorious inch of his body covers mine, his cock resting between my core making my hips buck instinctively, begging for him.

His lips claim mine in another scorching kiss, this one less frenzied than the last—deeper, soothing my soul with each stroke of his tongue. Knox lines himself up, entering me in one long thrust, both of us moaning into each other's mouths as he stretches me, seating himself fully inside me. I scrape my nails down his back as he begins to move, each stroke reaching a part of me that no one has before. My body sighs, singing its praises that he's inside of me.

"You feel so fucking good wrapped around my cock," he groans, his body shaking on a shudder.

My core clenches around him, squeezing him at his words. Knox drags his hand between us, picking up the pace as his thumb brushes my clit. I whimper as my hips buck wildly, meeting him thrust for thrust.

Knox's heavy-lidded gaze roves my body, his eyes pausing as he stares at us joined. "Look at you taking all of me, as if you were made for me."

I throw my head back as his words send flutters through my clit. I'm so close, I start begging, needing more of him, needing every single part of him. "Please, please, please."

Knox flares his canines, biting me in the crook of my

shoulder, marking me, staking me, claiming me. I moan, my eyes rolling into the back of my head as wave after wave of unending bliss overtakes my body. Shuddering around him, I come so hard my vision blurs entirely.

By the time I come back down to earth, Knox is kissing me again, slow and languid. He scoops me up, one arm holding me around my back while the other teases my sensitive nipple, making me pool with wetness, the pressure building again. "You're so beautiful," he whispers.

His hips arch up as he moves inside me again. He lowers his head, sucking hard on my nipple. I drop my head back on a moan as he licks away the sting.

I move my hips in rhythm with his, meeting his thrusts as he groans. Knox doesn't stop until his pace is relentless, stroking a part inside of me over and over as he enters me, making another orgasm build faster than before. I need to see him lose control; I need to make him feel what I feel. I run my hands through his hair, gripping it tightly, and his low-lidded, heated eyes lock with mine.

"I want to feel your pussy come around my cock again," he says on a deep groan.

Wetness trickles down my thighs at his crude words, my core pulsing. His fingers pinch my nipples again, making me whimper.

The pressure builds inside of me to an all-new height. My hips rock relentlessly, meeting Knox stroke for stroke as he picks up the pace, thrusting into me harder and faster. I'm a second away from exploding when I take one single finger, and snaking it around his back, I trail it slowly down his wings.

Knox explodes, chanting my name as his entire body shudders. His hips snap into me wildly as he comes, setting off my own orgasm. I milk every drop from him, stars exploding as my eyes roll into the back of my head. I slump onto his chest, both of us panting frantically, as we float back down to earth.

# Chapter Forty-Two

I stumble through the abandoned library, my chest heaving as my heart pounds wildly in my ears. Blood trickles down my thigh, leaving a trail behind me. The second I hear the doors slam closed I straighten, striding perfectly fine through the entryway, the old floorboards creaking beneath my boots as I turn. Reaching behind my back I take out my twin blades, flipping them in my hand as I lean against what used to be the sign-in desk.

The front doors blast open, sunlight streaming through the room, highlighting the dust floating in the air. I smirk at the pack of demon hounds. "Hello," I purr.

Fire arrows fly for them before they can respond. I lunge as they dart to avoid my arrows, right where I want them. Embedding two daggers into its throat and heart, the demon hound crumbles to the floor. A second one rushes for me before I can blink, a sneer on its mouth as its claws sink into my arm. I grab its disgusting leathery skin, locking my hands around its arm, and with a buck of my hips into its stomach, I hurtle it over my shoulder. The wooden floorboards crack beneath its body as it slams to the ground. A knife is poised in my hand before it can move, piercing its heart.

Then something smashes over my head from behind.

Stars explode in my vision as I crumble to the ground. Two boney leather hands tighten around my wrists, dragging me from the room.

"Cocky bitch," it spits.

My hair hangs over my face, hiding my feline smirk.

"Let me have—"

"She wants her unharmed," one spits, cutting the other off.

They drag me through the forest, taking me exactly where I plan to go. Unknowingly following the plan that I set in motion the moment my feet landed on the forest floor of the mountain, slicing myself open on a tree branch as Knox scattered my scent in all directions.

Sticks and broken bark scrape against my fighting leathers. I keep my head down as we near the compound. The unnatural energy begins to press into me, slithering against my skin, poking and prodding as it studies who I am. Pulsing with delight as it gets its answer.

I peek through my hair at the guards stationed around the large tree, their eyes unseeing, vacant of life as they step aside, letting us pass through the rotted core of the tree. The moment they drag me across the tree trunk border, my magic evades me, as if it was completely snuffed out.

Knox was right—they have magic wards.

I blink profusely as my eyes adjust to the darkness in the hall. I can't even see my own body.

The demons dragging me don't falter as they walk. Perhaps they have night vision. We turn corner after corner through the musty hallways before a yellow light burns around the corner. Fire lanterns are lit along the passageways.

The walls are made entirely of rock, as if they were hand-carved into the earth's core.

The pitter-patter of water dripping down the walls signals we're near a source of water. How far did we walk underground to reach water?

Boisterous laughter fills the hallways, sniveling and sneers joining in on the grating sounds. The noise increases as we descend further. An open door to my left has me dropping my head once more, but I peek under my shoulder in time to see a room full of every disgusting creature one has nightmares about.

Wendigos, demon hounds, shadowsteers, phookas, and even gremlins.

Every type of creature we studied in those demonic books is sitting in these rooms, walking these halls, waiting for orders from whomever is in charge.

We descend further into the tunnel system, each level mustier than the last, making me dream for the feel of the forest's fresh air above.

Halfway into the compound, cells and cages appear, metal bars embedded into the rock wall. It's too dark to see what's in them, yet as we pass hall after hall containing these, trepidation fills my gut. There's enough here to house thousands of Fae.

Every single one of them is empty…waiting.

We turn a corner to an empty hall. No cells or cages here, only a single flame ignited at the end, mounted into the wall next to a barred wooden door. My heart stops as the demons unlock the door and drag me inside. Floor-to-ceiling chains hang all along the round room.

They drag me to the back of the room, hauling my arms up as they throw my body against the stone wall with all their strength. My breath gets knocked from my lungs. I begin wheezing for air as they chain both my legs and arms to the side, mounting me to the wall as if in offering.

*That's exactly what I am.* The thought sends a cold shiver down my spine.

One of the demon hounds spits at my feet before they both leave the room, locking the door behind them. The only light to penetrate the room is the fire lantern lit beside the door on the other side. Its flames seem to twist toward the door, as if offering me comfort in this darkness, recognizing a kindred flame.

We're so far below ground no noise trickles into the room. The cheers from the creatures above me are long ago.

I don't fight. I don't even try to escape. I simply hang there as offering and wait.

Redemption whispers through my mind, his deep husky voice soothing my soul.

*Now, Angel.*

I smirk as I feel my magic return to me, breathing life once more as it fills me and surrounds me. Knox successfully destroyed the magic wards placed in the compound with the help of my veiling pendant.

Curling my fingers, flames erupt along my fingertips. With half a thought I have the chains melting off my wrists and ankles, the smell of metallic burning my nostrils as it sizzles, dripping onto the ground.

I rush to the door, melting the lock placed within the wood. I simply push it open, walking through it without uttering a sound. My body tingles as I make myself disappear and begin to hunt for the dark magic book.

My enemies dragged me exactly where I wanted.

I spear my power out, searching every hall and room for the book I know is hidden in these walls. I pause when something slithers along my magic, something wholly dark and not of this world. Crooking its finger at me to follow, to free it from its cage.

I turn, heading back down to where I came from. Descending deeper than before, into the heart of the tunnel system, the dark magic calls to me. No life breathes down here. I don't think even the demonic creatures dare to come past this point, for I hear nothing. The ice-cold temperature and the dark magic beckoning me are the only things to keep me company.

I pause at the end of a hallway, seeing it's a dead end. No doors, corners, or hallways appear to be near, yet I feel it, pulsing with life on the other side, calling me to free it. Placing my hands on the wall, I knock on the stone, pushing and prodding. It's behind the wall, I can feel it deep in my bones. My magic practically begs me to run.

One of my knocks rings hollow. I tap the area next to it, finding several more. With all my strength I push, holding my breath as the wall moves backward. My heart sinks as I peer into a room, and for the first time today, second-guess my plan.

The room is circular, every crevice alight with candles.

Endless worktops fill the room, littered with books, crystals, and vases of blood and potions. My stomach turns queasy as I enter, not daring to close the door behind me, for fear of being trapped in here. The very essence of the room feels corrupt and ancient, as if I'm trespassing on something that's alive and knows I'm here.

I scan the room for the book, praying I'll know it when I see it. I pass the leather sofa, disgusted that someone can be in here, sitting comfortably on a couch no less, and withstand the dark magic pulsing throughout the room. Something ancient and wicked crawls up my spine, mocking me as if to say, *Come find me.* I grit my teeth, blasting my power out, pushing it away.

I search the room top to bottom, knocking on the walls for any secret compartments, yet I find nothing. Absolutely nothing and no dark magic books.

I stop dead in my tracks.

*It's veiled.*

Of course it's veiled, and of course I don't have my pendant around my neck.

Panic claws its way up my throat, making it difficult to breathe. I close my eyes, fisting my hands at my side as I force myself to calm. If I wanted to hide something, what would I mask it as? I repeat the question in my mind, praying the answer will come to me.

Scanning the room, I look for anything that doesn't fit, anything out of place. Bottles, jars, potions, books, crystals, candles, cushions…a crown. Everything in this room screams of darkness and corruption, yet they have such a beautiful piece of jewelry displayed in a glass cabinet behind the desk, sitting in the dead center of the room.

Lifting the glass case, I gently pick up the bejeweled crown. The gold ornament sparkles as the candlelight shines on it, the white diamonds twinkling beside the blue gemstones. The diamonds and gems gradually grow in size until meeting in the middle. Peaking at the center sits the largest gem of all, the only one not to sparkle and shine.

I place it gently on the workbench before me. Closing my eyes I picture my pendant, what it feels like in my hands, how it feels when it pulses against my chest, as it glows and reveals those that are hidden.

As it reveals the truth.

I place my palms over the crown, slowing my breathing as gold light pours out of my hands, shining between my fingers. The crown begins to heat, sizzling at my touch, as if it's trying to squirm away. I grit my teeth, forcing more power out of me, pouring my very essence of pure magic into the crown as it tries to stay hidden.

*The truth.*

*Reveal the truth.*

I sing into my mind, repeating the words over and over as the crown pulls away from me. Suddenly my hands touch nothing but air. I open my eyes, and the worktop in front of me no longer houses a crown. Gazing down at my feet, I find a black leather book, the astronomical size of it alarming. It's almost as large as my torso, the ageing yellow pages over-flowing from its binder.

Triumph rushes through me.

I snatch the book off the ground, running out of the room as fast as I can, remaining invisible as I sprint through the halls. I'm about to smile with joy when suddenly a blaring sound surrounds me, so loud it makes me fumble. I don't dare stop running even as I hear doors on every level open and the unmistakable sound of beasts huffing and stomping along the floors. There's so many rushing throughout the tunnels at once the roof above me begins to shake, dust falling from the ceiling.

My eyes widen as I skid to a stop in the middle of the hallway as a creature enters, its size so large the tip of its bald head skims the ceiling. It's completely engulfed in shadows, its boney yellow rib cage poking out of its shadows as it walks.

I slap my hand over my mouth, holding back the bile that threatens to rise. Gratitude fills my heart that I have the power to make myself invisible. A sinking feeling in my stomach tells me the creature would have delighted in torturing me in unfathomable ways.

I don't dare try to run past the creature; its size alone fills the entire width of the hallway. Instead I follow it around a corner. The entire hallway beyond is full of various creatures, all as horrid as the beast in front of me. But that means Harlow, Lenox and the twins' diversion to lure the demons out of the compound is working.

Hall after hall, I trail behind demonic creatures until darkness swallows us whole. I use my hearing and senses to follow the stomping of boots and sniveling through the endless darkness. A sigh of relief escapes me when moonlight streams across the floor as I turn the corner, making my heart beat rapidly in my chest.

The moment my shoes connect with the forest floor I bolt, sprinting as fast as I ever have in my life as every type of demonic creature that exists pours out of the tree trunk behind me, taking off in all different directions, hunting the very trap Knox's court set for them.

I pay them no attention, keeping my gaze locked on the tree line in front of me, on the area Knox and I planned to meet. Pushing my feet to run faster, the landscape around me begins to blur.

I haven't heard Knox's voice since he told me he broke the magic wards. What if something happened to him? What if they found him hiding? Anxiety claws at my chest at the thought.

My throat constricts as I run around a tree, my gaze locking on sapphire blue eyes in the distance. I can't help the sob that escapes me. The full scope of being underground with so many demonic creatures hits me full force as I run into his arms. He holds me to his chest so tight I'm surprised the air doesn't get knocked from me. My hair flutters as Knox takes off into the sky, not spending a moment longer standing in the demon-infested forest. I cling to him, my arms wrapped around his neck, my legs around his waist, the book sitting between our chests and my head in the crook of his neck as I take him in. Relief flows through my body as his pinewood scent surrounds me.

Knox's grip tightens. "Did something happen?" he asks, viciously low.

I shake my head. I'm embarrassed to tell him my relief is from finding him alive and unharmed, after my anxiety told me otherwise. I open my eyes, looking over Knox's shoulder to see Hazel, Ace, Harlow, Lenox, and Axel emerge into the sky, their beautiful wings flapping wildly as they each take off into different directions.

I breathe another sigh of relief that everyone is unharmed.

The dark magic book in my arms seeps hope into my heart once more.

Lenox's howl of laughter booms throughout the halls the second I enter the house. "You made one of them soil themselves!"

"Harlow, what did you do?" Axel asks in awe.

They're lounging around in the sitting room, drinking and celebrating. Harlow is sprawled across a single sofa, her smile purely wicked. "I simply showed them a reflection."

"Whatever you did to make a demon soil itself, teach me," I say, plopping the dark magic book onto the coffee table. Its energy making everyone recoil.

"Horrid thing," Harlow spits.

"Indeed." I grimace. "The number of creatures down in that hell hole...It's an army of beasts."

"Did you see any of the missing Fae?" Axel asks, pouring himself a drink.

"No, but the tunnel system was so large it would have taken hours to search each cell." The sofa shifts as Knox settles in beside me, but his face is completely pale. "What's the matter?" I whisper. Not quietly enough I suppose around Fae ears. Everyone's chatter dies, glasses pause midair, all celebrations of stealing the dark magic book stop entirely.

"When Ace and Hazel held the guards down by the vines, I went into their minds. Every single one of them were completely gone, as if whoever controls them has locked them away in their own mind." Knox drags a hand through his hair. "I saw who's giving the orders, who controls them."

"Who?" Lenox barks.

"The queen's second-in-command."

My heart stops beating before picking up its pace, turning erratic. Nobody moves or speaks, the revelation making the temperature in the room drop.

"I don't think the queen knows. I didn't see her in any of the memories, only Emmalyn."

Axel's deadly quiet voice pierces the room. "Why would she do this? What does she have to gain?"

"The queen was meant to die that night. She wasn't supposed to arrive home later. Perhaps Emmalyn adjusted her plans when the queen escaped her death," Harlow chimes in.

Knox grimaces. "That doesn't answer why the queen's still alive today. She's had ample opportunity to kill her."

I furrow my brows. "What if she's controlling the queen?"

Lenox sets his glass down in front of him. "You're telling me there's a possibility that a possessed queen has been running the kingdom for nearly one hundred and fifty years?"

"That's why she never reinstated the court kings and queens," Knox breathes.

Axel sits forward in his seat. "We need to adjust our plans. The queen has spies everywhere."

"*Emmalyn* has spies everywhere," Lenox corrects, disgust lining his voice.

My stomach sinks. Every time we take one step forward in destroying this gods-awful spell, another mystery and question arises.

"You need to tell Nolan," Ace says. "Some of his men could be under Emmalyn's spell."

Knox nods as he stands, his body tense as he strides out of the room. My heart pangs. Every step closer to destroying the entrapment spell reminds him of his parents' death. Each new piece of information chips away at his wound of grief, reopening his heartache.

"So how was it?" Harlow drawls into the silent room.

I slump into the couch. "Terrifying. I was underground with hundreds of demonic creatures."

Harlow rolls her eyes. "Not that, you fool."

I cock my head to the side. What on earth is she talking about?

Hazel's cough draws my attention, her cheeks flushed as she sits next to Ace. "When Fae…uh …when Fae join…"

"Oh for fuck's sake, we can smell Knox on you," Harlow cuts in.

My eyes widen. *They can what?*

Lenox smirks. "When a Fae takes a lover, their scents mingle."

I grit my teeth. Why didn't Knox say anything? A warning would have been lovely right about now considering five nosey Fae are staring me down. They all look like a bunch of gossiping teenage girls. At least Ace has the decency to look sheepish.

I lift my chin. "That's none of your concern."

"It was about time," Hazel chirps, taking a sip of her wine.

My cheeks heat. Hazel has been calling it from the beginning. She'll want all the details.

Knox strolls into the room. "I've sent a messenger for him," he says, plopping down beside me. He looks around the room before slowly turning his head to mine, grinning. "What did I miss?"

"Care to tell me why you didn't inform me about mingling scents?" I say through gritted teeth. Lenox and Harlow burst out laughing, making my hands clench in my lap.

Knox stretches his arm on the back of the sofa, his fingers playing with my hair. "Slipped my mind."

*Insufferable bastard.*

Hazel's eyes shine with happiness as she changes the topic. "When should we go through the book?"

"Tomorrow. We all deserve some much-needed rest," Knox says. "I'll keep it in a safe place for now."

I stand, saying goodnight to everyone, exhausted after such an eventful day. Walking up the stairs I'm about to enter my room when Knox grabs my hand, dragging me down the hallway, his other hand carrying that god-awful book.

"What are you doing?" I ask.

"Taking you to bed," he says flippantly.

He leads me through his bedroom door, dropping my hand as he disappears into his closet, the sounds of metal clanging fill the space.

"That's very presumptuous of you," I taunt as he enters the room again without that horrid book.

He shrugs. "I sleep better with you."

His statement snaps my mouth closed. Knox doesn't shy away from anything, his emotions included.

My mouth begins to water as he peels off his shirt, his pants then dropping to the floor. His powerful body stalks forward, naked save for the boxers, the sight making my skin heat and tingle.

Knox stops so close I have to tilt my head back to look at him. His sapphire eyes droop, filling with heat, as his hands graze my stomach, moving lower until they connect with my pants.

The button of my pants pop, the zipper lowering. My shirt is the next thing to go, then I'm standing stark naked in front of him. His hands slide down my thighs, lifting me as he walks us over to the bed. Sitting on the edge, I straddle him, whimpering when my core connects with his hard steel.

"I thought we were going to sleep," I whisper huskily.

Knox leans forward, trailing kisses from my neck down to my chest, biting my nipple before soothing the sting with a swirl of his tongue. "Oh we will." He kisses his way up to my lips. "After I make you come." His fingers slide inside me in one thrust, his thumb rubbing my clit.

My hips buck, my body singing a sigh of relief that he's touching me.

"First I want to feel you come on my fingers," he groans, placing kisses along my jaw. "Then I'll have you wrap that pussy around my cock."

He smashes his lips to mine, the intensity in his strokes and touch unending, his tongue thrusting into my mouth at the same speed of his fingers. My hips start grinding on their own accord, the heat and pressure inside me building with each passing second.

I arch my back, thrusting my breasts into Knox's face as

he kisses a path to them. I sink my fingers into his hair as he sucks and nips my breasts, making the wetness between my legs pour.

I'm about to explode and he knows it.

"Oh gods," I moan as his canines flare, scraping over the sensitive buds.

Knox crooks his fingers inside me, stroking the spot that only he knows how to find. Brushing his lips against my ear, his warm breath sending chills down my spine, he growls, "Come."

It's the last thing I hear as my entire body climaxes from his demand.

My ears start ringing, my body shivering and quaking as I cling to him. My hips rock as I drag out my orgasm. I float back down to earth, shivering from the intensity to find I'm on my stomach.

"Lift up, Angel," Knox orders behind me.

Panting, my arms shaking, I lift myself, kneeling on all fours. I'm spread bare for him. His large hands scrape over my hips, pulling my ass higher in the air. His strong legs line up behind me, the length of his cock gliding between my legs making me whimper. "You're so fucking beautiful," he groans, entering me in one deep thrust.

My head falls down on a moan as his entire length is seated inside of me, filling me, stretching me. His hand wraps around my hair, yanking me back, as he ruthlessly fucks me from behind. His strokes are long and hard, his cock rubbing that spot inside of my core that makes my legs shake.

His hand in my hair twists my head to the side while the other cups my breast, pinching and rubbing my nipple. The pressure builds within me again, stronger than the last.

"Good girl, Delilah, squeeze me," he growls in my ear.

I wrap my arms behind me, burying my hands in his hair,

clinging to him as he thrusts inside of me mercilessly. The hand on my breast trails down, disappearing between my legs at the same time the hand in my hair wraps around my throat. When his thumb brushes my clit, I explode.

My mouth opens on a guttural moan. Knox smashes his lips to mine, eating up the sounds as I come around him, fucking my mouth with his tongue as he continues his relentless pace, still stroking my clit.

"That's a good girl, Angel. Come around my cock."

My jaw drops on a scream, his words setting off another orgasm, this one shredding my body from the inside out. Wave after wave of unending pleasure slams into me, my body going completely languid in Knox's arms. I whimper as he pulls out of me, turning me around to straddle him as he kneels on the bed.

"I need to see you when I come," he whispers in my ear, entering me slowly. All my muscles seize from the intensity, every prickle of my skin feeling alive, on fire.

Knox groans when he's seated fully inside of me. His hand wraps in my hair, tugging my head back gently until his heat-filled eyes lock with mine, making my breath hitch.

"So beautiful," he murmurs as his hips thrust. I moan when his head dips, latching onto my nipple as he sucks hard. "I love these so much." Electricity zips through my body, my core pulsing once more. "Fuck, Angel, I'm so close," he groans around my breast.

My hips buck, the sensitivity heightening everything as pressure builds in my core. I ride him faster, chasing the high that only he can give me. A shiver racks through Knox's body as he lifts his head, watching me as I meet him thrust for thrust.

His hips move wildly, his canines lengthening. "Open your wings," he commands.

As if he has complete control over my body, my wings unfurl behind me. Knox's thrusts become wild. He rests his forehead against mine, his mouth dropping open, our short pants mingling as he groans. His own wings flare behind him, straining as they spread wide.

I wrap my arms around his neck, holding on for dear life as he pounds me relentlessly, his control completely shattering as we ride each other, searching for the euphoric feeling only we can give one another.

Knox begins to pulse and swell inside me; I drop my hand between his shoulder blade at the same time his arm snakes around to my back.

"Come," he growls, as a single finger trails down my wings, shattering my world.

Every nerve ending in my entire body explodes by that one touch, shattering my mind and soul with the intensity that overcomes my body.

Knox comes on a feral growl as I do the same, using the tip of my fingers to tease and trail down his own wings. My name falls from his lips like a prayer as I scream, my core pulsing around his cock, milking every drop of his cum as the most intense orgasm crashes through my body.

Pleasure like never before sears into me, taking over my body as I shake uncontrollably on top of him, my body floating through stars as I collapse against him. My face falls into the crook of his neck as we sit in each other's arms, panting. I graze my fingers through Knox's soft hair, scraping my nails against his scalp.

His hands stroke my back, his fingers dipping over the ridges of my scars. "You're so beautiful," he whispers. My body tenses as I realize what he's feeling, what part of me he's calling beautiful. "Don't." His voice is guttural as he speaks. "Don't push me away."

I take a deep breath, willing my body to relax. I know that all of this is temporary. I know I can't get attached, yet my heart doesn't seem to understand that I can't have this. I vow to myself that no matter what happens, until the day I leave, I will cherish everything in this world.

Until the very last second.

# Chapter Forty-Three

E ach page of the dark magic book seals our doom. It's a horrid thing, its black leather marred with scratches and claw marks, the pages yellow and crumpled with age, as if the dark magic's very essence rots the book. The one thing that isn't scarred by age is the emblem on the front cover, an upside-down triangle surrounded by a circle, filled with swirls and twirls, that appears to be dripping with blood onto a human skull.

"We need a spell cleaver," Knox announces to everyone gathered in the study.

I frown. "What's a spell cleaver?"

"Those that specialize in spells. They have their main elemental magic and yet something else entirely. Magic that allows them to assess all other magic and the spells that are created with it."

Hazel inches forward on her chair. "It's an extremely rare specialty. Some Fae are born with the ability to cast, create, and undo spells. Any Fae can cast a spell yet the spell cleavers can create just about anything. They can also undo creation."

Nolan shuffles his feet into a defensive stance, moving the conversation back to work. "Are we sure we need one?"

Hazel grimaces. "The entrapment spell is more complicated than we thought. Emmalyn used multiple spells, combining them to create one giant clusterfuck of a problem."

I'd be shocked that she swore, yet there's no other way to describe what type of power and spell Emmalyn used to create this horrid ordeal.

"Can we trust a spell cleaver?" Axel mutters.

Harlow clicks her tongue. "I wouldn't."

Lenox rolls his eyes. "You don't trust anyone."

Harlow flings a manicured finger in Knox's direction, sweeping it around the room. "I trust everyone in this room." She pointedly stares him down. "Even the dog."

"I'm not a dog," Lenox mutters under his breath.

"You're as loyal as one. You follow Knox around like a lost puppy."

The insult hits its mark. Lenox's eyes shutter, pain filling them before it's gone in an instant. My heart twists. Lenox jokes around all the time, but I've never seen a better friend. He loves everyone in his court and will be loyal until the day he dies. He shouldn't be taunted for his loyalty and the kindness in his heart.

"Harlow," Knox snaps, his eyes full of thunder as he glares at her.

My spine stiffens. He's never barked at Harlow before. I frown, watching as Lenox's face hardens, shutting everyone as he focuses on the book. Harlow grimaces, seeing the repercussions of her words.

"I know a spell cleaver," Hazel says, breaking the tension. "I've known her all my life. She's the best if you ask me, and she can be trusted."

"How do you know?" Nolan asks, lifting his brow.

Hazel's swallow is audible. "Emory's the only one I trusted to ward my cabin when my daughter died. No one ever found my location over the one hundred and forty years I lived there."

Ace places his hand on her back, comforting her at the mention of Luna.

Hazel turns her kind eyes to Knox. "She lives in Cardania. I can take you to her."

Knox nods. "We'll leave first thing in the morning."

"Should we keep trying to decode this thing?" Harlow asks, grimacing.

"No, it's too complicated. Only a spell cleaver could understand it and know how to unravel the spell Emmalyn weaved," Knox says tightly.

Lenox walks out of the room without another word. Knox's brows furrow as he gazes at the door.

"I need to go check on the new guards, make sure they understand their assignments," Nolan says, breaking the silence as he exits the room.

Ace and Hazel are next to follow, muttering excuses to leave the room as Knox glares at Harlow.

"You better apologize to him for that bullshit you just pulled."

"It slipped, I wasn't thinking," she says, sincerity lining her eyes and, dare I say, guilt.

"I'm not the one you need to explain that to."

After a noticeably quieter dinner, I'm lying in Knox's bed, both of us naked after mind-shattering sex, his finger trailing up and down my skin as we lay in each other's arms. I lift my head, propping it onto my fist as I gaze at his beautiful face.

"What happened to Lenox?" I ask quietly. Knox's face visibly shudders. "If you think he wouldn't want me to know that's all right," I say after he's quiet for a moment.

"He wouldn't mind you knowing…It's just horrible. I hate thinking about it."

I wait patiently for the words to come, my chest tightening when they do.

"I've known Lenox since I was a young boy. We met in Azalea and became fast friends. His parents were horrible to him and used him against each other like a bargaining tool." Knox shakes his head in disgust. "As we grew up, we became closer. We wouldn't go a few days without seeing each other." His face pales as his eyes glaze over. "That's how I knew something was wrong. I hadn't seen Lenox in two weeks. It was unheard of for him to disappear. He practically lived at my house, and my parents treated him like he was their own." Knox falls silent, building the courage to speak again, his voice breaking as he does. "When I went to his house, I found…his father had murdered his mother, and killed himself after."

My heart sinks, ice coating my veins.

"His father had found out Lenox wasn't his own. In punishment he knocked him out while he was asleep, took him into the middle of the woods where no one could hear him scream, and locked him in a room he built into the ground. His father paid off a gremlin before he died to dump water and food daily, but the food was laced with poison that made his power useless." Knox rubs his eyes with the heel of his palm, dampness coating his thick black lashes.

"It was years before I found him. He hadn't seen sunlight or felt fresh air for over seven years. The bastard of the man that put him in there took all the necessary steps to make sure I could never find him with my power. I had to search every inch of the land myself by foot." Knox's voice cracks. "It took Lenox a long time to get better, and shortly after he did, my parents died. They treated him like their own, showering him with the love and kindness he never received. When they died it was as if he lost his true parents. It destroyed him as much as it destroyed me."

Silent tears roll down my cheeks as he finishes, my heart breaking for Lenox and what he had to endure, and for Knox, the man that never gave up on his friend, searching for him for seven years. I lean over, placing a gentle kiss on his cheek, my tongue tasting salt water as it connects with his tears.

"He has you," I whisper.

"Sometimes I feel like it's not enough," he croaks. "I will do anything for my people, yet no matter what I do, it's never enough. I keep failing them."

"You are more than enough," I say vehemently. "You have the kindest, most caring and loving soul. I see why your people love you and are loyal to you. No one else could make a better ruler." I sit up, dragging his gaze to mine. "You are not failing your people. The only way you could fail them is if you stopped trying and you have never stopped."

Knox stares at me so intently I swear I can feel it burning into my soul before he leans forward, kissing me deeply. My heart grows as Knox and the family he's created fills my heart.

"We'll make Emmalyn pay for the pain she's caused," I vow as he pulls away.

I'm in Knox's arms as he flies over the Water Court, Hazel and Ace leading the way in front of us, when I gasp. The entire city is surrounded by water, no forest to be found anywhere. White-stoned buildings fill the city of Cardania. Bridges arch over canals and streams, with each street framed by a body of water. Some buildings are even surrounded by waterfalls.

We land before a small two-story white house that sits on a busy residential street. A river separates us from the houses on the other side. Hazel marches up to the door, knocking three times.

Feet pad downstairs before the door opens to reveal a stunning woman. Her brown skin glows in the morning sun, deep ringlet hair falling to her shoulders. With sharp cheekbones, deep brown eyes, and pouty lips, Emory's gorgeous. Her entire face lights up as she smiles down at Hazel, towering over her. She looks to be about my height. "Hazel!" she exclaims, wrapping her arms around her in a tight embrace. "What are you doing here?"

"Can we come in?" Hazel asks hesitantly.

Emory lifts her head, gazing past Hazel's shoulder to us, as if just realizing Hazel isn't alone. I see the moment her internal walls go up, when her eyes land on Knox and Ace. Hazel frowns as she looks behind her, her eyes widening. "He's not a guard or warrior. This is the King of Azalea, Knox," Hazel rushes on.

Emory's spine straightens further, Hazel's words doing the opposite to relax her. I know exactly what it looks like to be afraid of men in power. I step forward. "We mean you no harm. I'd kill him myself if he ever laid a hand on a woman."

Emory snaps her eyes to mine, more assessing than uneasiness, understanding flashing through her expression.

That, I too know, the horrors that men put women through, and I will never stand aside to let it happen.

Emory tentatively steps back, opening the front door further. Knox gives Emory a kind smile as he passes. It does nothing to ease her tense shoulders. Walking through an open archway to a sitting room, two white cushioned seats face each other, a coffee table sitting in the middle. The room is designed with stunning colors of white and blue, in honor of her elemental court.

The moment Emory closes the door, Knox seals the house in a silent ward, making Emory snap accusing eyes to him. "We have to discuss sensitive matters," Knox explains.

Hazel cuts in, "We know how the entrapment spell was cast, but we need your help in breaking it."

Emory freezes, shock flashing in her brown eyes. "How?"

"Emmalyn, the queen's second. She cast multiple spells in one night, murdering the kings and queens as a sacrifice to channel the power into the dark magic spells," Knox explains.

Emory stumbles into the living room, taking a seat on her plush couch. She waves a hand in front of her. "You may as well sit down. I need a moment to process."

Hazel dashes out of the room, returning with a glass of water. She takes a seat next to Emory, handing the glass to her. Knox sits beside me on the couch, Ace taking the free space on the other side of me.

"How do you know this?" she asks after a moment.

"I think it may be easier if I show you," Knox offers gently.

Emory's eyes steel before nodding, her eyes going vacant as Knox shows her the memories. Once Emory comes back, her stunned gaze lands on me. "You took the book?" she asks in disbelief.

I nod. "Will you help us?"

"Of course," she answers. "I'll need to study the spells in the book myself, though."

Relief courses through me. We're one step closer to a world of freedom.

"It's at my home. Under the circumstances, can you study it there?" Knox asks.

Emory dips her chin stiffly. "Yes, I'll start tomorrow. There's certain elements that I'll have to prepare," she says, standing.

Taking that as our cue to leave, we shuffle toward the front door.

Hazel pauses in the living room, wringing her hands as she turns to Emory. "Is it safe for you to stay here alone with this information?"

"My wards are impossible to break. I'll see you in the morning."

Knox chimes in, "I can send someone for you—"

Emory holds up her hand. "I appreciate the gesture, Your Majesty, but I will have to decline."

"Please call me Knox. We're very informal in my court."

Emory clicks her tongue, ending the discussion.

We exit her house, taking off into the sky. The flight home is more freeing knowing that we now have a spell cleaver to help us. I can see it in Knox, Ace, and Hazel's faces.

Hope.

After a cheerful dinner of celebrating our success in finding a spell cleaver, I take a much-needed soak in the tub. It's always been my safe space to calm down after a long day, but we've been so busy lately that I've had to rush with bathing.

I step out of the clawfoot bathtub in my room. Wrapping a towel around my body I walk to the vanity mirror, running a comb through my wet tangled hair, when Knox appears behind me, making me jump. I don't have time to chastise him for scaring me because before I can speak, his warm hands are trailing down my back, pulling the towel down until I'm standing in front of him naked.

I watch in the mirror as heat fills his eyes, turning molten. "I can't keep my hands off you."

I turn around, peeling off his shirt, sighing as I see his bare chest. I run my hands up and down the smooth planes of his stomach, my mouth watering when his muscles bunch. "It's a good thing I have the same problem then, isn't it?"

Knox leans forward, sighing the moment our lips connect. I part my mouth, letting him devour me with his tongue, each stroke making my body tingle. Sparks ignite in my core, and wetness pools between my legs—just from his kiss. I drag my hand down his chest, delight sparking through me when he shivers from my touch.

I unbutton his pants, pulling them down along with his boxers. I capture his hard length when it springs free, soaking up the sound of Knox's moans in my mouth. I stroke him slowly, squeezing every time I reach the tip, circling the drop of moisture with my thumb. Knox's hands explore every inch of my body, never stopping in one place for too long as if he can't get enough of me. On the next stroke up his length, I squeeze harder, his hips bucking as he thrusts into my hand, his breathing turning shallow. I whimper when he pinches both of my nipples, my hips moving on their own accord, seeking his touch.

Knox growls when he notices my hips grinding air, begging for him. He bends, wrapping his hands around my thighs he picks me up, placing me onto the counter. The sting of the cold marble sends a shiver through me.

Knox's mouth leaves mine. I open my eyes, my breath leaving me as he begins to lower. It is the most glorious sight I have ever seen—Knox on his knees in front of me, naked.

"I kneel to no one but you."

Utter delight ravishes his face as he smirks. His tongue darts out, his eyes never leaving mine as he licks my center, swirling his tongue around my clit. I throw my head back on a moan, burying my hands in his hair as I tug him closer.

"You taste so fucking good," he groans, and I feel every vibration of it through my core.

"Oh gods," I breathe.

Knox's fingers enter me, pumping as he swirls, licks, and sucks my clit. I grind my hips shamelessly against his face, needing more, needing everything this man is willing to give me. Knox curves his fingers, stroking the part inside of me that makes me explode. My legs shake as the pressure inside of me builds.

"I'm so close, I'm so close," I pant.

Knox's husky rasp is what tips me over the edge. "Come on my face, Angel."

My hands cling to Knox's hair, my hips grinding against his face, as bliss shoots through my body.

My eyes are still closed when he kisses me, the taste of myself on his tongue making me moan into his mouth. Knox lifts me, lowering me to my feet as he spins me around to face the mirror, his hard cock resting on my ass.

I lift my droopy eyes to his, finding his blazing gaze already on me as he lowers his mouth to my ear. "I want you to watch as I fuck you."

A full-body shiver wracks through me from his words.

My knees buckle as he enters me in one hard stroke, my

head falling forward as I moan, his arm around my waist keeping me on my feet as his hips thrust. He wraps his other hand around my neck, pulling me back flush against his chest. "Look at you," he purrs. "You're so beautiful."

I whimper, his words making wetness trickle down my thigh.

His hand travels between my legs, circling my sensitive clit as his other hand teases my nipple, I close my eyes on a moan.

"Open your eyes Angel, look at what I do to you," he growls in my ear.

I open my hooded eyes. My body burns with fire as I look into the mirror to see his powerful body play mine like an instrument. He withdraws, glistening from my wetness, only to slam into me again. His eyes are full of heat so fierce it makes me moan, his gorgeous face filled with utter pleasure as he fucks me with abandon.

My core clenches around him at the sight of us.

"You're so fucking wet," he groans.

Fisting my hair, he twists my head to the side, fucking my mouth as passionately as he fucks me, kissing me with such ferocity my heart sings. I wrap my arms behind me, clinging to him, afraid that the intensity of what I feel will sweep me away entirely.

A feral growl leaves Knox's mouth at my thoughts. He moves so quickly I don't have time to process that I'm suddenly pinned against the bathroom wall, his length entering me again in one hard thrust. His shoulders shudder at the feel of me wrapped around his cock.

"Delilah, I—"

He smashes his lips to mine, kissing me fiercely, deeply, as he pours whatever he wanted to say into the kiss and I pour everything I feel into it. I nip Knox's lip, groaning when his wings snap out behind him. I scrape my nails down his back, unable to hold back on the intensity building within me. My legs start shaking around his waist, my hips grinding, meeting Knox thrust for thrust.

"You're. Mine." He punctuates each word with a deep, hard thrust. "I'm. Yours." I moan, digging my nails into his shoulders as I cling to him. "Say it, Angel."

Kneading my ass, he pulls me down onto his cock, swiveling my hips just right so that my clit brushes against his pelvic bone. "You're mine!" I scream. His thrusts become faster, more frenzied, as his cock swells inside of me at my words. "I'm yours…"

He shatters, saying my name like a prayer as he comes inside of me, his hips thrusting erratically as his power blasts throughout the room. His loud growl of pleasure topples me over the edge.

I come screaming his name as my world explodes around me.

# Chapter Forty-Four

T he next morning, Hazel and I wait for Emory to arrive in the foyer. Hazel wrings her hands behind her back, chewing on her lip. Hazel informed us to all be on our best behavior today; we desperately need Emory's help on the spell, and she doesn't take too kindly to trained warriors. Hazel told Lenox to shut his fat mouth, Nolan not to glare, and Axel and Knox to not do the "broody intimidating thing"—her words, not mine. Not surprisingly, Ace didn't get a tongue lashing, which Lenox pointed out and abruptly earned a smack in the stomach from Harlow because Hazel had already informed Ace last night, alone in her room.

A single knock on the door has Hazel rushing forward, revealing a stone-cold Emory on the other side. She's all business today after processing the information we dumped at her feet yesterday. She's wearing fine tailored clothing that represents the water element, cool tones and blue fabric. She strides into the room, offering a small welcoming smile as I do the same. I look down, noticing she's carrying a white leather case.

"They're all waiting in the sitting room. We would have

done this in the office but there's not enough space," Hazel chirps.

I look Emory dead in the eye and cut to the chase. "Knox and Ace are here—you met them yesterday. There's three other males, all trained warriors, and Harlow, another female."

Emory's spine straightens. "Thank you for the heads-up."

I turn, Hazel and Emory following behind me as they catch up. Hazel gives her a quick rundown on how she ended up in Azalea. I tense when she mentions the border cross; I can't think of that night without thinking about Easton.

My smile is strained when I enter the room. Everyone is sitting around the coffee table in an assortment of chairs and sofas. No one pays me a lick of attention besides Knox, who frowns, noticing my tense expression.

I can't get anything past this man.

*No, you can't. Care to tell me what upset you?*

I sigh, memories of the previous moment floating through my mind so Knox can see it for himself. I take a seat beside him as the girls enter the room. My body relaxes the moment his hand touches my lower back, staying there as he gently strokes the small area of exposed skin.

Hazel introduces Emory to everyone. I'm pleasantly surprised they all listened to Hazel's verbal warning and toned down on their antics for the day.

"I take it from the otherworldly essence pulsing throughout the room that that's the book," Emory states flatly, taking a seat in a chair at the end of the coffee table.

Harlow clicks her tongue. "Emmalyn has used several different spells, combining them to not only cast the entrapment spell around our lands but to mind control and create potions that poison Fae magic over time. Then there's also the issue of the stolen Fae."

Emory turns her eyes to me as I cut in. "There's a compound in the human lands. Kidnapped Fae have been sent there to work as slaves. They can't hear, see, or speak to those not working in the compound."

"So Emmalyn has created a clusterfuck of a spell," Emory says dryly.

Hazel chuckles. "That's what I said."

Emory leans forward in her chair. "Can you show me the individual spells?"

Hazel slides the open book to Emory. We all patiently sit in silence, staring at her as she reads. My stomach sinks as her face drains of color.

"She truly used the king and queens as a sacrifice," she breathes.

I place my hand on Knox's thigh on instinct, squeezing it in support.

"She couldn't have cast the spells individually; it would have been more taxing. It's easier to cast them together, all at once," Emory muses, turning the page.

Knox tenses beside me as Emory frowns. "What is it?" he asks.

"She would have needed to link it to something, to keep the entrapment spell secure," Emory says quietly, reading the next page.

"What would have enough power to hold such a dark spell?" Nolan asks.

"Anything with a life force to equal the power of the dark magic," Emory mutters, still not lifting her head from the book.

"Could destroying the object break the spell?" Knox asks.

"In theory, yes, but I don't think it's going to be that simple."

Lenox looks from Emory to the book, his lips tightening. "Why?"

Emory lifts her head as she grimaces. "The only thing I can think of with enough power equal to a source of dark magic this strong is the Tree of Life."

Knox's entire body locks, Lenox sputters out expletives, Axel outright looks disgusted, and Nolan's face has turned wholly white.

"That's why the land is dying," Knox whispers.

Harlow clicks her tongue. "Clever bitch."

My entire body turns to ice. "The very life force that's connected to magic, to the Fae in these lands."

"If we destroy it, everything and everyone in this land, including magic, would die." Axel shakes his head in disgust. "That's why she linked the spell to it. No one can destroy it without killing everything and everyone in these lands."

Hope faded from everyone's face this morning as Emory said nothing else would be big enough to hold the spell, that it indeed would be tied to the Tree of Life. What had bloomed in all their hearts, that made their smiles more carefree over the past couple of days, had been killed with one sentence. I refuse to watch another beautiful city of people lose hope.

"Take me to the Tree of Life," I blurt as I enter Knox's study.

He's seated in his chair behind the desk, placing the paper he was reading down at my entry. "Now?" he asks, standing.

Happiness soars in my heart. He never questions me or my ideas; he simply joins on each crazy and insane thought I have, and I adore it. I adore him for not controlling or diminishing my new confidence in speaking freely.

I smile up at him as he rounds the desk. "Yes please, if you're not too busy."

He lowers his head, laying a gentle kiss on my cheek before whispering into my ear, "Reports can always wait."

I ignore the flutters in my stomach from his words. In the foyer, when he holds out his palm for me to take, I simply slide my hand in his, wrapping my arms around his neck as he cradles me to his chest and flies.

I can't help but think to myself how different it feels compared to when I first arrived here months ago. When I would scoff, roll my eyes, and be displeased at how close I had to be to him.

As we approach, Knox whispers in my ear, "The Tree of Life is so beautiful at night. It's—"

His eyes narrow, his entire body beneath me turning to stone. My heart stops cold when I notice what made Knox so tense. Lines of guards march around the tree, all in the same gray fighting suits with the red emblem logo as the ones around the demonic compound.

I blink. "Are those the queen's guards?"

"They have never in my life had guards posted around the tree. This isn't the queen."

I wrap my hand around Knox's arm, clinging to him as tightly as I can as I make us invisible. My body crackles with energy before we disappear into the night sky. Knox's shields snap around us at the same time, masking our scent and energies from the guards below.

"We need to get a good count on how many there are," I breathe.

"There's too many to control. Even if we could break the spell, just getting in there would be a suicide mission."

I look closer at the tree, noticing an archway in its thick trunk, similar to the one at the compound. "This is how she made the compound; she already had a similar version to go off of to recreate," I whisper.

Knox continues circling as he counts how many guards are stationed around the tree. I stop listening once he reaches a thousand. I place my hand over my chest, the pendant resting on my breastbone cold. Nothing is veiled. Lifting my head, I scan the skies; they could be invisible like us, but I don't sense any aerial legions flying.

Knox reads my mind before I can ask. "The riders don't have the type of power to use invisibility. It's extremely rare. Even I can't do it."

If it was any other time, I would have teased him for the statement, yet looking down at the Tree of Life that keeps everything in these lands—including the man holding me—alive, turns my blood cold.

After scouting the area for other possible traps or armies of guards, Knox flies home, the ride more silent than ever. We stroll into the dining room to find everyone already seated for dinner.

"We found the missing guards. Over fifteen hundred are posted around the Tree of Life, each one as lifeless as the others."

Forks drop into plates, chairs squeak as they sit back, and wine sloshes over glasses.

"How did no one see them? Why are there no reports?" Lenox barks.

"That's what I'd like to know," Knox says, turning to Nolan.

Nolan's face turns red, rage simmering across his face. "Are you accusing me of treason, Your Majesty?" he asks coldly as he stands.

Hazel's eyes widen next to Ace as Harlow chokes on her wine.

"Since when do we address each other formally?" Knox asks, hurt lacing his words.

I take a step back to get out of the crossfire, when Nolan's eyes flick to mine, his face contorting and twisting. "Did you put the idea in his head?" he spits.

I lung for Knox's arm to stop him from snapping something he'll later regret, yet it isn't Knox that snaps, it's Axel. "Speak to her like that again, I fucking dare you," he says deadly quiet from his seat, his body locked tight, pulsing with anger.

"She's human! There's Fae trapped in the human lands near her house and you're telling me to watch myself?" Nolan bellows.

"She turned Fae before she crossed the border. Delilah was never human," Knox says casually, making the room turn silent once more. "Nevertheless, this discussion isn't about Delilah. It's about reports that I haven't received."

"I didn't hide anything from you. I truly haven't heard anything about guards being stationed there," Nolan swears solemnly, truth ringing in his words.

"That's all I wanted to clarify," Knox states.

Taking my hand, he leads me to my usual seat beside Axel. My stomach churns, my appetite completely lost. I don't know what I've done to make Nolan so distrustful of me. I've never hidden anything from anyone in this room. The second I look up, my eyes connecting with Nolan's bewildered face, he storms out of the room.

"Thank you," I whisper to Axel once everyone resumes eating. A small nod is my only response.

"I'm just glad I wasn't the one to get Axel's death glare." Lenox shrugs, digging into his food. "It's made grown men cry." Lenox shivers. "I still remember the first time he glared at me like that."

Harlow smirks. "Oh please do tell us what you did to piss him off."

Axel rolls his eyes. "Is this the Goddess Gaia incident?"

Lenox sputters, "It was more than just an incident! You threw me out the window!"

I throw my head back on a deep laugh; Hazel's gasp only makes me cackle harder.

Axel's face is animated, the most happiness I've seen in his eyes before. "That felt so satisfying," Axel says dreamily, making Harlow and Knox snicker.

"I could have died!" Lenox protests, flinging his arms out beside him.

Axel levels a stare. "You can fly, dipshit."

"You're lucky I could still fly with how drunk I was," Lenox grumbles.

"Please tell me what he did that made you, of all people, throw him out a window," I beg.

"The first day of spring is spent worshipping and celebrating Goddess Gaia, thanking her for the blessings she's sowed to you the year prior and praying for an abundant year ahead. It was nightfall and I was dead asleep. We had all been up drinking and celebrating the new harvesting. I thought we had *all* stopped and gone to bed." Axel pointedly glares at Lenox. "I wake up to Lenox's face right in front of mine, blabbering on about how he could hear the roots of Mother Gaia blessing the house's roof." Axel slides his gaze to mine. "Legend has it that Mother Gaia grows roots, blessing the houses of those that she's chosen to favor for the year." Axel shrugs. "I simply helped him get to the roof."

My stomach hurts from laughing so hard, my breathing starts to wheeze. "You thought you could hear Goddess Gaia's roots?"

"I was really drunk," Lenox mutters.

Hazel bursts out laughing at his reddening face, everyone around the table cackling with laughter as Lenox swears he heard the drag of the branches across the tiled roof.

The moment I enter Knox's room, his hands are on me, his lips trailing kisses down my neck. "You weren't kidding when you said you couldn't keep your hands off of me," I tease.

"You're so beautiful when you're happy. Every time I heard you laugh at dinner, my cock twitched."

"You're hard from my laugh?" I sputter in disbelief, chuckling.

"Yes, and I'm very happy to hear you laugh again."

I roll my eyes. "You're insufferable."

Knox bends as he picks me up, draping me over his shoulder. "You love my quirks."

My heart catches at that word, that very deep word.

*Love.*

I shove it out of my mind.

Digging my elbow into his back, I prop my chin up on my hand. "Care to tell me why you're carrying me over your shoulder?" With each step, we get further from the bedroom.

"I'm running you a bath."

I sigh. "You have absolutely no protest from me."

Knox lowers me to the ground as his dark chuckle rumbles out of his chest. Stepping away, he fills the tub, lathering the water with lavender oils. I begin taking off my clothes. Any decency I had around him left the moment he saw me naked.

Knox leans back, watching me with hooded eyes as I

slowly lower myself into the water, my muscles relaxing as the heat soothes them.

I open my eyes to find Knox also undressing. "What are you doing?"

"Having a bath," he states smoothly.

My mouth waters as he peels off his clothes. He wasn't lying before about how hard he is. His cock is pulsing as it stands to attention. Water sloshes everywhere as he enters. He offers his hand and I take it, letting him maneuver me so my back is flush against his chest, his long powerful legs bent beside me on either side as I sit between his thighs.

Knox picks up a bar of soap. Dunking it in the water, he begins lathering suds into his hands, the vanilla scent filling the bathroom. He nudges my arms and I lift them above the water, sighing further into him as he slowly begins to massage the soap into my skin. I tilt my chin back, my chest rising and falling as he reaches my neck, my breath hitching when his thumbs run down my pulse points. His hands slowly trail down to my breasts, kneading them, making my core clench with each featherlight, teasing stroke against my hard nipples. When his hands edge lower, a small whimper leaves me. His hands descend into the water and wrap around my thighs, spreading me wide. My lips part as I pant. I feel hot and needy from his teasing, a delectable form of torture.

"Let me take care of you," he whispers.

I sigh when his hands, lathered with lavender oil, begin to knead my back, massaging the tense muscles. I moan as he works a particularly tense spot. I close my eyes, my body going languid in his.

As each second passes that my body relaxes, my breathing begins to pick up, my breasts feeling full and heavy as he touches every part of me, except for where I need him the most. When his hands slowly glide to my breasts, I sigh as his large palms cup them, kneading the tender heaviness.

I arch my back as my lips part, my hips swiveling, begging for relief. Knox pinches my nipples, making a loud moan fall from my mouth as the pain sends electricity directly to my core.

"So sensitive," he murmurs.

My hips buck, seeking his touch as he teases my sensitive nipples, rubbing circles around the tight buds. His canines gently scrape down my neck, eliciting a full-body shiver.

"So responsive," he whispers, dragging his hand under water.

His fingers glide down my stomach, disappearing between my thighs. The moment they touch my clit I yelp so loud I surprise even myself. Knox groans into my ear as he slips two fingers inside me, slowly pumping me as his thumb swipes side to side over my clit. My hips roll with his movements.

"That's it. Ride my hand, Angel."

His words make my core clench around his fingers, his groan making my hips roll faster. Water sloshes over my sensitive nipples as he teases and tweaks them with his free hand. Tightness coils in my stomach, building with each passing stroke, turning my body to liquid heat as he curls his fingers inside of me, brushing that spot inside me that makes me feral.

"Come," he growls.

That one single word, the demand in his tone, makes me explode, shivering and moaning as ecstasy writhes through me, my hips jerking wildly as I ride out the orgasm.

I flutter my eyes open, turning around to face Knox, splashing water over the sides of the tub as I do. His eyes are hooded, his pupils flared as he pants. The sight of him so turned on from my own pleasure makes my skin tingle, pressure building within me again. I can never get enough of him. I straddle his thighs, raking my hands down his chest, my hand disappearing under the water. I lean forward, capturing his mouth as my hand wraps around his cock, squeezing. He grunts low into my mouth, his tongue darting out to stroke mine, slow and deep, as if we have all the time in the world.

His large velvet cock pulses in my hand, his hips bucking when I swirl my thumb around the tip. I situate myself, then lower onto him, moaning as he fills me to the hilt. Knox's head falls back, a deep groan leaving his mouth as I slowly begin to grind on him. His hands slide up my thighs, coming around to knead my ass, guiding the rhythm of my hips, picking up the pace. He opens his eyes, the intensity of them making my core clench around him, sending a shudder through his body.

"Beautiful," he whispers gutturally.

He lowers his head to my breasts, biting my sensitive nipple before he twirls his tongue around the hard bud. The tingling in my core expands to my whole body as he sucks hard on the other.

I sink my hands into his hair, gripping him tightly and shoving his face into my breast, needing more.

"You want to come, Angel?" he purrs around my breast.

"Yes," I beg. "Please."

"Say it," he orders, his hips picking up the pace of his thrusts. "Tell me what you want."

My head tips back as the pressure builds higher, heat pooling between my legs as my back arches, begging for him to touch me everywhere.

"I want to come around your cock," I pant.

Knox smashes his lips to mine as white light surrounds

us, the tub of water disappearing before we land in silk sheets. I yelp as I realize he teleported us to his bed.

His growl is feral as he rasps, "Say it again."

He stops moving his hips, making me squirm beneath him. "Knox," I whimper. "Make me come."

Knox lifts me up, and I only have time to wrap my legs around his waist as he places his hands on my shoulders, holding me down. He pounds in and out of me so hard and relentlessly, I scream.

His cock brushes against that spot inside of me with each thrust, the tightness in my core building so fast I can't control it. My body shakes around Knox. "Oh gods, oh gods."

"I may be your god, Angel, but you chant my name as I fuck you," he grunts.

I scream his name as his canines flare, biting my shoulder, claiming me. My hips buck wildly, trying to match his intense pace. Knox groans at every sound I make. Every whimper and moan has his cock expanding inside of me, stretching and filling me. When he snakes his hand between our bodies and brushes his thumb against my clit, I combust. Shaking uncontrollably, I gasp out his name over and over, my core clenching and convulsing around him.

My own orgasm sends him over the edge. His wings burst out when he comes as he whispers words nestled into the crook of my shoulder. Floating through my own bliss, I can't hear exactly what he says. Still inside me, he lifts his head, smashing his lips to mine. His cock twitches every so often as I soak up everything he pours into me.

# Chapter Forty-Five

I gasp awake in Knox's arms, breathing shallow. My hands shake as I run my fingers through my sweat-covered hair.

"What is it?" Knox murmurs, rubbing his hand up and down my back.

"Send a messenger for Emory," I croak.

Knox doesn't question me. Throwing the sheets off, he strolls into the dressing room, emerging fully clothed. "What do you want it to say?"

"That she needs to get here as soon as possible," I say, getting out of bed. The sunrise streaks through my windows as I walk down the hall to my room, Knox close on my heels. "I think there might be a way to break the spell."

Knox's eyes widen before he rushes out of the room in search of a messenger.

My hands shake as I rifle through my clothes, finally dragging tailored pants up my legs and throwing a white blouse over my head. I pray that Emory can get here fast.

Descending into the foyer, I pause as the front door opens. Nolan strides through, his sheepish expression making my stomach churn. He rubs the back of his neck, looking at the floor as he reaches me. "Can we go for a walk in the gardens?"

I tamp down on my urge to frown. "Why?" I ask hesitantly.

Nolan huffs out a breath. "I owe you an apology and an explanation."

I dart my gaze to the top of the stairs, wishing anyone would come down and interrupt us. But as I pull my eyes back, searching his face, I only find sincerity and, perhaps, embarrassment for the situation he's created.

I take a steadying breath, waving my hand to the back door. "Sure."

As we walk through the garden, passing the flowerbed trail, it seems like he's more nervous than I am, his cheeks tinted pink.

"I'm sorry for my recent outbursts. They were uncalled for and undeserved. I'm truly sorry for taking my anger and frustration out on you," he rushes out.

I feel the sincerity in every word he speaks. I turn to face him fully, stopping amongst the roses surrounding us, Knox's house looming in the distance. "Can I ask why my presence upsets you so much?"

He shakes his head, long blond hair swishing. "Your presence isn't unsettling." I look at him flatly, until a small smile twitches on his lips. "Your presence at the beginning was unsettling," he amends.

I jut out my chin. "Thank you for the honesty."

"I owe you an explanation." Nolan runs his hand through his hair as he begins to pace. "My mother and sister were amongst the Fae who were taken. I haven't seen them in over fifty years." His face twists in pain as he stops several feet from me. "It's no excuse, yet when you showed up—the only person who's been able to cross the border—I was skeptical, especially with the Fae being held as slaves in the human lands."

I close my eyes. Of course. The past few weeks of immense distrust and hostility makes sense. If it was Easton who had been taken and the roles were reversed, I would be just as skeptical.

"I know it wasn't logical to take all my frustration out on you. Grief works in odd ways sometimes, and each time I looked at you, I saw my missing family," he croaks out.

"I'm sorry about your sister and mother," I say hoarsely.

His face contorts in pain, silver lining his eyes. "Thank you."

"How did they disappear?" I ask hesitantly.

His Adam's apple bobs on a swallow. "We lived in the lower coastal region of Azalea. I had left earlier that day for the legion. There had been petty fights breaking out that Knox needed me to break up." His chest caves on a deep exhale. "I came home two days later to find the house empty. Dirty dishes from the morning I left were still in the sink, and when I searched their rooms, I found it trashed, windows shattered, furniture thrown around...They fought hard."

My heart breaks for the pain that coats his voice as he retells his nightmare. I place my hand on his forearm. "Perhaps our plan will work and you'll see them again."

He takes a step back, his head shaking. "What plan?"

"I need to speak with Emory first to make sure it will work, but I have an idea."

I expect to see a small glimmer of hope in Nolan's eyes, yet all I see is fear.

Emory walks through the sitting room door several hours later, waving her hand around the room. "You summoned me?" she teases, her brow quirking.

Knox closes the door behind them, taking a seat beside me. Everyone is sitting around the room once more, each more impatient than the next.

"What if there's a spell that can destroy and recreate the Tree of Life?" I ask. Everyone visibly deflates at my idea, except for Knox—he's the only encouraging face letting me speak.

"We already went over this," Emory says gently.

"Yes, but what if while I destroy it, I hold onto the lifeline in the tree that's pure? The core—its essence."

"I don't know any spells—"

"Phoenix rising," I say, cutting her off.

Knox stiffens beside me. The others look at me disbelievingly.

"You want to perform a phoenix rising spell?" Emory asks.

I lift my chin. "I saw the spell in my dream, the tree being burnt to ash, destroying the lifeline of the dark magic, while I hold onto the core of the tree's essence and rebuild it."

"That's an incredibly strong spell, Delilah," Ace murmurs anxiously.

"I have access to my full power."

Emory shakes her head. "The tree itself is powerful. You'd have to use up almost every last drop of your magic. If you don't complete the spell before you burn yourself out the tree will die and—"

"If you overuse your power...you can permanently burn out," Lenox whispers, eyes wide as he cuts Emory off.

I look around at everyone's shocked and anxious expressions, yet there's a small slice of hope, I can feel it. Noticeably, Knox has been silent the entire time. When I turn to him, his face is pale. I bite my lip, anxiety coursing through me at seeing his own worry.

"Knox?" I whisper.

"What if I do the spell with her?" he asks, lifting his stricken gaze to Emory.

Emory grimaces. "None of us have enough power for a spell of this magnitude. You'd burn out before you even started."

Knox's swallow is audible.

I square my shoulders. "What are the chances of it killing me?" I ask Emory.

Lenox's mouth opens and closes at my words, Axel leaning forward in his chair as if the threat of my death is sitting in this very room and he must stop it. Hazel has withdrawn into herself, Ace's worried expression mirroring her own, while Harlow openly assesses me, sizing me up. Emory bites her lip, her brows furrowing in concentration. A light flowing energy surrounds me, probing. Emory's magic.

The calm energy snaps away. "You have more than enough magic for the spell. If you don't use your power before the spell, you'll be fine."

"Will it take long for you to teach me the spell?" I ask.

"The spell itself is simple. It's the magnitude of the life force in the tree that's tricky," Emory explains.

"Let's do it then," I decide.

Lenox sputters, "Just like that? This is your life on the line!"

My eyes soften. "I'm the only one that can do the spell and we have no other options. Emory said so herself, I have more than enough magic."

Lenox's bewildered eyes snap to Knox. "And you're fine with this?"

I turn to Knox, his eyes searching my own. "It's Delilah's decision. If we don't help her she'll do it on her own, which is more dangerous."

I pat his thigh. "Smart man."

The room is silent before Axel snaps into his role of second-in-command. "We'll need a plan on how to get you in and out without using a drop of your magic."

After hours of detailed discussion and consideration for any pitfalls that could happen, we finally have a substantial plan. Harlow left hours ago to spy on Emmalyn and the queen, to get as much information about her as we possibly can. Sitting in front of a map of the Fae lands, I point to the center of the lands as everyone runs through their task for tomorrow once more.

"I've sent out a messenger demanding a mandatory meeting of the courts." Knox lifts his head, his gaze piercing Axel. "You need to delay the queen and Emmalyn for as long as possible. I don't care what bullshit you spew in that room so long as everyone stays occupied."

Axel smirks. "Spew bullshit to the queen. Understood."

I lean back in my seat. "While I fly Aurora to the tree, Knox will fly beside me, guarding,"

"Nolan will take the legions out on a mission for a 'threat' the queen received so the queen's second can't send any troops in," Knox adds.

Lenox's grin widens as he says, "While Ace and I light fires in the area surrounding the tree."

I nod. "The guards posted around the tree running strictly on orders—protect it at all costs. Knox saw as such when he dipped into their minds. If they see fires burning near, they'll have to leave their post to put it out."

"I can't believe I'm saying this, but...keep the fires going for as long as possible," Knox cuts in.

"Just don't burn the entire forest down," Axel mutters as Lenox smirks.

"Harlow will keep the beasts contained to the compound, transforming into whatever creature she sees suitable to keep the demons in their hole," I mutter.

"Any remaining guards that stay on their post around the tree will be met with Hazel's vines and my telepathy," Knox says, jutting his chin to Hazel.

"If there's more than we expect who stay on their posts, I can use my own earth magic to tangle them while helping Lenox set the fires," Ace chimes in.

"If either plan fails, Delilah has enough magic to make herself invisible, but that's the worst-case scenario. I don't want her using any magic before the spell if it can be avoided," Emory chimes in from her seat at the head of the coffee table.

"That takes care of Emmalyn, the kings and queens, warrior legions, the guards posted and the beasts...Are we missing anything?" I ask, looking around the room.

Knox shakes his head. "You just need to learn the spell."

Harlow bursts into the room, the doors slamming behind her as she struts to a chair. "I now know more about this bitch than she does."

Lenox rolls his eyes. "Always with the dramatic flare."

Axel snickers, snapping his mouth shut as Harlow's hard brown eyes slide to him. "Emmalyn has been the queen's second for over three hundred years, and she was born and raised in the Air Court, her father being the royal family's personal guard."

Ace leans forward in his seat. "How did a daughter's guard become second-in-command?"

"My thoughts exactly. The queen had a different second-in-command. One day she woke up and fired her, establishing Emmalyn as her second."

"I'm sure she received training for the position," Nolan offers.

Harlow's glare at Nolan is flat and emotionless.

Axel's brows furrow. "You think Emmalyn orchestrated it?"

"I think you can't create an entrapment spell without heavily planning it for years."

A chill runs down my spine.

How long has Emmalyn been planning all of this? How many people did she harm along the way to make her plans come to fruition, and why would she do any of this in the first place?

I leave Knox's court to their bickering, following Emory into Knox's study to learn the spell.

Emory clicks her tongue as she takes her seat in a wooden chair, wasting no time. "The phoenix rising is a simple purification spell. It's the recreation that we need to work—"

"I want to learn the spell in case I have to step in," Knox interrupts as he enters the study, taking a seat beside me on the sofa.

Emory doesn't voice it, but we both know it will be pointless. Even with the immense amount of power Knox has, he isn't at his strongest. The poison has been slowly blinding his magic for decades. But Emory simply nods, knowing there's no point in fighting Knox. He needs to feel useful and wants to know he can help me in any way he can.

"I was just explaining that the purification aspect of the spell is simple. It's the recreation of the life force we need to focus on, since that's what will use up most of her magic," Emory tells Knox.

His voice is laced with worry as he says, "I haven't taught Delilah any purification spells."

"She has fire magic. That's the purification element. All Delilah has to do is burn the dark magic while holding onto the core magic of the tree's life force. We'll practice on one of your trees in the garden."

"How do I rebuild the tree?" I ask.

"That's where your earth magic comes in. Has anyone taught you how to grow plants?" Emory asks.

"Yes, Hazel taught me weeks ago. I know how to make all sorts of plant life grow and flourish."

Emory leans forward. "You make plant life flourish because you connect with its life force, speeding up the growth. It's the exact same thing, the only difference being the sheer size of the tree."

I bite my lip. "Will I know when it's complete?"

"Yes, you'll feel it in your bones. You'll no longer feel like you have to physically hold it up. Once the spell is complete it's as if the weight of it has been lifted off you."

"It sounds too easy," Knox mutters.

"The spell is easy, rebuilding the life force of the tree isn't," Emory answers flatly.

Emory shows me the original phoenix rising spell, pulling an old leather-bound book out of her bag. We pour over the book until every word is memorized, until my eyes begin to blur and the words on the page swirl. Emory pushes me to continue reading, saying there's more power in knowledge. I recite the ins and outs of the spell in detail, recalling information about how it works and what to do. Once Emory is satisfied that I know every detail we head outside to the garden,

Knox a silent stand of support behind me as Emory coaches me through the spell.

My bones begin to feel heavy by the twenty-seventh time, a burnout looming as I burn, hold the tether of life, and revive the tree, over and over. I can no longer smell the flowers around me; an ashy scent coats everything. My body protests, pushed past the point of exhaustion, as I make the tree grow once more, my knees buckling beneath me. I can't help but close my heavy eyes, my eyelids feeling like grains of sand.

Knox's arms wrap around me as he cradles me to his chest. I listen to his strong heartbeat as it thumps wildly against my ears.

"She'll be fine, Knox. She mastered the spell by the third time. I just needed to know how long it took her to burn out," I hear Emory say.

Knox's strangled voice floats through my ears. "Does she have enough?"

"She has more than enough; she'll be fine. She just needs to rest."

I don't hear the rest of the conversation as sleep drags me under, so deep that I forget my own name as I fall into blissful darkness.

I awake later that evening to an empty bed, my bones tired and heavy. Looking at the darkened night sky through the window, I figure it must be close to midnight.

Sudden panic rushes through my chest, and my power sears through the house as I search for him. I breathe a sigh of relief when I feel him in his study.

Throwing the covers off I take one of Knox's white shirts, covering my naked body. I find Knox sitting shirtless at his desk, wearing nothing but gray sleep pants. Knox leans back in his chair, his brows furrowing. "What are you doing up? You should be resting."

I round the desk, sitting on the edge of the dark mahogany. "I'm no longer tired."

Knox places a hand on my calf, massaging the tense muscles.

"Why aren't you in bed?" I ask tentatively.

Knox shrugs sheepishly. "I wanted to run over the plans again."

I lean forward, placing a kiss on his cheek. "Do you feel better?"

He frowns. "I'm just worried."

"About?"

"You."

"You heard Emory, I have plenty of magic. It's not a risk."

Knox stares at me so intensely I have to force myself to sit still and not squirm.

"Why can't you sleep?" he asks again, changing the topic as he runs his hand up and down my calf.

Lowering my eyes, I play with the hem of his shirt I'm wearing. "I woke up and you weren't there."

"Ahhh," he murmurs. His hands grab my hips, dragging me across the desk to sit in front of him. He runs his hands up my inner thigh, parting them. "I think we both need to take our minds off tomorrow," he whispers, trailing kisses up the inside of my thigh.

My nipples tighten, poking through his shirt as my core begins to pulse. "I think that can be arranged," I say, running my fingers through his hair.

Knox licks a path from my knee to my hip, sending a

shiver down my body. He lifts my legs up, placing my feet on the desk, making me spread bare for him.

His eyes spark with burning heat as they lock on mine. My breath quickens as he lifts his white shirt that I'm wearing, his tongue darting out to lick his lips as his pupils flare. My chest heaves as he lowers his head, his eyes never leaving mine as he licks the entire length of my core.

My head drops back on a low moan as I tug his hair, trying to pull him closer to me. He slips two fingers inside me, pumping as his tongue swirls over my clit.

Air brushes against my back, the sounds of paper flying throughout the room and clutter hitting the floor as Knox uses his power of air to clear the desk entirely.

Black shadows swirl around me, and then my t-shirt buttons fly in the air, popping as my shirt is ripped open. A shadowed palm runs down my chest, pushing me to lay flat on my back. My hands are held together above my head, the shadows clutching my wrists, until I'm completely pinned down not only by Knox's body but his magic too. More hands appear, the featherlight touch of his shadows cupping my breasts, rubbing small circles around the sensitive, hard nipples.

"Oh gods," I breathe, squirming beneath his overwhelming touch.

I look over my stomach to see the top of his head between my thighs. The sight makes wetness pool from me, my core clenching around his fingers as my hips roll, grinding against his face.

"You taste so fucking good, Angel," he growls.

Shadows twirl around me as he feels every inch of my body with his magic. His bicep starts flexing, moving rapidly, and my body shivers as I realize he's touching himself to the sight of him pleasuring me. "Knox," I whimper.

My core clenches around his fingers. I'm on the verge of exploding when he curls his fingers, rubbing that spot inside of me as he commands, "Come on my face."

My orgasm rips through me, and I shamelessly ride it out as my hips buck wildly on Knox's face while he continues to lick my clit and pump his fingers. I need more, I need him inside of me. I have never felt so good yet empty at the same time.

Knox groans as he pushes out of his chair, his glorious length standing to attention. He wraps his hand around it, stroking himself. "Do you want me inside of you, Angel?" he drawls, his voice so low it sends shivers through me.

"Yes," I whimper.

He disappears, his dark chuckle coming from behind me.

I jump off the desk, turning to find Knox sitting naked on the couch, his arms spread across the back of it. He crooks his finger at me. "Come here."

A shiver races through my body at his demanding tone. I slowly stride around the desk, stopping in front of him.

"What do you want, Angel?"

"I want to taste you," I rasp.

His eyes flare, pupils dilating as magic erupts around the room.

I want to make this man come completely undone. The thought propels me forward. I peel off his shirt, letting it fall from my hands as I stand bare before him. I place my hands on his knees as I kneel, satisfaction filling my veins as his eyes heat at the sight of me.

Leaning forward, I capture his mouth, nipping his bottom lip, then scraping my canines down the length of his neck. My palms flatten against his chest, feeling the hard planes of his muscles ripple as his chest heaves. I lick across his collarbone, trailing kisses down his body. Knox wraps his hand around my head as I flatten my tongue against his nipple, wetness pooling between my thighs as he moans. My hard nipples brush against his warm skin, sending electricity through my body, as I lower myself further.

I wrap one hand around his length. Stroking it, I bring my mouth to the tip. I dart my tongue out, swirling around the mushroom-shaped head, licking off the pool of liquid that drips out. His jaw clenches, his hands fisting at his side. I open my mouth further, taking in his length. Knox's eyes turn heavy-lidded on a low groan, his hands sliding into my hair. He's so big I can't fit more than half of him inside my mouth. While the tip nudges the back of my throat, I stroke his lower half with my hand, working in tandem with my mouth, swirling the tip of his cock on each stroke upward and sucking.

"Fuck, Angel, nothing looks as good as your mouth wrapped around my cock."

His filthy words make wetness drip down my thigh. His nostrils flare as he scents the change in me, a knowing smirk playing on his lips. "I knew you liked it when I talked."

I can't help the moan that escapes me, the vibrations running down Knox's cock as I squirm on the floor, my core pulsing and begging to be touched again.

He puts his hands under my arms, lifting me to straddle him and entering me in one deep stroke. I throw my head back on a scream at the sudden intrusion, clamping around him. Knox sucks my nipple into his mouth while his hand teases and pinches the other one. My hips buck, matching him thrust for thrust.

"Faster, Angel, let me feel you squeeze me," he growls.

I whimper, his words sending waves of pleasure through my body. I grab a fistful of his hair, pulling his head back I lower my lips to his, gasping when his tongue strokes my own as wildly as his cock drives into me.

"Do you like my filthy words?"

"Yes," I pant into his mouth.

He slaps my ass, making me jolt forward, a surprised yelp falling from my lips. His palm rubs circles around the skin, soothing the sting as pleasure fills my core. He kneads my ass, using it to move my hips back and forth on his cock.

"Faster. Ride me faster," he grunts, his shallow breaths mingling with my own as we kiss. He slaps my ass again, the sting of pain making my core clench and the pleasure heighten. "That's it, Angel, let go. Make that pretty pussy explode around my cock."

On the next slap, my wings snap out as I throw my head back on a scream, wetness dripping down my thighs. Knox's growl of pleasure makes my legs shake. He latches onto my nipple, biting it at the same time he slaps my ass, rubbing soothing circles around the sting as he sucks my nipple.

The feeling that builds inside of me is so wild I can't control my hips as I rock faster into him, matching his thrusts, chasing the orgasm that's on the brink of exploding.

"You're so fucking beautiful," Knox groans, pulling my head down to his and kissing me with such ferocity stars spark in my vision.

Knox trails a finger down the center of my wings at the same time he sinks his canines in me. Holding on is the only thing I can do as I combust.

I scream Knox's name so loud I make his own feral growl leave his lips as my orgasm tips him over the edge. Both our hips jerk relentlessly as we milk each other's orgasm until the last second.

I collapse forward onto his chest, panting as Knox still shallowly thrusts, his orgasm unending. I smile as my canines puncture the crook of his neck, satisfaction coursing through me as he throws his head back on a deep groan, his whole body shuddering with the impact of the heightened orgasm.

Knox wraps his arms around my back, holding me to his chest as it rises and falls rapidly, both of us struggling to catch our breaths. "It gets better every time," he whispers, his words coated in awe.

I chuckle into his neck, burying my face further. My heart feels so full it could burst. We lie in each other's arms, neither one of us moving.

Knox's deep drawl brings me back. "In case something goes wrong, Delilah, I—"

I cut him off with my lips, pouring everything my heart feels into the kiss.

He can tell me tomorrow after our plan works. Tomorrow could have a multitude of problems—it won't work, we could be caught, we could be killed, or…we could be free. I have wanted to help free the Fae for months, and a small part of my heart hopes that in doing so I can free my own people. Yet with freedom comes cost. What if we free magic and all of this goes away? What if he sees his mate when his power returns? What if I have to leave it all behind tomorrow?

I kiss him with such passion that I feel him begin to swell inside me again. We stay joined, not daring to break the kiss as we slowly make love, both of us finding our orgasms once more as we pour everything we feel into that kiss.

I cherish Knox like it's the last time I'll ever have him.

# Chapter Forty-Six

The courts' kings and queens accepted the meeting Knox requested at the queen's grounds; everyone will be arriving at the castle in thirty minutes. Axel already left over an hour ago, wanting to ensure that everyone attends and stays there.

In the front foyer, I secure all my weapons for the flight, checking and triple checking that I'm prepared and ready. Aurora's already suited up for flight as she waits on the front lawn, probably terrorizing Knox's guards.

I turn my head, watching as Knox straps blade after blade to his immaculate body, his teeth biting his lower lip. He would never admit it, but he's been a ball of nerves today, uneasiness coiling throughout his entire body. Once Axel left, Knox went into a killing calm, so sharp and focused no one could penetrate it. He's completely transformed, allowing the trained warrior within him to take control, enhanced to a predatory level. I've seen Knox go into that warrior's mind, yet today is different. He's sharper, more aware, deadlier.

A warrior ready to fight for his people, his kingdom.

Knox snaps his head to the mantel clock in front of him,

turning his predatory gaze on mine. "It's time. Are you ready?"

I face Knox, feeling my own training take over my body, calm washing over me. "Ready."

On the front lawn, Aurora is just as poised and ready, as if she can feel the energy crackling in the air, the intensity. I mount her, tilting my head to see Knox already airborne in the night sky behind me, waiting.

"We have one shot at this, Aurora. Let's make it count," I whisper.

She takes off into the sky, her booming wings filling the silence as we fly for the Tree of Life—as we fly for freedom.

I scan the beautiful details of Azalea below me, the city glowing with lights, twinkling as bright as a star. I take in everything as we fly—the mountains, the forest canopy, the ocean. I take in everything built within these lands and pray to any gods that will listen that I don't destroy it tonight.

A horrible sick feeling slithers through my spine. I scan the night sky trying to find its source, watching as Knox pauses, hovering midair—he can feel it too. He slowly turns, scanning, putting his back toward the very thing that he searches for.

A shadow darker than the night's sky descends behind Knox, so large it makes my stomach sink. Its mouth opens to reveal rows upon rows of sharp white teeth glinting in the moonlight. Glowing red eyes snap open, illuminating the scaled horns atop its head as it aims for Knox.

Its dragon-like body is larger than those I saw at the aerial legion, but the dark shadows shrouding it tell me all I need to know—Emmalyn has summoned demonic dragons.

A scream leaves my mouth, piercing the sky with a warning, but it's too late.

The dragon knocks Knox to the side, red light pulsing

from the beast's hands. Its black talons snatch him as he spins in the air. Light flares around Knox, his magic withering in the dragon's hold, only to pulse, winking out completely.

The sight makes me explode.

I throw my hands in front of me, fire erupting from my palms, searing directly into the creature's heart. My flames fly faster than the beast. It releases Knox from its claws as it roars in agony, the fire turning the dragon beast to ash within seconds.

My magic completely incinerates it.

Aurora lunges for Knox as he freefalls through the air. My heart doesn't start beating until I see his wings flutter, relief coursing through me so strong I sag into Aurora. He disappears entirely before his strong arms wrap around me from behind, pinewood surrounding me.

"You weren't supposed to use your magic!" he barks.

"You weren't supposed to be in dragon talons!" I snap.

I lean forward, stroking Aurora's fur. "Keep going," I whisper. I slap my hands down on Knox's arms as he begins to move. "You're not going anywhere."

"Are you angry at me?" he asks incredulously.

"Yes! You could have died!" I scream.

A dark rumble of laughter floats into my ears as his chest shakes behind me. I swing my legs around, turning to face him. "Why are you laughing?" I ask through gritted teeth.

"Because you're adorable and you have an odd way of showing you care about me."

The adrenaline still coursing through my body makes me snap my mouth closed so I don't spew nonsense at him.

He narrows his eyes. "How much did you use?"

I scoff. "Not much."

He quirks a brow.

"I didn't use *a lot*," I amend. "But I can't use any invisibility magic now."

Knox's chest visibly deflates on a sigh. "Let's pray our plan works then."

I twist around, facing forward again as Knox wraps his arms around me, and I don't feel the least bit of shame as I cling to him. My heart is beating so fast I feel as if I might throw up. The image of him in the demonic dragon's claws will forever be ingrained in my mind.

I close my eyes, taking deep breaths, trying to go back into a killing calm.

When my heartbeat returns to normal and my breathing is even, I open my eyes to find the world on fire.

"Holy shit," I breathe.

Flames blast from all directions, creating a circle around the Tree of Life, a cage and a prison for the guards. When one fire goes out, another alights not too far away, burning brighter than the very sun itself. The flames dance and sing as they climb higher by the second.

"I think Lenox is enjoying himself a tad too much," Knox murmurs.

As we approach, I see most of the guards have left their posts to deal with the fires, threatening the very thing they've been compelled to protect.

I steer Aurora to an outcrop that we marked earlier. Lenox is under strict orders to not burn any fires near this area, to not draw any attention to Aurora and her hiding place. Thanks to her raven coat, she'll blend into the darkness of the night.

Knox and I dismount as she lands. Wasting no time, I give Aurora a pat. "If you see anyone turn up besides Knox's court, roar your heart out," I say, placing a small kiss on her snout.

Aurora nudges me, urging me to go.

I huff out a small laugh, then follow Knox through the forest.

The fires surrounding the Tree of Life burn so bright we have to keep to the tree trunks, hiding in the shadows as to not alert anyone of our presence. Sneaking up the edge of the forest I see the few guards still lingering by the door are held down by vines and tree trunks sprouting from the forest floor, courtesy of Hazel. Knox pauses on the tree line, dipping into each of their minds.

"Now," he whispers.

We take off running as fast as we can, Knox never leaving my side as I pray that no wayward guards catch us entering through the tree's archway. Instead of feeling relieved as we cross through unnoticed, I gag, covering my mouth and nose with my hand. I place the other on my stomach, trying to ease the waves of nausea.

The entire core of the tree is rotted. Black sap drips from the walls, my boots sticking to puddles of it on the floor. The outside of the tree looks as if nothing has changed, revealing nothing about the absolute wrongness of its core. I've never smelt something so horrid in my life.

Knox gags. "How Emmalyn got away with all of this for so long is unfathomable."

He takes my forearm, leading me through the halls of the tree. It's similar to the beasts' compound, except instead of stone walls is wood, though decomposing as dark magic infests its core. Like a parasite.

The further we walk the stronger the smell gets, each step intensifying as the rot encompasses our senses. Knox turns a corner, revealing faint white light glowing at the end of the hallway, obscured by shadows—

I gasp as I look around the circular area, disgust rolling through my stomach.

It's the tree.

Utter shock makes me stumble back. Darkness suffocates the core of the tree, the heart of Aloriah's magic. Faint white light tries to glow from between cracks in the sticky black sap, but the dark magic spell is completely suffocating the life of this very world, slowly killing everything and everyone in it.

I snap into action at the thought. Rushing forward, I square my shoulders, parting my feet into a steadying stance, preparing my body for the assault that's about to begin.

"Take it one step at a time," Knox says beside me.

His presence is comforting and soothing as he supports me.

Without another word I close my eyes. Taking a deep breath, I tunnel down into my magic, submerging myself into my well of power. Swimming to the bottom of its depth. I open my eyes as fire builds throughout my body, my eyes alighting with embers. I spear my power into the tree, feeling as if I'm wading through mud as I search for the pure essence of the tree's core, the divine magic. The tether of its life force, nestled at the bottom, barely pulses with life as it's devoured by the parasite of the dark magic.

I cling to it with everything I have as the world around me explodes. The floor beneath my feet shakes as the tree is engulfed with flames. The sap smells worse as it burns, as I burn it all to the ground, purifying and cleansing. The tether of life in my hands sighs as the dark magic erupts in flames, turning into nothing but ash swirling in the sky.

The kernel of life in my palms thanks me as I save it, thankful that I returned to it. That's why its energy beckoned to me the first time I flew past the Tree of Life. It knew I could help it, save it, free it.

The wood surrounding us cracks and crumbles, then the deafening boom of the trunk falling shakes my very bones. The light from the fires around us bursts, the white glow of the moon shining through the cracks, burning my eyes as the tree begins to flutter into nothing but cinders.

I can hear Knox's faint cough in the distance as the smoke becomes stifling. I make everything outside of myself and this tether of life disappear until it's only me standing there with a small kernel, an orb of white glowing light—a seed to grow a new world.

Standing on a pile of ash, with nothing surrounding us but the night sky and the burning forest, I begin to build life once more. Pouring everything I have, everything that I am into this small tendril of life, my entire body glows as white light pours out of me and into the life force of the tree's seed.

I have been dreaming about these lands and its people my entire life. My safe space was next to a veil of the truth the entire time. I have never been able to help my own people, but I was destined for this. I feel it in my very soul. I have lost and sacrificed what I love to be here. For this moment in time, I can help people, free them from their misery, from the horrors inflicted upon them.

My breathing comes faster, my chest heaving as I pant. Sweat glides down the nape of my neck as each drop of magic I pour into the seed begins to weigh on me.

Building its roots, the tree's seven layers, the core to the heart of these lands.

The night sky starts to disappear around me once more. The trunk grows, encompassing me in its hollow inside. The weight on my shoulders becomes unbearable, as if I'm carrying its very essence—the weight of the Fae lands.

A guttural deep roar pierces the air around us. "No, no, no, I can't—"

"Stop? What a shame," a dark female voice coos, before magic as black as night slams into me.

I grit my teeth as wave after wave of unending dark magic slams into me. Knox's protection shield buckles as it holds off the assault that Emmalyn throws my way.

"A protection shield, how adorable," she croons.

Her greasy black hair flutters in the wind from the assault of her power, a sneer marring her face as hate-filled blue eyes glare at me. Where did Knox go? His shield surrounds me, wavering against the force yet holding strong.

*He's still alive.*

As long as that shield holds, he's still alive.

My feet begin to slide on the floor as every bit of my strength tries to hold onto the life force blooming from my hands while also holding off Emmalyn's dark magic.

"What a clever human you are...or should I say Fae?" she drawls, cocking her head.

I don't take my focus off the spell. The moment she pulls my attention away, she can strike, killing everyone I've come to care about. I'm so close, I can feel it. My bones are screaming with the weight of it, the sheer size and magnitude of power in the room as the Tree of Life becomes a phoenix rising, life birthing from the very ashes that destroyed it.

My breathing becomes shallow as my magic starts to fade, faster than the spell. I furrow my brows, shaking my head as I try to concentrate. Why does my magic feel like it's escaping faster?

A roar fills the room as Aurora charges in, Knox leaping

off her back as shadows and darkness blast from his hands. Knox's power slams into Emmalyn as Aurora pounces, holding her down with all her weight, those sharp claws piercing Emmalyn's skin. The scream that escapes Emmalyn isn't Fae, isn't human, isn't of this world. The sound grates down my skin as it makes me want to shrivel away.

I blink rapidly as my vision starts to blur. I grit my teeth, my knees wanting to buckle as my power drains.

I'm not done yet. I shouldn't be burning out.

Panic like never before overtakes my body as I realize why Emmalyn didn't outright attack me. Her blasts of power were a distraction as she drained my magic.

Emmalyn's a siphon.

My eyes water as my body collapses, stars exploding into my vision as I scream from the pain of my heavy bones hitting the floor. My chest heaves as I pour every ounce of strength I have left in me to finish the spell.

I can't stop. I refuse to be the one to kill this beautiful world.

Even as my life slowly drains away.

My heart begins to slow, dizziness overtaking my mind and stars exploding into my vision. I slide my heavy eyes to Knox, taking in every last detail of him. I sigh with relief as Aurora latches her teeth into Emmalyn, tearing her limbs from her as Knox lifts his sword.

The last thing I see, that I'll ever see, is Knox dragging it across her throat, black blood pouring out of Emmalyn as darkness pulls me under.

# Chapter Forty-Seven

## KNOX

The blade in my hand has never felt lighter as I drag it across Emmalyn's neck, black blood oozing out of her wounds as Aurora tears her limb for limb, making sure that nothing is left of the woman that took away everything and everyone I loved.

The moment I heard Aurora's roar, I took off, only to find her charging for me in the open field. That's when my heart stopped dead, sensing Emmalyn with Delilah in the room I had left.

The sword in my hand clangs to the floor as it slips through my fingers, my heart stopping cold as I turn around to find Delilah crumbled on the ground. Her magic drains from her as she continues the spell even in darkness.

A desperate roar rips from my throat as I feel her fading, already past the point of burnout.

*She doesn't know I love her.*

It's the one thought that kills me, that cleaves my heart in two as I watch her chest barely rise and fall. A piece of my heart...my very soul dying alongside her.

I can't lose her; I refuse to lose her.

I just found her.

Power erupts, exploding throughout the lands of Aloriah, so strong and unyielding it makes my body fly across the room. Hurtled against the rebuilt tree wall as power and freedom return to the Fae lands.

Delilah's magic has completed the spell.

I scream in pain as my power floods my body, awakening from a slumber of over one hundred and forty-eight years, along with a tether so strong it knocks the very breath from my lungs.

I crawl to Delilah, my nails cracking and breaking as I heave myself across the floor, holding onto that tether inside of me, clinging to it with all my strength, as one word repeats in my mind.

*Mate.*

*Mate.*

*Mate.*

I was right all along. Delilah's my mate.

I pour myself, my essence, my own life force, everything that I am into that bond as I pick up her limp body and hold her to my chest.

*Please.*

*Please.*

*Please.*

I can't lose her. I'd rather die than lose her.

An array of boots storm the hallway, along with Aurora's whimpers. I fling my power around the room, shielding us as I roar in defiance. I hear Axel's cry of shock as he comes to a skidding halt, seeing Delilah's lifeless body in my arms.

Tears run down my cheeks, falling onto her as I cling with

everything I have inside of me to that bond, to that tether between us. "Please, Angel, please wake up," I beg.

A scream pierces the room as Hazel falls to her knees, pounding on the shield.

I can't drop the shield. I can't.

Every instinct inside of me is screaming with a passion so violent, so strong, it commands me to kill anyone who dares come near her when she's so vulnerable. I pray to every god that will listen to save her.

I will give anything—including my own life—to save hers.

No sooner do the words float through my mind does her chest stop moving in my arms. Every primal instinct in my body explodes as I scream so hoarse my voice cracks, power blasting out of me in every direction as the bond between us flickers and dies. My power howls, crying out in protest as her life slips away. It ripples down the bond, one last feeble attempt, begging her beautiful heart to beat once more, for her chest to rise again, for those captivating ice-blue eyes to open.

I lower my head to hers, my tears flowing without abandon as I beg, plead in her ear to breathe.

"Stay with me," I croak. "You can't leave me, Delilah." I close my eyes, sobbing into the crook of her neck as silence greets my ears. "I can't lose you. I love you."

My breath hitches.

There's a tug.

Not from outside of me, but from within me.

I pull my head back, my heart beating erratically in my chest as I feel another tug on the bond, as if she too is clinging to me, her essence fighting to stay in this world.

I hold my breath as I wait, as I pray, my entire body shaking beneath hers as I stare at her pale face.

Delilah's lips part as a whoosh of air enters her mouth, her lungs breathing with life once more. My shield around the room snaps, crumbling as I clutch her body to mine, sobbing with relief.

"Knox."

Her small broken whisper makes my heart pound.

I shake my head, unable to speak, unable to form words as I hold her in my arms, feeling her heartbeat beside my own once more. No one comes near us, but I hear their cheers of joy and smell the salt of tears as everyone cries in relief.

A small delicate hand touches my cheek, her thumb stroking back and forth. "I didn't kill you," she says in awe. "I didn't kill magic."

"No, Angel, you saved me," I whisper on her lips.

That tether between us pulls once more, uniting our very souls as I kiss my mate.

# Chapter Forty-Eight

I awake to darkness, panic clutching my chest as fear slithers along my spine. Darkness so similar to where I disappeared to, the utter cold of nothing. I breathe a sigh of relief as I smell pinewood. The bed dips, moments before water splashes in the bathing room. My eyes burn, my head pounding as the light from the bathroom assaults my eyes. A dark blurry figure freezes as they enter the room. Turning, Knox disappears again before the candlelight dims.

I sigh as his hands gently scoop me up as he cradles me to his chest, his warmth seeping into my cold bones. Without letting go of me, Knox lowers into the tub, the warm water on my bare skin making me sigh.

I stay seated in Knox's arms, my head against his chest as I listen to the steady beat of his heart, the sound soothing my soul.

I take a deep breath, only to be met by the smell of ash. The putrid smell from inside that tree clings to my hair, making bile burn my throat. Knox moves me forward, wasting no time in wetting my hair. He grabs the vanilla-scented shampoo that sits on the edge of the porcelain tub.

My heart flutters in my chest; he brought my belongings in his room.

His fingers gently sink into my hair, scrubbing my scalp as vanilla overpowers the smell of ash and death. I sigh and close my eyes as he carefully washes my hair, my heart warming at his gentleness. His hand cups my chin, tipping my head back ever so slightly as he pours warm water over my scalp, rinsing the suds from my hair.

Once he's done, he places a featherlight kiss against the back of my head before his arms surround me once more, pulling me back to his chest.

I open my mouth to speak, finding my tongue dry, my throat raw as if I swallowed razor blades. My voice cracks as I say, "I heard you, wherever I went...I heard you."

Knox's body stiffens under mine, his arms tightening around me.

"Is it true—are we mates?"

He's silent for a moment, the tension in the room intensifying around us. "Would that bother you if we were?" he asks, his voice hoarse.

I turn to face him. His face is guarded, his eyes filled with fear as if he's waiting for my rejection. "No," I whisper. "I couldn't imagine being anyone else's mate."

Silver lines Knox's eyes as his body deflates, relaxing once more in the water.

"Did you know?" I ask.

Those sapphire eyes flit back and forth, searching mine. "I suspected."

My brows tug low. "Why didn't you tell me?"

The corner of his lips twitch. "I hate to break it to you, but you have a habit of pushing me away."

His words make my own lips twitch. He has a point.

My humor dies. "What happens now?"

His eyes soften at my question. "Whatever you want. I'll take whatever you give me."

I search his face, only to find truth. "This complicates things."

"Does it?" he drawls smoothly.

"Extremely."

He shrugs. "We can figure it out tomorrow."

"Tomorrow?"

"Right now, I'd like to be with you, without the weight of the world suffocating us."

Knox stares at me so intensely, my heart lurches as he hides the flash of pain in his eyes. I know he's going to blame himself for what happened to me for a long time.

"Is everyone okay?" I croak.

Knox dips his head. "Everyone's fine. They're celebrating."

"Thank you for saving me," I whisper.

His eyes shutter closed as his breath leaves him. "Don't thank me, not for that."

"It wasn't your fault, Knox."

"If I didn't leave the room, she wouldn't have drained your magic."

I lean forward, placing my hand on his cheek, forcing him to open his eyes. "It wouldn't have made a difference; she would have still drained my magic. I don't want you to blame yourself. I refuse to let her cause any more pain," I argue. "If it wasn't for you, I wouldn't be sitting here right now."

Knox's sapphire eyes search mine, seeing the truth in my words. He gently places his hands on my hips, lifting me to straddle his own. He leans forward, placing a featherlight kiss on my lips. Tears line his eyes as he pulls back. "I thought you were dead," he rasps.

I stroke his cheeks, catching a tear that escapes. "I know," I whisper.

"I'm going to have the image of you lying dead in my arms ingrained in my mind for as long as I live." He gives me a small smile. "I'll have to create a lot more memories with you to outweigh it."

My heart catches, my pulse skyrocketing at what he's insinuating. I know we need to talk about what's going to happen, what this means for us. However, that talk can wait. Knox is right—we can spend one night together, without the weight of the world pressing down on us.

"Did she steal my magic?" I whisper. I haven't dared to touch that well, not wanting to feel the grief of that loss if it's not there.

"No, Angel." He strokes my hair gently. "She sped up the process of your burnout."

Relief courses through me, my body slumping forward with the force of it. "What happened?"

Knox tenses beneath me. "Everything that could have gone wrong did. Axel is—"

"Is Axel okay?" I ask, sitting up.

Knox's lips flatten into a thin line. "Physically yes."

I narrow my eyes. "What aren't you telling me?"

"Axel is torn up, blaming himself for not reaching you in time. When he realized Emmalyn had disappeared, he flew as fast as he could." Knox sighs deeply. "He got to the tree as you stopped breathing."

Tears well in my eyes. "That's not his fault. It's no one's fault but Emmalyn's." Her name makes bile churn in my stomach. The only relief I feel is that Aurora tore her into pieces.

Knox shrugs. "He doesn't see it that way, especially not after he realized we're mates. I think he already suspected."

"I'll talk to him," I whisper. No one should feel guilty, let alone Axel. He was given orders and he fulfilled them, regardless of what he thinks.

Knox's voice breaks the silence in the room. "She let me."

"What?"

"Emmalyn."

My body stiffens. "What about her?"

Knox's brows pull low. "She let me kill her."

I shake my head. "No she didn't. She knew she was caught. There was no way out for her."

"No. She *let* me kill her."

I peer into Knox's eyes, the sheer conviction I find making my heart sink. "Why do you think that?"

"She didn't fight me. Why would she go through all this trouble, decades of planning and control…only to let me kill her? Why?"

My stomach drops as Knox's words process in my mind. "I don't know," I whisper.

I can't think about it anymore. I don't want to think of that horrid woman and what she did. I look at Knox, his heart and his feelings swimming in those sapphire eyes. I felt the pain and sorrow he felt in those moments too, and I never want him to experience it again.

Staring into his eyes, I open my heart to him. "I dreamt of you, of this city." Knox pulls back, astonishment on his face. Before he can speak, I continue, "Why do you call me Angel?"

"It was the only word I could hear in my mind when I saw you."

My heart melts. "I dreamt about the Fae lands for years. As I got older I started to dream about a Fae man. I never saw his face but he smelled like pinewood and ocean. He called me Angel…It was your voice."

Knox's eyes widen as a small smile spreads across his lips. "You've been dreaming of me?"

I roll my eyes. "Don't let it go to your head."

"Oh, I intend to," he croons.

I laugh as I slump forward, nestling into his warmth. "Where is everyone?" I ask.

The shield around the room drops. Music, laughter, and cheers pour into the space.

"I had to silence the room so you could sleep," he grumbles.

"Touch my hair one more time and I'll incinerate you!"

I burst out laughing at Lenox's boisterous voice. "How much have they had to drink?" I ask.

"They haven't stopped since we arrived home hours ago."

A smile spreads across my face as the weight of what I did comes crashing into me. "I truly did it. I broke the entrapment spell."

Knox places a kiss on my cheek. "You did, Angel."

Hours later, I bounce out of bed, dragging Knox with me as renewed energy sizzles through my body. "We have lots to celebrate."

"Are you sure you're feeling up for it?" Knox asks, frowning.

"Absolutely. I deserve some fun."

Knox walks into his dressing room, changing into his usual black suit pants and white linen shirt. "I'm warning you; they'll tease us mercilessly about the bond."

"Are they not happy about it?" I ask nervously.

Knox chuckles before placing a small kiss on my forehead. "No, Angel, they adore you. However, they find great joy in harassing me."

My cheeks heat, gratitude filling my heart as I change into the soft dress Knox hands me. If I had to put on fighting leathers or any tight-fitted clothing, I think I would vomit. I need to give myself at least a week of no fighting or training.

Knox offers me his hand as we descend the stairs and enter the sitting room. There, I find Lenox, Harlow, Nolan, and Axel, all of them absolutely hammered.

"The lovebirds have finally tired themselves out!" Lenox slurs. Knox simply holds up a vulgar gesture, ignoring Lenox's cackles as he pours us drinks. "That was quick. What's the matter, Knox? Your age catching up to you?"

"Do I need to teach you a lesson on manners?" Knox drawls from the bar cart.

"Nope, just getting it out of my system."

"Is it out?" Axel teases.

Lenox makes a big show of putting his fingers to his lips, his face scrunching in concentration. "Nope," he chirps as he lunges for me, wrapping his arms around my stomach and twirling me in the air. "Welcome to the family," he whispers in my ear.

My cheeks heat from the warm sentiment. The only family I've ever truly had was Easton and Annie. Even if he's inebriated, it means a great deal to me that Lenox would consider me as family in his eyes.

"What the fuck did you say to her to make her blush?" Axel yells.

Knox's power rumbles through the room, making my eyes roll. "Axel, don't poke the bear."

Axel throws his head back, chuckling.

"Does this mean you're Lenox's new mummy?" Harlow taunts.

Lenox snorts wine out of his nose, spraying it all over the floor. Laughter roars through the room. I take my own wine, plopping onto the sofa besides Knox, nestling into his warmth as he wraps an arm around my shoulders.

"I'm not a child," Lenox grits through his teeth.

Harlow throws her hair over her shoulders. "You act like one," she mutters. Her sultry eyes lock on mine as she lifts her wine glass. "Congratulations," she says, smiling.

"Thank you."

"It was about time. I was going to lock you two in the cellar until you figured it out," Axel mumbles, his words slurred.

I chuckle. I haven't seen Axel this drunk before, and it's highly entertaining. I scan the room, frowning. "Where's Hazel?"

"She's off screwing Ace," Lenox announces.

My mouth drops opens as I snap incredulous eyes to Knox.

He winces. "I knew I forgot to tell you something."

"They're mates! I knew it!" I yelp, jumping with joy.

"Everyone knew it," the group mumbles in unison.

"What happens now? What happens to the beasts and the guards?" I ask.

Lenox shakes his head at me as Harlow clicks her tongue. "One problem at a time. The rest can wait for tomorrow."

"We go to the queen tomorrow to explain everything we found and why we didn't tell her in the first place," Knox whispers into my ear.

Trepidation fills my stomach; I hope she's as nice as this court.

"I found it highly enjoyable seeing Harlow with an ugly

face for once." Lenox waves his hand around, his drink sloshing over the glass.

She groans and visibly shudders. "Ugh, don't utter another word. I never want to be one of those fat things again."

I chuckle, nestling further into Knox as I drink and celebrate with everyone, relishing in the newfound freedom that we created.

# Chapter Forty-Nine

**M**y throat constricts while I try to suck air into my lungs as I stare at the tall imposing castle looming above us. I've been here before, yet under entirely different circumstances. Standing on the cobbled driveway of the queen's castle, Knox lays his palm on my back, offering silent support as I calm my breathing. He's assured me multiple times that although the queen may be old-fashioned, she is nothing like my father. No matter how many reassurances Knox whispered to me this morning, I still couldn't tamp down my anxiety.

I take a step forward, each one making my heart beat faster.

Two guards step aside as they open the black wooden door, the hinges squeaking as they do. A castle servant greets us in the foyer, guiding us to the throne room.

The castle is vastly different since the last time I was here. Instead of live music, laughter, and dancing, we're met with silence. The squeaking of our shoes the only sound to be heard.

The servant walks through a large archway, stopping at

the threshold. "Your Majesty, Prince Holloway of Azalea and his companion have arrived," the man says, bowing low before exiting the throne room.

*Holloway.*

My heart skips a beat at hearing Knox's name.

My gaze roams the room. Settled on a tall golden throne, an older Fae, looking no more than fifty, sits poised as she stares at us, a warm smile on her lips. "You may enter," her silky voice calls.

Knox's shoulders square before he approaches, keeping pace beside me. He doesn't bow as he reaches the end of the throne, merely dips his head in greeting. A king speaking with a queen.

"I suppose you know why we're here," he drawls, sliding his hands into his tailored pockets.

"Yes, unfortunately I do," she says solemnly. "Did you catch the monster who cast it?"

"Emmalyn," he says casually.

There's not an ounce of shock in her expression. Not so much as a muscle twitch.

"I suppose you already knew that." Knox continues.

The queen turns her head to me. "When your griffin dumped her carcass at my door, the black blood was explanation enough. I just wanted to hear it myself, to confirm it to be true."

I gulp at that; I had no idea Aurora had so much sass in her. I say nothing, having no words for what Aurora did and why.

"I'm sorry you had to find out that way," Knox adds.

"I have to admit, I'm ashamed I didn't notice the signs earlier." Her gaze slides back to me. "How did you do it?"

"Phoenix rising spell," I reply, hiding my clammy hands behind my back.

Her warm eyes assess me. "How did you turn into Fae?"

Her voice is soft as she speaks, her eyes holding kindness, yet it's not a question. It's a demand, from a queen. Authority rings through her voice.

I tamp down on my knee-jerk reaction of shock. She truly does have spies everywhere.

My gut screams to lie, to withhold a part of the truth. I don't have answers as to why I'm Fae, so technically my words are part-truth, part-lie. "When I crossed the border I found out I was Fae. I have a feeling I'll turn back into a human when I leave."

The queen accepts my response, dipping her head once.

"We need the guards to round up the remaining demonic beasts," Knox chimes in.

"I'll see to it. As a thank you for freeing us."

Knox dips his head.

"Is there anything else I should be made aware of?" the queen asks.

Knox slides his hands into his pockets. "When will the court reinstatement commence?"

Her head pulls back as shock flits across her face. "In time, after the courts get their affairs in order." The Queen of Air stands. Descending the dais, she bows her head as she stops before us. "Thank you for coming," she says, giving us each a tight-lipped smile before exiting.

That's the politest dismissal I've ever seen.

Knox places his hand on my lower back, guiding me as we walk out of the castle.

Outside, Fae line the streets, celebrating their freedom with drinks and cheers of joy. The skies are filled with Fae flying far and wide past Aloriah's lands for the first time in nearly one hundred and fifty years.

"Why did you lie earlier?" Knox asks gently once we've stepped onto the streets.

I shrug. "I was nervous. I didn't want to tell her I don't have any answers as to why I'm Fae." That's another thing that I've lumped into the "tomorrow" section. If I start thinking about it and what it means, my head begins to pound.

Knox wraps his arm around my shoulder, bringing me closer as he kisses the top of my head. "How does a celebratory meal sound?"

I chuckle. "What's the difference between our usual dinners and a celebratory one?"

Knox's smirk turns feline. "More alcohol."

I throw my head back on a laugh as we make our way back to Knox's home.

# Chapter Fifty

I wake up covered in sweat, a scream leaving my burning throat as I jolt awake.

Knox is beside me in a heartbeat, rubbing my back. "It was just a dream, Angel," he soothes.

I shake my head, throwing the covers off me as I get out of bed, rushing into the bathroom just in time as bile burns my throat. Knox's large hands sweep my hair behind my head, rubbing circles along my back as I hurl the entire contents of my stomach.

I stand on shaking legs, my ears ringing and hands trembling as I get changed. "I need you to take me to the mermaids," I wheeze.

Knox wastes no time. Without questioning me, he changes into his fighting leathers, blades strapped to his back. "Do you want to fly or teleport?"

"Teleport. I think I'll vomit again if I'm in the air," I whisper hoarsely.

Knox pushes my hair behind my ears, gently kissing my forehead as white light surrounds us, the floor beneath me disappearing and the forest's ground replacing it.

I lift my head, stumbling into Knox's arms as I find the entirety of the mermaid pod in the swimming hole, waiting for me. The leader of the pack bobs in the water at the front, her white hair glowing in the moonlight, shining brighter than the mermaids around her.

I kneel on the edge of the riverbank, threading my fingers through the forest grass to stabilize me.

Her face is just as cold as the first time I saw her.

"It isn't over, is it?" I croak.

Fear like no other fills my heart as horror flashes across the mermaid's eyes.

"It is only the beginning," she whispers.

# A Note From The Author

To those that made it this far, from the bottom of my heart thank you for giving my book a chance.

If I told my younger self that I not only love to read but that I wrote a book … well let's just say we would be attending her funeral. Books will forever hold a special place in my heart. At the age of nineteen, I immersed myself in the world of fiction and was lucky enough to be dragged out of a dark abyss.

Books have been there for me through thick and thin, helping shape the person I am today and I hope for some, Heir of Broken Fate will do the same. In whatever capacity that may be.

This story is near and dear to my heart for many reasons and that's why I can't thank the following people enough.

To my beautiful editor, Makenna Albert, for shedding tears for Easton and helping me on this crazy journey.

The incredibly talented Thea Magerand for bringing my vision to life in a way that even my imagination couldn't dream of.

To my psychotic and crazy mum and sisters, thank you for supporting me in everything that I do. I love you to the unicorn universe and back.

To my furbaby, Lola, who will never read a word of this but was there every step of the way, thank you for being my soul pair.

To Charlie … I love you the most.